# THE PERFECT KISS

"He would take you in his arms and kiss you long and hard in spite of your protests," Harrison said. "The way he has wanted to do from the moment he met you!"

"That's what you think a man like Ellsworth would do?"

"That's what I know a man like Ellsworth would do."

"And what about you, Harrison?" She stared up at him, knowing even as she said the words, these were dangerous waters. "What would a man like you do?"

"Me?" His gaze slipped from her eyes to her lips. "I would never take advantage of a beautiful woman on a darkened terrace."

"Why not?"

"It would be . . . dishonorable."

"And you are an honorable man?"

"Most certainly."

"And you would never take advantage?"

"Never."

"Not even if you thought that because of her ancestry she wouldn't protest?"

"Not even then." He paused. "And I would never think that."

"But what if she wanted you to kiss her?"

Their gazes locked for a long moment. He turned and her heart sank. He took a step. Then paused. "Damnation, Julia!"

He swiveled back and without warning pulled her into his arms and kissed her hard and long and quite thoroughly until her knees weakened and she thought she might swoon in his arms . . .

# BOOK YOUR PLACE ON OUR WEBSITE AND MAKE THE READING CONNECTION!

We've created a customized website just for our very special readers, where you can get the inside scoop on everything that's going on with Zebra, Pinnacle and Kensington books.

When you come online, you'll have the exciting opportunity to:

- View covers of upcoming books
- Read sample chapters
- Learn about our future publishing schedule (listed by publication month *and author*)
- Find out when your favorite authors will be visiting a city near you
- Search for and order backlist books from our online catalog
- Check out author bios and background information
- Send e-mail to your favorite authors
- Meet the Kensington staff online
- Join us in weekly chats with authors, readers and other guests
- Get writing guidelines
- AND MUCH MORE!

**Visit our website at**
**http://www.kensingtonbooks.com**

Some desires
are worth the scandal...

# THE
# Perfect Mistress

## VICTORIA ALEXANDER

ZEBRA BOOKS
KENSINGTON PUBLISHING CORP.
http://www.kensingtonbooks.com

ZEBRA BOOKS are published by

Kensington Publishing Corp.
119 West 40th Street
New York, NY 10018

All Kensington titles, imprints and distributed lines are available at special quantity discounts for bulk purchases for sales promotion, premiums, fund-raising, educational or institutional use.

Special book excerpts or customized printings can also be created to fit specific needs. For details, write or phone the office of the Kensington Special Sales Manager: Kensington Publishing Corp., 119 West 40th Street, New York, NY 10018. Attn. Special Sales Department. Phone: 1-800-221-2647

Zebra and the Z logo Reg. U.S. Pat. & TM Off.

ISBN-13: 978-1-4201-1705-9
ISBN-10: 1-4201-1705-X

First Printing: February 2011
10 9 8 7 6 5 4 3 2 1

Printed in the United States of America

*I have no true regrets, Dear Reader. You should know that from the beginning. Oh, certainly, I have not always chosen as wisely as I should have. I have taken roads that might have been best ignored and made some decisions that, in hindsight, were not especially wise, but even the most egregious of those inevitably led to grand adventure. Indeed, one might say the more disastrous the choice, the grander the adventure.*

*I am under no illusions that what I now sit down to write will ever be read. The world is a far stuffier place than it was in my younger days. Still, I would like to have my life remembered in some fashion. So I take pen in hand to record my adventures. I dare not leave these memoirs to my children; they are entirely too proper and too concerned with the opinions of others to be trusted with my remembrances. They have never accepted the passion with which I choose to live my life; there is too much of their father in them to understand. Thus the estrangement between us for far too many years. I confess that perhaps that is indeed a regret, but there is nothing to be done about it now. If I had known my life would have caused such a rift I cannot in good conscience say I would have done anything differently, but I might have. Still, one never knows the consequences of one's actions until it is too late.*

*I should add that my realistic view of my children, and their respective natures, in no way negates my love. They are who the world has shaped them to be. I have heard it said that while many qualities are passed from parent to child, it is as often true that some traits skip one or more generations. I do hope that the granddaughter I have never seen inherits from me the joy I have found in life and my spirit of adventure. It is with that wish that I leave this to her. Perhaps she will find a use for it someday, be that public dissemination or private perusal. At this writing, I am in my sixtieth year and she is far too young to understand a lifetime that may at first glance appear to be little more than filled with scandal but was, in truth, quite glorious. At least, I found it so.*

*I have decided to entitle this in a most immodest manner as my nature has grown less modest through the years. Indeed, I see no need for undue modesty. I am who I am, for good or ill. I hope you take pleasure in the perusal of my reminiscences, but if you find them too scandalous for enjoyment, I make no apologies. As I said, I have no regrets. So I shall call this work what I, for the most part, was:* The Perfect Mistress.

from *The Perfect Mistress,*
*the Memoirs of Lady Hermione Middlebury*

# Chapter One

*London, 1885*

". . . and I would therefore be most delighted to publish your great-grandmother's memoirs." Benjamin Cadwallender's voice rang in Lady Julia Winterset's small parlor as if he were offering eternal salvation and choirs of celestial angels would appear at any moment to accompany his words.

She raised a brow. Eternal salvation was not what she sought from Cadwallender and Sons, Publishers but rather rescue of a more down-to-earth nature. Financial salvation as it were. "I must confess I am surprised, Mr. Cadwallender, that you would make such an offer on the basis of what little I allowed you to read. No more than a chapter if I recall."

"Yet what a chapter it was." He chuckled. "If the rest is even a fraction as interesting as what I have already read, *The Perfect Mistress, the Memoirs of Lady Hermione Middlebury*, shall be a rousing success."

Julia considered him. "Do you really think so?"

"Oh, I do indeed." He nodded vigorously. "I have mentioned this project, in a most discreet manner, mind you, to a few trusted colleagues and they concur. Do not underestimate the appetite of the public for works of this nature, especially if they are factual."

"By 'this nature' do you mean scandalous?"

"Well, yes, to an extent. But as Lady Middlebury has been dead these past thirty years, and the incidents she reveals are older yet, it is not nearly as disreputable as it might be if she were alive today and in the midst of—"

"Her adventures?" Julia said with a smile.

"Exactly." Mr. Cadwallender's handsome face flushed. "Admittedly, the writing itself is not as fine as Mr. Trollope's or Mr. Dickens's or even Mrs. Gaskell's or Mrs. Carik's but, as it is written in your ancestor's own words and in a remarkably engaging and enthusiastic style, a certain lack of polish can be overlooked. Particularly given the nature of the, er, adventures she relates."

"And you think it will sell well?"

"Lady Winterset." He lowered his voice in a conspiratorial manner. "Scandal sells books. I predict this will be a book that will be the subject of a great deal of discussion, which will only make those who haven't read it wish to do so."

"I see. How very interesting."

"And profitable," he said pointedly.

"That too," she murmured.

There was a time, not so long ago, when she would have considered the word *profitable* in a conversation somewhat distasteful. Proper ladies did not discuss matters of a profitable nature nor did they discuss finances with anyone other than their husbands. Indeed, if anyone had asked her before her husband's death three years ago, if she had a head for finances, aside from administering the household accounts, she would have laughed. But everything had changed since William's death. Thus far, she had managed to stretch the little savings her husband had left with frugal living and an eye toward a bargain. Nonetheless, if she did not take action soon, she would be penniless. She had far too many responsibilities to permit that to happen. Life had changed and so had she.

Three years ago, the eminently proper wife of Sir William Winterset would have been shocked at the very thought of making public her great-grandmother's scandalous remembrances, even if she had no idea of the work's existence until recently. The woman she had become was different, stronger hopefully, than the woman she had been. That woman was dependent upon her husband. This woman depended on no one but herself and would do what she must to survive. Even though she had not finished her reading of her great-grandmother's memoirs, what she had read thus far, as well as odd dreams triggered by her reading, convinced her that her great-grandmother would not only approve of Julia's plan but applaud it.

She drew a deep breath. "I assume you have a sum in mind for the rights of publication."

"I do indeed." Mr. Cadwallender pulled an envelope from his waistcoat pocket and placed it on the table between his chair and hers.

Julia picked up the envelope, pulled out the paper inside, unfolded it, and stared at the figure written in Mr. Cadwallender's precise hand. Her heart sank but she refused to let disappointment show on her face.

"That figure does not take into account continued royalties which I expect to be considerable," Mr. Cadwallender said quickly.

She refolded the paper and replaced it in the envelope. "It does strike me as rather meager, Mr. Cadwallender." She cast him her most pleasant smile. "For a book you expect to be a rousing success."

"Yes, well . . ." Mr. Cadwallender shifted in his chair. "Might I be completely candid, Lady Winterset?"

"I expect nothing less."

"As well you should." Mr. Cadwallender paused, his brow furrowed. "My grandfather began the publication of *Cadwallender's Weekly World Messenger* nearly eighty years ago. When he began publishing books as well, he named the firm Cadwallender and Sons, overly optimistic as it turned out as he only had one son and several daughters. That son, my father, surpassed his father and sired six sons as well as two daughters. My two older brothers, myself, and my next younger brother joined in the family business as was expected." He directed her a firm look. "Do you have any idea what it's like to be in the position of a middle son in both one's family and one's business?"

"No idea at all. I imagine it could be somewhat awkward."

"Somewhat? Hah!" He snorted and rose to his feet to pace the room. "My voice is heard only after my father and my two older brothers have had their say. I am consistently overruled in any matter in which my opinion differs from theirs. My ideas are scarcely ever considered." He paused in midstep and met her gaze. "And I have ideas, Lady Winterset. Excellent ideas. The world is changing. We are a scant fifteen years from the dawn of a new century. Progress is in the air and we must seize the opportunities for change and advancement. Don't you agree?"

"Yes, I would think so," she said cautiously.

He stared at her for a moment then recovered his senses. "My apologies. I should not allow myself to be carried away in this manner.

"Nonsense, Mr. Cadwallender. There is no need to apologize for the passion of one's convictions." She smiled. "But I fear I don't see what this has to do with my great-grandmother's book."

"Lady Winterset." Mr. Cadwallender retook his seat and met her gaze with a fervor akin to that of a missionary converting heathens. "I think this book will be a very great success. The sort of success publishing houses are built upon. That establishes a publisher as a legitimate force in the market."

"I don't understand." She pulled her brows together. "As you mentioned, Cadwallender and Sons has been in business for a very long time. Its reputation is well known."

"It is indeed. However, the reputation of Cadwallender Brothers Publishing has yet to be established." He grimaced. "Not unexpected as the company has yet to publish a single book."

She shook her head. "I still don't—"

"My younger brother and I have started our own firm. We have experience, funding, and investors confident of our future. Neither of us are averse to the hard work that lies ahead and I have no doubt as to our ultimate success." He met her gaze. "I would very much like *The Perfect Mistress* to be our first offering."

"I see." She studied him for a moment. "You're going to compete against your father?"

"My father has decided to turn over the management of the company to my brothers. I do not wish to spend the rest of my life engaged in battles I cannot win. Furthermore, the publishing of books is of far less importance to them than the *Messenger,* which has always been the primary focus of the firm. My brothers are intent upon launching additional publications as well." He squared his shoulders. "I do not see this as competition as much as the development and expansion of a field they have little interest in. A field, I think, that is the way of the future."

"Your enthusiasm is commendable, however—"

A knock sounded at the door and immediately it opened.

"Beg pardon, my lady," her butler, Daniels, said with his usual air of cool competence. "Lady Smithson and Lady Redwell have arrived."

"Oh dear." She glanced at the ormolu clock on the overmantel. "I didn't realize the time." She rose to her feet, the publisher immediately following suit. "Mr. Cadwallender, my initial inquiry was predicated on the upstanding reputation of Cadwallender and Sons. I am not at all certain I have the . . . the courage required to trust the fate of this book to a new venture. I fear, therefore, I shall have to query another publisher and—"

"Lady Winterset." Mr. Cadwallender clasped her hand in his and met her gaze directly. "I beg you not to make a hasty decision. Please give me the opportunity to further plead my case. I assure you, you will not regret it."

She stared into his earnest, hazel eyes. Very nice eyes really that struck her as quite trustworthy, even if that might be due as much to his fervor as anything else. Still, there was no need to make a decision today.

"Very well, Mr. Cadwallender." She smiled and withdrew her hand. "I shall give your proposal due consideration."

"Thank you," he said with relief. "Perhaps I can arrange for a higher advance as well. May I call on you again in a day or two to discuss it further?"

"Of course."

"Again, you have my gratitude." He smiled and his eyes lit with pleasure, very nice eyes in a more than ordinarily handsome face. "I am confident, Lady Winterset, this is the beginning of a profitable relationship for us both." With that, he nodded and took his leave, offering a polite bow of greeting to her friends who entered the parlor as he left.

"I can see why you are late," Veronica, Lady Smithson, said in a wry manner, her gaze following the publisher. "I would certainly forgo tea with my friends for a liaison with a man like that."

"It was not a liaison," Julia said firmly.

"Still, he is quite dashing, isn't he?" Portia, Lady Redwell, craned her neck to see past the parlor door and into the entry hall. "If one likes fair hair and broad shoulders . . ." Her gaze jerked back to the other women, a telltale blush washing over her face. "Not that I do. Although, of course, what woman wouldn't? That is to say . . ." She raised her chin. "One can appreciate art without being in the market for a painting. That's what I meant."

"Yes, of course you did," Veronica said in an absent manner, her attention again on Julia, much to Portia's obvious relief.

Of the three widows, Portia was the most concerned with propriety. Veronica had, on more than one occasion, observed privately that it was those who walked the narrowest paths that were the most likely to plunge over a cliff when the opportunity presented itself. Fortunately for Portia, or unfortunately in Veronica's view, Portia had yet to so much as peer over the edge of a cliff.

For that matter, neither had Julia. But she had discovered a great deal about herself since her husband's death. Her character was far stronger than she had imagined. One did what one had to do to survive in this world. As for propriety, while she had always considered herself most proper in both behavior and manner, it was no longer as important as it once was.

"If it wasn't a liaison," Veronica continued, "which, I might add, is a very great pity as surely Portia agrees, given that she is an excellent judge of art . . ." Portia offered her friends a weak smile. "Who was he and what sort of profitable relationship is he confident about?"

Julia narrowed her eyes. "How much of the conversation did you hear?"

"Not nearly enough." Veronica breezed farther into the room, settled on the sofa, and began taking off her gloves. "You should call for tea."

"I thought we were to have tea at Fenwick's?" Julia said slowly.

"We were." Portia moved past Julia and seated herself beside Veronica. The three women had first met several years ago at the reading room at Fenwick and Sons Booksellers, which did seem to attract young widows who had little else to occupy their time. Indeed, it had become something of a unofficial club for ladies, as well as the home of the loosely organized Ladies Literary Society. It was Veronica who had suggested to the elder Mr. Fenwick or perhaps one of the sons—as they were all of an indeterminate age, somewhat interchangeable, and nearly impossible to tell apart—that the reading room could prove profitable by simply offering refreshments. Although Veronica had never admitted it, Julia suspected her suggestion had carried with it financial incentive. It would not surprise Julia to learn Veronica was now a part owner of Fenwick and Sons. "But you failed to appear at the appointed time."

Julia glanced at the clock. "I am scarcely half an hour late."

"Yes, but while Veronica and I are rarely on time, you are always punctual." Portia pinned her with a firm look. "Your note said you had something of importance to discuss. When you did not appear, we were naturally concerned."

Julia folded her arms over her chest. "You were naturally curious."

"Regardless." Veronica studied her closely. "It was

concern that compelled us to fly to your rescue." She raised a brow. "Tea?"

"Of course," Julia murmured and stepped out of the room to direct Daniels to have tea prepared. She would have much preferred to have had refreshments at Fenwick's rather than here. It wasn't that she did not like her modest home, it was simply not as grand as either Portia's or Veronica's. As such it pointed out the vast differences between her life and that of her friends. Now, as she often had in the past, she marveled that they had become friends at all.

At first it seemed the three women had nothing in common save that they were all of a similar age and their respective widowhoods had begun at very nearly the same time. Veronica's husband had been involved in the sort of financial dealings open only to those of great family wealth. Portia's had been a literary sort, something of a scholar from what she had said. And Julia's husband had been engaged in the practice of law. Three years ago, their husbands had died within months of each other of accident or illness or mishap. That they had forged a true friendship was attributable only to the whims of fate and perhaps the fact that they had met at a time when each needed a friend who was neither a relation nor considered them an obligation. And now they had come to rescue her.

Julia fetched her great-grandmother's manuscript from the library and returned to the parlor. She took a seat, keeping the memoirs on her lap. "This is what I wished to discuss with you."

Veronica eyed the stack of papers curiously. "And what, may I ask, is it?"

Portia sniffed. "It doesn't look very interesting."

"Appearances, my dear Portia, are often deceiving." Julia drew a deep breath. "Do you recall my telling you that my grandmother's brother died oh, about six months ago?"

Portia brightened. "And you have at last received an inheritance? Monies that will allow you to take care of the responsibilities that should have rightfully been his?"

"Yes, and no." Julia shook her head. "His property went to a relative so distant I was not even aware of his existence. As for money, well, it seems he had none to speak of."

"Of course not." Portia's expression hardened. "Vile creature." Portia could not understand a family not caring for its own. Her parents had died when she was very young and her aunt and uncle had taken her in.

"This"—Julia laid her hand on the manuscript—"is my inheritance. It was left to my mother by my great-grandmother. For reasons unknown to me, although I have my suspicions, my great-uncle kept it in his possession."

"And now that it is rightfully yours, what—" Veronica paused to allow a maid to enter with a tea cart then take her leave. She waited until the door closed to continue. "Now, what is it?"

"These are my great-grandmother's memoirs."

Portia sighed with disappointment. "Oh yes, that is interesting."

"Julia, dear," Veronica eyed her thoughtfully. "Who was your great-grandmother?"

"Lady Hermione Middlebury." Julia held her breath.

"Oh my," Veronica murmured. "That is interesting."

"Why?" Portia's impatient gaze slid from one woman to the other.

Veronica chose her words with care. "Is this the same Lady Middlebury who was reputedly the mistress of—"

Julia nodded. "Yes."

"And involved in the scandal surrounding the prince of—"

"That too." Julia winced.

"And the rather infamous incident with a prime min—"

"Yes, yes, all of that." Julia waved away Veronica's words.

"Well, I don't know what either of you are talking about." Portia huffed.

"My apologies, Portia." Julia paused to gather her thoughts. "My great-grandmother was widowed at an early age and then proceeded to live her life exactly as she pleased."

"In a most . . . independent manner," Veronica said with an amused smile.

"By 'independent' do you mean scandalous?" Portia asked.

"Of course." Veronica poured a cup of tea. "But it was a very long time ago."

Julia cleared a space and set the manuscript on the cart. "She passed away more than thirty years ago."

"Still," Portia said, "scandal is scandal."

"As I was saying," Veronica continued, "these are the memories of a woman who has been dead for these past thirty years and her . . ."

"She calls them adventures." Julia wrinkled her nose.

"Amorous adventures, no doubt," Portia said darkly.

"Adventures? How delightful. Oh, I do like that." Veronica paged through the manuscript. "The amorous adventures of a woman long in her grave may well have been scandalous when they occurred. But today, they are more in the realm of . . ." She thought for a moment. "Oh, history, I would think, as those who shared her adventures are long dead and buried as well."

"History?" Portia stared at the manuscript as if she

wasn't sure if she wished to spirit it away and read it in the dead of night or burn it. "I daresay no one would look at this as history."

"The history of society as it were, for better or ill," Veronica said in a superior manner. "These amorous exploits of Julia's great-grandmother happened so long ago they are only of interest in a literary sense."

"More prurient than literary, no doubt." Portia directed a warning look at Julia. "Some people have very long memories."

"And some people are fast reaching a point of financial ruin." Julia tapped her fingertip on the manuscript. "Hopefully, this will provide salvation." She drew a deep breath. "My finances are dwindling quickly."

Veronica stopped paging through the manuscript and cast a startled look at the other woman. "Why haven't you said anything?"

"It's rather embarrassing to admit that one's resources are limited," Julia said with a wry smile.

Surprise crossed Veronica's face. "Even among friends?"

Julia nodded. "Especially among friends."

Veronica huffed. "I tell you everything. Why, you know very nearly all my secrets."

Portia ignored Veronica, directing her words to Julia. "You should marry again. That would solve all your problems."

"I would very much like to marry again," Julia said, her tone a bit sharper than she intended. "However, it was not easy to find the right man once."

"It would be much easier if you were looking for financial stability rather than love," Veronica noted, not for the first time.

"At this particular moment, I would turn my life over

to a man without hesitation if it would mean financial salvation," Julia said staunchly.

Veronica raised a brow. "You do not lie well, my dear. You would beg on the streets before you wed a man you did not care for." She paused. "How bad is it?"

Julia blew a long breath. "I have approximately three months before my circumstances are serious."

Veronica frowned. "I thought I noted a look of concern about you in recent weeks."

Julia grimaced. "I have not been sleeping well."

Veronica leaned toward her and lowered her voice. "Do allow me to give you what you need. I have more money than I could possibly spend in a lifetime."

"I cannot take your money, although your offer is most appreciated," Julia said.

"Why ever not? She certainly has the money." Portia poured her tea. Veronica's spending habits were the subject of great amusement and, on Julia's part, who had to watch every penny, some envy. "Why, the amount she spends on hats alone would fund a small country for a year."

"Longer probably," Veronica said, the fanciful concoction of feathers and flowers on the hat she wore today bobbing with her movements. "I see no reason not to indulge myself as I have the means to do so. And I simply adore a hat that makes a statement."

"Oh, your hats make all sorts of statements." A wicked light sparked in Portia's eye. "I would say the statement that particular hat makes is—"

"I don't think that's necessary." Veronica cast Portia a narrowed look. "Or wise." She turned back to Julia. "Nor is your refusal to take my money." She met her friend's gaze and took her hand. "I have never had a great number of friends but I understand friends do things like this for one another. And, in truth, I have come to think of us as somewhat more than friends. You are the sister I have never had."

Julia swallowed the lump that abruptly rose in her throat. "I never had a sister either."

"And I've never had a real sister," Portia said quickly, not to be outdone, and fairly slapped her hand on top of her friends'. "And, while my finances are not as vulgarly excessive as Veronica's, I too have a tidy fortune. I should like to give you money as well."

Julia stared at Portia, glaring at Veronica, then met the other widow's gaze and the gleam of amusement in her eye. Both women laughed and Portia huffed. "I am quite sincere, even if a bit tardy."

"I know you are." Julia smiled. "And I am most grateful." She withdrew her hand, settled back in her chair, and considered her friends. "That you would both make such an offer touches me more than I can say, however I cannot—"

"Of course you can. You simply won't. Pride, my dear, is not nearly as becoming as you might think." Veronica straightened. "But do understand this, regardless of your refusal, the offer—both offers I assume—stand."

"We do not want to see you destitute." Portia flicked her gaze over Julia's serviceable but well-worn dress and wisely kept her opinion on the topic of Julia's wardrobe to herself. "You will never find a wealthy husband if you look like you need one."

"I should quite like to marry again, but as no potential suitor has yet to appear on my doorstep, I must take matters into my own hands." Julia nodded at the manuscript. "This might well be my salvation and, like any true miracle, arrived just when I needed it."

Veronica raised a brow. "Left to you by your late great-uncle then?"

"Not exactly." Annoyance sounded in Julia's voice. "According to her memoirs, my great-grandmother had always intended for this to be left in the care of my mother as she thought her children were too proper to appreciate it."

Veronica nodded. "Byron's memoirs were burned after his death, by friends I believe, who were concerned as to the scandal they might cause."

"For reasons unknown to me, it instead fell into the hands of my great-uncle who did not see fit to give it to my mother."

"No doubt because of its scandalous nature. You can scarcely blame the man for that." Portia's brow furrowed. "I never knew you had a scandalous great-grandmother." She glanced at Veronica. "And why is it that you know about this Lady Middlebury and I don't?"

"My grandmother quite enjoys a good story and considers them even better if they include an element of truth." Veronica smiled with the memory.

"Gossip?" Portia scoffed. "My family has never been prone to gossip."

"How sad for you, my dear." Veronica cast Portia a sympathetic look then turned her attention back to Julia. "I, for one, think this is fascinating. Why haven't you mentioned this before?"

"There is much about my family I don't know. I always thought we were quite ordinary, but apparently we are a family of many secrets." Julia thought for a moment. "I did know that my great-grandmother was considered quite notorious in her day but she died before I was born and my mother rarely spoke of her. I know as well that she was not close to her children—my grandmother and her brother—and spent the later years of her life living in France." She shook her head. "But I didn't even know my grandmother was still living until six years ago when my parents died."

"Which is when you became responsible for her support," Veronica said slowly.

"A responsibility that should have fallen to your great-uncle," Portia pointed out, again.

"It's all quite tangled and convoluted. After all, including me, it encompasses four generations." Julia paused in an apologetic manner. "And you have heard much of this before."

"And like any good story, we shall enjoy hearing it again." Veronica refilled her cup.

"My great-grandmother and her children were estranged. She lost her husband at twenty-four, the same age I was when I lost William." Julia sipped her tea. "Spouses do not seem to live overly long in my family."

"There's something to be said for that," Veronica said coolly.

Julia bit back a smile. In spite of Veronica's skeptical comments, she knew full well her friend had cared deeply for her late husband.

"My mother and my grandmother at some point had a falling-out which led to their estrangement for a time although I have never known why. But then, as I understand it, she became ill—"

"Mad." Portia nodded sagely.

"She's not mad," Julia said quickly. "Eccentric, yes, but—"

"You told us she hears voices," Portia said. "That's the very definition of mad."

"She's not mad." Julia's tone was sharper than she intended even if she didn't quite believe her own words. "She has lived quietly in the country for years with a housekeeper who is more friend than servant. Indeed, they . . ." She hesitated then looked at her friends. "They both seem quite happy. I first went to see her when my parents died and I learned of her existence—"

"Kept secret because of the madness no doubt," Portia said under her breath.

Julia met Veronica's gaze. "I had to meet her and see for myself, you understand, how ill she was."

Veronica nodded. "And?"

"And, I would not call her mad." Julia smiled. "I thought she was delightful. Quite witty and most amusing."

"And her voices?" Portia asked. "Were they witty as well?"

"I visit whenever I can and her company is most enjoyable. And"—Julia turned to Portia—"I have never seen behavior that I would truly call mad. Certainly her memories are muddled on occasion. She has a tendency to speak of matters long past as if they were yesterday—gentlemen callers and treasures lost and found and paths not taken. But it seems to me she is merely eccentric which, as a woman of advanced age, she has earned the right to be."

"Perhaps the voices simply don't speak to her when you are there." Portia's smile was entirely too sweet and not the least bit legitimate.

Veronica frowned. "You're being exceptionally nasty today, Portia. What on earth has possessed you?"

Portia opened her mouth to issue a sharp retort then apparently thought better of it. "My apologies. It's my mood I'm afraid." She rolled her gaze toward the ceiling. "My cousin is having yet another dinner party tonight. Inevitably I shall be seated next to the most eligible gentleman there who has been invited with the sole purpose of marrying me."

Veronica smirked. "Again."

Julia stifled a laugh. In recent months, Portia's loving and well-meaning family had apparently decided it was time for her to remarry. While she did indeed wish to marry again, her family's interference did not sit well. The woman who had never had a rebellious bone in her body found herself in the unfamiliar role of mutineer.

"Whether she is truly mad or merely odd with the eccentricities of age scarcely matters. After my husband died, I wanted to bring her to London to live with me but she refused. She insists she is happy where she is." Julia shook her head. "But I am reaching a point where I can barely support one household let alone two. Therefore . . ." Resolve straightened her spine. "I shall sell my great-grandmother's manuscript and use whatever it fetches to support her daughter. The gentleman you saw here is a publisher."

Portia gasped. "Surely you're not serious?"

"I have never been more serious in my life."

"I'm not sure publishing will provide you with the funding you need," Veronica said thoughtfully.

"If it sells well, it should provide a steady income." Julia wasn't sure if she was trying to convince herself or her friends. Still, she had nothing else.

"Perhaps it isn't scandalous enough to sell well." Portia's gaze settled on the manuscript. "As your friends, it might be wise if we all read—"

"It is a risky proposition." Veronica thought for a moment. "I think Portia's suggestion might better serve."

Portia glanced at the other woman. "What suggestion?"

"Blackmail," Veronica said in an offhand manner.

"I suggested nothing of the sort." Portia huffed then paused. "Did I?"

Julia stared. "I don't recall blackmail being mentioned nor would I consider such a thing."

"You should," Veronica said, "although *blackmail*

might be the wrong word as it implies something, well, wrong."

Julia's brows drew together. "Probably because it is."

"What did I suggest?" Portia said.

"You said some people have very long memories." Veronica nodded at Julia. "There are no doubt any number of people who would prefer that past scandals stay in the past."

"Don't be absurd." Julia waved away the comment. "You said it yourself. My great-grandmother's adventures were half a century ago. No one cares about those scandals now but hopefully they are interesting to read. However, I shall allow you to judge for yourself." She selected a section she had copied and handed it to Veronica. "This chapter is about a gentleman related to you."

"How delightful," Veronica murmured, and paged idly through the pages.

"Isn't there anything in there about a relation of mine?" Portia craned her neck to peer at the manuscript.

Julia shook her head. "Not that I've found thus far."

"We have never been a scandalous lot. Still . . ." Portia eyed the manuscript with barely concealed longing. "It would be advisable to look. Just to make certain, you understand. For no other reason than that."

"Of course not." Veronica's innocent tone belied the amusement in her eye.

"Besides, who among us is better suited to assess just how scandalous the work is?" Portia said primly. "I know scandal when I see it."

"Then you should certainly read a chapter." Julia selected another section she had copied, anticipating Portia's request, and handed the pages to her friend.

Portia frowned at the small number of pages. "Is that enough? To be able to ascertain the scandalous nature of the work, that is. Perhaps I should read more?"

"I'm certain when you finish reading, Julia would be happy to provide you with more," Veronica said smoothly. "For purposes of assessing the level of scandal, of course. Nothing more than that."

"My life is exceptionally dull," Portia said under her breath, leafing through the pages. Her gaze jerked to her friends as if she were surprised by her own words. "Not that I am interested in this in any way other than to help my dear Julia."

Veronica smiled. "We never thought otherwise."

"Not for a moment," Julia added, casting Portia a reassuring smile.

It was indeed odd that this disparate trio had become friends but friends they were and, Julia suspected, friends they would be for the rest of their days. She sent a silent prayer of thanks heavenward for these women, adding an additional prayer that the memoirs were indeed scandalous enough to provide true financial salvation even if that might not be the type of request the Almighty would be amenable to granting. Still, she would be most grateful if he would consider it.

And perhaps, she cringed to herself at the absurd thought, she would have to thank her great-grandmother as well.

# Chapter Two

"This is unacceptable." Harrison Landingham, the Earl of Mountdale, glared at the pages laid out on the desk in front of him. "Completely unacceptable."

"If you think the first page is unacceptable . . ." Amusement gleamed in his sister-in-law's eyes. "Wait until you read the rest."

"Good Lord," Harrison muttered. What he'd read thus far was bad enough. He didn't dare consider what the rest of these memoirs might contain. "This family has avoided scandal in the past and scandal will not touch us on my watch."

"More's the pity," Veronica murmured.

He glanced up. "I do appreciate your bringing this to my attention, however."

She smiled pleasantly. "I thought you would find it interesting."

He raised a brow. " 'Interesting' is the very least of what I find it."

Veronica shrugged. "I found it rather amusing as well."

"That comes as no surprise," he said coolly. His late

half brother's wife was exactly the type of woman who would find something of this scandalous nature amusing.

Seven years ago, when Charles had announced his intention to marry Veronica Wilton, Harrison had done his best to dissuade him. Not that she wasn't lovely with her dark red hair and tall stature and, indeed, her family was more than acceptable, her father was a viscount after all. But there was something in the woman's manner, as if she were far more intelligent than anyone else and found the rest of the world amusing in its stupidity, that he found most irritating. In his experience, intelligent women were prone to making their own decisions and never overly concerned with the propriety of those decisions. Still, he had to admit, in many ways he had been wrong about her. While he never did understand what his brother saw in her aside from her appearance, and certainly one required more in a wife than a pretty face, she had made Charles happy and they seemed to have truly cared for each other. Which somewhat redeemed her in Harrison's eyes. In this world, could one ask for more?

Veronica laughed. "Goodness, Harrison, Charles would have found it amusing as well."

"Charles found much amusing that I do not," Harrison said in what struck even him as an overly stodgy manner. While they shared the same mother, the two brothers could not have been more dissimilar in temperament.

Charles was nearly seventeen years of age when his widowed mother had married Harrison's father and had promptly borne another son. Harrison had adored his older brother in spite of the disparity in their ages. But it wasn't until he was an adult that they had become close even though the characters of the two men were decidedly different. While Charles was brilliant in all matters of finance, he had lived his life with a devil-may-care attitude and a passion for wine and sport and women—especially women. He was well past his fortieth year when he had at last decided to marry. No one was more surprised than Harrison by his brother's decision and his choice. He had rather expected his brother to fall head over heels for an actress or another unsuitable sort rather than a woman who, in spite of Harrison's initial concerns, was still a fitting match for the Earl of Smithson.

In recent years Harrison had been searching for an appropriate wife of his own. He was well aware of his responsibilities and his duty to provide an heir, as his half brother had failed to do. Charles's title had passed to a distant cousin upon his death. Harrison had no intention of allowing the same fate to befall his heritage. Indeed, he was currently considering several suitable candidates for the position of Countess of Mountdale, young ladies of good family and unblemished reputation. That he hadn't selected a wife yet he attributed only to the fact that he had yet to find one he considered absolutely right and had nothing at all to do with the lack of particular affection he felt for any of them. Affection would come in time.

"Even Charles would not be amused to see the infidelities of his father available at a bookseller's for all the world to read."

Veronica raised a brow.

"Well, perhaps he would." His brother had always been amused by scandal. "But his father is dead and mine is very much alive. However this . . ." He cast a disgusted look at the pages in front of him. "The scandal this will cause will kill him."

Veronica laughed. "I very much doubt that."

Harrison drew his brows together. "My father is seventy-six years of age and—"

"He is the youngest elderly gentleman I know."

"His constitution is not what it once was," Harrison said staunchly.

"How is your father's health?"

"Acceptable." Harrison ignored the fact that his father's physicians pronounced him the picture of health, save for stiffness in his knees. "Regardless, it is a risk I do not intend to take. Now, you say this friend of yours—"

"You needn't say *friend* as if it were an obscenity." Veronica's brows pulled together in disapproval. "She is a very nice woman and I am fortunate to count her among my friends."

"Very nice women do not publish the scandalous memoirs of their ancestors."

"Very nice women who have financial responsibilities do what they must to meet those responsibly. Goodness, Harrison, she's not pandering in the streets."

"This is not substantially better," he said. "What did you say her name was?"

"I didn't. It's Lady Julia Winterset."

Harrison raised a brow. "The wife of Sir William Winterset?"

"The widow of Sir William Winterset."

"The barrister?"

"I believe so. Did you know him?"

"I knew of him. He had a fine legal mind and an excellent reputation. And he was of good family as well." Harrison huffed. "No doubt this has him turning over in his grave."

"If he had provided adequately for his widow, if his good family had not abandoned any responsibility toward his wife upon his death, there would be no need to turn over in his grave and he could rest in peace," Veronica said sharply.

"Yes, I suppose." Harrison drummed his fingers on his desk. "Obviously, I shall have to deal with this myself. I shall request a meeting with your friend and persuade her of the error of proceeding with this venture."

"Such persuasion to consist of nothing more than your gallant manner and charming disposition?" Veronica said mildly.

Harrison glared at his sister-in-law. "I can be quite persuasive and most charming when the occasion calls for it."

"Harrison." Veronica rolled her gaze toward the ceiling. "Have you listened to a word I've said?"

"Each and every one."

"Apparently not." Veronica leaned forward and met his gaze. "Julia Winterset is badly in need of funds. If the state of her finances was acceptable, I daresay she would never think of selling her great-grandmother's memoirs. She is very nearly as proper as you are." Veronica shrugged. "Or at least she used to be."

"What do you mean?"

"When you have lost a husband, when without warning you find yourself completely dependent on your own resources, you have very few choices other than to take your life in your own hands. If you wish to survive." She shook her head in a long-suffering manner, as if he were entirely too stupid to understand. "I met Lady Winterset two years ago. I have watched her since then. She has changed, grown if you will. She has become quite independent and discovered a strength of character I suspect she ever knew she had."

Harrison glared. "If you are trying to make a point, Veronica, you are not doing it well."

"My point is that while Lady Winterset is a woman of intellect and grace and any number of other sterling qualities, she is also desperate. Desperate women do what they must do and they do not easily succumb to fine words and charming manners."

"Still, if she is indeed intelligent, she shall surely be reasonable as well." Even to his own ears, the assertion sounded absurd. Women, intelligent or not, were rarely reasonable. "I have no doubt that I can convince her that making this . . . this *rubbish* public will cause her and all involved irreparable damage."

"Talk alone will not suffice. As I see her financial circumstances, she has only two recourses open to her. As she is not averse to marriage, she can wed a man of substantial fortune—"

"Excellent, then she should do so at once."

Veronica stared as if he had grown another head. "It's not as easy as that. One simply doesn't snap one's finger and a suitable husband appears. Marriageable men with wealth and position, men like yourself, are not easy to come by."

Harrison gasped. "Surely, you're not suggesting I marry her?"

"Don't be absurd." Veronica waved away the comment. "While I have no doubt Julia meets your absurdly high standards, and you could certainly do worse although she could certainly do better, you and she would never suit."

"Excellent, as desperate is not something I am seeking in a wife," he snapped, ignoring an odd twinge of annoyance. "And her other recourse?"

"She has no jewels to speak of, no property aside from her house, and nothing of any value whatsoever." She shrugged. "Therefore there is nothing she can do but sell her great-grandmother's memoirs. She already has one publisher interested."

"Who?"

"A Mr. Cadwallender."

"Cadwallender? The name sounds vaguely familiar."

"Oh, if you had met Mr. Cadwallender you'd remember. Tall, blond hair, brownish eyes with a hint of green if I recall, most dashing in appearance."

He stared at her as if she'd lost her mind. "I don't care."

"I just thought it should be mentioned." She shrugged. "You should know what's involved. In terms of how much charm you need to expend."

"Very amusing." He again drummed his fingers on the desk. "If I cannot convince her not to publish them perhaps I could offer her a reasonable sum to simply eliminate all references to my father."

"Reasonable?"

"Outrageous then." He thought for a moment. "Better yet, I could buy them myself."

"And they will never see the light of day?"

"Never," he said grimly. Indeed, once the memoirs were in his possession, they would be destroyed.

Veronica narrowed her eyes. "I don't know that she would like that."

"Nonetheless, once they were mine she would have no say in the matter."

"No, of course not." Veronica sighed. "And I think her concern at the moment is more about her finances than preserving her ancestor's adventures. That's that then." Veronica gathered her things, rose to her feet, and adjusted the tilt of her hat—a truly obnoxious concoction of indiscernible things that might have been alive at one time. Harrison stood to escort her to the door. "I have other matters to attend to today so I shall take my leave."

"Veronica." He circled the desk. "I am most grateful to you for coming to me with this."

"Harrison, while our connection is tentative at best, you are still Charles's brother and he was quite fond of you. And I am quite fond of your father. While I do think he would be rather amused by the public airing of an affair he had in his youth, I fear the outrage of his responsible son would cause him undue concern. I told you of this for him, not for you."

"Regardless of your motives, you still have my gratitude."

She studied him for a moment. "Will there ever come a day when you approve of me?"

"I don't disapprove of you." And indeed he didn't disapprove of Veronica, only her manner.

"But you don't like me."

"Nonsense." He scoffed. "I don't dislike you. You are my late brother's wife and you made him happier than I had ever seen him." He forced a smile. "How could I possibly dislike you?"

"That is what I have always wondered. I am quite easy to like, you know." She started for the door. "Many people do."

He chuckled. "I have no doubt of that."

She glanced back at him. "And now your smile is genuine. It's a very nice smile, Harrison, when you mean it. You should mean it more often."

"Veronica."

She paused. "Yes?"

"I am curious. I have wealth and position and I am not unattractive. Indeed, I am considered something of a catch. Why do you think Lady Winterset and I would not suit?"

"Goodness, I thought it was obvious. While I suppose Julia might suit you—"

He snorted.

"—you would not suit her at all." She shook her head. "You live in a world of right and wrong, proper and improper, black and white. There is no compromise in your life, no shades of gray if you will. Charles bemoaned that fact about you. He often said, 'If Harry' "—Harrison winced at the name—" 'would try not to be so perfect all the time, perhaps he could find a little enjoyment in life.' "

Harrison frowned. "I find a great deal of enjoyment in life."

She ignored him. " 'Perhaps he might even have a little fun.' "

"I frequently have fun."

" 'Perhaps he might even find a wife. He is a handsome devil after all.' Charles's words, not mine," she hastened to add.

"I am looking for a wife."

" 'A wife,' he would say, 'who would bring joy to his days and not merely credit to his name.' " She cast him an overly sweet smile. "Like his brother did."

"I know precisely what I want in a wife and the appropriate candidate would be as different from you as night is from day."

"Would she?"

"Yes. She would have a sense of propriety, of her place and position in the world. She would be conscious at all times of her position as my wife, as the Countess of Mountdale and future Marchioness of Kingsbury. She would be an excellent hostess, a model of decorum. Well bred, perfect manners, and while beauty is not necessary, I would prefer she not be unattractive."

"So you want a well-bred, well-trained monkey?" She shook her head. "You can't choose a wife the same way you choose a financial investment."

"A wife *is* a financial investment."

Astonishment widened her eyes, then she laughed. "My God, you can be pompous, Harrison."

He blew a frustrated breath. "You, Lady Smithson, are the most annoying woman I have ever met."

"Thank you, Harry." She grinned, no doubt amused by her use of his brother's name for him. "That's the nicest thing you've ever said to me."

"I do hope your friend is not as annoying as you are."

"Goodness, why on earth would I have a friend who wasn't?" She nodded and, before he could respond, swept from the room.

No doubt all of her friends were annoying. Annoying women probably found each other through some sort of magnetic attraction that bound them together to create havoc for sane, rational men like himself. Not that it mattered.

Harrison was not about to allow a desperate, annoying woman—no matter how many sterling qualities Veronica alleged she had—to drag his family's name through the muck and mud of scandal. If this Lady Winterset was indeed as desperate as Veronica had led him to believe, why, she would be putty in his hands. He had the finances to sway even the most stubborn negotiator. And regardless of Veronica's assertions, he could indeed be quite charming and most persuasive. Any number of women he could name would agree. No, Lady Winterset had met her match. There wasn't a doubt in his mind of his success.

Even if she was indeed as annoying as his sister-in-law.

*. . . and indeed, there is an importance about the first meeting with a new gentleman that cannot be discounted.*

*When a man you have never met before takes your hand and raises it to his lips, his eyes never leaving yours, well, even at this very moment it makes me quiver simply to think about it. His eyes carry a promise of all sorts of things you dare not consider but enter your mind nonetheless. And you can no more break the spell than he.*

*However, more often, a first meeting is a tentative thing. With many gentlemen it is only after a long acquaintance that affection grows, that the fire flames.*

*And then there are those gentlemen whose very presence makes you want to throttle them thoroughly. Such a gentleman is either genuinely not to your liking and should be given no further thought. Or he can be very dangerous to your heart, and quite, quite delightful. Do remember, Dear Reader, there is a fine line between intense dislike and overwhelming desire . . .*

from *The Perfect Mistress,
the Memoirs of Lady Hermione Middlebury*

# Chapter Three

It scarcely mattered how long she stared or how many times she looked away and then looked back, the figures written in her fine hand on the pages of her account book did not change. The numbers indicating the small amount of money remaining did not grow larger, the sums of bills owed to merchants refused to shrink. Even the frugality which ruled her life these days made little difference. She leaned back in her chair behind the desk in the library and sighed. If only William had not died . . .

How many times had she thought that in the last three years? A hundred? A thousand? More? Not that it mattered. She could no more turn back the hands of the clock or the pages of the calendar and prevent him from falling under the wheels of a careening carriage than she could magically add a hundred or so pounds to her bank account. Utter nonsense to dwell on what might have been. From now on, *if only* was a game she would no longer play. She drew a deep breath, straightened, and continued her perusal of the accounts, with an eye toward determining if she could indeed accept Mr. Cadwallender's offer.

There was nothing left to trim when it came to the expenses of the London house. She had already cut her staff back to Daniels, the housekeeper, the cook, and one maid. Not that the staff had been much larger when William was alive. She would not be in the predicament she was now in if William had had more of a head for finances. He had always been more concerned with causes that needed a champion, precisely why he had been awarded a knighthood, and with clients who needed his help, rather than those who could afford to pay him in a timely manner. His wealthy family had given them an allowance even though they were not pleased by his choice of profession or wife. Still, he was the brother of the current Baron Holridge, the youngest of four sons and a Winterset. As such, he could not be allowed to wallow in gentile poverty. Pity they felt no such responsibility toward his widow.

Within days after William's demise, the family's solicitor had called on her to inform her the allowance would cease. If she and William had had children, it would be a different story the solicitor had said, with a look that indicated their lack of offspring was entirely her fault. After all, William had three brothers and a sister, and as Julia was an only child, their childless state was obviously her fault. She had been both stunned and furious but had, as a proper lady did, held her tongue rather than tell the overbearing, pompous Winterset spokesman that she would rather beg on the streets than continue to take so much as a penny from William's family. Still, at that moment, she had some savings and never imagined begging on the streets might well be her fate.

She turned the page of the account book and studied the expenses of her grandmother's support in the country. Here too there was nothing to be trimmed. Her grandmother and Mrs. Philpot—as much a companion as housekeeper really—lived simply in a small cottage. Mrs. Philpot's wages were scarcely more than the roof over her head and the food she ate. Even so, on her next visit, Julia would have to tell them the day was fast approaching when they would have no choice but to join her in London and make certain they understood.

She studied the figures carefully. If Mr. Cadwallender would increase his offer she might well be able to survive on that for the next few years, longer if she let go the cottage and moved her grandmother to London. She refused to consider what might happen after that. But if Mr. Cadwallender was right in his assessment and the book did well, there would be royalties and she might be financially sound well into the future. Dear Lord, she hoped so. Other than that absurd notion of finding a new husband with money, she had no other options.

At least she was clear-headed this morning and had slept soundly through the night, undisturbed by the dreams that had plagued her ever since she had begun reading Hermione's memoirs. She did indeed think of them as Hermione's rather than her great-grandmother's. It was decidedly difficult to read accounts of romps with royalty, dalliances with noblemen, and amorous adventures with gentlemen whose names she recognized and think of the woman involved as Great-Grandmama. The dreams themselves had been strange. One would have thought she might have dreamt of the incidents she read about but instead, Hermione had come to sit at the foot of her bed and chat about her life. Thus far, Julia had been reluctant to respond and had simply stared and listened, all the while reminding herself that she was asleep.

Hermione had accepted her silence and had chatted about whatever section of the book Julia had most recently read, clarifying a vague point here, elaborating on an escapade there. She was quite explicit and her descriptions embarrassingly erotic, or would be embarrassing if they were not the product of a too-active imagination Julia never knew she had, fueled by Hermione's memoirs. Usually, weariness would overcome her, the dream would fade, and she would slip back into a sound sleep. Oddly enough, she could remember these dreams upon waking with a clarity she'd never experienced with her dreams before. As such they were difficult to put from her mind even in the light of day. Worse, they at once reminded her of the intimacies with William she admittedly missed as well as those completely improper they'd never shared. That was a thought she immediately dashed from her mind although it did seem to resurface with every new dream. It was most annoying even as it was altogether too arous—

A knock sounded at the door and heat washed up her face. Nonsense. No one could possibly know what she was thinking simply by looking at her.

"Yes?"

The door opened and Daniels stepped into the room, carrying a small silver salver that bore a single calling card. "A gentleman is here wishing to speak with you, my lady."

He crossed the room and presented the tray with a slight flourish. Even in these times of limited finances, Daniels refused to let her circumstances affect his demeanor. She bit back a smile. Poor dear. While he might well have felt suited to a much loftier household, his sense of loyalty was stronger than his ambition. He would remain with her until the time came that she forced him to go.

She picked up the card and studied it. It was of the finest quality, elegant in its very simplicity bearing only a small embossed coat of arms and a title.

"How very interesting," she murmured.

"I can tell him you are engaged and send him on his way if you wish, my lady," Daniels said. The butler was as protective as he was loyal. She sighed to herself. He deserved better.

She smiled. "Tempting, Daniels, but not necessary."

"Shall I show him into the parlor then?"

"Yes. No." She glanced around the library. William had often worked in this room late into the night. While it was even smaller than the parlor, there was an air of businesslike competence here she suspected she would need. "I shall meet with him here."

"Very well, my lady." Daniels nodded and left the room.

Julia rose to her feet. Much better to stand than to allow his lordship to look down on her. She drew a deep breath.

Daniels opened the door and stepped aside to allow the earl to enter. He strode into the room with an almost visible air of purpose and determination. He was taller than she'd expected and far more attractive as well with brown hair of a shade so deep it was nearly black and eyes almost as dark. His shoulders were impressively broad, his jaw square and set with resolve. His nose was narrow, noble, and his lips a shade fuller than one would have thought attractive on a man. Veronica had spoken of him, of course, but had only mentioned his dashing presence in passing. She tended to speak more of his unyielding nature and annoying sense of propriety. His clothes were perfectly appointed, his style elegant and quite perfect in an understated sort of way that spoke of wealth and breeding. Julia could see by the way he entered the room and approached her that this was a man used to being obeyed, to getting exactly what he wanted. Without thinking she raised her chin slightly and met his gaze. Her stomach fluttered. This was obviously not a social call. He stepped closer and she could see his eyes were blue, the deep unrelenting shade of a winter night.

She adopted a cordial smile and nodded, grateful they were separated by the desk. This seemed a man it would be wise to keep as far away as possible. "What a pleasant surprise, my lord. Especially as we have never met."

A touch of annoyance glinted in his eyes then vanished. He offered a polite smile. "To my everlasting regret, Lady Winterset."

She gestured at the only other chair in the room, a worn wingback positioned off to one side of the desk, then took her seat. It was only after she sat down that she realized the lamp on the corner of her desk obscured his view and he had to lean to see around it. She'd never noticed before; she couldn't recall the last time she'd sat behind the desk with someone in the chair. "May I offer you some refreshment?"

"Thank you but no, I shall not be here long." He shifted toward one side of his chair and peered around the lamp. "This is not a social call."

"I thought not." She leaned slightly to see around the lamp. It was an ornate thing with an amber glass shade. Its bronze base was the figure of a woman with wings folded against her back, a fairy she'd always thought as a child but as an adult thought it was perhaps more a fanciful depiction of some other sort of mythical creature. Her mother had given it to her when she and William had set up housekeeping because Julia had always loved it whereas her mother had not. She really should move it but it was there in the first place because of its oddly comforting presence. Besides, she suspected he was more disconcerted than she. It was an advantage she preferred not to lose. "Please, go on."

"I have been informed by Lady Smithson that you are

in possession of the scandalous memoirs of Lady Middle-bury."

She nodded and settled back in her chair, obscuring his view of her. "I am indeed, my lord."

He shifted again to aim a disapproving look at her. "I must tell you, Lady Winterset, I have read the portion you gave to Lady Smithson and I am most disturbed by it."

"Imagine my surprise," she said under her breath. She should have known Veronica would show him the pages Julia had given her. Not that it mattered.

"To read about the dalliances of my father with a woman who was . . ."

She raised a brow. "Who was what, my lord?"

He narrowed his eyes. "Completely improper, thor-oughly scandalous, and without any sort of moral stan-dards whatsoever."

It was all she could do to keep the anger that rushed through her from showing on her face. Anger was not the way to deal with this self-righteous snob. No, she needed to remain calm and collected. Besides, Hermione herself would freely admit to her improper, scandalous nature. However, as Julia discovered with each page she read, her great-grandmother did have certain moral standards. They simply did not conform to those of the rest of soci-ety.

She folded her hands on top of her desk and smiled slowly. "Then her memoirs should sell extremely well."

His brow furrowed in a forbidding manner. "They will not sell at all if I have anything to say about it."

She leaned slightly to one side, partially obscuring his view of her once again. "But you don't, my lord."

He huffed, stood up, towering over the desk, and a prickle of alarm stabbed her although surely she had nothing to fear. This man's sense of proper behavior would never allow him to resort to violence against a woman. He grabbed the wing chair, moved it to a spot directly in front of the desk, set it down with a thud, then sat back down and glared at her.

She bit back a satisfied grin. "So you read what I gave Lady Smithson."

He snorted. "I did indeed."

"Did you not find it interesting?"

"I found it deplorable."

"But did you not find the writing of it"—how had Mr. Cadwallender put it?—"engaging and enthusiastic?"

"I found it offensive and appalling."

"The story itself then. Did you not find it intriguing?"

"Not in the least. I found it scandalous and disgraceful."

"I see." She leaned forward slightly and met his gaze. "The particulars then." Even as she said the words, a blush washed up her face but she couldn't seem to stop herself. "Did you not find them . . . exciting?"

"I found them disturbing. Extremely disturbing." Shock sounded in his voice. "I do not find reading about the misdeeds of my father to be the least bit arousing."

She raised a brow. "I did not say arousing, I said exciting."

"I know what you said even as I know what you meant. This is my father we are speaking about!"

"Just as my great-grandmother is the subject of discussion."

"But she is dead and he is very much alive." He clenched his teeth.

"And is he as scandalized as you by the thought of publication of this book?"

He hesitated for no more than the space of a breath. "I have not felt it necessary to bring this to his attention out of concern for his well-being."

"What a thoughtful son you are." She smiled pleasantly.

"Indeed I am." He leaned toward her. "Lady Winterset, let me be clear on this point. I find nothing enjoyable about reading of the . . . the amorous dalliances of my father and I have no desire to discuss intimate details of his past with him."

"I can well appreciate that, my lord."

He stared at her in surprise. "Then you understand?"

"Most certainly." She raised a shoulder in a casual shrug. "If Lady Middlebury was alive, I can't imagine discussing her adventures with her. Why, I would be dreadfully embarrassed."

"Exactly." The tense line of his shoulders relaxed a bit. "Then surely you can see why I do not wish the public to read of this . . . relationship with your great-grandmother."

"I can see it quite clearly."

"Excellent. I did not expect . . ." He cast her a genuine smile and it struck her as both very nice and little used. "I have a request then to make of you."

"Yes?"

"Lady Smithson has made me aware of your financial difficulties so I understand your need to sell the memoirs for publication. However, I would be most appreciative if you would remove all reference to my father from the book." In spite of his polite tone, it was clearly a demand more than a request.

"No doubt you would be. However . . ." She shook her head regretfully. "I'm afraid I can't possibly do that. As you said, the state of my finances is such that I have no choice but to sell this manuscript. Eliminating the section about your father would diminish the overall value of the work."

He stared in disbelief. This was a man obviously unused to being refused. "But my father is alive whereas I suspect the majority of the other companions Lady Middlebury lists are not."

She nodded. "That does seem to be true, at least given what I have read thus far."

"Scandal has never touched my family, Lady Winterset." A warning sounded in his voice. "And I refuse to allow it to do so now. I realize your family—"

Her spine stiffened. "Contrary to your implication, my family has, as well, been scandal free in recent generations."

"Yes, of course. My apologies." He drew a deep breath and leaned forward. "May I be completely candid with you, Lady Winterset?"

"Please."

He paused, as if trying to decide just how candid he wished to be, then drew a deep breath. "My father has lived a somewhat, shall we say colorful, private life and has not always been as discreet as one would hope. My family has, however, managed to keep his indiscretions from becoming public through the years due to my efforts and those of my mother before me. It has not always been an easy task."

"I can imagine."

He considered her for a long moment. "If you will not remove references to him from this book, let me propose something else." He pulled an envelope from an unseen pocket and laid it on the desk. "I am prepared to purchase the memoirs myself. You will find the sum I have in mind to be most generous."

She picked up the envelope, pulled out a paper that was as fine in quality as his calling card although she expected no less, unfolded it, and read the amount he had written.

"Most generous indeed," she said thoughtfully. Lord Mountdale's offer was nearly twice that of Mr. Cadwallender's, enough to support her household and her grand-mother for several years. "Still, my lord, if the manuscript is published, there will be royalties well into the future. An ongoing income if you will."

His brows pulled together. "Surely you do not expect me to provide continuing funding indefinitely?"

She narrowed her eyes. "I don't expect anything of you at all. But I must consider the future."

He gestured at the page still in her hand. "That is a considerable, even exorbitant, amount of money."

She nodded. "It is substantial."

"Well?" Impatience sounded in his voice.

"Let me ask you this." She met his gaze directly. "If I sell you the memoirs, what do you intend to do with them?"

Confusion crossed his face. "Nothing."

"Nothing?"

"Well, I shall destroy them, of course."

"Of course you will." She refolded the paper, "Then I fear I must decline. My grand-grandmother entrusted the record of her life to my mother and now it is my responsibility. I cannot allow her manuscript to be destroyed."

He stared in disbelief. "But it is a great deal of money. And you need money."

"Indeed it is and indeed I do but I must think of tomorrow as well as today." She shook her head. "If the book sells as well as I have been told it has the potential to do, it shall provide income for years."

"Be reasonable, Lady Winterset," he said in a stern manner. "Do not let misplaced sentiment cloud your judgment."

"This has nothing to do with sentiment," she said sharply. "I am being extremely practical. What you're of-fering, in spite of its generosity, is finite. It will not last forever."

He continued as if she hadn't said a word. "I do not know a great deal about the business of publishing but I do know the success or failure of a venture is always a gamble. What I am offering you is a certainty. As for the future, you are, well, a very beautiful woman. Surely you will remarry someday and no doubt soon. Then you will not have to worry about money."

She gritted her teeth. "As much as I do appreciate what was no doubt a compliment buried somewhere in your words, I have no intention of marrying anyone for financial stability. And, as I have no prospects at the present time, my marrying again is as much a gamble as the success of *The Perfect Mistress*."

He frowned. "The what?"

"*The Perfect Mistress*. That is the title Lady Middlebury gave to her memoirs."

"Oh, that is indeed"—he fairly spat the word—"perfect."

"Little in this world is perfect, my lord. My great-grandmother certainly was not. I am not. Even you are not perfect." Julia rose to her feet. "As much as I do understand your concerns I cannot allow them to prevent me from doing what I think is best with what is essentially my legacy."

He stood, his lips pressed into a hard line. "This is a poor decision on your part, Lady Winterset."

She shrugged. "It is neither my first nor do I suspect my last."

He cast a disgusted look at her lamp. "And that is the ugliest lamp I have ever seen."

She rested her hands on her desk, leaned forward slightly, and lowered her voice. "Your cravat . . . is crooked."

His hand shot to his neck to check the item in question.

She smiled sweetly and straightened. "My apologies, I was mistaken. It was the angle, no doubt."

His jaw tightened. "No doubt."

"Good day, my lord."

"I warn you, Lady Winterset, I do not give up easily."

"Lord Mountdale, you were candid with me. I should like to be honest with you as well."

"I prefer honesty."

She nodded. "Most people do." She chose her words with care. "For much of my life, I have done exactly what was expected of me. My behavior has been eminently proper. I avoided even the suggestion of scandal and I did as I was told. I have reached a point in my life when necessity dictates that is no longer of importance."

He stared at her with a hint of disdain. "It must run in the family then."

She shook her head. "What?"

"A complete disregard for proper behavior, the courting of scandal and moral lassitude." He glared. "You are exactly like your great-grandmother."

It was all she could do to keep from vaulting over the desk to pummel him into insensibility. Not that she could truly have bested him or that she had any abilities in that regard whatsoever, indeed, she had never even slapped a man's face. At this moment however, she suspected she could at the very least inflict noticeable damage on that too handsome, too smug face.

"And you, my lord, are a self-righteous, condescending, arrogant ass. As for my being like my great-grandmother." —she forced a cordial smile—"I certainly hope so." She pulled her gaze from his, sat down, and shuffled the papers on the desktop as if there was a great deal that needed her immediate attention and he was no longer of interest. "Good day, my lord. Daniels will see you out."

She sensed him staring at her although she refused to look up. "This is not over, Lady Winterset. I do not give up this easily."

"I never imagined you would," she said coolly, still refusing to give him the satisfaction of meeting his gaze. "Good day."

He hesitated for another moment then she heard him stalk to the door, open it, and snap it closed sharply behind him.

She released a relieved breath and sank back in her chair.

Dear Lord. She rubbed her hand over her forehead. What an irritating, sanctimonious beast the man was. She might well have given his offer serious consideration had he not been so . . . so . . . well, the man made her want to resort to violence. She was not, nor had she ever been, a violent person. Why, she scarcely ever raised her voice. But with the Earl of Mountdale she wanted nothing so much as to wrap her fingers around his neck and squeeze the very life out of him.

As for being exactly like Hermione, she did indeed hope she was. Oh, not when it came to her amorous escapades, but her great-grandmother had a strength and a spirit of independence Julia was coming to admire more and more. She had lived her life precisely as she pleased with no apologies and few regrets. One could do far worse than to emulate those qualities.

The earl's offer was tempting and she hoped she had not been foolish to turn it down. Still, she had no doubt she would hear from him again. He was not a man to accept no for an answer.

She was rather proud of herself for not losing her temper. She could only pray that when next she met his lordship she again would have the strength to restrain from surrendering to physical violence.

Although, she blew a long breath, she had never before met a man whose face deserved to be slapped as much as his did. And never met a man to whom she wished to do just that.

Until now.


As much as he hated to admit it, even to himself, he was wrong.

Harrison strode to his carriage, ordered his driver to return home in an even more curt tone than usual, climbed in, and tried to regain a semblance of calm. No, he was completely wrong about Lady Winterset. She was not at all as annoying as Veronica. Veronica was a sheer delight in comparison. Lady Winterset was by far the most annoying woman whose path it had ever been his misfortune to cross.

Not that she wasn't lovely. Only a blind man would fail to notice Lady Winterset's beauty. Her eyes were the shade of flawless emeralds and flashed with green fire when she was angered as she obviously had been more than once during their discussion. Her hair was fair, the color usually found on paintings of Renaissance angels, with an unruly curl. Even as he had spoken with her he watched several tendrils escape her admittedly proper coiffure to drift around her face, like the whisper of a halo. The thought had occurred to him, briefly and immediately discarded, when he had watched that pale gold strand caress the peach blush of her cheek, what a perfect match she might have made in those days when she was concerned with propriety and the avoidance of scandal. Not for him, of course. At least not now. She was entirely too intelligent and independent although she did have an admirable sense of familial loyalty, even if misplaced.

He blew a long breath. He had not handled that at all well. Veronica had told him that Lady Winterset was in dire financial straits and he had assumed that meant she would succumb to his generous offer. As lovely as she was, he had noticed a tension in the set of her shoulders as if they bore the weight of the world, a paleness that bespoke of a lack of sleep, and a few fine lines of worry creasing her brow. But he hadn't taken into account what else Veronica had told him about Lady Winterset's nature. No, he should have handled that better.

Now, he was obviously going to have to begin anew. She was clever but she was still only a woman and he was certainly smarter. And as stubborn as she may be, he was not about to give up. He would acquire those memoirs and prevent his family from becoming embroiled in scandal. His mother had taught him scandal was to be avoided at all costs. She had spent most of her life trying to keep his father's indiscretions quiet. He had always thought that was part of what had hastened her death. Still, he could never bring himself to blame his father. Neither his father nor his mother had been happy in their marriage. When he was younger and had been enamored of foolish notions like love he had wondered if they had ever felt that particular emotion toward one another. And if they had, when had it vanished? Well, he was certainly not going to predicate his marriage on love. If it existed at all, it was far too fragile and fleeting to last a lifetime. Charles, of course, had felt differently and had on occasion talked to his younger brother about the joy love with Veronica had brought him.

As much as he regretted the very idea, he would now need his sister-in-law's help. Veronica had scoffed when he had mentioned his powers of persuasion and charm and, admittedly, he had employed little persuasion and even less charm, but with very little effort he certainly could. And if Lady Winterset liked him, surely she would be more agreeable to selling him the manuscript. How difficult could it possibly be to get the woman to like him? He simply had to spend some time with her, socially perhaps.

And that he would put in Veronica's capable hands. He'd pay a call on her at once. She couldn't possibly refuse to help. She was a member of his family after all, no matter how tenuous the bond. Besides, it would be in her friend's best interest as well as his, especially if he increased his offer. He smiled with satisfaction. One way or another, Lady Hermione's memoirs would be his.

Even if he had to rely on the help of one annoying woman to best another.

# Chapter Four

"You want me to do what?" Veronica stared at him in that way she had, as if the level of his intelligence was far too low to justify his existence.

"I thought about it all the way here and it's a brilliant idea." Harrison paced the width of Veronica's parlor, his mind occupied with the details of what he now thought of as *The Plan.*

"It doesn't sound especially brilliant to me."

"That's because you don't see it the way I do."

"As much as I am eternally grateful for that, let me see if I understand any of this." She paused to pull her thoughts together. "You want me to have a soiree—"

"Nothing elaborate. Simply a dinner."

"*Simply* a dinner?" She sighed. "Very well then. A dinner so that you may use your powers of persuasion and your considerable charm on Julia to convince her to sell you her great-grandmother's memoirs so that you may destroy them."

"Exactly." He grinned.

"The obvious flaws in this plan are too many to mention." She shook her head. "Why a dinner? Why not a small gathering of some sort?"

"A dinner allows me to be seated next to her. Besides, I have impeccable manners."

"Yes, that will sway her." She scoffed. "I know when I am interested in a gentleman, the correct usage of the proper fork is always a considering factor."

He ignored the note of sarcasm. "If I am next to her at the table she cannot escape and will be forced to speak to me. I am prepared to raise my offer, by the way. I am considering some sort of trust or annuity that will pay her annually but right now she will not give any offer from me due consideration."

"Not surprising as you acted like an ill-mannered boor."

"I did not . . . well . . ." He paused. "Ill-mannered boor" did seem to describe his behavior with a disquieting accuracy. "I insulted her lamp."

"Goodness, Harrison, don't you know anything about women?"

"I know a great deal about women," he said in a lofty manner.

"Then you would know insulting a woman's style of décor is not unlike telling her her waist is a bit thick or saying yes when she has asked if her bustle makes her bottom look large."

"I didn't see her bottom," he muttered although admittedly, the rest of her figure was exceptional. She was shorter than he by nearly a head with a form nicely curved and lushly rounded in all the appropriate places. He mentally shook his head to clear the intriguing image.

She rolled her gaze toward the ceiling. "As for this dinner, how many guests would you like?"

"I don't know, thirty perhaps."

"You want me to have a dinner for thirty people?" Disbelief sounded in her voice.

He glanced at her. "Too many?"

She sighed. "I suggest we make up the guest list before deciding on a number. As I understand your somewhat garbled initial explanation, you wish me to invite—"

"I don't care who you invite for the most part but I do wish to have some of the literary set present."

"Why?"

"So that the conversation may be casually directed toward the uncertainty of publishing." By God, this was brilliant.

"I see," she said slowly. "You wish Julia to understand Lady Middlebury's memoirs might not ultimately prove as lucrative as your offer."

"Precisely. If you could invite a few authors perhaps."

She raised a brow. "Would you like some poets as well? Perhaps an artist or two? Maybe a violinist?"

"Don't be absurd. Why would we need artists or violinists?" He paused in midstep and glared at her. "You are not taking this at all seriously."

"It's not like hiring servants, you know. I can't simply send a note to an employment service requesting an upstairs author and a scullery poet. For goodness' sakes, Harrison, where do you propose I find such people?"

"I assumed you knew some. You are a well-known hostess after all."

"Well yes, there is that," she said grudgingly, somewhat mollified. "I suppose I have met, on occasion, an author or two, at someone else's affair . . ." She paused.

"You've thought of something."

"Perhaps." She sighed. "Lady Tennwright has a literary salon every other month or so. She knows everyone who has ever so much as picked up a pen. She insists on inviting me and usually I manage to avoid attending. I find her extremely pretentious. If I make any overtures to her whatsoever she will assume we are the best of friends. Still, I suppose I could ask her if she could—"

"Provide you with names? Excellent." He beamed at her.

She stared. "Whatever is wrong with you?"

"Nothing at all." He drew his brows together. "What do you mean?"

"You're pacing, you're smiling, and God help us all, you're positively enthusiastic."

Shock coursed through him. "I am, aren't I?"

"You are indeed." She shook her head. "It's most disconcerting. You arrive unannounced, which I cannot recall you ever doing even when Charles was alive, ranting about my giving a party so that you can charm Lady Winterset."

"I want those memoirs," he said firmly.

"Then you should have been charming when you met with her today."

"Yes, I should have," he said sharply. "But I wasn't and I must go on from here."

"At least sit down. All that pacing is driving me mad."

He took the chair nearest hers then leaned toward her. "I realize this is a large favor to ask of you, especially as I am someone you do not particularly like."

Her eyes widened in surprise. "Goodness, Harrison, I don't dislike you. I believe, as Charles did, that you have a great deal of potential, if you would only get that very large stick out of your—"

"Veronica," he said sharply.

She huffed and glared at him. "Honestly, Harry, I have always wanted a brother and have never had one save for you. As such I do wish we could get on better."

He stared at her for a moment. "And I have never had a sister. In spite of your marriage to Charles I have been reluctant to think of you in that respect. For that you have my apologies and my assurance that from this point forward I will indeed regard you as my sister." He meant every word, even as he realized a sister would certainly lend greater assistance than a mere sister-in-law. A sister would work with him. A sister would be an ally. He cast her a genuine smile. "But from what I have heard from friends who do have female siblings, our squabbling is not unusual."

"Well then, we shall carry on, I suppose." She blew a resigned breath. "When do you want this dinner?"

"As soon as possible."

"A week from now would be awkward but perhaps manageable."

"Tomorrow would be excellent."

"Tomorrow would be impossible. You might as well ask me to dance naked on an elephant in Piccadilly Circus while playing the flute! Except that I cannot play the flute. That would almost be easier."

He grinned. "But you, of all the people I know, would have no difficulty dancing naked."

She gasped. "You're teasing me! Good God! Are you ill? Dying?"

He chuckled. "I have never felt better."

She stared at him for a moment then her eyes widened and she sucked in a sharp breath. "God help us all, you like her!"

"Who," he said innocently although he knew full well who she meant.

"Julia!"

"Nonsense. I find her even more annoying than I find you." He scoffed. "Granted, she is quite beautiful if one likes all that angelic hair and flashing emerald eyes."

Veronica's brow rose. "Angelic hair? Emerald eyes?"

"It's a description, Veronica." He shrugged. "Nothing

more than that." He paused. "She looked vulnerable and weary though, as if she was bearing a great burden."

"She is."

"As a gentleman I naturally feel an urge to protect those weaker than myself."

"Make no mistake, she is not weak."

"No, I did notice that." He forced a casual note to his voice. "What kinds of traits does she like in a gentleman? I assume women talk about such things."

Veronica's eyes narrowed in suspicion. "If you don't like her, why do you want to know?"

"If I am to be as charming as possible, knowing the kind of man she likes would be most beneficial."

"If you are to be as charming as possible, you shall have to change your manner. You shall have to be far less stuffy and much more pleasant and friendly. You should also try not to be quite so dignified every minute."

He started to respond then realized she was probably right. "I can do that."

"We shall see." Veronica studied him closely. "She likes men who have a sense of humor."

"I have a sense of humor."

Veronica scoffed. "Not that I've noticed."

"What else?"

"She prefers men who appreciate her mind as well as her appearance."

"Yes, she would, wouldn't she?" He thought for a moment. "Is she dreadfully intelligent?"

Amusement twinkled in Veronica's eyes but her tone was somber. "Dreadfully."

"That can't be helped, I suppose." He nodded. "Anything else?"

"She likes what all women like. Consideration, thoughtfulness, a man who will worship the very ground she walks on. Who could not bear to live if she was not in his life. A man who would sacrifice what he wants most for her."

He stared. "You sound like you're reading from a romantic novel."

"You asked what women want and there you have it." She shrugged. "For most women, such a man is only found between the pages of a novel. They are forced to settle for far less. For some of us however . . ." She drew a deep breath. "I found all that with Charles. And should I ever find it again, I shall snatch the poor man up before he can take so much as a single breath." She cast him a wry smile. "Although I have no desire to marry again."

"Nonsense, all women wish to be married," he said staunchly. "You are still young and quite lovely. If it were not for—" He caught himself.

"For my independent, stubborn nature?" She laughed. "Yes, well, that is a hindrance. But one never knows what might transpire in life."

"I suppose not." He chuckled.

She stared at him then shook her head as if to clear it. "Harrison, I swear on my mother's grave I have seen you smile more today than I have in the entire seven years I have known you."

"My apologies for that, Veronica. I shall endeavor to be more . . ." He searched for the right word. "Amusing in the future."

"That will be interesting." She considered him for a moment. "Julia is not what you are looking for in a wife."

"Most certainly not. You have already said we would not suit."

"It bears repeating." She paused. "Of course, marriage would be one way to get legitimate possession of the memoirs."

"But as much as I am willing to pay." Harrison shook his head. "That price is entirely too high."

They discussed the details of Veronica's dinner for a few minutes more before Harrison took his leave, wondering why he hadn't reached this point with her long ago. Certainly he found her annoying and she was entirely too intelligent for her own good. But she was family and he liked this whole idea of having a sister. After all, wasn't it already his duty to watch over her? Didn't he owe that to his brother? And wasn't it a responsibility he had shirked? Well, no more. For a man who prided himself on living up to his responsibilities, it was something of a shock to realize he hadn't when it came to his brother's widow.

He left Veronica's with an newfound spring in his step and an odd sense of exuberance. He could not remember the last time he had felt anything remotely resembling exuberance but surely it was many years ago. Perhaps it could be attributed to facing a challenge, a goal that could not be easily achieved. Much in life had not been the least bit difficult for him.

And blast it all, when had he become so grim and overbearing? Certainly, he had taken over all of the family responsibilities from his father, which carried with them a sobriety his father had never displayed. But no sense of humor, indeed. Why, he found any number of things amusing, and if he did not show that amusement it was only because it would be frivolous to do so. He was certainly not a frivolous man and had no intention of becoming one. Still, he could be a little less of an ill-mannered boor.

His carriage rolled toward home and the oddest thought popped into his head and refused to go away. It would be a lucky man who got to worship the ground beneath Julia Winterset's feet.

*   *   *

"You haven't listened to a word I've said, have you?"

The now-familiar voice drifted through Julia's head and she groaned. Blast it all, another dream. It began as it always did, with Hermione's voice and Julia dreaming she opened her eyes.

"I have had quite enough of this nonsense," Hermione said. "Do sit up and greet me properly."

Why not? It was only a dream. Julia struggled to sit up, and sighed. "Good evening, Hermione." She yawned. "Or is it morning?"

"Much better." As usual, Hermione sat at the foot of her bed. "Now then, this will come as something of a shock as I suspect as you are very nearly as stubborn as I. I fear it runs in our blood."

"Oh, fortunate me."

"Sarcasm, my dear child, is not becoming in a lady."

"My apologies," Julia muttered, heat rising in her face. As always, she marveled at the vividness of these dreams.

"Brace yourself, my dear." Hermione leaned forward and met her gaze directly. "I am not a dream."

Julia snorted. "Don't be absurd. I have been dreaming of you since I began reading your memoirs." She shook her head. "I cannot believe I am arguing with a dream."

"You're not arguing with a dream. You're arguing with—dear me, how shall I put this?" Hermione thought for a minute. "There's really no good way to say it. You're arguing with a ghost."

"A ghost." She scoffed. "Utter nonsense."

Hermione raised a brow. "I assure you, I am quite real. Although *real* is a relative term I suppose, but I am as real as a ghost can be."

Julia studied her closely. "If you're a ghost, why can't I see through you?"

"You could if I wished you to but I don't. I find that transparent nonsense to be quite unnerving and that's from my point of view. I can't imagine how it would be from yours. Why, I might be extremely frightening and I really don't wish to frighten anyone." She aimed a stern look at Julia. "But I am tired of being ignored."

"I haven't ignored you." Julia narrowed her eyes. "If you're a ghost, why do you look like that?"

Hermione glanced down. "I think I look very nice. I always did love this dress."

It was indeed an exquisite deep blue silk, with dropped shoulders and puffed sleeves, trimmed in lace with small bunches of violets attached here and there.

"You look like you're going to a ball."

"One never knows," Hermione murmured.

"You died when you were in your sixty-seventh year. You don't look much older than I am."

"This is how I appeared when I was eight-and-thirty." She smoothed her hand over her throat. "My neck had not yet begun to sag, there were only the tiniest wrinkles at the corners of my eyes from laughter. I rather liked them. And my breasts . . ." She smiled smugly. "My breasts were magnificent, as you can clearly see."

Julia smiled in spite of herself. "They do look very nice."

"While I was somewhat of a remarkable beauty in my youth—"

"And humble," Julia said under her breath.

"—at eight-and-thirty, I was clever and I was confident and I was strong. All of which creates the kind of beauty that lingers in a man's eyes and in his dreams. Eight-and-thirty was a very good year for me." She sighed with the memory. "It is one of the . . . oh, benefits, I should say, of, well, death that one is allowed to appear as one wishes depending on the occasion, of course."

"That's the most ridiculous thing I ever heard."

"Then you have never heard the story about a crowned

head of one of those tiny European countries, a scullery maid dressed as a poodle, and a pony. Now that, my dear, was ridiculous."

Julia stared. She certainly did have an excellent imagination.

"But I digress." Hermione gestured in a nonchalant manner. "Where was I? Oh yes." Her eyes narrowed. "I am not a dream, I am not something you invented. I am not a result of indigestion or imagination. I am a ghost like Scrooge's Marley or Hamlet's father."

"Ah-hah." Julia aimed a triumphant finger at the alleged specter. "They were both fictional, concocted from man's imagination as surely as mine has conjured you."

Hermione's brows drew together in a forbidding frown. "Lord Mountdale was right, I see."

Julia narrowed her eyes. "What do you mean?"

"Why, he found you most annoying." Hermione's expression brightened. "And how would I know that if I were not a ghost? If I have not been watching over you?"

"You would know that because I know that." She shrugged. "It was obvious." Indeed, she'd never met anyone she was as certain disliked her as much as Lord Mountdale did.

"Even to the dead?"

"Apparently."

"He is dashing, though."

Julia shrugged. "If you like that sort."

"What woman in her right mind doesn't like that sort? The sort that is tall and handsome with piercing blue eyes that seem to caress you with every look—"

"They did not!" Although why would her dream say they had if they hadn't?

"And his hands. Did you notice his hands? You can tell a lot about a man by the size of his hands. And Lord Mountdale's hands—"

"That's quite enough!" Odd, Julia couldn't remember noticing his hands but obviously she had. "This is absurd."

"Not as absurd as when Lady Ridgemont had her portrait painted dressed as a mermaid." Hermione shook her head. "Sea green was not the woman's color and fish scales are never attractive."

Julia glared. "You're digressing again."

"I am, aren't I? I do hate it when I do that." Hermione thought for a moment. "I was about to mention that in addition to his handsome face and his ha—"

"Stop that!"

Hermione continued without pause. "He is extremely wealthy and would make someone an excellent husband."

"Would he indeed?" Was Julia really thinking such a thing? Surely she must be if the idea would surface in her dreams. Still, it was a revelation she was not willing to accept. Why, she didn't like the man and he didn't like her. Nor did he like her lamp.

"The gentleman has everything you need. Marriage to him would solve all your problems. And you could scarcely do better."

"Marriage to Lord Mountdale is out of the question. Furthermore he has nothing to do with this discussion." Julia directed a firm look toward Hermione. "We were discussing your . . . your nature."

"I assure you, I am indeed a ghost."

"Prove it, then." Julia folded her arms over her chest and nodded. "Go on. Prove you're a ghost and not a dream."

"What do you suggest I do?"

"I have no idea." Julia shrugged. "Something ghostly, I suppose."

"I'm not going to vanish and reappear, change my appearance, float near the ceiling, that sort of thing. I don't do parlor tricks." She sniffed. "Besides, anything of a ghostly nature you will simply attribute to the idea that you are dreaming." She heaved a heartfelt sigh. "I should have appeared to you during the day when there wasn't a doubt in your mind as to your wakefulness. Perhaps to-morrow—"

"No," Julia said without thinking.

"No?" Hermione raised a brow. "Then you do believe me."

Julia shook her head. "No, I don't. I simply don't want the idea that you may pop up at any minute haunting my thoughts all day."

"Haunting your thoughts?" Hermione grinned. "What a telling phrase."

Julia sighed. "I am now going to bury my head in my pillow and force everything from my mind, thus ending this dream."

"You can bury your head in the desert sands for all the difference it makes, I shall not go away," Hermione said in a tone that was as pleasant as it was determined. "I have no idea how I shall prove my nature but prove it I shall. We shan't accomplish anything until I do," she added under her breath.

"What do you wish to accomplish?" Julia said slowly.

"Why, I am here to help, of course."

"At the moment you can help by allowing me to get some much-needed rest."

"If I'm a dream then you are asleep and already getting rest."

"I have scarcely had a decent night's sleep since I began reading your memoirs."

Hermione cast her a satisfied grin. "They are stimulating, aren't they?"

"They are scandalous, disgraceful, and completely out-rageous."

"They should sell very well then."

Julia smiled wryly. "Yes, they should." She drew a deep breath. "And you have my thanks for writing them."

"It was entirely my pleasure." Hermione smirked. "In so many ways."

Julia groaned. "Good Lord."

"I know. You have not reached page one forty-seven yet. What if I tell you what's on that page? It's not something you already know. That should prove I know things you don't."

"My dear Hermione, I can very nearly guess the type of incident that will be recounted on page one forty-seven."

"Yes, well perhaps." She thought for a moment, then smiled slowly in an entirely too wicked manner. "What if I told you a secret you couldn't possibly know and would never suspect?"

Julia narrowed her eyes. "What kind of secret?"

"About your Lord Mountdale."

"He's not my Lord Mountdale."

"It's the reason why he, and his mother before him, are so concerned with scandal."

"How very interesting. Still . . ." Julia shook her head. "That sounds like gossip to me."

"And?"

"And I try not to indulge in gossip."

"Gossip, my dear, serves a necessary purpose. Without gossip, how does one ever learn anything of interest?" Hermione rolled her gaze toward the ceiling. "Besides, you won't be indulging in gossip, I will. You'll just be listening. Although the point is moot as this isn't gossip. This is something I know for a fact."

Without warning, Hermione vanished from the foot of the bed to reappear at once sitting beside Julia, close enough to speak low into her ear. Dream or not, it was most unnerving. Julia realized she felt Hermione's presence although she had no sense of her substance. Even in a dream it was enough to make a shiver run up her spine and so disconcerting that it took a moment for Hermione's words to sink into her mind.

"Good Lord!" She stared. "I can't believe I could ever come up with such a far-fetched idea."

"You didn't." Hermione huffed. "It's the truth and something you would have no way of knowing."

"That is true, I suppose." Julia thought for a moment. "However, I have no way of finding out if it's true, I certainly can't ask him."

"Oh, I don't think he knows."

"Then how am I to know if this is indeed a fact and not something my sleeping mind has concocted?"

"You are a clever woman, my dear. I'm sure you will think of a way." Hermione slipped off the bed. "And then you will have to accept that I am precisely what I say I am."

Julia sighed. "I suppose I will. Although . . ." She shook her head. "The dreams of you were bad enough. The very idea that my great-grandmother's ghost would be here, in the flesh—"

"Not exactly," Hermione murmured.

"—speaking with me as if she were alive, revealing secrets—it's hard to believe."

"No, dear. What is hard to believe is the time Lord Albemarle and Lady Ed—"

"Enough!" Julia huffed. "I do not want to hear another scandalous story about people who are long dead and best forgotten."

"I'll tell them you said so," Hermione said in a wry tone.

Julia groaned.

"Try to remember, child, that while the dead do not

mind being thought of as dead, we do hate to think we've been forgotten."

"*You* will never be forgotten."

"You are a dear girl and most thoughtful." Hermione cast her a brilliant smile. "Now, go back to sleep or else you shall have nasty bags under your eyes in the morning and will not look anywhere near your best. You should always endeavor to look your best, you know. One never knows who one might run into unexpectedly."

"I am asleep," Julia said firmly.

"I shall return when you are prepared to accept the reality of my existence."

"I can scarcely wait." Julia sighed and lay back down, pulling her covers up around her. She refused to look to see if Hermione was still standing by the bed. Not that it mattered. Her great-grandmother was not a ghost but simply part of a dream. As for this secret she had revealed about Lord Mountdale, it couldn't possibly be true and was nothing more than the deepest recesses of Julia's mind dwelling on what might take his lordship down a peg.

Still, as she drifted deeper into sleep, the thought lingered that if the secret were true then Hermione was indeed a ghost and Julia's problems might well be just beginning.

*. . . and needless to say he swore me to secrecy.*

*It is always beneficial to know those secrets a gentleman does not want revealed. Not that I would ever encourage use of secrets in an untoward manner. Blackmail and the like are never acceptable unless one has no other recourse and there is something of great importance at stake. But the very fact that a gentleman, or anyone, has trusted you with that which they hold most precious is a gift that should not be valued lightly.*

*Now, however, he is long in his grave and I do not consider his secret to be as devastating as it is amusing. Dear Reader, you can well imagine my surprise when he appeared in what can only be called . . .*

from *The Perfect Mistress,*
the *Memoirs of Lady Hermione Middlebury*

# Chapter Five

Julia loved this time of year. The leaves were beginning to turn and there was the faintest hint in the air of the crisp days to come.

It was a scant hour and a half by train to the village where Julia's grandmother resided and no more than a ten-minute walk from the station to her grandmother's cottage. The village was decidedly picturesque with aged buildings, brick or timbered. She strolled past the parish church and well-tended church graveyard. It was easy to see why her grandmother loved it here. After the busy streets of London, the single road that wound through the village was quiet and tranquil. It was at this point in her walk, where the cottage first came into view, that Julia inevitably felt a sharp twinge of annoyance.

Not at her grandmother—the old woman couldn't help being eccentric or even a bit dotty. Not at the need to travel from London as often as she could manage it. And not at the unexpected expense of her grandmother's support that had become her responsibility when her parents had died.

But at her parents, especially her mother, who had chosen to keep her grandmother's existence secret, even from their daughter. No doubt due to shame as to the state of her mental faculties. Still, it made no sense at all. Certainly Lady Eleanor Everett was a little peculiar perhaps and yes, she did tend to talk to people who weren't there even if that might well run in the family. But Julia had visited her as often as possible after she'd learned she was alive, and very nearly once a month since William's death, and didn't think she was truly mad. Just old and possibly . . . sad.

Mrs. Philpot opened the cottage door at Julia's knock. Tall and thin, brisk and a bit stern, Harriet Philpot and her husband had worked for, in truth, cared for, Lady Everett since she had first moved to the cottage more than thirty years ago. Mr. Philpot had died a decade ago and now his sons maintained the place.

"How is she?" Julia asked after they exchanged greetings.

Mrs. Philpot's lips flattened into a disapproving line. "She's fine, she's always been fine, she'll always be fine."

While Julia appreciated Mrs. Philpot's protective nature toward her grandmother, she could never understand why this particular question always elicited such a curt response.

Mrs. Philpot showed her into the small parlor where Eleanor sat near the window reading as she always did, then took her leave. She did indeed look fine and far younger than her seventy-five years. She was small of stature, her hair nearly white and curling softly around her head. One could easily see she must have been quite lovely in her younger days. It struck Julia that she looked very much like an older version of the specter who appeared in her dreams. But, of course, she would.

"Grandmother?"

Her grandmother glanced up from the book and raised a brow.

Julia laughed and sat down in the chair beside her. "My apologies, *Eleanor.*"

"It would be different if I had known you as a child, dear," Eleanor said as she did every time Julia forgot to call her by her given name. "Having a grown woman call me Grandmother reminds me of how very ancient I am. And reminds me as well that I can do nothing about it." She sighed. "It's most upsetting."

Julia bit back a grin. "I am sorry."

"I know you are, Julia." Her green eyes twinkled. "My only consolation is that one day you shall be in my shoes. And while they are very comfortable they are as well very worn and sadly out of style."

Julia smiled then drew a deep breath. "I have a matter of some importance I must speak to you about today."

"A matter of some importance?" Eleanor closed her book. "Well, well, that will be a change."

Julia widened her eyes in surprise. "What do you mean?"

"Darling, when you visit we chat about the weather. Autumn is in the air today, which means winter is not far behind. I did so love winter once. Riding in sleighs, wrapped in furs." She sighed. "It has been a very long time since I rode in a sleigh and the cold no longer has the appeal it once did."

"Eleanor," Julia began.

"Sometimes we discuss literature. I should recommend the book I am now reading. It's quite naughty." Eleanor met her granddaughter's gaze directly. "But then naughty does tend to sell books, doesn't it?"

Julia stared. "So I have heard."

"Often, you listen to me ramble on about nothing of any significance whatsoever, which unfortunately, is the way my thoughts wander when left to their own devices. When your husband was alive you would frequently tell stories about his work. Now, you sometimes comment on public events which I am already familiar with. We are in the country, dear, not on the moon."

Heat washed up Julia's face.

"Then we have tea and one or another of us will mention the quality of Harriet's scones. How does she get them so light? Admittedly, they are usually exceptional unless she is cross as she tends to be on occasion."

"They are tasty," Julia said under her breath. She was a grown woman with responsibilities, not a child to be chastised. Still, she couldn't dispute anything Eleanor had said and she was not at all proud of herself.

"And when we're done with tea, you ask if there is anything I need. And I say I have everything I need, which is true enough, thank you for asking. Then you kiss my cheek and take your leave."

Julia stared. "It sounds dreadful."

"It's not at all dreadful. I cherish every minute that you are here even if I suspect that I am an obligation you could easily forgo."

"Eleanor—"

"The truth, if you please."

Julia chose her words with care. "It is true that I consider my visits to be somewhat obligatory but it is also true that"—she met the older woman's gaze—"I enjoy your company and I enjoy our visits. Even if I am sometimes at a loss at to what to say."

"Are you?" Eleanor chuckled. "Goodness, dear, you have never asked me about the past, your mother, or my family. At my age, there is a great deal of past to speak of. And while much of it isn't the least bit interesting, I daresay there have been moments now and then which are well worth relating."

"I've been coming here for six years. Why didn't you say anything?" Julia tried and failed to hide the defensive note in her voice.

"Pride," she said with a shrug.

"I had no idea. You could have mentioned something."

"Yes, I could have but I was afraid. I assumed you didn't wish to speak about anything other than the mundane. The mundane is very safe, you know. No one ever got offended by discussion of the uncertainty of English weather in the spring.

"I didn't want to talk about matters that might keep you from coming back. Your mother never visited nearly as much as you do and every time I tried to talk about anything of significance, I wouldn't see her again for a very long time. When she died"—a shadow of sorrow passed over her face—"and you began coming to see me, I was so pleased I didn't want to do anything that might make you stop." She leaned forward in a confidential manner. "This is my home, and while I am happy here, Harriet is not the brilliant conversationalist she might appear. An obligatory visit from you is better than no visit at all. Even in your darkest days, you brought life to me. And frankly I miss, well, life."

"Good," Julia said simply.

"Good?" Eleanor huffed. "That's a rather rude thing to say to an old woman."

"I don't mean it to be but it will make things easier."

"Ah, then now we have come to the matter of some importance." Eleanor folded her hands on her book and beamed. "This is exciting."

"Shall I fetch Mrs. Philpot? This concerns her as well."

"Harriet," she called, then lowered her voice. "She's right outside the door, you know."

Mrs. Philpot appeared at once.

Eleanor waved her to the nearby settee. "Julia has a matter of some importance to discuss."

"So I hear," Mrs. Philpot said wryly and took her seat. "Go on, girl."

Julia paused to choose the right words. "I know when William died I asked you to come to live with me in London and you refused."

"She didn't want to be a burden," Mrs. Philpot said.

Eleanor heaved an overly dramatic sigh. "I didn't want to be a burden."

"I do not consider you a burden," Julia said. "However, the state of my finances is not good. I have taken certain steps but they are speculative at best. While I may be able to support two households if all goes well, I cannot guarantee that. Therefore it is time, past time really, for you to reside with me in London."

Eleanor studied her thoughtfully. "Are you saying I would be more of a burden here than I would be in London?"

"Yes, and no." Julia searched for the right words. "I'm saying my finances are such that it is time to do what I have wanted to do for a long time." She took the older woman's hand. "You are all the family I have and I would rather like to talk to you every day, even if all we talk about is the weather. I know this is your home—"

"My home, dear child"—Eleanor cast her a brilliant smile—"should be with my family." She glanced at Mrs. Philpot. "It's time I think."

"Past time," Mrs. Philpot said. "Past time as well to tell her everything."

Eleanor cast the housekeeper a quelling glance. "I think not."

"She thinks you're mad."

"Not at all," Julia said quickly.

"She's as sane as I am," Mrs. Philpot said.

"Oh, that's a ringing endorsement," Eleanor said under her breath.

"She simply likes people to think she's mad so that they leave her alone. Your mother got the idea in her head that she was addle-brained and Lady Everett did not do anything to dissuade her." Mrs. Philpot huffed. "She didn't come here because her family wanted to hide her away but because she wanted to hide from the rest of the world."

Eleanor glared. "And I have done a fine job of it."

"Too fine." Mrs. Philpot's tone softened. "My dear friend, it is not too late to pick up the pieces of your life. Even at your age, you can begin anew."

Eleanor sighed. "I admit, I have been something of a coward."

"You have wasted a great deal of time," Mrs. Philpot said sternly.

Eleanor met her friend's gaze. "You really don't think it's too late?"

Mrs. Philpot snorted. "You're not dead yet."

Eleanor shook her head. "But most everyone I know is. Still, I suspect there are a few hardy, lingering souls about."

"Grandmother." For the first time, Eleanor did not correct her. "Is this true?"

"I do hope so. Surely, everyone I once knew is not dead."

"Not about that." Julia drew her brows together. "About you allowing people to believe you're mad."

"Madness, like beauty, is often in the eye of the beholder. I have allowed people to see what they expected to see," Eleanor said with a dismissive shrug. She nodded toward the housekeeper. "Harriet, we should begin packing at once."

Julia stared. "That's it then? You'll come to live with me?"

"It's been a long time since I have so much as stepped foot on the streets of London. I admit, it's something of a frightening prospect. Still . . ." Eleanor smiled. "I should hate to end my days knowing my spirit remained weak and insipid to the very end." She thought for a moment. "I would think that's the kind of thing that would haunt you even after death." She shook her head. "And I, for one, should very much like to rest in peace after I'm gone."

Julia turned toward the housekeeper. "Mrs. Philpot?"

Mrs. Philpot shook her head. "I shan't be coming with you."

Eleanor smiled a sad sort of smile. "I knew you wouldn't."

"My sons and their families are here. They've talked about me coming to live with them for a long while." Mrs. Philpot's lips twitched as if she held back a smile. "I suspect they just want me for my scones."

"As do we all," Eleanor teased, and Julia realized these women were as close as sisters. And, in truth, hadn't Mrs. Philpot been her grandmother's family? Once again, anger at her mother and regret for all the lost years washed through her.

Eleanor met her friend's gaze. "You'll be all right then?"

"Of course I will," Mrs. Philpot scoffed, but Julia was certain parting would be difficult for both women. She rose to her feet. "It's time for tea."

"And scones, if you please." Mrs. Philpot left the parlor and Eleanor sighed. "I shall miss her scones."

"My cook makes excellent scones," Julia lied.

Eleanor drew a deep breath. "When shall I come?"

"As soon as you wish."

"I have my affairs to put in order here. Oh, nothing of true significance really. I do think, however, or rather, I should like . . ." Eleanor began, excitement sounding in her voice.

Mrs. Philpot returned within a few minutes with the tea and Julia could scarcely get a word in. The two older ladies discussed what needed to be accomplished before anyone could move anywhere, her grandmother with an animation Julia had never seen before and the usually forbidding Mrs. Philpot perilously close to enthusiastic.

Regret washed through Julia. Not only because she hadn't known this lady in her childhood, but because she hadn't taken matters into her own hands years ago and insisted Eleanor come live with her. Now, Julia noted she was very nearly as excited as the older women. If truth were told, in spite of the companionship of her friends, her life was more than a little lonely.

By the time Julia prepared to take her leave it was decided that it was foolish for her to return simply to fetch Eleanor. They agreed that Eleanor would travel to London, escorted by one of Mrs. Philpot's sons, as soon as arrangements could be made.

"Very well then," Julia said, rising to her feet. "I shall see you soon."

"Sooner than you expect, perhaps." Eleanor beamed. "My clothes are long out of fashion and I may decide not to bring them with me, which would eliminate a great deal of packing. I would much rather acquire an entirely new wardrobe in London."

Julia winced. "Eleanor, there really isn't money for an entirely new wardrobe. A gown or two perhaps."

"Nonsense. We can sell my treasures," Eleanor said blithely. "Our treasures really. They are as much yours as they are mine."

Julia glanced at Mrs. Philpot who rolled her gaze toward the ceiling. Eleanor had been talking about her treasures since Julia's long-ago first visit. "Of course we can. Still, the market for treasures may not be as we hope."

"No, I suppose not." Eleanor sighed, then her expression brightened. "I know." She rose to her feet and hurried out of the room.

"They're pretty enough but not worth anything." Mrs. Philpot shook her head. "She told me years ago they were of no value. Nothing but paste. Copies her mother had made."

Eleanor returned, her hand fisted in front of her. "Hold out your hand, dear."

Julia dutifully held out her hand and Eleanor dropped a gold chain bearing a large pendant. Julia turned the pendant over in her hand and caught her breath. She didn't know a great deal about jewelry but this looked to be a lovely copy of a brilliant green stone, perhaps an emerald. Pity it wasn't real.

"Take that to a jeweler's, dear, and find out what it's worth."

"I'll do just that." Julia slipped the necklace into her bag.

"I really do need new clothes." Eleanor beamed. "And hats. Oh, I do love hats."

"Then we shall purchase new hats for you," Julia said, vowing somehow to scrape together enough for a minimal wardrobe. She bent to kiss the older woman's cheek. "I shall see you soon."

Eleanor cast her a brilliant smile. "We shall have a grand time."

"Indeed we shall." Julia smiled and opened the door. She would have to hurry if she was to make the next train back to London. She was to meet Veronica at Fenwick's in a few hours.

"Julia." Eleanor stepped closer and lowered her voice in a confidential manner. "About the madness . . ."

Julia shook her head. "There's nothing more you need to say."

"Oh, but I do." Eleanor paused. "To say I hear voices is not entirely accurate."

"That is good to know."

"I only hear one and she is most persistent." Eleanor held her breath. "Do you mind terribly?"

"Well, as long as it's just one," Julia said somberly. "We simply don't have room for an entire chorus. My house is not nearly large enough."

Eleanor studied her carefully. "You're teasing me." She smiled. "I like that. Now, be off with you and I shall see you soon." She nodded and turned to close the door.

"Did you tell her the voice belongs to a dead wo—" Mrs. Philpot's voice was cut off by the solid wooden door and Julia nearly stumbled.

What on earth? Surely her grandmother didn't . . . she couldn't possibly . . .

Julia drew a steadying breath and started off at a brisk pace. Time enough when her grandmother came to London to discuss whose voice she did or didn't hear. And exactly what that meant. Now she had a train to catch.

Julia had done a fine job thus far today of putting the question of whether Hermione was a ghost or a dream out of her head, even if it was never far from her thoughts. With any luck, Veronica would be able to confirm whether the secret Julia had been told was legitimate or just a product of her own far-fetched imagination.

If indeed Eleanor wasn't mad, Julia had no doubt as to whose voice she heard. And if this secret was true, well, she wasn't entirely sure which was worse.

To be truly mad or merely haunted.

*　*　*

"And how was your grandmother?" Veronica asked with a smile and sipped her tea.

Julia had arrived at Fenwick's a few minutes early and had impatiently waited for her friend. But once Veronica had arrived, Julia couldn't seem to find the right words. This was not the kind of question one simply blurted out. Of course, it wasn't the kind of thing that effortlessly slid into the conversation either.

"Very well actually. She has apparently only been feigning madness all these years, for the most part." Although there was that one voice. "She did agree to come to London to live with me."

"It's about time." Veronica shook her head in a chastising manner. "You should have insisted on this long ago. Why, if it was my grandmother—"

"You have known your grandmother all of your life whereas I have only known mine for a few years. If only . . ." Julia caught herself. "It scarcely matters. The past is over and done with."

"The past is always with us."

"In more ways than you know," Julia said under her breath.

"Take as an example, oh, I don't know, your great-grandmother's past," Veronica said casually. "That certainly is still with us."

Julia stared at her for a moment then laughed. "I should have known you would go directly to Lord Mountdale."

"He is family . . ." Veronica studied her cautiously. "You're not angry with me then?"

"Not at all."

"Good." Veronica heaved a sigh of relief. "I must confess, I felt somewhat torn. Loyalty to you versus loyalty to

Charles's family. Although I really didn't think one precluded the other as I do want what's best for everyone." She paused. "Harrison mentioned he's willing to increase his offer."

"Is he?" Julia asked in an offhand manner and sipped her tea. "And does he still intend to destroy the manuscript?"

"I'm afraid so."

"Then I have nothing to discuss with him." In truth, his lordship's desire to destroy Hermione's manuscript was little more than an excuse to refuse to have anything to do with him. Still, she might come to a point when she had to accept his offer. It was very lucrative after all. If only he wasn't so infuriating.

"I see." Veronica sipped her tea. "Oh, by the way, I have decided to have a small dinner party next week. I do hope you can come."

"I should check my calendar," Julia said in a serious manner then laughed. "If I had one. I daresay if I did, there would be nothing of importance on it."

"Then you'll come?"

Julia nodded. "I shall be delighted."

"You hardly ever accept my invitations, you know. You won't change your mind?"

Julia stared at her friend. "No, I assure you I will be there."

"Promise?"

"Whatever is the matter with you?"

"Promise you will attend my party."

"Very well, I promise." She sighed.

"Excellent." Veronica smiled with satisfaction.

"Now, tell me about this party and why are you so insistent I attend."

"You never go anywhere, really. You've only been to

my parties when I've forced you to attend. You never meet anyone new." Veronica shook her head. "You should get out more."

"I never have anywhere to go."

"And now you do," Veronica said simply.

Julia studied her suspiciously.

"You needn't look at me like that. This is just a small gathering really. Just a few . . . people."

Julia raised a brow. "By 'people,' do you mean eligible men perhaps? If you intend to throw marriageable men in my path as Portia's family has been doing—"

"I wouldn't think of such a thing." Veronica's brows drew together. "Not that it isn't a good idea, and certainly I will have some eligible men in attendance. I am inviting both you and Portia after all and I do so hate it when the numbers aren't even." Veronica drew a deep breath. "And Harrison will be there."

"Then perhaps you should redefine 'people,' " Julia said wryly.

"He realizes, when he called on you, he might have been a bit of a—"

"Vile, sanctimonious, beast?" Julia smiled pleasantly.

"In my family, we prefer ill-mannered boor," Veronica said loftily then grimaced. "My apologies, Julia. This whole dinner idea was Harrison's. He knows he behaved badly and he would like another chance to at least prove to you that he is not a—"

"A beast?"

"Or a boor." Veronica studied her. "You will still come, won't you?"

"I did promise. Why are you doing this for him? I thought the two of you didn't get along."

"We never have but now he wants to be, well, my brother." Veronica smiled weakly. "I've never had a brother and have always wanted one. When one's family is as small as mine is . . . Surely you understand."

"Of course," Julia murmured. "I understand completely. My family is even smaller than yours. I think it's very nice that you and his lordship have put aside your differences in the spirit of family unity."

"We shall see." Veronica smiled. "I daresay it won't be easy. We have always clashed. He has never really approved of me. Still, I did sense a change of attitude in him. Odd, really, but surprisingly pleasant all the same."

"I suspect he can be pleasant on occasion," Julia said, although she really suspected nothing of the sort.

Veronica laughed. "Given your encounter with him, I can't imagine why you would think that, although he is quite handsome. I know that has always encouraged me to give a man the benefit of the doubt."

"There is that." Julia paused. "May I ask you something about him?"

"Anything."

Julia hesitated then plunged ahead. "Is it true that he was conceived out of wedlock?"

Veronica's hand stilled, her teacup halfway to her lips. "What?"

Julia held her breath.

Veronica's eyes widened. "Where on earth did you hear that?"

Julia shrugged. "It doesn't matter."

"Of course it matters." Veronica set her cup down hard and stared at her friend. "With Harrison's concern about scandal, if this were to get out—"

"It won't. You have my promise on that. And my information comes from a very discrete source."

"Regardless"—Veronica shook her head—"Harrison doesn't know."

"Good Lord." Julia gasped. "Then it's true?"

Veronica paused then blew out a long breath. "Yes, Charles told me years ago. Harrison's father was quite the rake in his day. Only age has slowed his amorous pursuits. He is still most charming and I can only imagine what he was like in his younger years. Charles thought, and I must say I agree, that was why his mother was always overly concerned with even so much as a hint of scandal."

"A trait she instilled in Lord Mountdale."

"Exactly." Veronica nodded. "No one knows about this. Charles told me his mother married Harrison's father and they went off to Italy for nearly two years I think, long enough for them to return with Harrison without anyone so much as suspecting the truth." She met her friend's gaze directly. "But how on earth did you find out? If Harrison knew, it would devastate—" She sucked in a hard breath. "Dear Lord! Is it in the memoirs?"

Julia shook her head. "I don't think so."

"Then how . . ."

"If I told you, you wouldn't believe me."

Veronica studied her. "Tell me anyway."

"It sounds, well, mad."

"There are worse things than sounding mad."

"Indeed there are." Julia drew a deep breath. "Ever since I began reading her memoirs, Hermione, my great-grandmother, has been appearing to me in what I thought were dreams. She sits on the foot of my bed and discusses her life. It's been most disturbing."

Veronica nodded. "And explains why you have looked so tired of late."

"Yes. At any rate last night, she appeared . . ." How did one say something like this?

"And?"

"Well . . ."

"Go on," Veronica said impatiently.

"Last night . . ." Julia mustered her courage. "Last night she said she wasn't a dream but a ghost."

Shock colored Veronica's face.

"Needless to say, I didn't believe her."

"Who would?"

"So I asked her to prove it." Julia shrugged. "Which led her to tell me this secret that no one knew."

Veronica stared.

"Well, say something."

Veronica shook her head. "I have no idea what to say."

"It was bad enough when she was a dream. Now . . ."

"Now . . ." Veronica picked up her tea and took a sip, her hand trembling slightly. It was most disconcerting. Veronica was never shaken but apparently the idea that her friend was seeing ghosts was enough to upset even her.

"I don't know what to do."

"I don't think there's anything you can do." Veronica chose her words with care. "Given the veracity of the information she revealed to you, something you would have no way of knowing, apparently the only thing you can do is accept it. It's really rather exciting in its own way." Veronica shook her head. "You, my dear friend, are being haunted."

Julia rubbed her hand over her forehead. "So it would appear."

"Tell me one thing." Veronica leaned forward and lowered her voice. "Is she as amusing in person as her writing?"

"More so really." Julia's gaze met hers, Veronica's usual sense of amusement sparkling again in her eyes. At once the absurdity of the discussion struck her and she choked back a laugh. "This is not funny."

Veronica chuckled. "Oh, but it is." Veronica tried and failed to adopt a somber expression. "I've never met anyone who has seen a real ghost before."

" 'Real' being a relative term."

"Do you think I could meet her?" Veronica glanced around the tearoom. "Can you get her to appear here?"

"She doesn't do parlor tricks." Julia met her friend's gaze and the two women burst into laughter.

"That would be most undignified." Veronica giggled. "Is she transparent? Can you see through her?"

"She appears as solid as you or I." Julia shrugged. "Solid, as well, being relative." She paused. "Do you believe me then?"

"You know what is the best-kept secret I have ever known. That in itself would make me believe you."

"You don't think I'm mad?"

"Not in the least." Veronica took her friend's hand. "You are the most down-to-earth, sensible, rational person I know. Now if Portia had said something like this—"

Julia laughed.

Veronica sobered. "What does she want? From what I have read about this sort of thing, ghosts usually have a purpose."

"I have no idea. Up until last night, I thought she was nothing more than a dream."

"You need to ask her then."

"I shall. Now that I know she's"—Julia nearly choked on the word—"real."

"Relatively speaking."

"You have no idea what a relief it is to share this with someone." As hard as she had tried today, she could not put the idea of Hermione's ghost out of her head. Now, it was as if a weight had been lifted off her shoulders.

"I can well imagine."

"But do promise me you won't say anything to anyone."

"Absolutely not." Indignation sounded in Veronica's voice. "I would never reveal your confidences to anyone. Other people are not nearly as accepting as I am about things of this nature."

Julia arched a brow. "Things of this nature?"

"I have no idea what else to call it." She thought for a moment. "But I certainly wouldn't mention this to Portia if I were you. One never knows how she might react, and she's never been very good about keeping secrets."

"Portia would be the last person I would tell." Julia shuddered. "I can't even imagine what she might say."

"I can." Veronica grinned. "Are you sure you can't get—you call her Hermione?"

"Lady Middlebury is too formal and Great-Grandmother"—Julia shuddered—"doesn't seem right, given the intimate nature of her memoirs."

"I can see that. I do have a request though."

"Oh?" Caution edged Julia's voice.

"Do ask if she might make an appearance at my dinner party. We can seat her next to Harrison." Veronica grinned. "A ghost would be so much better than a violinist."

. . . should never judge a gentleman simply on appearance alone. I have met any number of gentlemen whose faces could easily melt even the most steadfast female heart, but beneath the visage, there was little of note to commend them.

I remember one of the most magnificent men it has ever been my pleasure to cast my eyes upon, a distant relative of one of the Scandinavian royal families. His hair was the color of palest wheat, his eyes as blue as the summer sky, and his smile promised all sorts of carnal delights. He was tall with nicely broad shoulders. I have always been nearly as fond of broad shoulders as I am of a well-chiseled masculine derrière. It is my considered opinion that a man should look every bit as delicious walking away as he does upon his approach.

My recollection is that he might have been a lesser baron with a given name of Leif or Gunnar or Odell. Unfortunately, the moment he opened that seductive mouth, one realized this was a creature to whom God had given the gift of incredible beauty but bestowed little else. It was deeply disappointing.

The most important qualities to look for in a man are not a handsome face or how he looks without a shred of clothing, although that is always commendable. A man needs intelligence and a modicum of humility. Not a great deal as involvement with an arrogant man is much more interesting than with a man who is overly unassuming. An arrogant man knows his own worth, and if he is clever as well, knows yours.

*Furthermore, there is little more attractive in a man than an astute sense of the absurd. A man who can laugh at the amusing moments in life as well as laugh at his own foibles, is a man to be treasured. There is nothing as delightful or as seductive as a man you can laugh with. As for Leif—Gunnar—Odell, well, my adventure with him . . .*

from *The Perfect Mistress,*
*the Memoirs of Lady Hermione Middlebury*

# Chapter Six

Julia handed her wrap to the footman who greeted her in the entry of Veronica's grand house. For a moment she regretted refusing Portia's offer of transportation, but Portia was nearly always late and Julia much preferred to arrive at an event at the appointed time. Even so, right now, it would have been nice to have someone by her side. It wasn't as if she'd never been to a party alone before. Certainly during her first year of mourning she had refused most invitations although she had been to a few gatherings at Veronica's in the past year or so. Still, those occasions were rare and nothing quite as elegant as this evening.

She moved to the entry of Veronica's parlor and paused, it was absurd to be at all nervous. At least she was well rested tonight. Hermione had not made an appearance since she'd revealed Lord Mountdale's secret. Julia wasn't sure if her absence was good or very, very bad.

She glanced around the parlor. Small gathering, indeed. She heard more guests arriving behind her and there were probably as many as twenty people here already. Not that the room seemed crowded. Veronica's parlor was at least three times the size of her own, maybe four. It must be nice to be able to entertain in a grand manner in a grand house without concern as to the undue extravagance of such entertainment. Julia pushed the unworthy thought aside. She wasn't jealous of her friend's financial solvency really, and she certainly wouldn't wish her own monetary problems on anyone. Still, she sighed to herself, it would be nice.

Veronica caught her eye from across the room and started toward her, skirting around guests, stopping for a word here or to cast a smile there. Most of the gentlemen stood, many of the ladies were seated, and it did look to be a lively crowd. This might be an enjoyable evening after all.

"Julia, my dear." Veronica took her hands. "You look lovely."

Julia smiled her thanks. Portia had insisted on loaning her a gown as most of Julia's were deemed to be out of style and not nearly elegant enough.

"I am so glad you came."

"I had little choice," she said wryly. "You did make me promise."

"Indeed I did and I shall do so every time I host a party from this day forward. I have been sadly remiss in my responsibilities as your friend in allowing you to hide away like a hermit." She tucked Julia's hand into her elbow and led her around the room, stopping at the various clusters of guests to make introductions and exchange pleasantries.

Julia knew a moment of discomfort when Veronica introduced her to the Marquess of Kingsbury, Lord Mountdale's father. Not that the elderly gentleman wasn't most pleasant and charming, but because she had read of his dubious adventure with Hermione. Much to her relief, he didn't mention her great-grandmother or the memoirs and Julia wondered if he knew about them, although surely his son or Veronica had mentioned them.

"You are going to have a delightful evening," Veronica said as they continued.

Julia raised a brow. "Am I?"

"I am certain of it."

"Then I gather Lord Mountdale sent his regrets."

"You are a silly goose." Veronica nodded at a point across the room. Lord Mountdale stood speaking with another gentleman, nearly as tall, almost as dashing. "Of course he's here. And he's requested to be your partner for dinner."

Julia pulled up short and glared. "Surely you did not agree."

"Don't forget this dinner was his idea. In fact he has called on me or sent me a note nearly every day this past week to check on how plans were progressing. As if I don't know how to plan a proper party." She sniffed and Julia bit back a smile. You could say very nearly anything you wished about Veronica's failings and it wouldn't bother her in the least. But woe to the person who questioned her skill as a hostess. "And he has asked a great many questions about you. He intends to try very hard to be pleasant and charming."

"It will be difficult for him, no doubt," she said under her breath.

"No doubt." Veronica laughed. "But Harrison has never had to put forth any effort whatsoever to gain whatever it is he has wanted. You shall do him good."

Julia narrowed her eyes. "I shall do him nothing at all."

"Did I say you?" Veronica's eyes widened innocently. "I meant to say this. This situation that is. The pursuit of the memoirs." She considered her friend thoughtfully. "Although, now that I think about it, you would indeed do him a world of good."

"Veronica." Julia shook her head. "I have no interest in your newfound brother."

"Excellent, as he says he has no interest in you either. I have already told him the two of you would not suit."

"Oh? And how did that topic arise?"

"I'm not entirely sure." Veronica shrugged. "One thing led to another and I found myself telling him that while you might well be perfect for him, he would not suit you at all. He is entirely too stuffy, too proper, and too unyielding."

"So I have noticed." Julia paused. "Just as a matter of curiosity, mind you, nothing more than that, why do you think I would be perfect for him?"

"Darling Julia, you are the cleverest woman I know, aside from myself, that is. Harrison detests intelligence in a woman." She smiled in a wicked manner. "You would drive him quite mad because you would never bend entirely to his will."

"I bent to William's will." She huffed. "I was a most proper and obedient wife."

"Perhaps, but William, from what you have said, was a rational man used to compromise. Besides, even if you do not see it, it's apparent to me, you are not the same women who lost her husband three years ago. That Julia would never consider selling scandalous memoirs." Veronica drew her brows together. "Do you realize how different you are?"

Julia cast her a reluctant smile. "Yes, I believe I do. I'm not sure that's altogether good."

"It's nothing short of wonderful." Veronica took her arm again and they started off. "As for Harrison, while it would be a great deal of fun to watch you lead him on a merry chase, I think you can do far better. And Harrison has a very strict list of what he wants in a wife."

Julia snorted back a laugh. "He has a list?"

"You sound surprised." Veronica chuckled. "Of all the men I know, Harrison is the one most likely to select a bride based on a strict list of the attributes he requires in a wife."

They paused before an older couple chatting with two gentlemen and a young, lovely blond woman. Veronica introduced Miss Celeste Waverly and her parents, a Mr. Roberts and a Lord Minden.

When they continued, Veronica leaned closer and spoke into her ear. "Her father is the youngest son of the Earl of Guilesford. She meets all of Harrison's requirements. The family fortune is immense. Miss Waverly has been trained since birth to be the perfect bride for someone exactly like Harrison. Her breeding is impeccable, her manners flawless, her education appropriate."

"And she is not unattractive," Julia murmured, wondering why she found the idea of the pretty young blonde with Lord Mountdale so disconcerting.

"She is a pale imitation. There is no substance to her, no spark. She is an empty vessel waiting to be whatever the man she weds wishes her to be." Veronica sniffed in disdain. "She is exactly what Harrison says he wants. I have already introduced them." She smiled. "We shall see."

"What are you planning?"

"Nothing untoward, I assure you. I am simply being sisterly. My *brother* has expressed his desire for a certain type of woman and I am presenting him with one. God help him." She glanced around the parlor. "We shall go into dinner as soon as the other guests arrive. I see Portia is not here yet." She sighed. "We must do something about her alarming tendency to disregard the very idea of punctuality."

"It seems to me, you are rarely anywhere at the appointed time."

"I am an entirely different matter."

Lord Mountdale noticed their approach and met Julia's gaze, a warm smile lighting up his face. She nearly stumbled.

"Why is he looking at me like that?" The oddest sense of panic fluttered in her stomach.

"It's called a smile. He doesn't use it often, which is a very great pity," Veronica added. "Now, do allow him to be charming. He intends to ignore his innate reserve and be at his most agreeable as evidenced by the smile."

"It's rather frightening, isn't it?"

"You have no idea," Veronica murmured, and they stopped in front of Lord Mountdale and the other gentleman. "Harrison, you remember my dear friend, Julia, Lady Winterset."

"Indeed I do." His dark gaze met hers and his smile lingered in his eyes. A genuine smile. She had caught a fleeting glimpse of it during their first encounter but tonight there was something decidedly different. As if he had changed or she had. Nonsense, it was nothing more than Veronica's talk about how they would never suit. Still, the oddest sensation fluttered in her stomach.

"And Julia"—Veronica nodded at the other gentleman—"I should like you to meet Mr. Ellsworth. Mr. Ellsworth, may I present Lady Winterset. Mr. Ellsworth is a celebrated author, you know."

"John Eddington Ellsworth at your service, my lady." He took her hand and raised it to his lips, his gaze locked on hers. A distinct glimmer of admiration shone in light brown eyes that nearly matched the color of his hair.

"Mr. Ellsworth." Julia tried not to stare but it was impossible. John Eddington Ellsworth was one of the best known and most popular authors in the country. Nearly as popular as Mr. Dickens although, of course, Mr. Ellsworth was alive. "I have read your work."

A smile quirked the corner of his mouth. "If you didn't like it, please be so good as not to tell me. I would be devastated if one of the loveliest women it has ever been my pleasure to meet does not like my work."

"*The* loveliest," Lord Mountdale said quickly.

Julia slanted him a quick glance. He was indeed trying to be charming. Perhaps a bit too hard. She turned her attention back to the author and pulled her hand from his. "Then you have nothing to fear." She glanced at Veronica. "I had no idea you knew Mr. Ellsworth."

"My repertoire of friends and acquaintances is remarkably varied." Veronica waved her hand in a blithe manner. "You would be surprised."

Lord Mountdale snorted.

"Lady Smithson and I met at a literary salon at Lady Tennwright's," Mr. Ellsworth said smoothly. "She was kind enough to invite me this evening."

"It's to be quite a literary evening," Veronica said smugly.

"A literary evening?" Julia studied her friend. "I wasn't aware that you enjoyed literary evenings."

"I enjoy all sorts of things," Veronica said in a lofty manner. "We also have two poets in attendance as well as one of my cousins who fancies herself a poetess. If we are lucky the gentlemen will read some of their work after dinner." Veronica's eyes twinkled with amusement. "If we are very lucky, my cousin will not."

"Still, one never knows when one might discover a new literary talent," Mr. Ellsworth said in a kind manner.

"I have read her efforts, Mr. Ellsworth. If simply being

able to rhyme head with dead is talent then she is blessed indeed. However, it is my duty as a hostess to shield my guests from such unbridled brilliance."

Julia choked back a laugh.

Veronica looked at her pointedly. "I had hoped for more interesting entertainment."

"Lady Winterset." Mr. Ellsworth's brow furrowed. "Your name sounds familiar. Have we met?"

"Not that I can recall," Julia said with a smile. "Perhaps you knew my late husband, Sir William Winterset?"

"No." He shook his head. "And I can't for the life of me imagine forgetting you."

"You are too kind." And entirely too polished. But then, Mr. Ellsworth's reputation for amorous pursuits rivaled that of his literary efforts. He had been involved in more than one public scandal to his benefit. Scandal did indeed sell books.

He studied her for a moment then realization dawned on his face. "I have it." He flashed her a practiced grin. "I believe you and I have a great deal in common and a common acquaintance as well."

Julia raised a brow. "Do we?"

"Mr. Benjamin Cadwallender." He leaned closer to her and lowered his voice. "He has mentioned your ancestor's book to me and I must agree it should be a rousing success."

She stared at him. "Do you really think so?"

"I do indeed." He straightened. "Perhaps we can discuss your venture further at another time."

"Isn't publishing a somewhat risky endeavor, Mr. Ellsworth?" Lord Mountdale asked casually.

The author nodded. "It is true, my lord, that one never knows how a work will be received. However, when one's material is particularly intriguing or when one already has a certain literary reputation"—he flashed a confident smile—"the risk involved is far less."

"Fortunately, the risk of dinner being overcooked has just been minimized as I see Lady Redwell has finally arrived." Veronica turned to Julia. "Mr. Ellsworth has agreed to escort Portia in to dinner."

Julia grinned. Portia adored Mr. Ellsworth's books. "Oh, she'll like that."

"I thought so." Veronica addressed the author. "I should introduce you. Mr. Ellsworth?"

"I would be delighted." He offered Veronica his arm and they started across the room, leaving Julia alone with Lord Mountdale.

Lord Mountdale chuckled. "He is every bit as interesting as I have heard."

She studied him curiously. "You sound amused."

"I am amused by a great many things."

"Are you?"

"I am indeed." He shrugged. "I simply don't often reveal my amusement."

"Why not?" she said without thinking.

He was obviously taken aback by the question. "I don't know. I suppose I have always considered it undignified to show one's amusement."

"And is it undignified as well to smile as if one truly means it?"

"No, it isn't." He smiled wryly. "I am a man of many flaws, Lady Winterset, as I'm sure Veronica has mentioned. She has recently pointed out this particular fault out to me. Even though I have never seen it as such, my"—he cleared his throat—"stuffy manner is one flaw I am endeavoring to change."

"Because you wish to convince me to sell you the memoirs?"

"That, Lady Winterset, would be an added bonus." He grinned, an unabashed, heartfelt grin that unexpectedly caught at her breath.

Good Lord, she'd noted when she'd first met him that he was handsome. Now, he was, well, more. This was absurd. She didn't like the man. It would take more than a smile that bespoke of all sorts of . . . of possibilities to make her feel otherwise.

She drew a steadying breath. "I think I should tell you, Lord Mountdale—"

"My given name is Harrison."

She widened her eyes. "Yes, I know."

"And yours is Julia."

"I know that as well." She shook her head. "In spite of your newfound determination to be less stuffy, calling one another by our given names would be entirely improper."

"Quite right, although I had rather hoped you and I could be friends." He smiled. Again. "Please go on."

"Yes, well, as I was saying . . ." This was ridiculous. She was well equipped to deal with the stern, pompous Lord Mountdale. This . . . this *Harrison* was altogether too appealing. She wasn't used to being flustered by a man and she did not like it one bit. As for being friends, that too was absurd. "I know that this party was your idea in hopes of changing my mind about the memoirs."

"It was, but it was not to convince you to change your mind about the memoirs. Merely to change your mind about me so that you will at least continue to allow me to plead my case."

"I suppose it is unfair of me to reject your offer simply because . . ."

"Because you don't like me?"

She shook her head. "I didn't say that."

"I don't believe it was necessary to actually say it."

"My apologies, my lord. I do not usually base my opinion on a single meeting. Especially when emotions are involved."

"No apology is necessary. I realized the moment I left that I had been overbearing, demanding, and didn't give due consideration to your concerns." He shook his head. "I was a . . ."

"Ill-mannered boor?"

"Among other things I can think of, ill-mannered boor being the kindest. In addition"—he winced—"I insulted your lamp."

She bit back a smile. "It's a very sensitive lamp."

"And I apologize for calling it ugly. It's really quite . . ." He searched for the right word. "Interesting."

"On behalf of my lamp and myself, I accept your apology."

"Then, as this is neither the time nor the place to discuss what is essentially business, I suggest we say no more about it tonight and enjoy what promises to be a pleasant evening." His gaze met hers. "Don't you agree?"

"I do." She nodded with relief.

He glanced behind her. "I see it is time to go in to dinner." He held out his arm. "Shall we?"

"Of course." She smiled and took his arm.

"One more thing, Lady Winterset, and then we shall set the topic of our last meeting aside hopefully forever."

"Yes?"

He leaned close and spoke softly into her ear. "My cravat is never crooked."

It was a brilliant idea when he conceived it and it was progressing just as brilliantly.

As was the plan, he was seated next to Lady Winterset—or rather, Julia. As improper as it was, he could not

help but think of her as Julia, as that was how Veronica re-
ferred to her. It had been his idea as well to seat Lady
Redwell and Mr. Ellsworth across from them—the author, to enable him to direct the conversation to the va-
garies of publishing, and Lady Redwell, because she was
the only other person Veronica had said Julia would know
at the table. While he fully intended to devote most of his
attention to her, he did not want said attention to seem too
obvious.

Veronica's cousin, Miss Evangeline Nelson, sat on Mr.
Ellsworth's other side. She was a chatterbox with literary
pretensions and obviously thrilled to be sitting next to the
famous author. Unassuming in appearance, Miss Nelson
was the kind of lady one would pass on the street without
a second look. Still, in spite of her endless babble, her enthusiasm and excitement gave her an air of animation that
was almost attractive. Her ongoing chatter, while somewhat annoying, had the unexpected benefit of eliminating
any possibility of awkward silences. It was also quite
amusing to watch both Miss Nelson and Lady Redwell
vie for the attention of Mr. Ellsworth.

"I think that's a brilliant idea for a poem," Lady Redwell said to the gentleman beside her.

One of the poets Veronica had invited, neither of whom
Harrison had ever heard of, sat beside Lady Redwell,
across from Harrison. The other poet was next to Julia but
was engaged in a heated discussion with the guests on his
left about the merits of various literary movements or
some such nonsense. Still, Harrison vowed to read some
of the gentleman's work in gratitude for leaving Julia's attention free.

"What do you think, Julia?" Lady Redwell asked her
friend.

"I think it is most interesting," Julia said thoughtfully.

His gaze caught hers and he realized she was hard-pressed to keep from grinning.

"And you, my lord?" Lady Redwell tilted her head in a flirtatious manner. He had already noted, much to his surprise, Lady Redwell was unfailingly flirtatious. "What do you think?"

"I agree with Lady Winterset," he said. "It is an interesting idea. Even somewhat provocative."

"I think it's extraordinary." Miss Nelson fairly bubbled with enthusiasm. "I only wish I had thought of it. Don't you think so, Mr. Ellsworth?"

"In theory perhaps." The author chose his words with care. "I would never denigrate anyone's idea, as an idea is simply a place to begin. One never knows when an idea, no matter how unique, might become the basis for a literary work. However, I do think there are some ideas that are perhaps not as conducive . . ."

Julia leaned toward Harrison and spoke under her breath. "You have no idea what they're talking about, do you?"

"Is it that obvious?"

"Perhaps only to me. And perhaps only because you agreed with me." Amusement shone in her eyes. "In truth I think it's a dreadful idea. I would never wish to read poetry about this year's cricket season."

He frowned in a mock serious manner. "For many people it is an extremely passionate subject and well suited to verse."

She laughed, a delightful sound that echoed in his blood. "Perhaps, but I cannot imagine anything quite so absurd as *Ode to a Winning Batsman*."

"Or *Sonnets from the Portuguese Cricketers*?"

Julia stared. "My lord, was that a joke?"

"I think it might have been," he said in an overly

somber manner and again she laughed. Yes, indeed, this was going well.

He had decided in the past week that it would not be enough to merely charm her, he would become her friend. She would be much more willing to turn over the memoirs to a friend rather than someone she detested. Yes, they would become friends and he would acquire the memoirs, remaining friends afterward because it would be most ungentlemanly to do otherwise. Besides, there was something about the woman that made him want to befriend her. According to Veronica, Julia was all alone in the world, with no family to speak of. Regardless of her intelligence or independent nature she was still only a woman. And what woman couldn't, on occasion, use the advice and guidance of a gentleman like himself, a friend, who was much better versed than she in the ways of the world and in particular, finance? The very idea appealed to his sense of chivalry. He quite liked this plan even if he wasn't entirely sure how to accomplish it.

He'd never realized before but he didn't, in truth, have friends. He had never especially considered them necessary. Besides, until his death, he'd had Charles who was as much a friend as a brother. Oh, he had a fair number of acquaintances, gentlemen he would converse with at his club and greet in passing on the street. Now, watching Veronica and Julia and Lady Redwell, he wondered if he wasn't missing something although, of course, they were women and friendships between men were a decidedly different thing.

"It is my considered opinion, with talent and skill," the poet across from him began in a pompous manner, "one can produce excellent if not exceptional . . ."

"Do you like poetry, Lady Winterset?" Harrison asked.

Her eyes widened in surprise. "Yes, of course. Don't you?"

"I am fond of Shakespeare's sonnets." He thought for a moment. "'Shall I compare thee to a summer's day? Thou art more lovely and more temperate.' That is fairly straightforward. One understands exactly what Shakespeare is saying. However, I must confess, for the most part I much prefer prose to poetry. Most poetry is too obscure, too vague if you will for my liking." He nodded at the poet across from him. "I daresay any poetry he might compose about the cricket season would have us scratching our heads at the conclusion wondering who had won and who had lost."

She smiled. "Probably." She tilted her head and considered him. "But you consider poetry vague?"

"All that imagery, one thing being said when something entirely different is meant." He nodded. "I do indeed."

"You find . . ." She thought for a moment. "'She walks in beauty, like the night, of cloudless climes and starry skies. And all that's best of dark and bright meets in her aspect and her eyes vague'?"

For a moment he debated the merits of honesty. "Not entirely, and admittedly the words are very nice, but why can't he simply say she is the loveliest woman he has ever seen?" His gaze met hers. "And everything he's ever thought was wonderful, everything he's ever wanted but never knew he wanted before now, is right there in her presence. In her eyes."

She stared at him for a long moment and he couldn't believe he had said such a thing. What had gotten into him? At last she shook her head slightly and smiled. "I believe, my lord, he said exactly that." She drew a deep breath. "You are not a romantic, are you?"

"I've really never thought about it." He shook his head. "But I fear I am too practical and rational to appreciate the language of poetry."

"What a shame," she murmured.

"Perhaps." He cast her a rueful smile. "That too may be one of my flaws."

"Is there no poetry other than Shakespeare's you appreciate?"

"I will confess," he said slowly, "there is a line or two that through the years has lingered in my mind."

"Oh, do tell." She leaned closer and lowered her voice. "I promise to keep your secret. That you are not so practical and rational as you appear. And even you can see the beauty in something as vague as poetry."

Again his gaze met hers and he ignored the voice in the back of his head that said this was too revealing and too fraught with meaning. "'How sad and bad and mad it was—But then, how it was sweet.' "

She raised a brow. "Robert Browning."

"It's a favorite of my father's and it has always struck something of a chord in me."

"And I believe I was wrong."

"Oh."

A teasing light shone in her eye. "There might be a touch of the romantic about you after all."

"And is that a good thing?"

She smiled slowly. "Yes, I think it is."

". . . and I would dearly love for you to read my work," Miss Nelson said to Mr. Ellsworth.

"I should like nothing better," Mr. Ellsworth said in a most gallant manner even though the look in his eyes said the man would rather have his thumbs cut off.

Miss Nelson gasped. "Even better, I have brought a few pages." She glanced around the table. "I could read some of it tonight."

The question hung in the air for an endless moment.

"I'm sure we would all be delighted." Harrison's manner was every bit as gallant as Mr. Ellsworth's and every bit as feigned.

"Delighted," Portia said under her breath.

"That was very kind of you," Julia said softly for his ears alone.

He looked at her and shrugged. "It was nothing, really."

"You have made her evening a success." She cast him an approving smile. "Possibly at our expense."

"No doubt we shall bear up admirably," he said in a no-nonsense manner. His actions were little more than polite. Any gentleman worth the name would do the same. Or at least should. Julia was giving him entirely too much credit. Still, he would take it.

A peal of laughter sounded from the far end of the table and they glanced in that direction. Miss Waverly and her parents were seated some distance away but even from here it was apparent she disapproved of the unrestrained expression of mirth. As any proper lady would.

"She is lovely, isn't she?"

"Miss Waverly?" he asked, his gaze still on the young woman. He had met her earlier in the evening and had immediately decided to call on her. Whether Veronica intended it or not, and knowing Veronica she knew exactly what she was doing, Miss Waverly appeared to be everything he was looking for in an appropriate match.

"Yes."

"Indeed she is." He studied the young woman for a moment more. Excellent posture, flawless manners, she did indeed look to be quite perfect. Abruptly he remembered his own manners and turned back to Julia. "My apologies, Lady Winterset."

"Whatever for?" she said coolly.

"It's most impolite to . . ." To ignore the lady he hoped to make his friend for the one who might become his wife. "To stare."

"No apologies necessary. You weren't staring at me after all." She smiled in a pleasant yet remote manner and returned her attention to the quail on her plate and the conversation across from her.

Damnation. Everything had been going so well. He groped for something to say but he'd never been good at idle conversation.

". . . even, so, I must confess a preference for light opera," Lady Redwell said. "Lady Smithson and I attended the Mikado some months ago and we thought . . ."

"Do you like theater, Lady Winterset?" Harrison asked.

"Yes, I do." She sighed. "Quite a lot really but I rarely seem to attend. Do you?"

He nodded. "I do."

"I thought it might be too frivolous for you."

"Not at all," he said quickly, although in truth he did find some offerings somewhat frivolous. "And you like poetry."

"Yes, my lord." She considered him for a moment. "I like poetry, I like to read. I have always had a fondness for Shakespeare but I like novels as well. I enjoy art, galleries and museums. I paint and sketch a little but not very well. I enjoy the out of doors, especially at this time of year. My husband used to take a walk in Hyde Park every morning before he went to his office. I often accompanied him. Now, I find I still enjoy a morning constitutional although I admit I am not able to do it every day. Now then." Annoyance sounded in her voice. "Is there anything else you wish to know about me?"

He ignored the question and drew his brows together. "You walk alone in the park every morning?"

"I'm not entirely alone. You would be surprised at the number of people who are about at that hour."

"I must disagree, Lady Winterset. I myself ride or walk

in the park nearly every morning and I encounter no more than a handful of people."

"You are probably right. I am usually engaged in my own thoughts so I pay no real notice."

"Lady Winterset." He leaned closer. "Do you think a woman walking alone in the park is wise?"

"I have yet to have any difficulties." She shrugged. "The sun is well up and I feel perfectly safe."

"Still." He paused. "Do you have a dog, Lady Winterset?"

"A dog?" She shook her head. "No."

"You should consider getting one if you insist on walking alone in the park."

"I suppose." She cast him a grudging smile. "I always wanted a dog as a child."

"You are no longer a child, and if you want a dog you should have one."

"I understand they are superb companions." She studied him. "Do you have a dog?"

"There are dogs at the estate in the country but they are hounds and used for hunting. Working dogs." He shook his head. "Not pets. It is difficult to keep a dog in town."

"I see."

She sounded distinctly disappointed.

"I don't have a dog at the moment but I am considering acquiring one soon," he lied. A furry, messy, problem of a beast. He snorted to himself. When Hades froze.

"Are you?" She arched a delicate brow. "What breed?"

"Breed?" He searched his mind for a breed of dog and couldn't think of one. "I have not decided. Something substantial I should think."

"Not a lap dog then?" Amusement danced in her eyes as if she knew he was lying, although why shouldn't he have a dog? He did enjoy the dogs at the estate. And a man with a dog was surely much more likable than a man who thought a dog was a great deal of trouble.

"Most certainly not." He paused. "Perhaps, when I have my dog, you will allow me to accompany you on your morning walk one day."

She glanced past him toward the other end of the table. "Perhaps you should be asking Miss Waverly that question."

"I am asking you."

"Because you wish to be friends?"

"Exactly." He nodded. "And because I think a woman shouldn't be walking alone in the park. It's not safe."

"Because a woman is unable to take care of herself?"

"Even to a capable woman of independent nature I don't think that can be debated," he said without thinking

"Not only on walks alone but in other matters as well?"

"Women, my dear Lady Winterset, no matter how competent, are still merely women." Even as he answered he knew it was a mistake. Still, he couldn't seem to help himself. It was as if his words had a life of their own. "A woman needs a guiding hand as it were from a husband or father or brother or—"

"Friend?"

"Yes," he said staunchly.

"Then a woman should choose her friends wisely, don't you agree?"

"Without question."

She smiled in a pleasant but dismissive manner and pointedly turned away to join in the conversation on her other side.

He pressed his lips together in annoyance. He should have known better than to speak his mind on the topic of the capabilities of the fair sex. He wasn't an idiot after all, or perhaps he was. But he had no intention of lying to further the cause of friendship. And damn it all, he would get a dog.

Through the final two courses of dinner, his attempts to engage her in further conversation were stymied at every turn. If he ventured a question, she would respond politely then return to chat with other guests. She busied herself with involvement in the discussions on her other side or across the table. Still, it did give him the opportunity to study her. She was indeed dreadfully intelligent and far too clever to do what she didn't think was wise simply because of friendship. This was not going to be easy.

Still, he considered the evening at least moderately successful thus far. Even if he hadn't yet managed to pull Julia and Mr. Ellsworth into a discussion of the risky nature of publishing, there would certainly be time later between the readings from one poet to the next. And while he hadn't planned on it, if Miss Nelson's work was as questionable in quality as Veronica had implied, it might help his case.

Veronica signaled the end of the meal and announced the ladies would retire to the parlor to allow the gentlemen no more than a half an hour for their brandy before the poetry recitations would begin.

He rose and assisted Julia with her chair. She turned to leave with the other ladies then turned back.

"Lord Mountdale, I congratulate you. Your purpose this evening has been admirably achieved."

"It has?" he said slowly.

"You said you wished to change my mind about you and you have succeeded."

His spirits lifted with satisfaction and he smiled modestly. "Excellent."

"While your manner on our first meeting was not conducive to cordial relations—"

"My fault entirely," he said quickly.

"—you do seem to have made a concerted effort this evening to convince me to give you another chance. And, as Veronica seems convinced of your sincerity—"

"Oh, I am nothing if not sincere," he said in as sincere a manner as he could muster

"—I can do no less." She smiled cordially. "Therefore I will not refuse to consider any further offer you may put forth."

This was good.

"I assure you, you will not regret it."

"Furthermore, I do accept your offer of friendship. It's most kind and one can always use another friend. And I know that, as my friend, you only want what's in my best interest."

This was extremely good.

"Without question," he said staunchly and seized the moment. "And what is in your best interest is to receive the most income possible in the most guaranteed manner possible from Lady Middlebury's memoirs."

"Ah, and there we differ, as friends often do."

"But—"

"I should tell you, my lord, the more I read my great-grandmother's memoirs the more I feel I know her. Her work is not merely an accounting of her adventures but is filled as well with her observations on the relations between men and women." She leaned closer, laid her hand on his arm, and gazed into his eyes in a knowing manner. "And some excellent advice regarding those relations as well."

Good Lord. What kind of advice would her great-grandmother . . . He swallowed hard. "Indeed."

"Oh my, yes. It would be a shame, my lord—why, it would be a travesty if her words were not allowed to be read by the world."

He stared. "The world?"

"The *entire* world." She removed her hand and smiled. "The world could certainly use more good advice just as a mere woman could always use the benefit of a guiding hand. Don't you agree?"

"I—"

"However, I will certainly give due consideration to any further offers you might wish to make. Because you"—she cast him a smile so brilliant he swore he felt it somewhere deep inside—"are my friend." She nodded and joined the rest of the ladies on their way out of the room.

He stared after her. The sense of triumph he'd noted a minute ago still lingered, if now a bit fainter and uncertain. Still, the evening was indeed successful for the most part. Julia had left the door open for him to continue to pursue the memoirs and had agreed to a tenuous friendship. The vaguest glimmer of a new idea teased the back of his mind and, God help him, he needed a new plan. And he had met Miss Waverly. Yes, it had been a most efficient evening.

A wave of satisfaction bolstered him and he ignored the voice in the back of his mind that wondered why Miss Waverly was at the bottom of that list of accomplishments.

And Julia was at the top.

*. . . and the count knew exactly what he wanted or more precisely who. Men are odd creatures in that regard. Often what they think they want isn't what they want at all. A wise woman recognizes that, a truly clever woman uses it to her advantage.*

*That is not to say that, on occasion, donning the costume of a shepherdess or a Roman slave girl is not greatly amusing for all concerned even if, as was the case in this instance, the count was intent upon . . .*

from *The Perfect Mistress,*
*the Memoirs of Lady Hermione Middlebury*

# Chapter Seven

"I never imagined you to be a coward." Hermione's chastising voice drifted into her dreams and at once Julia was fully awake.

She sat up and glared at the figure as always at the foot of her bed. "Where have you been?"

"San Remo, Brighton, Trouville. Seaside resorts, hunting lodges, palaces." Hermione scoffed. "Where do you think I have been?"

"I have no idea where those who are no longer alive go when they're not haunting those of us who are still living." If Julia hadn't been sitting up in bed, she would have tapped her foot with impatience. "Well? Where have you been?"

"Hither and yon. Here and there," Hermione said in an offhand manner then grinned. "You missed me, didn't you?"

"I most certainly did not."

"Come now. I am not that easily fooled. You, no doubt, have a great many questions for me other than where I have been."

"A great many, yes, but let's start with why you haven't returned since you proved that you were, well, real."

"I don't want to wear out my welcome."

"Hah! You don't convince someone that you're a ghost and not simply a dream and then just vanish."

"Most of the people I know vanish all the time," Hermione said under her breath.

"I think it's rather rude."

Hermione smiled in a overly sweet manner. "I have earned the right to be rude."

Julia ignored her. "And what do you mean—I was a coward?"

"That's obvious, dear." She ticked the points off on her fingers. "First, you left Lady Smithson's tonight before the gentlemen rejoined the ladies, thus avoiding that handsome, arrogant Harrison."

"Lord Mountdale, if you please."

"Ah, but you have begun to think of him as Harrison."

"That's not the least bit significant and no doubt only because that is how Veronica refers to him." And, in some odd way, this evening he had become much more Harrison and much less his lordship.

"Secondly, you did not stay long enough to hear Lady Smithson's cousin's poetry." She shook her head. "I never thought any descendant of mine would be quite so faint-hearted."

"My head ached." Admittedly, it had been more of a twinge but it had promised to develop into an ache if she'd had to continue to parry with Lord Mountdale—Harrison. The man was exhausting. She had spent the entire meal thinking of witty, clever things to say. It had seemed wise to leave when she'd had something of an upper hand.

Harrison was not all as she had expected. He proved to be an engaging but not overbearing conversationalist. He was attentive but not overly so, conversing as often with Portia, Miss Nelson, and the lady on his other side. Oh, there was that moment when he had studied Miss Waverly with an assessing gleam in his eyes that had she had found most irritating. Ignoring the woman sitting next to you for a woman you found more desirable was the height of bad manners. Still, it struck her that the man had made an effort to be cordial, and given all that Veronica had said about him and what she had seen for herself, it could not have been easy for him. His behavior was almost endearing.

Until he had apparently been overcome by his own staunch beliefs as to the capabilities of women to manage their own lives. That had been most annoying and made even more so because her position was not of her choosing. She did not choose for her husband to die nor did she choose independence. She did not choose for her finances to be limited. And she certainly did not choose to be born female.

"That's not all you found annoying," Hermione said under her breath.

Julia glared. "Do you read my thoughts as well?"

"Your thoughts are fairly easy to read." She paused. "She is quite pretty and very young. The older men get, the more they like them young and pretty."

"Who?"

"Miss Waverly, of course."

"Nonsense." Julia sniffed. "I scarcely exchanged more than a handful of words with her. Not nearly enough to find her annoying or anything else for that matter."

Hermione stared at her in a knowing manner.

"You may know my thoughts but I have no idea of yours," Julia snapped. "What are you not saying?"

"What is obvious even to a dead woman. Miss Waverly is entirely wrong for Harrison even if he thinks she's exactly what he wants." Hermione shrugged. "If he is as clever as he thinks he is, he will realize the truth before he marries her. I can't tell you the number of gentlemen I have known who have wed because a lady has met some strict list of criteria, only to discover, when it was entirely too late, that they have forgotten the most important attribute of all."

"Love?"

"Love is always an added benefit because love overcomes most obstacles." She shook her head. "But I have known men who have married for what they thought was love who then discover, after the first flush has faded, that there is nothing left and nothing to look forward to through the years. I have known men who have dismissed love as being unnecessary. Their unions too ultimately provide little happiness on either side. And I have known men who have found true love, but I don't think even that is enough." She thought for a moment. "A man needs a woman who will be a match for his mind as well as his heart. A woman who will disagree with him and challenge him. A woman he can respect and argue with and lose to as often as he wins. That is what makes the blood race in a man's veins and that is what makes him truly happy to be with one woman for the rest of his days. It's the adventure, my dear, that makes life worth living. Don't let anyone ever tell you otherwise." She met Julia's gaze. "Most men, and most women for that matter, never find that."

"Did you?"

"You haven't finished the book, have you?"

Julia shook her head.

"I would never reveal the ending of a book. You shall have to wait." She paused. "But, as turnabout is indeed fair play, let me ask you. Did you find that with William?"

"I loved William," Julia said staunchly

"And who wouldn't? He was a very nice man."

"Yes, he was. And kind and generous. And handsome." Julia wasn't sure why she needed to defend her late husband or her marriage but she did. "And we were very happy. I would have been quite content to have spent the rest of my days with him."

"One can scarcely ask for more than content in this life," Hermione said pleasantly. "If only his financial acumen had been . . . well . . . had existed at all."

"He was a good man."

"Yes, he was. As, I believe, is Harrison under all his stiff and stodgy ways." She leaned forward and pinned Julia's gaze with her own. "If you were to marry Harrison, your troubles would be at an end."

"You made that same ridiculous suggestion the last time you were here." Julia glared. "Do you intend to bring this up every time you visit?"

"Yes, because it's not the least bit ridiculous. It is, in truth, an excellent idea."

Julia drew her brows together. "If you claim to know my mind, I fear you are sadly mistaken. I have not for a moment considered marrying Lord Mountdale. Nor, I am confident, does he have any inclination toward me."

"Not yet," Hermione said with a smile.

"Not ever." Julia huffed. "I will admit that he was most agreeable tonight and charming and very . . . likable. And there is something quite appealing about a man who wishes to be your friend."

"Hmph."

"What does that mean?"

"It means he wishes to be more than your friend."

"Don't be absurd." Julia shrugged. "And he only wants my friendship because he thinks it will help him acquire your memoirs."

"But you cannot be swayed because you are made of sterner stuff."

"Indeed, I am." She thought for a moment. "However, I have agreed to give due consideration to any further offer he might make."

"Thus keeping Harrison in your life." Hermione nodded. "Very good."

Julia ignored her. "But I will never turn your memoirs over to anyone who intends to destroy them."

"I should hope not." Hermione sniffed. "It's not as though I dashed them off in an evening, you know. It took me several years to compile my adventures, my observations, and my advice. Why, my very life is laid out in my book."

"So I have noticed. And quite an"—Julia cleared her throat—"adventurous life it was too."

"Wasn't it?" Hermione grinned with satisfaction. "I did so hate to see it end."

"You shall live on forever through your book." Julia blew a long breath. "And, apparently in your . . . visitations."

Hermione sighed. "Apparently."

"Will you be with me forever?"

Hermione plucked absently at the bedclothes and shrugged. "Darling, I have no idea. I have a few thoughts on the matter and I have heard rumors—people do talk, you know—but I'm not sure why I'm here at all. I have always kept an eye on you, your mother, and grandmother but I was never able to speak to your mother or to you either until you began reading my memoirs."

Julia cast her an accusing look. "You talk to my grandmother though, don't you?"

A distinct look of guilt crossed the dead woman's face.

"I suspected as much. You do realize that's why people have thought she was mad."

"That's not my doing," Hermione said quickly. "If one wishes not to be bothered, the easiest way to keep people at a distance is to let them believe something is wrong with you." She shook her head. "No one wants to get too close to a madwoman. Or men who have monkeys for pets."

"I'm not entirely certain I'm not mad," Julia said under her breath. "Here I am speaking to a woman who doesn't exist."

"But I do exist, as I believe I have proved by revealing the detail of Harrison's—"

"You needn't say it," Julia said quickly.

"A fact you couldn't possibly have known."

"A fact even he doesn't know."

"Which is to your advantage," Hermione said in a sage manner. "It is always good, my dear, to know more than your adversary. Or your newfound friends."

"Hermione, my pet, are you coming?" A gruff male voice sounded from somewhere behind the foot of the bed.

Julia gasped and clutched the covers tighter around her. A shadow formed behind Hermione then slowly took shape.

"Goodness, Victor." Hermione rose to her feet and addressed the still-indistinct figure. "I don't know why you are so impatient. It's not as though we don't have all the time in the world."

"I was impatient before my death and I see no reason to change now." The figure solidified somewhat into a distinguished older man dressed in the fashion of more than half a century ago. "You found it charming."

"No, dearest, I simply let you think I found it charming."

He chuckled and looked at Julia, a definite twinkle in his eye that didn't make up for the fact that she could see right through him. Her stomach churned. "Death hasn't changed her a bit, you know."

Julia shrank back against her pillow. "Who is this?"

"Where are my manners?" Hermione shook her head. "Julia, allow me to introduce—"

"No, no!" Julia pulled the covers over her head. "I don't want an introduction. Just make him go away."

"She's not very hospitable, is she?" Victor said in a distinctly wounded tone. "I don't make appearances to anyone."

"Yes, I know, dear," she said, and Julia suspected if she had looked, she would have seen Hermione pat his—she shuddered—transparent arm. "Julia," she said in a no-nonsense manner, "come out from under those bedclothes at once. You're being rude."

"I'm being rude?" Julia pushed the covers off her head and glared. "This is my bedchamber and he was not invited. For that matter"—she narrowed her eyes—"neither were you."

"And yet here I am." Hermione huffed. "Goodness, Julia, I should think—"

"I can see through him!" Julia's voice rose to a high pitch. "It's . . . it's . . ."

"Most unnerving. Of course, I should have realized. Victor," she said sharply, "pull yourself together at once. You're scaring my great-granddaughter."

Understanding broke on Victor's face and at once he became substantially more, well, substantially *more*. "I say, I am sorry. One tends to forget the social niceties when one is dealing mostly with the dead."

"Understandable, my dear." Hermione nodded. "However, we do need to keep in mind that she is not used to our kind. I am the only spirit she knows."

"Why do you need to keep that in mind?" Julia stared at the unearthly couple. "Is he coming back?"

"Not if I'm not wanted," he said loftily.

"My apologies." Julia forced a calm note to her voice. "I am not used to entertaining gentlemen, living or dead, while I am in bed. It makes me somewhat, oh I don't know, unwelcoming!"

Victor inclined his head toward Hermione and spoke out of the side of his mouth. "She resembles you in appearance but she doesn't take after you at all otherwise."

"More so than she imagines, I think." Hermione frowned at her companion. "Why are you here?"

Victor raised a brow.

"Oh yes, of course. It completely slipped my mind. We must be off and you should go back to sleep." She looked at Julia and shivered. "You're going to look simply dreadful in the morning otherwise."

"You're leaving?" Julia stared. "Just like that."

Hermione shrugged. "Just like that."

Beside her, Victor started to fade but Hermione smacked his arm with a fan Julia hadn't noticed before and Victor immediately became solid again. He glanced at Julia and nodded a bow. "Again, my apologies."

With that he vanished. It wasn't as bad as watching him fade but it was still most disconcerting.

"When will you return?" Julia asked. "I still have a number of questions."

"Read the book, dear, I'm sure all the answers are there. As for when I will be back, I don't know." She shook her head and sighed. "I don't seem to have a great deal of control over that. I suspect I will be here when you need me." And then she too was gone.

Julia slid down under the covers and stared unseeing at the ceiling. Sleep? Hah, not anytime soon.

Now she didn't just have one ghost, she had two. And who knew how many more of Hermione's gentlemen might appear? Victor might be only the beginning. Victor? She pulled a pillow over her face and groaned. A Victor played a prominent role in chapter five.

Then there was Hermione's ongoing suggestion that she marry Harrison. Not that he would be interested even if she was, which, of course she wasn't. Not in the least. She freely admitted, he had been different tonight and not at all difficult to like. And while his offer of friendship still struck her as suspicious, he had seemed sincere.

But she was not what he wanted in a wife and he as far away as possible from what she wanted. She wanted . . . another William. Exactly. She was happy once, she could certainly be happy again.

She thrust aside everything that had transpired this evening and tried to go to sleep. But it was something Hermione hadn't actually said that stuck in her mind like a relentless refrain.

Content was fine unless one longed for adventure.

"I assume you are curious as to why I asked you here today." Harrison handed Mr. Ellsworth a glass of brandy and waved him to the chair in front of his desk.

"Indeed I am, my lord." Ellsworth glanced around the library and took his seat. "It is not often I get a summons from an earl."

"It was an invitation, Mr. Ellsworth, not a summons."

Harrison settled in the chair behind his desk and studied the author. He was unquestionably handsome with a man-about-town air that was equal parts disreputable and literary. A combination that was, no doubt, irresistible to women, which explained Ellsworth's substantial reputation with the ladies. Why, just last night, Harrison had watched as one woman after another flirted with the author, some in a most outrageous manner. Even Julia appeared to appreciate the man's questionable charms while Miss Waverly had paid no heed to the author at all. For a young woman, she was remarkably poised and proper. His resolve to call on her strengthened.

Ellsworth raised a brow. "It did sound like a summons."

"My apologies." He chose his words with care. "I do have a proposition that may prove most beneficial to us both."

Ellsworth sipped his brandy and considered him. "And what might this proposition involve?"

"From your comments last night I understand you're aware of the book Lady Winterset is interested in having published."

"Ah yes, the memoirs." Ellsworth nodded. "They should be most successful."

"I would prefer that they never see the light of day."

"Oh?"

"Let me be blunt, Mr. Ellsworth. There are portions of the memoirs that detail the involvement of Lady Winterset's ancestor with a member of my family. I do not want that incident to become public fodder. I do not want my family embroiled in scandal."

"I see, my lord," Ellsworth said smoothly. "How can I be of service?"

"I have attempted to purchase the memoirs from Lady Winterset to avoid publication. However, as she knows my intention is to destroy them, she has thus far refused my offer."

Ellsworth nodded. "Understandable."

"Something you said last night about ideas triggering stories made me think if perhaps there wasn't a better way to achieve my purpose. Something not quite as straightforward."

"You wish to deceive her?"

"I wouldn't say 'deceive.'" But in truth, his idea was rather less than honest. "Lady Winterset will not sell me the memoirs but she might sell them to you."

"To me?" Ellsworth's brows drew together in confusion. "Why would I want them?"

"To use as the basis for one of your own books." Harrison couldn't hide a small note of triumph. This was another brilliant idea. "Think of it, Mr. Ellsworth. A story by John Eddington Ellsworth based on the true escapades of Lady Middlebury. Why, it would fairly fly off the shelves."

"Indeed it would," Ellsworth said thoughtfully.

"That is the argument you will use to approach Lady Winterset."

"It is a very interesting idea," Ellsworth murmured. "And most commercial. With my name and Lady Middlebury's stories it could indeed be a rousing success." He grinned and raised his glass. "A brilliant idea, my lord. I should have thought of it myself."

Harrison stared at him. "You do realize you aren't actually going to write this book."

Confusion furrowed the author's brow. "I'm not?"

"Good Lord, no. The only thing worse than having the actual memoirs published would be to publish a fictional version of them."

"Then I'm afraid you have me at a disadvantage. What do you intend?"

"It's really very simple. I want you to approach Lady Winterset with an offer to buy the memoirs and tell her you wish to base a book of your own on them. Once she sells you her ancestor's work, you turn it over to me."

"Won't Lady Winterset notice when I don't write the book? Won't she want the memoirs back?"

"You tell her another more pressing project has claimed

your attention but you do fully intend to write her great-grandmother's story at some later date."

"I see." Ellsworth studied him for a moment. "Tell me, my lord, if I am not to write this book and I must say I do like the idea, then what do I, forgive my candor, but what is the benefit to me of your plan?"

"First of all, I have given you an excellent idea. You are an acclaimed, successful writer—you can certainly write the fictional memoirs of a fictitious mistress."

"I can indeed but it won't garner the same public attention as it would if it were based on a real person. The reading public loves scandals taken from real life."

"Yes, but, as you admitted last night, it's impossible to predict how a book will be received." Harrison directed him a firm glance. "Even a book written by you."

Ellsworth paused for a moment, no doubt considering recent reviews which Harrison believed included words like *trite* and *stale*. "Quite right."

"In return for acquiring the book for me I am prepared to offer you a great deal of money, payment, as it were, for services rendered. An amount equal to that which I am willing to pay for the memoirs." He slid an envelope across the desk. "In here you'll find what I am willing to offer for the memoirs as well as a token advance payment. To seal our agreement."

Ellsworth picked up the envelope and pulled out the paper and the banknotes. He studied the amount Harrison had written then refolded the paper, replacing it and the notes in the envelope.

"Extremely generous," he murmured, setting the envelope back on the desk. "I assume, given the amount here, you wish me to acquire the memoirs by whatever means necessary."

"Good Lord, no!" Harrison pulled his brows together.

"I don't want you to bash her over the head in the dead of night and steal away with the book."

"My lord, I may not be of noble birth"—Ellsworth's eyes flashed—"but I consider myself a gentleman. I would never resort to outright theft."

"I want this to be above board and legitimate. Nothing illicit or illegal. That would spawn an even greater scandal, and the purpose is to prevent any scandal at all."

"Legitimate, you say?" Ellsworth's brow rose. "Even though it is predicated on a fabrication?"

"One does what one must." He ignored the accuracy of Ellsworth's assessment and nodded at the envelope. "That sum is enough to pay off your debts and allow you to continue to live in the manner to which you are accustomed. At least for a while."

Ellsworth eyes widened with surprise. "How did you know about my debts?"

Harrison shrugged. "It's been my observation that a man does not live the type of life you do without incurring debts."

Ellsworth chuckled. "True enough."

Harrison leaned forward and met the author's gaze. "As much as I am not completely familiar with the publishing world, I do know that the proceeds from any book, no matter how successful, accumulate over time. I know your work is popular but even a writer of your stature could use an influx of funds."

Ellsworth swirled the brandy in his glass and smiled wryly. "Always."

"Then, Mr. Ellsworth, do we have an agreement?" Harrison rose to his feet behind the desk.

Ellsworth downed the rest of his brandy in one long swallow, set his glass down, and stood. "It seems to me I have nothing to lose and very much to gain." He picked up the envelope and slid it into his waistcoat pocket. "Yes, my lord, we do."

"Excellent." Harrison nodded, circled around the desk and walked Ellsworth to the library door. "I suspect this will not take long. Lady Winterset's finances are somewhat precarious and she must make a decision soon."

Ellsworth nodded

"I do expect to be kept apprised of your progress however."

"Certainly." The author paused at the door and considered Harrison. "Might I say, my lord, that Lady Winterset does not strike me as the type of woman who would take this sort of ruse at all well should she discover your plan."

"Then we must make certain she does not discover it."

"Of course." Ellsworth nodded a bow. "Good day, my lord."

"Good day."

Ellsworth took his leave and Harrison returned to his desk, buoyed by a sense of confidence and satisfaction. It was a perfect plan. Ellsworth was a well-known author and highly respected. Even Julia had not been completely immune to his charms last night.

The thought pulled him up short. Surely Ellsworth did not plan to acquire the memoirs through any sort of seductive means? Harrison certainly did not want him to . . . to *seduce* Julia into selling him the manuscript. He should have made that clear to the man and would do so at the first opportunity. Not that Julia would be receptive to Ellsworth's seduction. At least he thought she wouldn't. She was entirely too clever to allow her head to be turned by a man of Ellsworth's questionable reputation. Still, her thoughts were no doubt filled these days with her great-grandmother's questionable advice, and who knew how that might influence her. Not that Harrison cared who Julia might become involved with romantically. It was none of his business really. But as the instigator of this plot and more, as her friend, he did not want to cause her harm or worse, heartbreak.

"Is that wise?" His father stood in the doorway, leaning on the silver-headed cane that had become as much a part of him in recent years as his gray hair.

"Wise?"

The Marquess of Kingsbury hobbled into the room. "I've never known you to be devious."

Harrison busied himself with the papers on his desk. "I am not being devious."

His father snorted and settled in the chair in front of the desk.

"How much did you hear?" Harrison said under his breath without looking up.

"Enough."

Harrison did not respond but he could feel his father's gaze on him.

"I don't care, you know." The older man sighed. "About the memoirs."

At that, Harrison looked up. "How do you know about the memoirs?"

"Veronica told me. She thought you had already mentioned them." Father met his gaze directly. "You should have told me."

"I did not want to upset you."

"Rubbish." He snorted. "You didn't tell me because you suspected I would find the whole thing amusing." Laughter shone in his eyes. "And indeed I do."

"There is nothing amusing about scandal." Harrison winced to himself at the pompous note in his voice.

"When you get to be my age, the idea of being embroiled in scandal, no matter how long ago the incidents in question might have occurred, is rather exciting." He chuckled. "Brings back all sorts of fond memories. Makes you feel young again."

Harrison fixed his father with a firm look. "Nonetheless, it is my responsibility to prevent scandal from touching this family."

"And you take your responsibilities entirely too seriously."

"One of us should."

"And I have left it to you. My apologies." Father sighed. "It's entirely my fault, I suppose."

"Of course it is. If you hadn't been so indiscreet and free with your favors—"

He laughed. "I have no regrets on that particular score. Admittedly, if I had my life to live over I might not make all the same decisions. I do have a few regrets but there is not a great deal I would change. I have enjoyed my life and as there is more behind me than ahead, I daresay not everyone can say that." He sobered. "No, my apologies, my boy, are not for how I have lived but for what I have done to you."

"To me?" Surprise coursed through Harrison. "What have you done to me?"

Father shook his head. "I thrust the responsibility of managing this family's affairs upon your shoulders far sooner than I should have."

Harrison shrugged. "You were ill and there was no other choice."

"Yes, but I recovered. Rather quickly if memory serves. I should have relieved you of those duties then." He shook his head. "But I confess I had no desire to do so."

"That was ten years ago. I was more than prepared to accept my responsibilities."

"Through no fault of mine."

"Are you displeased with my management?"

"Not in the least. You are far more capable and competent than I ever was. We would no doubt be penniless by now if I had not handed the reins over to you." Father heaved a resigned sigh. "You have both a natural affinity for finances and estate affairs, as well as a passion for such things, that I never had. It must have come from your mother's side of the family. My passions run in an entirely different direction."

"Is that a compliment?"

"Yes." He shook his head. "And no." He paused. "I am quite proud of you, my boy. You should know that."

Harrison raised a brow. "But?"

"But you take life entirely too seriously."

"And you have never taken it seriously enough."

"Perhaps." The old man grinned. "Although perhaps that's what has kept me alive as well." He sighed. "I worry about you, my boy."

"You needn't." Harrison's manner was gruff, as if to hide the fact that he was oddly touched by his father's concern. They rarely spoke about anything of substance.

Father considered him for a long moment. "I would like, just once, to see you do what you want to do rather than what you think you should. To surrender to desire rather than be a slave to duty. To listen to your heart and not your head."

"As you have?"

He chuckled. "We are extremes, you and I. Opposite ends of the spectrum as it were." He met his son's gaze. "The perfect man would be a combination of us both."

"No man is perfect, Father."

"Nor is any woman. No matter how perfect she may appear," his father added in an overly casual manner.

Harrison narrowed his eyes. "Are you trying to say

something specific or is this just random philosophizing on your part?"

"I'm trying to say there is no one less suited to you than your Miss Waverly."

"She is not my Miss Waverly. I have not yet begun my campaign to win her hand." He frowned. "How do you know of my interest in Miss Waverly?"

"How do you think?"

"Of course." Harrison huffed. "Veronica."

"Do not forget, I too met Miss Waverly last night. And I saw the way you looked at her."

He heaved a resigned sigh. "And how did I look at her?"

"You looked at her as though assessing a good investment."

"She is," he muttered. "As well as a per—appropriate choice for a match."

"The appropriate choice for a match is the woman who captures your heart."

"Love?" Harrison leaned back in his chair and crossed his arms over his chest.

"Exactly."

"Because that served you so well?"

Father shook his head. "No, because I passed it by."

Harrison studied him. "I know there was no overt affection between you and Mother."

"Nonsense. We were very fond of each other. But no, she was not the great love of my life nor was I the love of hers." He paused for a long moment. "Love did not seem so important then. In hindsight, I think it was the only thing that was important. Still, circumstances and all that." He shrugged. "What's done is done. I hate to see you make the mistakes I made."

"There is little chance of that," Harrison said wryly.

"No, you shall no doubt make mistakes entirely different but mistakes they shall be." He rose to his feet. "I think this scheme you have hatched to wrest the memoirs from Lady Winterset is a mistake."

"Father." He sighed. "It is not as if I am going to steal from her. She will get a very handsome payment. Enough to ease her financial woes for some time to come."

"She will be furious when she learns the truth."

"I have no intention of allowing her to learn the truth."

"Secrets, no matter how old or how well kept, inevitably surface. Usually when they are least expected."

"Lady Winterset is not my concern."

"Pity." He thought for a moment. "She resembles her great-grandmother, you know. That fair hair and green eyes must run in the blood."

"I did not know, nor do I care."

His father ignored him. "She was a fine woman and I was very young." He chuckled. "She taught me a great deal."

"So I have read."

"Ah, yes. Veronica said you had a copy of the pertinent chapter." He paused. "I should like to read it."

Harrison widened his eyes. "Why on earth would you want to do that?"

"It is about me, after all. I should like to make sure it's . . . accurate."

Harrison groaned. "One can only hope it isn't."

"Given the look on your face, I suspect it must be." Father grinned in a wicked manner. "And I do want to read it."

"Very well." Harrison opened his top desk drawer, pulled out the scandalous pages, and handed them to his father.

"Memories, my boy." He glanced at the papers in his hand. "There is a point in life when what has passed is so much more interesting than what lies ahead." He looked up and met his son's gaze. "This plan of yours, it's beneath you. And I don't like it."

"Are you forbidding me then?"

"I gave up the right to forbid you to do anything long ago. Although I remain the official head of the family until I breathe my last, in truth, that title belongs to you." He scoffed. "Not that there is much family remaining to speak of. You do need to marry, you know. Continue the line and all that."

"I fully intend to, Father."

"Miss Waverly is not the woman for you."

Harrison's jaw tightened. "Father."

"She is yet another mistake."

"Well, then she will be my mistake," he said. "Not that she is."

"Hmph. We shall see." Father turned and walked awkwardly toward the door. "I do intend to live long enough to dance at your wedding, regardless of whether or not I agree with your choice of bride."

"I appreciate that."

He paused at the door. "Charles wouldn't approve of it either."

"Of what, Father?" Harrison said in a weary manner.

"Miss Waverly and your scheme to get the memoirs."

"Charles is dead."

"He was a good man." Father stepped through the doorway.

"He was exactly like you," Harrison called after him.

"That's what made him a good man." The door closed behind his father.

Harrison sank back in his chair and blew a long breath. He didn't like being chastised, especially for doing what he thought needed to be done. But his father was right: this plan of his was beneath him. Brilliant perhaps but not especially honorable. Still, one did what one had to do to protect one's family. Besides, whether Julia took his offer or accepted Ellsworth's proposal, she would be well provided for financially. And those tiny lines of worry around her eyes that marred her lovely face would vanish. He was doing this as much for her as for his own purposes. If it required a bit of deception to accomplish, so be it.

Damnation. He got to his feet and paced the room. It was all Julia's fault really. If she'd been reasonable, blast it all, if she'd simply joined the others for the poetry recitations rather than fleeing, he would have had the opportunity to continue to talk to her. Charm her. He had no doubt he had been most charming. At least until he had begun talking about the capabilities of women. Not that he wasn't right. Still, he was intelligent enough to understand that was not the way to curry favor with her. Perhaps he should send her flowers as way of an apology although he really shouldn't need to apologize for expressing his opinions. He blew a long breath. Women were odd, inexplicable creatures. He should probably send Miss Waverly flowers as well, to pave the way for his first visit.

He had chatted with her for a few minutes after the gentlemen had rejoined the ladies. Admittedly her conversation had not been as stimulating as Julia's but that was to be expected. Miss Waverly was younger and much less experienced socially than Julia. And possibly not as clever, although if she was, she was too well bred to display her intelligence. Even while talking to Miss Waverly, he had noted a certain disappointment that Julia had gone. He had to admit, while it hadn't been easy, he had quite enjoyed their conversation. Perhaps there was something to be said for cleverness in a women after all.

At least in a friend.

*. . . and, as he knew how very much I like surprises, he planned something quite extraordinary. If you don't know already, Dear Reader, I should mention that a surprise a man thinks is brilliant and delightful and that which a woman feels is brilliant and delightful are very often completely different. Nonetheless, as long as there is sufficient thought put into the surprise, even if it is to a woman's mind rather less than brilliant and delightful, it can still be most appealing. Indeed, there is nothing as attractive in a man as effort, no matter how misguided. Although one should tend to avoid gentlemen whose surprises involve exotic animals that require a handler. Unless, of course, one is intrigued by such things . . .*

from *The Perfect Mistress*,
the Memoirs of Lady Hermione Middlebury

# Chapter Eight

This was a true delight and one thing in her life she enjoyed without hesitation. Even better, it cost nothing whatsoever.

Julia reveled in the crisp feel of the morning air and set off at a brisk pace. It had been several days since she had last taken a morning constitutional. She just couldn't seem to find the time although, in truth, she couldn't understand why not. The park was no more than a few minutes' walk from her house and while the hour was still early, the streets were already filling with traffic.

She stepped through the park gate and paused, pulling a deep breath of air into her lungs. There was something refreshing and invigorating about the park in the morning. It seeped into her soul and made the very world around her seem brighter somehow, almost as if she wasn't in the midst of London but rather in the country somewhere, very far away. Where all was calm and serene and soothing.

There was scarcely anyone about at this hour, although the park was far from empty. There would be riders already on Rotton Row but that was on the opposite side of the park and she never went anywhere near there. This afternoon, the park would be crowded with carriages and pedestrians. But at this time of day one could imagine one was very nearly alone and she relished the solitude. It gave her the opportunity to think, to sort things out in her mind. To calm her soul.

She'd received a letter from her grandmother yesterday explaining that it was taking longer than expected to pack her things but she did plan on being in London very soon. Julia hoped she hadn't changed her mind. If necessary, Julia would fetch her herself. She quite looked forward to her grandmother's arrival and being able to share her life with the older woman. She sighed. Not that she wasn't already sharing quarters with an older woman, but of course that one was dead.

She absolutely refused to consider what might happen when Hermione and her daughter were under one roof with her. Perhaps her mother would make an appearance as well? No, that was even more absurd. Her mother's entire world had consisted of her father and Julia had had little place in it. It was fitting that they had died together in a boating accident as neither one of them could have lived without the other. It was their lack of concern about their daughter that had made her discovery of her grandmother's existence that much more upsetting. She could have had at least one relation who might have made her a part of their life, rather than an afterthought. She'd often wondered if his large family wasn't one of the things that had attracted her to William. She snorted to herself. And hadn't that turned out well.

Which brought her circle of thought back to her finances. And the memoirs. And Harrison.

He had sent her flowers yesterday. Yellow roses with a note attached asking to call on her. No doubt to continue his quest to buy the memoirs. Pity, he had no idea roses made her sneeze. Still the gesture was nice enough.

She had told him she would give his offer consideration and she fully intended to do so. Although, the more she read of the memoirs and, God help her, the more she talked to Hermione, the less inclined she was to sell the book to anyone who intended to destroy it. Regardless of how much they offered. Still, she looked forward to the next encounter with Harrison. She had rather enjoyed sparring with him.

"Lady Winterset," a man's voice called, and she jumped, her thoughts at once returning to Harrison's comments about ladies walking alone.

She swiveled toward the voice to see Mr. Cadwallender hurrying toward her, a smile on his handsome face. She breathed a small sigh of relief. "Good day, Mr. Cadwallender."

"Good day, Lady Winterset. And a fine morning it is too." He grinned. "Which could only be made better if you allow me to accompany you."

"I must say I'm surprised to see you here this morning. I can't recall the last time, if ever, I have run into someone I know at this time of day." She studied him for a moment. "It's most unusual."

"And delightful." He held out his arm. "Shall we?"

She smiled and took his arm. "You must admit, our encounter seems something more than mere coincidence."

He chuckled. "I confess then, you have caught me."

"Oh?"

"It's not a coincidence. I was hoping to see you."

"And you thought you would do so by lingering about the park gate in the early-morning hours?" she said slowly, not sure if she should be concerned or flattered. "On the off chance that I might happen by?"

"Not exactly." He grimaced. "I suppose I should tell you everything."

"That would be appreciated."

"I knew you were in the habit of walking in the park in the morning because . . . well . . ." He paused, obviously to collect his courage. "My servants spoke to your servants. I only wanted to know if there was anything you particularly liked, and I learned you liked this."

"I see." She thought for a moment. "And you wanted to know what I like because you wish to assist me in making a decision about publishing the memoirs?"

"Yes." He smiled in a sheepish manner. "Well, for the most part. We haven't spoken for nearly a fortnight and I am eager to proceed as well as impatient."

"And?"

"And?" He looked at her in confusion.

"You said for the most part, which naturally leads me to assume there is something more."

"Indeed there is." He drew a deep breath. "I do hope I am not overstepping my bounds."

She smiled. "That is yet to be determined I think."

"Yes, of course." He cleared his throat. "Lady Winterset, I believe we have a great deal in common."

She raised a brow. "Do we?"

He nodded. "We do indeed."

"And what might that be aside from the fact that I have a book you wish to publish?"

"Well . . . you like the theater and so do I."

"Everyone likes the theater, Mr. Cadwallender."

"Quite right. Let me think." His brows pulled together then his face brightened. "You like a good book as do I."

She cast him a wry glance."

"Yes, yes, I know." He sighed. "Everyone likes a good book."

"I'm afraid your servants did not do a very good job of gathering information from my servants."

"Apparently not," he said under his breath.

"Did they mention that among the things I like are diamonds and emeralds? Oh, I do adore a brilliant emerald," she said with a heartfelt sigh.

He stared at her for a moment then realized she wasn't at all serious. He grinned. "Every woman likes diamonds and emeralds."

She laughed. "Indeed they do."

"I hope you like surprises as well."

"It would depend on the surprise, I suppose."

They rounded a corner and, nearly hidden behind a tree, was a small table set for tea and two chairs. A servant stood nearby beside a parked carriage.

"Oh, how delightful. I wonder who—" She stopped and glanced at the publisher. "This looks rather familiar, Mr. Cadwallender."

"It should." He chuckled. "There was a similar incident recounted in the portion you've allowed me to read of Lady Middlebury's book."

"I see." Of course, in Hermione's memoirs, it was not a small tea table in the morning in a public park. It was a decadent dinner with champagne and berries, set under the stars in the private park of a royal duke with musicians playing hidden behind a stone wall. "Is this then the surprise?"

"Do you like it?" He held his breath. "I know it's not exactly Lady Middlebury's adventure but we are in the middle of London and it is morning and—"

"Mr. Cadwallender," she interrupted. "Its charm is exceeded only by its unexpected nature. I find it completely delightful."

"Good." He grinned. "Then will you join me for breakfast? Just tea and scones but—"

"It would be my pleasure."

He escorted her to the table and assisted her with her chair, then sat down. The servant immediately poured tea then moved a discreet few steps away.

"I must say the morning air does tend to stimulate the appetite," he said, slathering clotted cream on a scone.

She sipped her tea. "Tell me, Mr. Cadwallender, how did you know I would be here this morning?"

"I didn't." He shrugged. "I've done this every morning for the last three."

She stared. "Have you really?"

He grinned. "The element of surprise, Lady Winterset, is not easily arranged."

"I am most flattered." She paused. "You could have simply called on me, you know."

"I could have and I fully intended to but then I was, oh, inspired."

She laughed. "I shall have to thank my great-grandmother for inspiring you."

He cast her a quizzical look.

"In my prayers, of course," she said quickly. "But the more I read of her book, the more real she has become to me."

He nodded. "It's the mark of a good book and an intriguing character."

"Oh, she is certainly intriguing," Julia murmured.

"Lady Winterset." He chose his words with care. "When I said we had a great deal in common . . . well . . ."

"Yes?"

"I should very much like to call on you," he said, the words coming out in a rush.

"To discuss the book, of course. You are most welcome at any time." She shook her head. "And I do apologize for my hesitance in making up my mind. But it does seem a rather substantial decision and I—"

"That's not what I mean," he said quickly. "Oh I do wish to continue to further discuss the memoirs and my plans and all that, but I should very much like to call on you in a more personal manner. That is . . . well . . ."

She stared in disbelief.

"You are a widow and I am unmarried and I was most impressed, during our first meeting and . . ." He drew a deep breath. "I think you are the most remarkable woman I have ever met and I should like to call on you with the purpose of hopefully, at some point, engaging your affections."

"I . . ." She shook her head. This was the last thing she had expected and most definitely a surprise. "Mr. Cadwallender—"

"Benjamin. My given name is Benjamin and I would be honored if you would call me by my given name."

"I couldn't possibly. That would be most improper." Still, why not allow him to call on her? He was clever and ambitious and handsome. And he had gone to all this trouble to impress her and re-create, even if on a much smaller scale, one of Hermione's adventures. Obviously, he was a thoughtful man and very nice as well. Besides, it wasn't as if she had suitors lined up at the door. She cast him an encouraging smile. "For now, at any rate, but we shall see. And yes, you may call on me."

He stared, his smile broadening to a delighted grin on his face. "Excellent. I say, this is good. Very good."

She laughed. "I hope you continue to think so."

"I cannot imagine ever thinking otherwise," he said in a most gallant manner.

"So, Mr. Cadwallender." She took a bracing sip of tea. "Tell me how your new enterprise is faring."

"Better than I had anticipated," he began, the light of passion in his eyes. "We have already acquired works from several authors. Admittedly, none of them are as well . . ."

It wasn't at all difficult to listen to Mr.—Benjamin go on about his new business. The gentleman's enthusiasm was contagious and Julia found herself making comments and even suggestions. Now here was a man who obviously valued a woman who had a head on her shoulders. Who knew her own mind and did not need male guidance. Not like another man she could name. Not that she cared, of course.

Still, she couldn't help but wonder what it might be like to have someone else, someone most annoying, appreciate her mind as much as her face.


Harrison strode down the park path, rounded a corner, and pulled up short. What on earth were those people doing, sitting at a table, having breakfast under a tree in the park? How completely absurd. He stared for a moment longer. Good Lord, was that . . . He stepped behind a conveniently placed tree and peered around it. That was Julia! And who was that man with her? He had asked Veronica, in an offhand manner so that she would not make anything more of the question than it was, if Julia had any suitors and she had said no. Unless Veronica didn't know. Nonsense. This was exactly the sort of thing Veronica would know. Cadwallender! Who else but the publisher could it be? The gentleman with Julia was exactly as Veronica had described him. And obviously doing his best to charm the memoirs out of Julia. Well, two could play at that game.

Harrison turned and hurried back to the park gate, stopping the first street urchin he found. He gave the child a coin, instructions, the promise of another coin if he was successful, then sent him into the park. Harrison followed at a cautious distance. This was yet another brilliant idea. It struck him that he had had several since first meeting Julia, but then she was the type of woman with whom one needed to be on one's toes. The type who required brilliant ideas.

The boy approached the table and spoke to Julia's companion. If Harrison was wrong and this wasn't Cadwallender, then there was no harm done. After a few moments the gentleman nodded and dismissed the boy. He hurried back toward Harrison with a broad grin on his face. Harrison's smile matched the child's. He gave him the promised coin and sent him on his way. Cadwallender rose to his feet reluctantly and started off. Harrison picked up his pace and approached the table.

"Good day, Lady Winterset." He took the chair Cadwallender had vacated and sat down. "Breakfast in the park? What a charming idea."

"Lord Mountdale." Julia's eyes widened in surprise. "What on earth are you doing here?"

"Why, I was just taking a morning walk." He drew an exaggerated breath. "You were right, you know. It's most invigorating."

Her brows drew together in suspicion. "You said you rode in the park in the morning."

"Usually I do but after our talk the other night, I decided to walk instead." He glanced at the tea offerings. "And imagine my surprise to find tea and scones. Do you think your companion would mind? I do love scones."

"Mr. Cadwallender was called away to his office. A matter of some urgency apparently." She shrugged. "Do help yourself."

"Excellent." He selected a scone, broke off a piece, and took a bite. "Very good."

She studied him curiously. "I must say your appearance is most unexpected."

"As is yours." He swallowed the mouthful of scone, noting with satisfaction that it was somewhat dry. "I never considered that I might find you having a tryst with a suitor in the park in the morning. Rather early for that sort of thing, don't you think?"

"It was not a tryst." She huffed. "Indeed, I was as surprised to see Mr. Cadwallender as you were to see me."

He smiled in a noncommittal manner although it was all he could do to hold back a satisfied grin. He glanced at a nearby servant, obviously Cadwallender's, who was too well trained to allow more than a hint of his confusion to show in his eyes as to why the publisher had been replaced. "A fresh cup if you please."

The servant hesitated. "Of course, my lord."

He fetched a cup from a nearby carriage and placed it on the table.

Julia raised a brow. "Would you like me to pour?"

"That would be most appreciated. I'm not good at pouring tea. Excellent at pouring brandy however. I rarely spill a drop."

"Because pouring tea is something a woman is better suited to?" she said, and filled his cup. If he didn't want hot tea in his lap he'd best watch his words.

Still, he couldn't seem to help himself. He met her gaze. "Without question."

"You are most annoying, my lord." She set down the teapot and picked up her cup. "I don't believe for a moment that this meeting is a mere coincidence."

"There's nothing mere about it. I think it's smashing."

"Are you trying to be charming again?"

"Yes, indeed." He flashed her a confident smile. "Am I succeeding?"

She tried and failed to hide the smile in her eyes. "As I said, you are the most annoying man I have ever met."

"Excellent. Then my stock in your eyes has risen."

She shook her head in confusion. "What?"

"A moment ago, I was merely annoying."

"Most annoying," she said pointedly.

"Ah, but now I am the most annoying man you have ever met." He sipped his tea. "I think that's progress."

"To what end?"

"We have agreed to be friends. Surely you can forgive annoying in a friend. After all, Veronica is annoying and you are her friend."

"Veronica is not annoying."

He snorted.

She bit back a smile. "She can be a bit opinionated."

"Only a bit?"

"She's intelligent and she sees no need to hide her intelligence." She studied him curiously. "You don't like intelligent women, do you?"

It was a trap as surely as anything he'd ever seen. He choose his words with care. "I admit intelligence is not something I seek in a woman. Although I do appreciate it"—he caught her gaze and smiled—"in a friend."

"Then, as my friend, do tell me." She leaned forward and gazed into his eyes, as if to judge the truth of his words. "Is our meeting in the park this morning mere chance or were you looking for me in hopes of continuing your crusade?"

He gasped and clasped his hand over his heart. "You wound me, Lady Winterset. To think that you attribute such ulterior motives to something as innocent as a carefree walk in the park."

"And?"

"And I admit when I set out this morning," *or yesterday morning,* "I was not opposed to the idea of crossing your path."

"I see."

"Besides, you did not respond to my note."

"I intended to do so today."

"However, my intention was not to advance my cause." Even as he said the words he realized they were more or less true. "But to advance our friendship."

She stared at him for a long moment as if trying to determine his sincerity. At last she shrugged. "Very well." She rose to her feet and he stood at once. "Now, if you will excuse me, I shall be on my way."

"Allow me to escort you home," he said in as gallant a manner as he could muster.

"There's no need. My house is but a few blocks from here. No more than a ten-minute walk."

"Then surely you will allow a friend to accompany you for a mere ten minutes." He held out his arm and she reluctantly took it. "Especially as it does not appear your companion is returning."

"He was not my companion," she said quickly. "He hopes to be my, or rather my great-grandmother's, publisher."

"How interesting." They started toward the park gate. "And this well-planned rendezvous was his way of trying to convince you to sell him the memoirs?"

"Rendezvous?" She laughed. "Goodness, my lord, you do have a unique way of looking at things."

"I simply saw how he was looking at you." He shook his head in a solemn manner. "It was not the look of a publisher interested only in a book."

"He did ask to call on me," she said, in an offhand manner.

He nearly stumbled. Not merely at her words but at the mildly smug note in her voice. Still, why shouldn't she be smug? She was a lovely—no, beautiful—woman who, from everything Veronica said, deserved to be courted and wooed and won. Not, however by a man whose ulterior motives were questionable. His own motives weren't the least bit questionable. He'd been very straightforward. He wanted the memoirs and he wanted her friendship. If one helped him achieve the other, well, there was nothing wrong with that. Not really. He ignored the voice in the back of his head that said just maybe there was. Still, Julia knew exactly what his intentions were. Could the same be said for Cadwallender? And even an intelligent woman could lose her head over romantic nonsense and a handsome face and, God help them all, breakfast in the park.

"And?" she prompted.

"And what?" He stared at her.

She sighed. "I didn't think you were paying attention. My lord, if you truly wish to be friends, the very least you can do is listen to what I am saying. It's not a great deal to expect from one's friends."

"My apologies," he said smoothly. "I was swept away by the mellifluous nature of your voice and the poetry of your words which naturally distracted me."

"Poetry?"

He nodded. "Poetry."

"You don't like poetry."

"Unless it comes from your lips."

She laughed. "You needn't try so hard to be . . . whatever it is you're trying to be."

"Charming." He shrugged in a offhand manner. "Thoughtful. Attentive."

"Thus far, you're not doing well in terms of attentive. Although, the roses were most thoughtful and I thank you."

"It was my pleasure."

"I asked you about your dog."

"What dog?"

"The dog you said you were going to acquire." She glanced at him, amusement in her eyes. "Unless of course that was simply something else you said in the interest of being charming."

"Not at all." Indignation rang in his voice. "I have every intention of getting a dog, any day now."

"Of course you do." She smiled as if she didn't believe him for a minute.

"If I recall, I advised you to get a dog as well. As a matter of safety," he added.

"I am perfectly safe." She cast him a sidelong glance. "Why, the most eventful thing that has ever happened to me in the park was being invited to breakfast al fresco."

"About that." They paused in front of a house, small for Mayfair but respectable. He drew his brows together. "Why are we stopping?"

"This is my house."

"Oh." He glanced around. "This is still Mayfair?"

"This is not your end of Mayfair but mine." She gazed up at the house. "This was a wedding gift from my late husband's family." She scoffed. "The only thing they couldn't take back. All I have left."

He studied her. The look in her eye was thoughtful, without remorse. What kind of woman wasn't angry over the unfair turns her life had taken? Admiration washed through him.

"And there are bills to be paid." She cast him a wry smile. "And memoirs to be sold."

"Yes, of course." It was on the tip of his tongue to mention his new offer but he caught himself. Now was not the right time. It might not be the right time to mention another matter that had been on his mind since he had spoken with Ellsworth. Still, he was compelled to say something. "Lady Winterset." He chose his words with care. "You should consider that gentlemen who are aware of, or interested, in the memoirs, well, you should be cautious." He paused. "They might think you are exactly like your great-grandmother."

She choked. "What?"

"There is the possibility that—"

"Like my great-grandmother?"

"Yes, well, in terms of character and so forth."

"Character?"

"She was . . ."

"What?"

"Free with her favors." He drew a deep breath. "A tart."

"And you think Mr. Cadwallender asked to call on me because he thinks I am likely to follow in Hermione's footsteps?"

"I didn't say that," he said quickly. In truth, he was thinking of Ellsworth. "I just think it's something you should keep in mind."

"Because a gentleman would not be interested in calling on me otherwise?"

"Don't be absurd." He scoffed. "You know as well as I do that's ridiculous. You know full well how incredibly compelling and damn near irresistible you are."

She gasped. "I know nothing of the sort. What utter nonsense."

He ignored her. "And as your friend, it is my responsibility to, well, protect you."

Her eyes widened. "To do what?"

"To protect you. I know you won't take this well—"

"I have been protecting myself for three years."

"I know. Still"—he looked her directly in the eye—"one can always use help from a friend."

She stared at him in shock. "Do you really want to be my friend?"

"I do."

"This is not just part of your plan to get the memoirs?"

"No." He shook his head. "I am not abandoning that but it has nothing to do with our friendship."

"You are as confusing as you are annoying."

"To no one as much as to myself," he said under his breath.

"Very well." She drew a deep breath. "I shall quite value your friendship, Harrison."

"And I yours, Julia." He took her hand in his.

"And as we are friends, do tell, how did you get rid of Mr. Cadwallender?"

He stared directly into her eyes and knew from the moment the words were out of his mouth, she didn't believe him. "I didn't."

"No, I didn't think so." She turned to go into the house then turned back. "And as for being just like Hermione. The more I read about her life, the more I get to know her. Why, I often feel that she is actually speaking to me."

He stared.

"And the more I get to know her, the more I like her. The more I admire her courage and her strength. She lived her own life in her own way without undue apology and without regrets." She leaned closer and met his gaze. "As for being like her, perhaps not in the past but I do hope so in the future."

With that, she turned and strode into her house. Harrison stared after her. He had no idea if that had gone well or very, very bad. Still . . .

He grinned, turned on his heel, and strode toward his end of Mayfair. She had called him Harrison.

*. . . and then he professed his love and of course, I reciprocated. In that moment, in that time and place, I did indeed love him. And why wouldn't I? He was charming and handsome and even his brief moments of needless jealousy were most endearing. Did I promise to love him forever? What an absurd idea. I knew myself better than that and more, I knew him.*

*Love is at once remarkable and confusing, Dear Reader. I have always firmly believed the more love there is to be had, the better we all are. But it can, as well, be a weapon and it can, unfortunately, also be a lie. And while I don't believe one can love too often and certainly never too well, one should always be cautious when a declaration of love comes too soon. The words themselves are entirely too easy to say . . .*

from *The Perfect Mistress,*
*the Memoirs of Lady Hermione Middlebury*

# Chapter Nine

Julia paced the width of her parlor and tried not to scream out of sheer frustration. As she had paced and controlled herself for the last hour. How dare he suggest that Benjamin, or any man for that matter, would only be interested in her because they assumed she would be as easy in her virtue as Hermione had been. Was he being a protective friend or did he think that of her as well?

"That was most impressive. I must say I wasn't sure that you were up to the challenge."

Julia uttered a small scream.

"Well, that was rude."

Julia glared, yanked open the door, and yelled to her servants who would no doubt come running at her scream. "There was a mouse. Nothing to worry about, it's gone." She slammed the door behind her. "What are you doing here?"

"I came to give you the courage of your convictions," Hermione said in a lofty manner.

"But you only come out at night."

"My dear child, I do not *come out* like a debutante in

her first season." She scoffed. "I appear. Thus far I have chosen only to appear at night."

"Nonetheless, I would prefer that you not appear when I least expect you! And I expect you at night when ghosts are supposed to appear."

"Goodness, Julia, it's not as if there were rules for this sort of thing. There is no guidebook to the hereafter." She lifted a shoulder in a casual shrug. "One simply gets in the carriage and goes. Admittedly, it would be nice to know if there was an end to the journey, but on the other hand, to continue to exist at all is not unpleasant." Her voice softened. "You should not allow a mere man to upset you like this, my dear."

Julia drew a deep breath. "I don't know what to make of him."

"Him being Mr. Cadwallender or him being Harrison?"

"Harrison." She shook her head. "I don't trust him."

"But?"

"But . . ." She sighed. "I want to."

Hermione nodded. "There is something irresistible about a man who wishes to take care of you."

She cast her a sharp glance. "I don't need to be taken care of."

"Nonsense, darling. Even the most capable woman needs someone to take care of her. As does the most competent man."

She narrowed her eyes. "That makes no sense at all."

"Of course it does. I'm not talking about physical need but rather . . ." She thought for a moment. "Needs of the heart as it were."

Julia arched a brow. "Love?"

"Yes." She shrugged, "Love, affection, friendship. One often leads to the other."

"Are you saying that Harrison might, well, that love might be involved?"

"I'm not saying anything of the sort." She paused. "At least not yet. But his feelings toward you are very strong." She studied the younger woman thoughtfully. "As are yours for him."

"Indeed they are," she snapped. "Feelings of annoyance, irritation, anger."

"Fine line, my dear," Hermione murmured.

"Did you hear what he said? Of course you heard what he said." She resumed pacing. "He said gentlemen who know about you might think I am exactly like you."

Hermione chuckled.

Julia huffed. "It's not the least bit funny."

"Nonsense, it's most amusing. And it is your legacy, I'm afraid."

Julia stared. "But I'm not like you. At least not when it comes to your adventures. I would like to be more like you, you know, in other ways. Your strength, your courage, your independence."

"My dear child." Hermione cast her a loving smile. "You already are like me."

She shook her head. "No, I'm not. I am too cautious and quite cowardly."

"You don't see it but I do." Hermione paused for a moment. "You have weathered the death of a husband, not an easy thing to do. You took the loss of your income in stride and found a way to finance your future."

"Thanks to you," she said pointedly.

"Rubbish." Hermione shrugged. "The memoirs give you the means, nothing more than that. You could have hidden them away or destroyed them yourself. Instead, you've chosen to use them to your benefit." She shook her head. "You know full well they will be viewed as scandalous. It takes a great deal of courage to flaunt convention."

"But it's not my scandal."

"It will be."

"Yes, I suppose." Julia sighed. "Still, I don't have a choice."

"Certainly, you do. You did not accept Harrison's first offer nor Benjamin's for that matter. Someone lacking strength would have accepted either at once and been grateful to have been done with it." She pinned Julia with a firm look. "It's not easy to do what one needs to do and I am proud of you."

Julia smiled wryly. "A moment ago you said you weren't sure if I was up to the challenge."

"I didn't mean the challenge presented by my book or even of doing what you have to do. You're well up to that." Her eyes twinkled. "I meant the challenge of resisting the urge to strangle Harrison with your bare hands."

"It wasn't easy." She shook her head. "He drives me mad and makes me want nothing more than to box his ears and yet . . ."

"Yet, there is something about him."

"Yes, there is." She drew her brows together. "What is going to happen next?"

"Goodness, how would I know?"

"Well, I assumed—"

"I'm dead, darling, which does not mean I can see into the future." She sniffed. "I do not do parlor tricks and I do not tell fortunes."

"Pity."

"You cannot imagine my own disappointment. One would have thought death would bestow substantially greater benefits as so much has been lost. I do manage to see a great deal of what is currently happening but not everything. And I cannot say what will happen. Still"—

she grinned—"I can try. Nothing ventured, you know."
She tilted her head up, closed her eyes, stretched her arms
out, palms facing toward the heavens.

Julia choked back a laugh. "You look ridiculous. What
are you doing?"

"Trying to see into the future as you requested."

"I did no such thing." Julia crossed her arms over her
chest and watched in amusement. "Are you seeing anything?"

"One moment, if you please. These things take time.
Ah, yes." Her brow furrowed. "I see . . . I see . . ."

Julia laughed. "What do you see?"

"You are going from famine to feast, my dear. In addition to Harrison and Benjamin, there will soon be one
more gentleman on your doorstep."

"I thought you couldn't see into the future."

"I can't." She dropped her arms and opened her eyes.
"There is a gentleman coming up your front walk."

Julia's eyes widened. "Now?"

"This very moment." She glanced at the clock. "And I
must be off. Other matters to attend to."

"What other matters?"

"You'd be surprised." She laughed and vanished.

"That's most unnerving, you know," Julia called, ad-
dressing nothing but air. "I do hope you don't plan to
make a habit of this."

Hermione's laughter lingered in the room. A knock
sounded at the door and Julia jumped.

"Yes?"

Daniels opened the door and glanced around as if
looking for someone. She sighed. Good Lord, her servants were soon going to think she was as mad as everyone had thought her grandmother to be.

"A Mr. Ellsworth is here, my lady," Daniels said in his
usual cool manner.

"Mr. Ellsworth?" Her brows rose in surprise. "Show him in."

"Yes, my lady." Daniels glanced around once again.

"And you had best have someone set some traps," she said weakly. "The mice, you know."

"Yes, my lady, at once."

A moment later he showed Mr. Ellsworth into the parlor.

"Good day, Lady Winterset." The author strode across the room to take her hands in his. "How delightful it is to see you again."

He was unquestionably most attractive with a slight gleam of delightful wickedness in his hazel eyes. Add to that his potent air of confidence and she could understand why the celebrated author was as well known for his amorous adventures as he was for his literary endeavors.

"It's nice to see you too, Mr. Ellsworth. And most surprising." She pulled her hands from his.

He raised a brow. "Too much?"

She smiled. "Entirely too much."

"My apologies." He grinned. "I could not resist."

"Well, do try your best," she said wryly.

He chuckled. "It will be difficult."

She stepped away and chose to sit on a chair then gestured at the sofa. "Please sit down and tell me why you're here."

"Why, I wish to further the acquaintance of a beautiful woman, of course." He sat on the end of the sofa closest to her chair and leaned forward. "And you are quite lovely, Lady Winterset."

"And you are entirely too charming. Furthermore, I don't believe you for a moment."

"Really?" He chuckled. "Most women do."

"I am not most women," she said primly.

"Exactly why you are so appealing."

Despite his forward, most improper manner, or perhaps because of it, there was something undeniably charming about the man and she smiled in spite of herself. "Why are you here, Mr. Ellsworth?"

"Do I need a reason? It's not enough that you have captured my heart?"

She laughed. "What utter nonsense. Although I do say you live up to your reputation."

He grinned. "It is well earned."

"I have no doubt of that. But I seriously doubt, on the basis of a few words at dinner, that I have captured your heart."

"A heart has been captured by far less."

"Not mine and I doubt yours either," she said firmly. "Furthermore, I have no desire to become one of your string of conquests."

He winced. "That's rather harsh."

"I daresay it's not harsh enough." She considered him curiously. "Now, do tell me. To what do I owe this visit?"

"I have something of a proposition for you."

"Oh?"

"Not that kind of proposition, although . . ."

"Go on," she said coolly.

"Very well." His expression sobered. "What I am proposing is a partnership of sorts. I would like to purchase Lady Middlebury's memoirs and incorporate them into a book of my own."

She shook her head in confusion. "You want to do what?"

"I want to use excerpts from the memoirs verbatim, then expand on them. Turn them into fiction, as it were." He leaned toward her in an eager manner. "I want to combine her true exploits—"

"She calls them adventures," Julia said under her breath.

"Even better. I envision taking her adventures then

adding dialogue, setting, and so forth to make them come alive to the reader." His brow furrowed in thought. "We can call it *The True Adventures of a Lady of Pleasure*—"

Her brows rose. "A lady of pleasure?"

"It does need a good title," he said. "Something to grab the reading public's attention."

"My great-grandmother entitled it *The Perfect Mistress*."

"*The Perfect Mistress?*" He thought for a moment then nodded. "Yes, I like that. Very well then. We could call it *The Perfect Mistress: The True Adventures of Lady Middlebury in Her Own Words and As Told by John Eddington Ellsworth*."

"That's rather long, isn't it?"

He scoffed. "Not in the least."

She considered the idea. It was not bad, not bad at all.

"Think of it, Lady Winterset. With your ancestor's scandalous tales and my literary prowess, this book could be my most successful to date." He smiled in a less than humble manner. "And I have had some impressive successes."

"Indeed you have, Mr. Ellsworth. But do answer one question."

"Anything."

"If I am to sell you the memoirs and you are to write the book"—she cast him a pleasant smile—"where is the partnership?"

"Oh." He stared at her. "Perhaps I misspoke."

"Or perhaps you intended to offer a percentage of the royalties from sales, in addition to the payment to purchase the memoirs, and simply forgot to mention it."

"Yes." He nodded slowly. "That must be it."

"I thought as much." She beamed at him. "Now then, did you have a figure in mind? For the memoirs themselves?"

He nodded, produced an envelope, and presented it with a flourish. She sighed to herself. This must be how men do business. Once more, she opened an envelope and studied the figure written. It was quite generous and quite familiar, matching the offer from Harrison. Although selling to Harrison meant the memoirs would ultimately be destroyed whereas with Mr. Ellsworth's proposal they would live on, at least in some form.

"Quite generous, Mr. Ellsworth." She eyed him thoughtfully, "You must be very certain as to the success of this proposal."

"Oh, I am, I am indeed." Confidence rang in the man's voice.

"Very well then," She nodded and stood. At once he jumped to his feet. "I shall certainly give your proposal serious consideration."

He stared in disbelief. "Serious consideration? Is that all?"

She nodded. "Very serious consideration."

"You do realize that I am considered a most successful author?"

"Of course."

"One of the most popular writing in England today?"

She stifled a smile. "I realize that as well."

"And what I am offering is very nearly certain success?"

"I do recall you saying that one never knows how a work will be received."

"Well, yes, but . . ." He stared at her for a long moment. "My apologies, Lady Winterset, I believe I have not given you the credit due you."

"In what way, Mr. Ellsworth?"

"I assumed you would jump at the opportunity I presented you."

"Did you?" She shook her head. "Oh dear, I do so hate to disappoint."

His gaze narrowed. "You are not swayed by my celebrity?"

"No, I'm afraid not."

"Nor impressed with my past success?"

"Even though it is most impressive." She shrugged. "No."

"And you seem to be immune to my considerable charm as well."

"Surely I'm not the first?"

He choked.

"Well, perhaps I am." She tried and failed to hold back a grin. "Although I do find you most amusing."

"Well, that's something, I suppose," he muttered. "I warn you, Lady Winterset, I do not take rejection well. I intend to pursue this."

"I did agree to consider your proposal." She walked to the parlor door and opened it.

"Yes, that too." He started to leave then turned back. "You are a most unusual woman."

"And just today I was called remarkable as well." And hadn't Harrison called her compelling and irresistible? She'd been too irritated to heed his words at the time. Now, she couldn't help but wonder what they meant and why he had said them.

"Indeed you are." A grudging smile spread across his face. "It's not very often that I meet a woman who is not impressed by my fame."

"Then this is a new experience for you."

He laughed. "And not one I wish to repeat. However you . . ." He drew a deep breath. "Lady Tennwright is having one of her salons two days from now. I am the guest of honor and I would be honored if you would accompany me."

"That would be most improper. However . . ." She smiled. "I would be delighted to attend and I shall see you there."

His expression brightened. "That will do nicely. We can continue to discuss the disposition of the memoirs and why you are not swept away by my charm and wit and celebrity."

"Oh, that does sound like fun." She smiled. "Might I bring along a friend?"

He raised a suspicious brow. "A gentleman friend?"

"I was thinking Lady Redwell might enjoy accompanying me. She sat next to you at dinner."

"Lady Redwell?" Recognition crossed his face and he smiled. "Ah yes, delightful lady. Oh, do bring her."

"Because she is appropriately impressed with you?"

"Well, yes." He grinned in a most immodest manner. "I shall need some adoration to renew my flagging spirits."

"I doubt that your spirits will flag for long." She cast him a pleasant but dismissive smile. "Good day, Mr. Ellsworth."

"Good day, Lady Winterset." He studied her for another moment then nodded and took his leave.

She closed the door behind him then leaned back against it and blew a long breath.

"Well, what do you think of that?" she said aloud and waited. There was no response. "Never a ghost around when you need one." Again, there was no response save silence.

She pushed away from the door and resumed pacing where she had left off. Now she had three offers for the memoirs. Benjamin's, which was very much a risk but could provide a source of income for years. Harrison's and Mr. Ellsworth's, both of which were equal in initial payment but Mr. Ellsworth's offered long-term income as well. Fortunately, there was no need to make a rash decision. Very soon, she would no longer have the expenses of her grandmother's cottage, which would ease her financial strain and allow her more time to decide which offer to accept.

It was an interesting dilemma. Of the three, Benjamin struck her as the most trustworthy. Mr. Ellsworth produced no doubts whatsoever. She was absolutely certain she couldn't trust him. As for Harrison, as much as she wished to trust him she wasn't at all sure she could.

Which only made her wonder why she wanted to.

"More tea, my lord?" Celeste Waverly smiled in what Harrison assumed was supposed to be a most beguiling manner. And indeed it might well have been most beguiling if it had not seemed so well practiced.

"Yes, thank you."

He had come to call on Miss Waverly this afternoon as a first step toward making her his wife. As much as she encompassed all his requirements, it still seemed wise to get to know the young woman before declaring his intentions. After all, they would be together for the rest of their days.

It was the appropriate time of day to pay such a call and as was proper, they were not alone. Miss Waverly's mother sat on the other side of the parlor appearing to be engrossed by her embroidery although Harrison was certain she was listening to every word.

"Lovely weather for this time of year. Don't you agree, my lord?" Miss Waverly said brightly.

"I do indeed." He nodded. "Do you like autumn, Miss Waverly?"

"Well." She paused to consider the question and an annoying voice in the back of his head questioned why she needed to consider something so simple. "I like that the weather is cooler and that soon it will be winter. And I shall be able to wear all sorts of lovely furs. I do like furs. Then of course Christmas will be upon us and there will be any number of balls and entertainments. Do you like to dance, my lord?"

"Yes, I do." He nodded. "I make an appearance at those events that I am obligated to attend although I admit I do not attend many balls."

"Oh, but you should." Her lovely blue eyes widened. "There is nothing I enjoy more than a grand ball. The dresses and the music and the excitement. Why, last spring, my own coming out ball was . . ."

Miss Waverly continued chatting about parties and gowns and her friends and Harrison smiled and nodded and added an appropriate comment whenever she took a breath. He resisted the urge to drum his fingers impatiently on the arm of the sofa and wondered why he had been nervous about approaching her house today.

Certainly, he had never called on a young lady before. He had never met anyone he wished to call on. Besides, he considered it inappropriate to do so unless his intentions were of a permanent nature.

Not that he had never been with a woman in a carnal sense before. Charles had made sure of that in Harrison's youth. And indeed, through the years, Harrison had had a fair number of women in his bed. Women who wanted nothing more from him than he had wanted from them. Cordial interludes on both sides but nothing of significance. If Charles was here he would point out that while he may have taken women to his bed, he had never taken one into his heart. Harrison started at the idea. Where on earth had that come from?

But Charles was a romantic whereas Harrison was most practical. In considering Miss Waverly's qualifications to be his bride, Charles would certainly point out that in spite of her sterling qualities, nothing was as important to a successful marriage as love. Utter nonsense of course. Harrison had never had so much as a twinge of any sort of feeling that might approximate love. Of course, Charles would laugh and say neither did he until he met Veronica and would further add that the men in Harrison's family did not seem to find love or even the right wife in their youth. His eyes would twinkle and he would add they were far too clever for that.

Perhaps it was because he was now seriously considering marriage that these odd thoughts about love and what his brother would say if he were here came to mind. But it was his duty to marry an appropriate woman. She would, after all, ultimately be the next Marchioness of Kingsbury.

"And then, my lord, my friend Grace, surely you know her family. Her father is . . ."

Miss Waverly was the perfect candidate. Well bred, well trained, her family background was impeccable, she would no doubt be an excellent hostess and a perfect wife. And she was young enough to be most pliable. There was no sense of independence or extreme intelligence about Miss Waverly. No, indeed. She would never defiantly stare at him and refuse to do as he thought best. She would certainly not court scandal in any way whatsoever. She would do as she was told, without question. This was a woman who knew her place in the world.

"Do you like poetry, Miss Waverly?" he said without thinking.

"Oh, yes, I do," she said eagerly. "I quite like poems about love and romance and being carried away by grand passion. They are so . . . so romantic. Although I will confess, I don't like poems that do not rhyme." She wrinkled her pretty nose. "I find poems that don't rhyme most confusing. It isn't really a poem if it doesn't rhyme, is it?"

"No, I suppose not." He smiled weakly. "And literature? What do you like to read?"

"Read? Well . . ." She paused for a moment. "Books really seem to take a great deal of effort and time but I quite like magazines. Why, I was looking through *La Mode Illustré* just the other day and this year's fashions are très, très chic. I was thinking that the current fashion of . . ."

Harrison kept a pleasant smile plastered on his face and ignored the feeling of horror that rose within him. Surely Miss Waverly's shallow manner was due to her inexperience and youth, and with time and the proper guidance she would become more, well, substantial. She was very young after all.

"Might I ask you a somewhat personal question, my lord?" she said with her perfectly proper smile.

A faint sound that might have been a groan came from her mother although he might have been mistaken. Miss Waverly's parents had been most pleased when he had asked to call on their daughter. And why shouldn't they be? He was wealthy and of excellent lineage and was considered a catch for any ambitious family.

"Yes, of course."

"I was just wondering how old you are."

"I have just passed my thirty-third birthday."

Her eyes widened. "As old as that?"

"I'm afraid so."

A faint smile curved her lips. "How very nice." She paused then fluttered her lashes at him. "I have always heard that a lady needs an older man to guide her along the proper path."

"Quite right." He nodded in agreement although he really wasn't sure what to say. Not that he didn't, in truth, agree with her.

After the requisite amount of time considered proper

for this type of call he bid her good day and took his leave, ignoring a faint sense of relief. It was absurd, of course. Miss Waverly was everything he looked for in a bride. She couldn't be more perfect if someone had taken his list of requirements and checked them off one by one.

Still, in the carriage on his way home, he considered what it would be like to spend the rest of his life with a woman who met all his qualifications. His household would be well run, his meals served on time, his needs attended to. She would spend some of her time in appropriate charitable pursuits. When they entertained it would be correctly done, not too lavish but properly elegant. She would look well on his arm when they attended the opera. She would provide him with children and would attend to their care, hiring well-trained nannies and governesses. Indeed, she would run his life with order and efficiency. She would not cause him an undue care in the world. His world would be exactly as he wished it to be.

Dull, boring, staid and stuffy, Charles would have said. Harrison ignored the thought.

He entered the house and noticed an envelope addressed to him on the silver tray that sat on the table in the entry. No doubt it had been delivered while he was out. He opened it and read the note.

It was a brief report from Mr. Ellsworth. It seemed Lady Winterset had not leapt at his offer. He smiled in spite of himself. Good for her. She was far too clever to accept any offer for the memoirs in a rash manner, without due thought. The author's note went on to say his meeting with her was but his first move and he hoped to make additional progress two days from now, when they attended a salon at Lady Tennwright's. Harrison's brows drew together and once more the idea that Ellsworth would try to seduce an agreement from Julia popped into his head.

He absolutely could not allow that to happen. Ellsworth was working for him and seduction was not part of the plan. Damnation, if anyone was going to seduce Julia, it would be him!

Good Lord! Shock coursed through him and he sucked in a hard breath. Where in the name of all that was holy had that idea come from? He certainly had no intention of seducing Julia, not that she would allow him to do so at any rate. It was quite obvious that while she might accept his friendship, his considerable charm was wasted on her.

Absently he strode into the library and slammed the door shut behind him. And as her friend he would certainly not allow that . . . that . . . womanizer Ellsworth to seduce her. No, whether she wanted to admit it or not, she did need someone to watch out for her at least in this particular instance. She certainly couldn't count on Veronica to do so. Veronica would probably encourage her to have an *adventure* with the man. As for Julia herself, the more she read of her great-grandmother's memoirs, the more she might be inclined to do just that. Why, hadn't she just this morning declared that she intended to be like Lady Middlebury in the future? Might not that future be as early as two days hence?

Not if he had anything to say about it. He paced the floor. As much as he abhorred the very idea of literary salons he would make an appearance at this one. He'd be by Julia's side every minute, even escorting her home if necessary.

There was no way on earth he would allow Ellsworth to make Julia yet another one of his conquests. Especially given Harrison's role in it. The last thing he wanted was to be the cause of her unhappiness. She could be dreadfully hurt by a man like Ellsworth. Underneath all her strength and independence he suspected there was a fragile heart that could easily be broken. He would confess his role in

Ellsworth's proposal and give up all hope of acquiring the memoirs before he would let that happen. Because she was his friend, he amended quickly. For no other reason.

Still, as he sat down to write a note to Lady Tennwright and a second to Veronica, he couldn't dismiss the question lingering in the back of his mind.

When had rescuing Julia become more important than acquiring the memoirs?

*. . . and then his lips met mine. Even now, it fairly makes me swoon simply to think of it. Regardless of age or circumstances, Dear Reader, there is nothing that can compare to the first time your lips meet his. There is the moment your eyes meet. Your chin raises, his head lowers, and for the briefest fraction of a second, time itself stops. You hover between one heartbeat and the next, unable to breathe, unable to think. And then his lips touch yours. Of course, that sort of first kiss usually follows considerable flirtation. Gazes meeting across a crowded ballroom. The casual touch of a hand brushing against yours. A clandestine meeting under the stars.*

*And then there is the unexpected first kiss. Why, it hasn't so much as crossed your mind that you and he would kiss. One moment, you are thinking nothing of any consequence and the next his lips are pressed to yours and you realize with the suddenness of a storm in the summer that this is indeed what you have longed for somewhere deep in your soul. What you never even knew you wanted. Abruptly everything between you has changed and will never again be the same. And the possibilities, well, the possibilities take your breath away.*

*But when the marquis's lips claimed mine it was not at all unexpected. We had danced around this moment for some time and now that it was upon us, it was merely the beginning of what would ultimately be one of the most . . .*

from *The Perfect Mistress,*
*the Memoirs of Lady Hermione Middlebury*

# Chapter Ten

"She is quite in her element, isn't she?" Julia's heart unexpectedly skipped a beat at the familiar voice behind her.

She smiled but did not turn around, her gaze lingering on Portia. "I assume you're speaking of Lady Redwell."

Harrison chuckled. "She's like a child in a candy shop."

Portia was indeed having a grand time. They'd only arrived within the past quarter hour and Julia had scarcely done more than chat with their hostess but already Portia had been engaged in one flirtatious conversation after the other. With Mr. Ellsworth of course, who was surrounded by other admirers, as well as with one of the poets who had attended Veronica's dinner.

"Her late husband was a literary sort as I understand it although I don't think he was terribly successful. She's quite impressed by literary fame."

"So it would appear." He paused. "Are you?"

"To a certain extent I suppose. I daresay I don't know anyone who isn't." She turned to face him. "It must be incredibly difficult to craft a story or poetry so that it captures a reader's attention. I am most admiring of anyone who can do that well. As for the fame that accompanies success . . ." She shrugged. "That in itself is not especially impressive to me."

The faintest hint of relief shone in his eyes although she might have been mistaken. He nodded toward Portia and Mr. Ellsworth's other admirers. "Then you are the exception."

"Perhaps." She studied him for a moment. "You have the oddest habit of appearing where I least expect you. I had the distinct impression literary evenings were not to your liking."

"I am trying to broaden my horizons," he said. "After our discussion the other evening about poetry, I thought I was being somewhat narrow-minded and—"

"Stubborn?"

"Possibly." He paused. "I have been known to be stubborn on occasion."

She gasped in mock surprise. "You? Stubborn? Imagine my surprise."

"I would think you of all people would recognize stubborn."

She laughed. "Perhaps I would."

"And, as I am trying to improve relations between myself and my late brother's wife, I thought it would be a nice gesture on my part to escort Veronica here tonight."

"Did you?" Her brow rose. "I have never known Veronica to require an escort before. Veronica alone among the ladies of my acquaintance never hesitates to go wherever she wishes unaccompanied."

"Well"—he shook his head in a mournful manner—"it was not easy to convince her."

"And you did so because you wish to broaden your literary horizons?"

"Absolutely." He paused. "And I knew you would be here."

"How on earth did you know that?"

He chuckled. "A gentleman never reveals all of his secrets."

Veronica must have mentioned this evening to him. It was all Portia could talk about yesterday when the three women had met briefly for tea at Fenwick's. Portia had been in something of a tizzy at the very thought of being again in Mr. Ellsworth's illustrious literary presence; Veronica was late, as usual, for an appointment with her dressmaker; and Julia hadn't felt at all her usual self but rather restless and preoccupied. She couldn't get Harrison's comments out of her head. That nonsense about gentlemen thinking she was like Hermione. Surely no honorable gentleman would think anything of the sort. And he had called her compelling and irresistible. Even William had never called her anything of the kind but had rather praised her as sensible and practical. Yes, her mirror told her she was pretty if a little too somber-looking and tired around her eyes. But she'd passed her twenty-seventh birthday and was a widow with no family to speak of and no money. Scarcely what anyone would call compelling or irresistible. Anyone but Harrison apparently. And the man did seem to have the strangest urge to protect her, which was altogether too, well, nice. He was as confusing as he was annoying. Yet she wasn't at all annoyed to see him now but oddly pleased.

"You don't strike me as a man who has secrets, my lord."

"That's because I hide them well."

"Which is the very definition of secret," she said wryly.

"Oh, I am a man of many secrets, Julia." He leaned close and lowered his voice confidentially. "I am most mysterious."

She stared at him for a moment then caught the gleam of amusement in his eyes and laughed. "You are not at all mysterious."

His eyes widened in disappointment. "Not even a little?"

"I am sorry." She shook her head. "No."

"Hmph. I shall have to work on that." His brows drew together. "But I am wearing you down. Not only am I now the most annoying man you've ever met but you must admit, every time we meet, you find me more charming than the time before."

She started to protest then smiled. "Yes, Harrison, I believe I do."

"How . . . wonderful." Genuine pleasure curved his lips and his gaze locked with hers. His dark blue eyes, the sky at midnight, simmered with something unknown. For the briefest of moments she couldn't seem to breathe. "Julia—"

"Lady Winterset." Mr. Ellsworth abruptly appeared at her side. His assessing gaze slipped from her to Harrison and back. He took her hand and raised it to his lips. "I am delighted that you decided to join us."

The author obviously thought grabbing her hand at every opportunity was gallant and dashing but she found it both presumptuous and irritating. She cast him a polite smile and pulled her hand from his. His brow rose slightly and his smile was a bit too knowing. Most irritating. "I am quite looking forward to the evening, Mr. Ellsworth. I understand you will be reading for us later."

"I intend to read something from my newest book," he said smoothly. "It has only been available for a few weeks but perhaps you've already read it?"

She shook her head. "No, I'm afraid not."

"Then I shall make sure you have a copy. Personally

signed, of course." He glanced at Harrison. "Good evening, my lord."

Harrison nodded coolly. "Good evening."

"Mr. Ellsworth has made me an interesting offer for the memoirs," she said.

Harrison raised a brow. "Oh?"

"Yes, my lord." The author nodded. "I believe Lady Middlebury's words combined with my own fictional retelling of her adventures would be a rousing success."

"It's a most intriguing idea," Julia said with a smile, studying Harrison closely.

Harrison frowned in a forbidding manner. "And I would prefer the memoirs not be published in any manner whatsoever."

"Obviously we are of two minds on the matter." Mr. Ellsworth shrugged. "It is fortunate then that the disposition of the memoirs and their literary fate is in the capable and quite lovely hands of Lady Winterset." He flashed her an altogether too intimate smile.

Harrison's eyes narrowed slightly. "I am certain she will make the appropriate decision." He paused. "It does strike me however that we have been entirely too free in our discussions of Lady Middlebury's work."

"Too free?" She laughed. "Goodness, my lord, it's not as if we will be reading selected portions tonight."

"Or choosing parts and acting it aloud," Ellsworth said in an overly innocent manner.

Julia flashed him a quick look. If she didn't know better she'd think the author was deliberately baiting Harrison.

"Free in our discussions, Lady Winterset." His gaze hardened. "I would hate to have anyone overhear. It might provoke talk, rumor, gossip. Even scandal."

"Scandal sells books," Ellsworth murmured.

"Perhaps, but there will be considerable scandal surrounding this book should it be published in any manner whatsoever." He cast Julia a warning look. "Some of which will inevitably fall on you."

"I am aware of that." Indeed, she'd known from the moment she'd realized she had no other means of financial salvation but to sell the memoirs that there would be some scandal attached to Lady Middlebury's great-granddaughter. She was not pleased at the idea but it was unavoidable.

"Yet another reason not to expose them to the public at all," Harrison said.

"Nonsense." Ellsworth scoffed. "I daresay whatever scandal falls on Lady Winterset will be minimal. And should she accept my proposal, I shall do my very best to see to it her name is kept out of it." He cast her an apologetic smile. "As much as possible of course."

"Of course." She didn't for a moment think Ellsworth would live up to that particular promise. The more scandal, past and present, surrounding the book, the better it would sell. Besides, there was something about Ellsworth that was not at all trustworthy. Perhaps it was his self-serving nature. This was a man who would throw her to the wolves of gossip or anything else without hesitation if it would further his position.

"I would strongly suggest," Harrison began, "that until Lady Winterset makes her decision, any further discussion be held in private. Away from the hearing of anyone who might be inclined to gossip or speculate about exactly what is included in Lady Middlebury's memoirs."

Ellsworth frowned. "I don't think—"

"Thank you, my lord," Julia said quickly. She wasn't at all pleased with Harrison telling her what to do, but he had an excellent point. "I think that's both wise and prudent."

Harrison aimed a smug smile at Ellsworth whose eyes narrowed slightly.

"If you will excuse me, Lady Winterset," the author said smoothly, "there are new arrivals I should greet." He leaned closer and lowered his voice. "Perhaps we can speak more in private later."

She smiled in a noncommittal manner. "Perhaps."

"I shall look forward to it." He looked as if he were about to take her hand again but thought better of it. "My lord." Ellsworth nodded, then turned to join another group of guests who were obviously more pleased to have his company than Harrison.

She studied the earl for a moment. Harrison watched the author with an odd gleam in his eye. "You don't like him, do you?"

He pulled his gaze from Ellsworth. "It's not a question of like or dislike. He is an excellent writer."

"I'm not talking about the author, I'm talking about the man."

"I would wager the man leaves a lot to be desired," he said casually. "You are aware of his reputation?"

"He is a well-known literary figure, Harrison." She cast him an overly innocent smile as if she had no idea that he was speaking of the man's amorous reputation. "He is highly regarded in the literary world."

"Julia." His brows pulled together. "I don't think—"

"Here you are." Veronica stepped up beside them. "And Harrison as well. Are you having a nice time?"

"Quite." His tone was clipped. "We were just discussing Mr. Ellsworth."

"Interesting man." Veronica's gaze flicked to the author. "And most charming."

Harrison snorted and Julia bit back a smile.

"You look lovely tonight, Julia." Her friend studied her for a moment.

Julia had chosen to wear what was very nearly her best dress. She had bought it right before William's death but had never had the opportunity to wear it. It was the height of fashion when purchased and she was grateful fashions hadn't changed so much as to prevent her from wearing it now. She was well aware that the deep emerald silk emphasized the green of her eyes. Her grandmother's pendant provided the perfect complement.

"Doesn't she look lovely, Harrison?"

"Exquisite." His gaze met Julia's and her heart skipped a beat.

Veronica leaned forward to get a closer look at her pendant. "That is exquisite as well."

Julia laughed. "It would be if it were real."

"Then it is an excellent copy." She straightened and glanced at Harrison. "Now, if you will forgive us, I have something of importance I must discuss with Julia." Before he could protest, Veronica took her elbow and steered her across the room toward the terrace doors.

"Where are we going?"

"Where we can speak in private." They stepped out onto the terrace. There was a chill in the air but it was not especially unpleasant after the stuffiness in the salon. Veronica glanced around but the terrace was empty. "This will do."

"Whatever is the matter?"

"Nothing really." She drew a deep breath. "I simply needed a breath of fresh air and feared coming out here alone. I have no desire for anyone with thoughts of romantic interludes to trap me in an unwanted liaison."

Julia widened her eyes. "What?"

"One of those poets, a less than successful one I might add, has been flirting outrageously ever since we arrived." She rolled her gaze toward the sky. "I'm not certain if he's looking for a patron or an affair or, God help us, a wife."

Julia choked back a laugh. "I've never known you not to be able to handle unwanted attentions before."

"I am trying to be on my best behavior," she said in a haughty manner. "And speaking of best behavior, have you noticed Portia's?"

Julia nodded. "It's rather hard to miss."

"Whatever has come over her? Not that it isn't pleasant to see her be less sedate than usual," Veronica added. "Still it's very odd. Has she said anything to you?"

"Nothing, but then I haven't asked." Julia thought for a moment. "Perhaps all those introductions to eligible men her family has orchestrated has pushed her into some sort of flirtatious frenzy."

"I have always said it's those who are least willing to bend who will ultimately snap." Veronica shook her head. "We should keep an eye on her. I should hate to see her fall in love with some unscrupulous writer who is interested only in her money."

"You're right, although I can't imagine she would be quite that foolish. She does have a practical side and alone among us is the most concerned with propriety."

Veronica arched a delicate brow. "Least willing to bend, remember?"

"Of course." Julia eyed the other woman curiously. "I must say it's not like you to be so concerned."

"Rubbish. I am always concerned about my friends." Veronica paused. "Which reminds me. Harrison was most insistent on escorting me tonight because he knew you would be here."

"He mentioned that."

"Do you know why?"

"I assume to continue his pursuit of the memoirs."

Veronica shook her head. "I think there's more to it than that."

"What more could there possibly be?"

"I think . . ." Veronica chose her words with care. "I think he likes you."

"Of course he likes me." Julia scoffed. "And I like him. We have agreed to be friends and thus far I think it's going very well."

"He wants to be your friend?" Disbelief sounded in Veronica's voice.

"Yes."

"And you wish to be his friend as well?"

"One can always use another friend."

Veronica stared then laughed. "Good Lord, he's a man. A very stuffy, very proper man but a man nonetheless. He wants more than friendship."

"Nonsense." Julia waved off the comment.

"Trust me, Julia. I have had experience in such things. I am the friendliest person I know, and every man who has ever alleged to want nothing more than friendship from me has ultimately desired something substantially less platonic."

"Don't be silly. You're not at all friendly. In fact, you are often something of a snob."

"I am not." Veronica huffed. "But I am not the topic, you are. Heed my words, Julia."

"Even if they are the most ridiculous words you have ever uttered?" She dismissed the fact that Veronica had always been most perceptive about people.

"They're not at all ridiculous." She shook her head. "There's something vaguely possessive in the way he looks at you. As if you are an undiscovered land and he has planted his flag."

Julia gasped. "Veronica!"

She shrugged. "I thought it was an appropriate analogy."

Certainly Julia had noted the way Harrison had glared at Ellsworth but that was no doubt due to their competition for the memoirs and not out of any desire for her. And, in spite of his denial, she was certain Benjamin's departure had been Harrison's doing. Which again might be attributed to Harrison's wanting to stop publication of the memoirs. Still, if Veronica was right, wasn't it possible that he was, well, jealous? "Why on earth would you think something so absurd?"

"Julia, darling, I have known this man for many years. I have never seen him express anywhere near the interest in anyone that I have seen him show for you. He asks endless questions. Every time I see him the subject is always you and he insists on being wherever you might be. Surely you've noticed."

"He wants the memoirs," Julia said.

"Of course he wants the memoirs." Veronica scoffed. "But he wants you as well."

Julia stared. The very idea was shocking and surprisingly appealing. "You're mad, you do realize that."

"Perhaps, but there is brilliance in my madness. Harrison is an intelligent man and they can be very dangerous." She shuddered. "God save us from intelligent men."

"We're talking about your newfound brother."

"Yes, and I love him as a brother, which doesn't mean he's to be trusted when it comes to you." Her gaze slid past Julia and she nodded. "Oh, he may use the memoirs as an excuse and he may say he wants to be your friend but the man can scarcely keep away from you. And to prove my point, he is coming out to join us now."

The opening of the terrace door sounded behind her.

Veronica leaned closer. "And if all that weren't bad enough, I'm beginning to think you want his flag planted."

Julia choked.

A moment later Harrison's voice sounded behind her. "Are you talking about me, Veronica?"

"Goodness, Harrison, you are conceited. We could be

talking about any number of things. You are as arrogant as those members of the Explorers Club who go around planting their flags everywhere." She slanted Julia a knowing glance then nodded. "But yes, we are. We have also been discussing Mr. Ellsworth. He's quite charming, don't you think?"

Harrison pressed his lips together in annoyance and ignored the question. "The readings are to begin in a few minutes and Lady Tennwright was looking for you. I believe she wants advice on arranging the chairs for the readings."

"Good Lord." Veronica groaned. "The woman seems to think I am her new dearest friend." She glared at Harrison. "This is all your fault, you know."

He smiled in an innocent manner.

"I suppose I have no choice but to go in." She started toward the door then glanced at Julia. "Are you coming?"

Harrison's gaze met Julia. "I should like to have a word with you first, if you don't mind."

"Of course you do," Veronica said under her breath.

"I don't mind at all," Julia said.

"I shall see you both inside in a minute then." Veronica squared her shoulders and went into the house.

"A word, Harrison?" She smiled up at him and realized he stood entirely too close than was proper. Not that it mattered. The man was her friend after all. "That sounds dreadfully serious."

"It is." He frowned. "I don't trust Ellsworth and I think you should be wary of your dealings with him."

"For goodness' sakes, I am not a fool." Why, she could touch him without scarcely any effort if she wanted. Not that she did. "I have no intention of making a hasty decision. While I do find his offer interesting, there is still much to consider."

"The memoirs are not my greatest concern."

"Then what is your concern?" she said without thinking.

"You." He paused. "As your friend naturally."

"I am not your concern. I am perfectly capable of taking care of myself."

"Not when it comes to a man like Ellsworth." He shook his head. "You have no experience with a man of his nature."

She scoffed. "I am scarcely an innocent schoolgirl. I have been married, you know."

"To an honorable man I assume?"

"He was most honorable."

"And was he a man who would never have taken advantage of a vulnerable woman?"

"Absolutely!"

"Then I was right," he said in a smug, superior manner. "You have no experience with men like Ellsworth."

"Perhaps not. But do you think I am so weak as to be swayed by his face or dashing appearance?"

His brows drew together. "You think he's dashing?"

"Yes, and I daresay every woman here would agree."

"You are not every woman."

"No, I most certainly am not and I would thank you to remember that."

"But you are—"

"But I am what?" Without warning something inside her snapped. She'd had quite enough. She ground out the words through clenched teeth. "Lady Middlebury's great-granddaughter?"

"Yes, but—"

"Then perhaps I should go in there and throw myself at Mr. Ellsworth!"

He stared in shock then his eyes narrowed. "Who is no

doubt expecting it. Whether you like it or not a man like that would certainly think you take after her. Not that you do in this respect," he added quickly.

"And if I do?" she snapped.

"What do you mean?"

"You don't really know, do you?"

He shook his head in confusion. "Of course I know."

"No, you don't. Oh, you know a great deal about me and yes, we have shared some discussions about poetry and dogs and I can't recall what else, but you don't know me. You have no idea if I take after Hermione or not."

"Regardless, I know the kind of man Ellsworth is."

She scoffed. "What kind of man is he?"

"He's the kind of man who would take advantage of a beautiful woman alone on a darkened terrace!"

"And am I the kind of woman who would allow such liberties?"

"He would not ask your permission!"

"Then he would take what he wanted?"

"Yes."

"And what would that be?"

"He would take you in his arms and kiss you long and hard in spite of your protests. The way he has wanted to do from the moment he met you!"

"That's what you think a man like Ellsworth would do?"

"That's what I know a man like Ellsworth would do."

"And what about you, Harrison?" She stared up at him, knowing even as she said the words, these were dangerous waters. "What would a man like you do?"

"Me?" His gaze slipped from her eyes to her lips. "I would never take advantage of a beautiful woman on a darkened terrace."

"Why not?"

"It would be . . . dishonorable."

"And you are an honorable man?"

"Most certainly."

"And you would never take advantage?"

"Never."

"Not even if you thought that because of her ancestry she wouldn't protest?"

"Not even then." He paused. "And I would never think that."

"But what if she wanted you to kiss her?" She wasn't sure where that had come from but the moment she said it she knew it was true.

He stared down at her.

"What if she didn't realize she wanted you to until right that very moment?" She held her breath.

"I might realize that I wanted to as well," he said slowly. "That I have wanted to for some time but perhaps I didn't realize it either."

Their gazes locked for a long moment. At last he drew a deep breath. "The readings are about to begin. We should join the others."

Disappointment throbbed through her. "Yes, we should."

He turned and her heart sank. He took a step then paused. "Damnation, Julia."

He swiveled back and without warning pulled her into his arms and kissed her hard and long and quite thoroughly until her knees weakened and she thought she might swoon in his arms. She slid her arms around his neck and clung to him, meeting his passion with her own. Desire swept through her. Her mouth opened to his and his kiss deepened. Good Lord, a part of her mind not fogged with an aching need to press closer, to feel his body next to hers, noted this was not the kiss of the stuffy Earl of Mountdale.

At last he released her and stepped back.

"And that, Julia"—he nodded—"is how an honorable man kisses a beautiful woman on a darkened terrace."

She stared and tried to catch her breath.

"The reading should begin any minute." He held out his arm. "Shall we?"

"Certainly." She struggled to regain a semblance of composure and took his arm, grateful for the support. She wasn't at all sure she could walk on her own at the moment.

A shadow flittered by the terrace door and she wondered if someone had seen them. Not that it mattered. At least not to her, although it no doubt mattered to him. It would be most improper for Harrison to be discovered in a passionate embrace with a widow who might soon be linked to scandal, even old, nearly forgotten scandals.

She glanced up at him. His expression was set, almost stern. In spite of the passion that she was confident they'd shared, did he now regret what had just passed between them? Regret what was obviously an impulse on his part. He opened the door and nodded for her to pass. Did he blame her for . . . enticing him? She groaned to herself. What had come over her?

Perhaps there was more of Hermione in her than either of them had thought. Was he embarrassed now for his actions? For succumbing to the flirtations of the descendant of a . . . a . . . tart? Heat washed up her face. How could she have been so brazen?

She drew a deep breath and smiled pleasantly as if her insides weren't churning. The chairs had been arranged while they were on the terrace and guests were taking their places. "Shall we take a seat?"

He paused. "I should sit beside Veronica as I am her escort for the evening."

It was as if he had slapped her across the face, but she didn't so much as flinch. "Yes, do that."

She found Portia and sat down beside her on a chair at the end of the row. Portia was too busy chatting with the gentleman next to her to do more than cast her a welcoming smile. Even if Harrison wanted to sit with her, there was no place for him at her side. Good. That was exactly what she wanted. She might have lost her head on the terrace but her senses had returned. Even if there was something of a tremble in her hands and a catch somewhere in the vicinity of her . . . no, it absolutely was not her heart.

Mr. Ellsworth took his place in front of the gathering and began to read from his latest work. She adopted a pleasant smile and attempted to pay attention.

"It was to be expected then that the first thing he intended, upon meeting at the arranged location . . ."

What had she been thinking? No, she hadn't been thinking at all and she should have been. She should be on guard against every single man who knew about the memoirs. Even if he appeared to be staid and too proper. She would be from this moment on. Oh, certainly in many ways, her lapse in judgment might have been understandable. Why, it had been years since she'd been kissed and longer still since she'd been kissed by anyone other than William.

It wasn't simply the kiss, although one could never call that kiss simple. She'd baited him, teased him, practically laid down a gauntlet and dared him to kiss her.

And he had certainly picked it up with enthusiasm.

"'. . . the scent of the garden in bloom, a rapturous mix of roses and violets and all the . . .'"

She slanted a discreet glance across the room at him. His brow was furrowed and he appeared to be absorbing every word Mr. Ellsworth read. As if he were aware of her perusal, he glanced in her direction and her gaze met his. At once she jerked her head forward and tried again to give the author her full attention.

" '. . . and it was, he thought, not inappropriate that he would find her here, of all places . . .' "

Ellsworth's gaze met hers and she cast him an encouraging smile. As much as she wanted to see if Harrison was still watching her, she refused to give him the satisfaction. The corners of the author's mouth curved upward slightly as if in response to her own smile. Nonsense, he could be smiling at any one of his throng of female admirers. Still, it would do no harm for Harrison to note this innocent flirtation. To wonder if she was succumbing to Ellsworth's charms. Indeed, it would serve Harrison right. Especially if the man thought so little of her as to think she would fall into the arms of a notorious womanizer. She cast Ellsworth her brightest smile and ignored the look of pleased speculation in his eyes. She would deal with the repercussions of this meaningless exchange later.

She ignored the thought that she might well be venturing onto a path she was ill-prepared to tread. She'd scarcely passed her first season when she'd married William. He wasn't the only man she had ever kissed but she could count that number on one hand and have several fingers left. Harrison was right in one respect: she had no experience with men like Ellsworth. Or men like Harrison, or very nearly any men at all.

Still, how hard could it be to carry on in a flirtatious manner? Why, Portia was certainly doing it well.

She might not be a tart by nature but, God help them all, she was a tart by blood.

# Chapter Eleven

What on earth had gotten into him?

Harrison stared at Ellsworth reading in a far too dramatic manner and tried to keep from stealing another look at Julia. It was impossible given that she was directly in his line of sight if he turned his head to the right and leaned forward slightly. He had already met her gaze once and she had pointedly turned away as if she couldn't bear the sight of him.

Not that he could blame her. He had been rather stunned by his behavior himself. Why, one minute he was explaining why she should be on her guard with Ellsworth and the next he was behaving in precisely the same manner. He should be ashamed of himself and indeed he was. Honorable man—hah! He was no better than that cad of a writer. He wasn't at all sure what had possessed him to take advantage of her like that. His intention had only been to provide her a measure of protection. After all, Ellsworth wouldn't be more than casually acquainted with her if not for Harrison's plan to get the memoirs.

His mind returned to the scene played out on the terrace. When had he lost control of the conversation? When had it stopped being about Ellsworth and had become about him? And what was that rubbish about his wanting to kiss her from the first moment they'd met? Utter nonsense. The first time they'd met he'd wanted to thrash her.

No, he had to admit, the first time they'd met she'd been as impressive as she was annoying. Her strength of character and resolve was as strong as any man he'd ever known and far greater than most. But as for wanting to kiss her . . . certainly he'd noticed the intense emerald of eyes so deep, a man could lose his soul in them. And yes, he'd noted the way unruly tendrils of golden hair had escaped to caress the sweet blush of her cheeks. And he had as well seen the vulnerability and weariness that lay beneath her determined manner, but the thought of kissing her hadn't so much as crossed his mind.

Until tonight.

Almost of its own accord, his gaze turned toward her. She appeared completely engrossed in whatever Ellsworth was babbling on about. Julia was wrong though; he did know her. Not merely the details of her life he had pried from Veronica but how she looked when the brisk autumn breeze heightened the color in her cheeks. And how her laugh reminded him of something extraordinary he had long ago forgotten, if he had ever known it at all, and how it echoed deep inside him. And how her green eyes flashed with fire when she was angered or glittered with humor when she was amused or simmered with something quite remarkable right before he'd kissed her.

Good God, perhaps he had wanted to kiss her from the beginning after all.

She smiled at Ellsworth and his stomach clenched. Surely she hadn't meant it when she said she'd throw herself at Ellsworth. She was entirely too intelligent to become involved with a man like him. Still, women, no doubt some of them intelligent, were apparently quite taken with the man. Harrison grudgingly admitted he was handsome enough. And even though Julia had claimed not to be awed by his celebrity, his literary accomplishments were most impressive. Why, the man could probably talk to her about poetry for hours. Worse, he could no doubt compose a poem just for her right on the spot. Something about how her eyes were like a day in May or some such nonsense. Even a sensible woman like Julia could fall prey to a man who used words as a weapon of seduction.

His gaze slid from Julia to the author and back. Damnation, the man was flirting with her right here in front of everyone. Not that he could truly blame him. He'd never seen her as lovely as she was tonight in that dress that precisely matched the color of her eyes. The woman was delicious enough to entice even the most stalwart soul. Oh, their flirtation was subtle—a gleam in Ellsworth's eye, an answering smile from Julia. A slightly upraised brow from him, the barest tilting of her head in response. Harrison might well be the only one who noticed but then he was the only one watching the two of them. It was shameless, that's what it was.

Well, he would not allow Julia to be taken in. No, Ellsworth's intrusion into her life was Harrison's doing and it was his responsibility to make certain no harm came to her because of it. Because he was her friend and because he liked her. Quite a lot. Furthermore, he respected her. He was not going to allow that reprobate to drag her into scandal and ruin her life. The fact that watching Julia and Ellsworth exchange glances made his stomach twist and his jaw tighten was due to nothing more than his sense of responsibility and friendship. Nothing whatsoever.

He was not a man to lose control of conversations or anything else. The kiss was merely a momentary loss of the reins he always tightly held. Regardless, it was still most disturbing and completely perplexing. This wasn't the first time he had been alone with a lovely woman on a secluded terrace but he'd never had the impulse—no, the need—to embrace her and ravish her lips as he wished to ravish her body and claim her soul. He started at the thought. Where in the hell had that come from? He didn't think of Julia in that way. Or at least he hadn't.

He pushed the disquieting thought from his mind. He'd have to apologize. Assure her it would not happen again. He'd send roses in the morning. That would ease things. Women loved flowers. She'd forgive him because, after all, they were friends. And the kiss meant nothing of significance to either of them.

He'd also put an end to his dealings with Ellsworth. He never should have initiated it in the first place. He'd pay the man what he had promised then send him on his way. Far away from Julia. Yes, that was the thing to do. With Ellsworth gone, Harrison would renew his efforts to procure the memoirs. First, flowers, then an apology, then he would increase his offer. It was brilliant.

He reluctantly pulled his gaze from Julia and turned his attention to their speaker. He narrowed his eyes and studied the man. He couldn't quite get the thought out of his head that it could have been Ellsworth out on the terrace with Julia in his arms. In that dress.

And that he would not allow. Tonight or ever.

"Are you feeling better?" Harrison asked as soon as the carriage rolled away from Tennwright House.

"I am excellent now that we are away from there." Veronica heaved a sigh. "But I wouldn't have been if I had been forced to stay one minute longer. That woman drives me mad."

Harrison stared. "But you said your head ached and insisted we leave at once."

"Goodness, brother dear, you know nothing about women." She snorted in a most unladylike manner. "I couldn't say I was bored beyond tears and I'd had quite enough of Lady Tennwright and more than enough of a presumptuous poet who was fairly falling all over me."

Indeed, the moment the reading had ended, Veronica had claimed a headache and demanded they depart. Which left him no time to seek out Julia and apologize. Not that he knew exactly what he would say although he had been going through various options in his head.

*My dear Julia, I don't know what came over me* sounded too lighthearted, like a line from a frivolous drawing room comedy.

*Forgive me, Julia, I had no right to impose myself upon you* was entirely too stuffy, and while he might well be stuffy, he did not wish to sound like it.

*I am sorry, Julia, for taking liberties but I could not seem to stop myself and you were quite irresistible in the moonlight* had potential although he had no idea if there had been moonlight or not.

It might be best simply to pen a note of apology to accompany the roses. He should send flowers to Miss Waverly as well and perhaps request to accompany her on a walk in the park. Odd, the idea of an outing with the woman he intended to marry held no particular appeal.

"Then there was no need for us to take our leave so precipitously?"

He couldn't see her eyes in the darkness of the carriage and yet he knew she was staring at him.

"To my knowledge, you've never liked these kinds of evenings. I assumed you'd be delighted to escape as soon as possible." Speculation sounded in her voice. "Why did you want to linger? It can't be because of your love of Mr. Ellsworth's work."

He scoffed. "Hardly."

"I see." She paused for a long moment. It did not bode well and he braced himself. "What happened on the terrace, brother dear?"

"On the terrace?"

"With Julia."

"With Julia?"

"Would you stop repeating everything I say. It will not buy you more time to devise an answer. Now . . ." She leaned forward and emphasized each word. "What-happened-on-the-terrace-with-Julia?"

He shrugged. "Nothing of significance."

"Given the way you couldn't keep your eyes off her during the readings, I don't believe that for a moment. What happened?"

"I might have kissed her," he said under his breath.

"You *might* have kissed her?"

"Well, yes."

"Either you did or you didn't." She huffed. "Did you kiss her on the hand or on the cheek?"

"Not exactly."

"Then exactly what did you do?"

"I pulled her into my arms and I kissed her quite thoroughly for what seemed an endless moment," he snapped.

She gasped. "You kissed your *friend*?"

"Apparently."

"Worse, you kissed my friend. My dearest friend!" A threat sounded in her voice. "I don't know what you're thinking, Harrison, but I will not have you toying with her affections."

"I am not toying with her affections!" Indignation rang in his voice.

" 'I kissed her quite thoroughly for an endless moment,' " she mimicked. "That sounds like toying to me."

"Well, it wasn't. At least I didn't intend it to be." He blew a long breath. "One minute I was warning her about Ellsworth—"

"Warning her about Ellsworth?" Her voice rose. "What kind of warning?"

"He is not to be trusted, Veronica. His reputation with women is appalling. He would take advantage of her without hesitation."

"So to prove your point you took advantage of her?"

"It wasn't like that," he muttered.

Now that he thought about it, he realized Julia hadn't pulled away from him. Indeed, she had slipped her arms around his neck and greeted his unexpected moment of desire with passion of her own. But obviously, as she refused to meet his gaze afterward, she regretted their brief lapse in judgment as much as he. And he did regret it, even if he couldn't get the memory of how her lips had felt beneath his and how her supple body had felt against him out of his mind.

"Dare I ask what it *was* like?"

"No," he said sharply.

"I see."

"What do you see?"

"Far more than you want me to, brother dear."

"You have no idea what you're talking about," he snapped. "And I would prefer that you refrain from calling me *brother dear*. I find it most annoying."

"Precisely why I shall continue to call you *brother dear*. It describes our relationship perfectly. Besides, I like it and the fact that you do not only makes me like it more." She fell silent and he readied himself for her next attack. Instead, Veronica drew a deep breath. "She is an intelligent woman and more than capable of taking care of herself. Still, I would appreciate it if you did not break her heart."

"Breaking her heart is the farthest thing from my mind." *What about my heart?* He brushed the absurd notion from his head. "It was a momentary aberration, nothing more than that, and I daresay Julia sees it the same way. It was an embarrassment to us both. I assure you it will not happen again."

"Really?"

"You have my word."

"Tell me, do you think Julia would agree that it was a momentary aberration and an embarrassment? That she would prefer it not happen again?"

"Yes, of course. Absolutely. No doubt she . . ." Without warning, the depth of passion he had felt and the certainty that she had shared it, if only for an instant, rushed through him. "Probably."

"Then I would say the pertinent issue to ponder here, brother dear, is not that you kissed her," Veronica said in a deceptively casual manner, "but whether she kissed you back."

His florist must be chortling at the Earl of Mountdale's newfound need to dispense roses across the city and the subsequent increase in his bills. Not that it wasn't worth it.

Harrison sat at his desk trying to concentrate on the varied and sundry items that needed the attention of the Earl of Mountdale or the Marquess of Kingsbury as he had done all morning and well into the afternoon with little to show for his efforts. His thoughts kept returning to last night. And the more he considered what had happened on the terrace, the more confused he became. It did no good to dwell on it so he tried to force it from his mind. With little success.

He had had flowers sent first thing this morning to Julia and had dispatched a footman with a brief note of apology as well. It wasn't at all adequate and he fully intended to provide a more appropriate apology in person as soon as he determined exactly what he would say. Why was this so blasted difficult? He was never at a loss for words. Perhaps it was attributable to his lack of sleep. He had tossed and turned all night, and when he had slept he had dreamed of Julia. Not merely of their searing kiss but of Julia and he in all manner of carnal activities. Obviously, his dreams were influenced by the erotic writings of her ancestor.

Or perhaps it was because, while he did feel he should apologize for his actions, he could not bring himself to regret the kiss itself. Most confusing indeed.

He had had flowers delivered as well to Miss Waverly along with a request to accompany her in the park this afternoon. He had already received a reply, no doubt thanks to her eager mother, regretfully declining his invitation for today but agreeing to accompany him tomorrow. He wasn't at all pleased by the delay. He would much prefer to get this courtship over and done with. Now that he had chosen an appropriate wife he would just as soon get on with it.

Somewhere in the back of his mind he heard his brother's laughter. He ignored it. Bad enough he had his dead brother's wife to contend with. He knew full well if Charles was here he would say getting on with it was not at all what one should be thinking about in regards to marriage. Charles would have grinned and added unless, of course, one was being forced to wed.

A small stack of papers fell on the desk in front of him

and he jerked his head up. "Father, I didn't hear you come in."

"So I noticed." His father sat heavily in the chair in front of the desk. "I don't know where you were but you certainly weren't here. Wool-gathering, Harrison?"

"I do not wool-gather," he said, and adopted a stern expression. "I have a great deal of work to do."

His father considered him for a long moment then nodded at the papers he had tossed on the desk. "I read it."

Harrison glanced at the top page. It was the portion of the memoirs Veronica had given him. "And?"

"The writing was quite lively I thought."

Harrison scoffed. "And?"

"And it's not entirely accurate."

"Yet another reason why it should not be published."

"Nonsense." His father leaned forward and met his gaze, a definite twinkle in his eyes. "It's so much better than I remember." He chuckled and settled back in the chair. "Deny it all you want, but I look bloody good in Hermione's version of our affair."

Harrison stared. "You most certainly do not!"

"Come now, Harrison. Your perception is colored by the fact that I am your father. Be honest with me, boy. If you were reading this adventure about another man, wouldn't you find the portrayal of him . . ." He flashed his son a wicked grin. "Splendid?"

"I most certainly would not." Indignation rang in his voice.

"Daring?"

"Not at all."

"Dashing?"

"Absolutely not."

"At the very least, extremely well-en—"

"Father!" Harrison snapped.

His father laughed. "I had no objection to its publication before reading it and I endorse it wholeheartedly now. I should rather like to be remembered for my adventures as a youthful scoundrel rather than as a doddering old man who continues to cast his eye on beautiful young women who, if they had any interest at all, would only want him for his title and wealth." He shook his head. "Sometimes I quite envy those who have died young."

"Yes, well, I would have missed you," Harrison said in a gruff manner. If truth were told, he had not only always loved his father but had secretly admired the devil-may-care way he had lived. In spite of his mother's disapproval. Odd that he had never told him.

His father's gaze met his and the old man smiled. "Thank you, my boy." He paused. "Dare I ask how goes your campaign?"

"In truth, I don't know." Harrison blew a long breath. "Somewhere along the way I seem to have lost sight of the goal."

His father's brow rose. "That doesn't sound like you."

"It's not me." He shook his head. "I thought I would become her friend and she might be more inclined to sell me the memoirs then but, in truth, I like her."

"Lady Winterset?" Mild surprise sounded in his father's voice.

"She's very clever, which is not something I look for in a woman. Indeed I find intelligent women annoying. Veronica being an excellent example."

"And Lady Winterset is not annoying?"

"Oh, she's most annoying and stubborn and has no idea of a woman's place in the world. She thinks she can take care of herself. Can you believe such a thing?"

"It's all hard to believe," his father said wryly.

"In spite of that, I find her company most enjoyable. She doesn't simper, she doesn't act like she's less intelligent than she is. She doesn't directly challenge every opinion I have but she makes it very clear that she does not agree."

"And she's quite lovely as well."

"Isn't she?" He absently tapped his pen on the desk. "Yet she doesn't behave like most beautiful women of my acquaintance. I'm certain she's cognizant of her appearance but it doesn't seem especially important to her. And well, last night . . ."

"Last night?"

"Last night she wore a dress . . ." He glanced at his father. "Green and it precisely matched her eyes. She was . . ." He shook his head.

"Breathtaking?"

Harrison nodded.

"Ah well, that explains it." His father chuckled. "I have always had a fondness for green-eyed women myself. Must run in the blood."

"That's not all that runs in the blood," Harrison said under his breath.

His father eyed him curiously. "Don't stop now. It's not often that you confide in me, and I must say I am enjoying this. Go on."

He drew a deep breath. "I kissed her."

"I see."

"I didn't set out to kiss her. I still have no idea what happened." He ran his hand through his hair, a gesture completely foreign to him. "One moment I was explaining to her that Ellsworth was a cad who wouldn't hesitate to take advantage of her. And the next minute . . ."

"You were kissing her."

"You were right about that, you know. About my plan with Ellsworth, I mean."

"I appreciate you admitting that." His father chuckled. "I am rarely right."

Harrison shook his head. "It was, well, wrong of me. And furthermore, has had repercussions I did not anticipate."

"It brought Lady Winterset to the attention of Ellsworth," his father said, nodding his head slowly. "That is awkward, given how you feel about her."

"She is a friend," he said staunchly. "Aside from a momentary lapse in judgment last night, I feel nothing but friendship for her."

"Yes." His father chuckled. "That's what I meant. Feelings of friendship." He considered his son thoughtfully then smiled. "Well, you have work to do so I shall leave you in peace." He stood with the help of his cane and started to the door.

"Father," Harrison said impulsively and rose to his feet. "If you have any . . . advice I would be most grateful to hear it."

His father turned and stared for a moment then a slow smile spread across his face. "I don't believe you have ever asked me for advice before."

"This whole business with Julia and Ellsworth's involvement and the way I feel about Ellsworth's involvement . . ." He shook his head. "It all seems completely out of my control and I have no idea what to do now."

"It's often completely out of our hands when the situation involves women. Especially women we care for. Even as friends," he added. "The best advice I ever received on the subject of the eternal conflict between men and women was to trust your heart. I didn't and have regretted it nearly every day since. Your heart, Harrison, will not fail you." He nodded then opened the door, paused, and turned back to his son. "Oh, and I would reconsider that nonsense about you feeling nothing more for Lady Winterset than friendship."

Harrison drew his brows together. "Why?"

"Because, my boy, when I asked how your campaign was going, I was not referring to Lady Winterset but to your pursuit of marriage with Miss Waverly." He smiled in a knowing manner. "That all that seems to be on your mind is your kissing the delectable Lady Winterset is most telling." He chuckled. "Most telling indeed."

Harrison stared at the closed door. What on earth did that mean? It wasn't most telling. It was . . . He had no idea what it was. Certainly Julia was on his mind whereas Miss Waverly was not. But that was only due to circumstances. It was nothing more significant that that.

And that nonsense about trusting his heart. It was all well and good to say that but his heart was as confused as his head and could not be trusted. One shouldn't leave something as important as one's future to the whims of something as fickle as one's heart. He had never done so before and had no desire to do so now. Indeed, he'd had no experience whatsoever in matters of the heart. Before now, it had never occurred to him to wonder why.

Or wonder as well if, for the first time, he might possibly be wrong.

. . . .*and because of that incident, it strikes me that I should explain why I have called this book of memoirs* The Perfect Mistress. *I am certain, Dear Reader, that my adventures have not struck you as being those of a mistress but of someone lax in moral character who flitted from man to man. First, I never flitted, and secondly, my character, in most aspects, was not at all immoral. I never stole, I never cheated, I never became involved with a man who was married, and I never sought to hurt anyone deliberately.*

*The accepted definition of* mistress *is that of a woman who allows a man to take care of her financial needs in return for carnal favors. I never allowed a man to pay for the necessities of life. Oh, I did accept gifts; it would have been foolish not to. One can sell the spare diamond or ruby if one's financial circumstances warrant such a thing, although it is always a dreadful shame.*

*But when I was with a man, I was faithful to him alone. I cost him nothing save his affection and I gave him my heart. If you have not noticed by now, in each and every instance, I gave my heart. And that is why I truly was the perfect mistress as well as why very nearly every one of my adventures ended well.*

*Still, the end of an adventure, no matter how much both sides agree that what was once shared is at an end, is always bittersweet. But the beginning—there is little to compare with finding a new love as I know I have mentioned before. Regardless, it cannot be said enough.*

*The very moment I met Sir Anthony and his dark eyes captured mine, I knew, indeed we both knew . . .*

from *The Perfect Mistress,*
*the Memoirs of Lady Hermione Middlebury*

# Chapter Twelve

"You can't avoid him forever, you know." Hermione sat once again at the foot of Julia's bed.

"I'm not avoiding anyone," Julia said, and sat up. She had been expecting a visit from Hermione for days and had discovered, much to her dismay, she slept no better on nights when her great-grandmother didn't visit than when she did as she was always anticipating her arrival. Besides, she was beginning, albeit reluctantly, to look forward to their chats. "I had no need to see Harrison today nor did he have any need to see me."

"But you wanted to," Hermione said with a knowing smile.

"Nonsense," Julia muttered even though Hermione was right.

In spite of her best efforts, she couldn't get the kiss they'd shared out of her head. She had never been kissed like that before nor had she ever responded with such unimagined passion. She had felt that kiss right down to her very toes and an ache of need had gripped her so fiercely she had wanted nothing more than to stay locked in his embrace forever. Why, even now, the memory of his lips on hers . . .

Hermione raised a brow.

Heat washed up Julia's face. "You needn't look like that. You have no idea what I'm thinking."

"I can't read your mind but the expression on your face is unmistakable."

"Regardless, Harrison obviously regretted kissing me the moment it happened. He couldn't wait to be rid of me."

"Or he was as confused as you."

Julia scoffed. "I doubt that. I've never met a man as less likely to be confused as Harrison Landingham. And no one as confusing."

"Men are often confused when they don't listen to what their heart is trying to tell them." Her voice softened. "Which is what makes them so confusing to women."

"Now you are being confusing as well." Julia's brows drew together. "What are you trying to say?"

"I thought your flirtation with Mr. Ellsworth was quite clever. Most discrete and nicely done."

Julia huffed. "You are changing the subject."

"Not entirely." She paused. "Harrison was well aware of it, you know."

"Was he?" Julia shrugged but was pleased nonetheless. "I didn't notice."

"No, you were too busy trying not to look at him."

"I didn't . . ." She sighed. "I couldn't."

Hermione nodded. "You were hurt by his manner, as you had every right to be. Although I'm not at all surprised that he was shocked by his action. It was most improper and defied everything he thinks he knows about himself. It was also a most impressive kiss. I must say, I was quite proud of you."

"Proud of me? For what?"

"How to say this delicately." She thought for a moment. "I was somewhat afraid that after marriage to William that you might not surrender to passion when it claimed you."

Julia gasped. "William was a very passionate man!"

"Was he?"

"Yes," she said staunchly. "Our marital relations were very . . . nice."

"Comfortable as well, no doubt?"

"Yes."

"And never the least bit surprising?"

"Not at all."

"Yes, darling, that's what a woman truly wants." Hermione nodded. "Intimacies that are comfortable, unsurprising, and *nice*."

"You needn't say 'nice' in that manner."

" 'Nice,' in this particular context, deserves to be said in that manner."

"I was very content with William," Julia said firmly, "in all respects."

"Tell me, Julia." Hermione studied her closely. "Did William's kiss ever make your toes curl?"

"My toes have no need of curling," she said in a lofty manner.

"But did Harrison's kiss make your toes curl?"

Julia clenched her teeth. "You know full well it did."

"Passion is an interesting thing, you know. And never better than when the heart is involved."

She shrugged. "My heart is not involved nor is his. We shared a moment of . . . of lust. It's nothing more than that."

Hermione snorted. "Lust, my dear, does not linger in the mind of a woman unless her heart is involved."

"And you are an expert on lust."

She chuckled. "I am indeed."

"But you know nothing of love."

Hermione cast her an offended look. "On the contrary, darling, I know a great deal about love."

Julia scoffed. "You went from one man to another."

"Yes, and I loved each and every one of them. I never bedded a man I didn't love." Her brows drew together. "Oh, there was that once, that was indeed nothing but pure lust and quite a lot of fun I might add."

"Dear Lord," Julia muttered.

"Love is not finite, Julia. One can love more than one man. Admittedly it's best to only love one at a time. But the fact that you loved William, and I have no doubt that you did, does not mean you cannot love someone else."

"I don't love Harrison. I find him . . . annoying and pompous and stuffy."

"At first, perhaps, but now?"

"Now?" She thought for a moment. "I don't know." In truth, the more she came to know him, the more she liked him. She drew a deep breath. "He is trying to be less stuffy and admittedly he has become somewhat charming. He was very kind to Miss Nelson when she had wanted to read her poetry, although he doesn't like even good poetry. However, he seems to think my virtue needs protection from men who would take liberties because of you." She ignored the thought that in a tiny way, it was endearing. "It's both arrogant and most annoying."

"That is arrogant of him and I can well understand your annoyance. Although one might consider that jealousy might play a part as well."

"I doubt that." Julia scoffed. "I will admit he's more amusing than I anticipated and more thoughtful as well."

"Ah yes, the roses. I noticed Benjamin and Mr. Ellsworth sent roses as well. I assume they're in the maid's quarters?"

"The maid is most appreciative." Julia nodded. "The note of apology that accompanied Harrison's however was brief and tersely worded."

"The man is confused, dearest. He's never had these feelings before and he has no idea what to do with them." She smiled. "He's not at all like his father."

"You loved his father?"

"I said I loved them all." She paused. "Albert was most delightful but in retrospect he was a dreadful mistake. Ripples in a pond, darling. One truly never knows what repercussions one's actions might ultimately have." She sighed. "But that is a story for another time."

"You think I'm in love with Harrison?"

"I think you are right on the edge of plunging into something quite extraordinary that will make you blissfully happy for the rest of your days if you allow yourself to do so."

Julia was hard-pressed to deny it. Even before last night, it had seemed something was happening between them. Still . . . She shook her head. "I don't know how I feel."

"Let me ask you this then." Hermione chose her words with care. "How would you feel if the memoirs were disposed of tomorrow and Harrison was out of your life forever? Or, even worse, if he married the insipid Miss Waverly tomorrow?"

The oddest sensation of pain and regret stabbed her somewhere near her heart and her breath caught. "Good Lord."

Hermione smiled with satisfaction. "I am never wrong about these things. Why, I remember once telling Lady Kentworthy that even though she was most insistent—"

"Ah-hem." A throat cleared somewhere behind Hermione. A male throat.

"Don't tell me that's another one of your paramours." Julia heaved a long-suffering sigh.

"I do hope so." Hermione grinned and glanced over her shoulder. "Gregory, darling, please show yourself. Julia finds disembodied voices to be most unnerving." She glanced at Julia. "At least I assume you do."

"It's remarkable what no longer unnerves me," Julia said wryly.

At once a gentleman snapped into sight standing behind Hermione. This one was tall and fair-haired and considerably younger than Victor. Julia wondered if he had died young or simply preferred to be seen at this age. Admittedly he was quite handsome.

"Lady Winterset." Gregory bowed in a polished manner. "How delightful to meet you." His gaze swept over her. "And in such a charming state of dishabille."

Julia grabbed her covers and pulled them up to her neck. She glared at her great-grandmother. "Are you planning on bringing your friends every time you come?"

"Not every time." Hermione rose gracefully to her feet.

"Aren't you going to introduce me?" Gregory smiled in a manner that made Julia instinctively clutch the covers tighter.

"Julia prefers not to be formally introduced to gentlemen who are dead," Hermione said with a shrug.

He frowned. "How very narrow-minded of her."

"Julia prefers not to be introduced, formally or otherwise, to gentlemen, dead or alive, while she is in her bed!" Julia huffed. "And I do wish you would stop inviting your friends here."

"I did not invite him." She looked at Gregory. "Did I?"

"No, my dear." He chuckled. "I simply followed you on wings of love."

"Utter nonsense." She lightly smacked his shoulder with

her fan and smiled. Julia had stopped wondering where the fan came from. "Gregory is every bit as charming now as he was when he was alive."

"More, I think," Gregory said with a grin. "Death has given me the opportunity to sharpen my wit. One does need a sense of the absurd in the hereafter, don't you agree?"

"I wouldn't know." Julia smiled weakly.

"No, of course not. What was I thinking? You'll know soon enough. We all do." He cast Hermione a fond smile. "I make her laugh."

"It's why I keep you around."

"That, and my considerable charm and dashing good looks," he said in a far-from-modest manner.

Hermione laughed. "That too."

A wicked smile curved his lip. "One would hope there are other reasons as well."

Julia had no desire to consider what those other reasons might be.

Hermione cast him a wicked look of her own.

"Shall we, my dear?" He held out his arm and Hermione took it.

"Are you leaving?" Julia asked.

"We have an engagement, dear." Hermione shrugged. "Life, or rather death, is somewhat more busy than one would expect."

"But I don't know what to do. Or how I feel or anything."

"I can't tell you that." Hermione scoffed. "I can only give you the benefit of my experience and considerable wisdom."

"Oh, thank you so much."

"Sarcasm, remember? Not becoming at all." Hermione favored her with a brilliant smile. "And you are most welcome. Gregory?"

"Good evening, Lady Winterset." He nodded and at once they both vanished.

Julia blew a long breath and lay back down. Not that she was going to sleep. Hermione had given her a great deal to think about as had, no doubt, been her purpose.

Was she falling in love with Harrison? She had no idea. She hadn't felt at all like this when she had fallen in love with William. That had been almost natural. They had shared the same likes and dislikes. Nothing about William had been the least bit difficult.

With Harrison she was constantly at odds. Not just about the memoirs but about everything. Still, there was something special about the man. In one respect, Hermione was completely right. Nobody, not even her husband, had ever made her feel like that. Wanton and irrational and as if her very bones were melting.

But as for love, well, it was all most confusing. Still, she couldn't ignore her immediate response when Hermione had asked how she'd feel if Harrison was abruptly gone from her life. Even now, she couldn't quite vanquish the feeling of loss that still lay in the pit of her stomach.

She wasn't used to feelings of confusion and she didn't like it one bit. Something needed to be done. Someone needed to do something. And obviously that someone was her. She needed to make a decision about the disposition of the memoirs as her finances were growing smaller every day. And she needed to confront Harrison. If the kiss they'd shared meant nothing to him, she needed to know that. And if it had, she needed to know that too.

She absolutely would not fall in love with a man who would not return her love. Even if that resolve might well be too late. Still, the very idea that Harrison might be jealous did oddly lift her spirits.

She rolled onto her side, closed her eyes, and tried to sleep. And smiled.

It did seem there was far more of Hermione in her than she had suspected and that probably wasn't altogether bad.

Harrison and Miss Waverly strolled through the park at a sedate pace. Her mother and a companion were a good ten feet behind them. Far enough to allow the couple privacy but still well within sight. As was eminently proper. Regardless, Harrison wasn't pleased by the presence of a chaperone. His intentions were entirely honorable after all.

In spite of himself, he couldn't help but contrast this walk with Miss Waverly with the walk he'd taken with Julia. There was no need for a chaperone with a widow, not that she had needed one of course. He chuckled to himself. Nor, he suspected, would Julia allow one even if one was required. And Julia could converse on any number of topics. Even when they were at odds, it was never boring. Miss Waverly's endless chatter on nothing of particular significance was, well, inane.

He couldn't discuss literature with her as she did not read books, and he had no interest in the ladies' magazines she did read. He doubted she read newspapers. Miss Waverly did not strike him as being interested in current events although she might well peruse the society pages. He wondered if she liked art but feared bringing up the topic. Miss Waverly didn't seem to notice his silence. But then why would she? She chatted more than enough for the two of them and did go on about the latest ball she had attended, what she had worn, and who she had seen. And she had the most irritating penchant for gossip.

"I heard something quite scandalous the other night," she began.

"Miss Waverly," he interrupted and tried not to sound stern. "I am not fond of gossip."

Her eyes widened. "Even about people you know?"

"Especially about people I know," he said. "I do not find gossip at all becoming in a young lady."

"That's what Mother says." Miss Waverly sighed and Harrison was at once relieved that she didn't take his comment as a chastisement and get annoyed. "Although she doesn't seem to think gossip on her part is the least bit objectionable. She is a dreadful gossip, you know, even if she does tend to learn the most interesting things. Why, only yesterday, she was saying . . ."

Harrison groaned to himself. Conversing with Miss Waverly was pointless. There was simply nothing to talk about. He had never thought the ability to converse in an intelligent manner was a particular asset in a wife, but now, the idea of spending the rest of his days with a woman who didn't seem to have an opinion on anything beyond fashion or parties, was most disturbing. Surely it was because she was so young and not because she didn't have a brain in her pretty head. The thought pulled him up short. He didn't like women who were intelligent; he never had. Still, intelligent women might be maddening but they were never boring. Veronica was certainly never boring. And Julia, well, he couldn't imagine ever being bored by Julia.

A woman walking a large, spotted dog passed by them. For the barest instant he thought it was Julia and his heart jumped. That too was most disturbing and no doubt due to his father's talk yesterday about trusting his heart.

"Do you like dogs, Miss Waverly?" he said without thinking.

"Oh yes, I do, my lord." She cast him a brilliant smile.

"Father doesn't like them. Mother had one when I was very young and Father hated it as it did seem to hate him. I don't have one now but I fully plan to have at least one when I'm wed." She fluttered her lashes at him and he smiled weakly. Not that it wasn't charming. It was simply well rehearsed. "I would very much like a small, fluffy sort of dog. One that would sit in my lap and play with a ball and that sort of thing. In truth, I would like several. It would be great fun. Oh, I can see it now."

"As can I, Miss Waverly." He could indeed see it. A flock of small, yapping beasts that would nip at his heels and leave hair on the furniture. Animals that were nothing but annoyances and wouldn't even provide proper protection on a walk in the park.

Miss Waverly launched into another recitation about something of no consequence and he was grateful for the respite. One thing to be said about the young woman, she required no particular attention from him save the occasional nod or assenting comment.

After he had spoken with his father yesterday, he had sent a note to Ellsworth, along with a bank draft, dissolving their arrangement. That should eliminate him from Julia's life. While she was quite lovely, she had no money, her position in society was practically nonexistent, and a liaison with her would not be of any real benefit to Ellsworth. Harrison was confident the man would now leave her be and move on to greener pastures.

"My lord." Miss Waverly stopped and turned toward him. "Might I be perfectly honest with you?"

"Please do, Miss Waverly."

"Mother says, and Father agrees, that when an eligible bachelor, particularly one who is older—"

He cringed to himself.

"—asks permission to call on an unmarried girl, he does so with the idea of marriage in mind." Her gaze met his. "So my question is whether that is indeed what you have in mind."

"Miss Waverly," he said slowly, trying to force words out past the fingers of panic that even now were wrapping themselves around his throat. "As we scarcely know one another, it seems entirely too early to be discussing even the idea of marriage. Don't you agree?"

"I do indeed." She beamed at him. "You are very wise." *Because of my advanced years, no doubt.*

"But I do think you should know, if you are inclined in that direction at some point, we have discussed it."

"We?" He raised a brow.

"Mother and Father and I, of course."

"Of course." As was most proper.

"And they would be amenable to this match."

He studied her closely. "And you, Miss Waverly? Would you be amenable as well?"

"Oh my, yes, my lord. I would be a fool not to be." She shook her head. "Why, you would be considered the catch of the year. Your wealth is sound and extensive and there has never been a hint of scandal about you. Even Mother is hard-pressed to find any gossip about you whatsoever aside from the fact that you have not been known to have asked permission to call on a young lady before. And while you are merely an earl now, you are heir to a much loftier title. You are really a perfect match." She leaned toward him and lowered her voice confidentially. "My dearest friend, Evelyn, has recently become engaged to an earl but he will never be more than an earl whereas you will one day be a marquess. Which means I would one day be a marchioness which is ever so much better than a mere countess. Evelyn would be quite green with envy. And as your father is so very old, I can't imagine it will be all that long before he has gone on to his final resting place." She paused as if she knew exactly what she'd said although he doubted it. "God rest his soul," she added.

"My father, Miss Waverly, is the picture of health." He offered his arm and they started off again. "I hope to have him with us for many years to come baring unforeseen accident."

"Yes, that would be dreadful," she murmured with no particular enthusiasm.

He didn't often think about becoming the Marquess of Kingsbury one day, it was simply an accepted part of his life. The fact that his father would have to die first was not something he wished to dwell on.

"I just thought you should know," she said. "About our . . . amenability that is."

"Quite right." He forced a pleasant smile. "Your candor is most appreciated."

"I thought you would like it." She beamed. "Now then, what was I saying? Oh yes. We were at a soiree with . . ."

Good God, how was he going to extricate himself from this mess? While Miss Waverly did indeed meet all of his qualifications, he couldn't imagine living the rest of his days with her. And her little dogs too. Certainly, the simple request to call on her was not an absolute declaration of intentions, although it was considered a first step. It was not surprising that Miss Waverly and her parents had discussed a match between them. But the more time he spent around her, the more sure he was that they would never suit. She might be quite perfect, well bred, eminently proper, and everything he thought he had wanted but actually being with the appropriate candidate had opened his eyes.

Somewhere, in the back of his head, he heard Charles laughing.

Perhaps he should trust his heart even if he had no idea

how to go about it. And perhaps the very fact that he was confused was significant. As was the realization that even with Miss Waverly by his side, all he could think about was Julia. The more he considered everything, the more perplexing it all became.

Worse, if he was wrong about the kind of wife he wanted, what else was he wrong about? And wasn't it past time he found out?

. . . *and, as she was my friend, I had to tell her. Even if in cases like this one very nearly always kills the messenger.*

*I have always found friendship interesting. It is my observation that friendships between men and women are only successful when their hearts are otherwise engaged. If not, the affection shared in friendship is often the beginning, which is the nature of men and women. The best marriages are those where husband and wife are friends as well as lovers. A man married to his dearest friend hardly ever strays.*

*Friendship between women is a different matter. The bond can be stronger than that between sisters as one has no choice in one's sisters. A true friend will walk through fire for you or with you. It is easier to have stalwart friends though than to be one, especially when it comes to matters regarding men.*

*I was not at all bothered when my adventure with his lordship ended by mutual accord and within days he was in her bed. But when I learned he was going directly from Agatha's bed to another's, all the while professing his undying affection for her, it seemed my course was clear if exceptionally difficult.*

*I knew she would not take it well and indeed my fears were confirmed when . . .*

from *The Perfect Mistress,*
*the Memoirs of Lady Hermione Middlebury*

# Chapter Thirteen

"I have never known you to be indecisive," Veronica said mildly and sipped her tea.

"It's a very big decision," Portia said. "She has three interesting offers and her future depends on which she picks."

The three friends sat at their usual table at Fenwick's. Julia thought they'd been lucky it was available. Four of the five tables in the tearoom were occupied by small groups of ladies very much like themselves. Fenwick's tearoom was obviously proving to be a good investment.

Veronica's brows drew together and she stared at Portia. "You're being very practical today."

Portia shrugged. "I am unfailingly practical."

Veronica scoffed. "Not that we've noticed."

"Which brings up an interesting matter," Julia said, eager to change the conversation to something other than her own dilemma. "You have been behaving quite oddly of late."

Portia's eyes widened innocently. "Whatever do you mean?"

"I mean you seem to have become an outrageous flirt," Julia said. "We noticed—"

"Everyone noticed," Veronica added.

"—at the literary salon the other night and before that at Veronica's party," Julia continued. "It's not at all like you. What has gotten into you?"

"Not a thing." Portia shrugged.

Veronica scoffed. "Come now, Portia, we are your friends and we are concerned about you."

"It's nothing really." Portia stirred her tea and refused to meet either woman's gaze. "I've simply been . . . well . . . practicing."

"Practicing? For what?" Veronica snorted. "The national tart championships?"

Portia's gaze snapped to Veronica. "I have not behaved like a tart."

"No, you haven't," Julia said quickly. "But a gentleman might think that your actions are not merely harmless flirtations but invitations. Believe me, I have read enough of Hermione's memoirs to know of what I speak."

"Thus far"—Portia leaned back and crossed her arms over her chest—"no one has accepted my invitation and I find it most upsetting."

Veronica choked on her tea. "Good God!"

Julia cast her a quieting glance. Anything she said right now would only exacerbate the situation. "What do you mean?"

"I thought perhaps if I was more flirtatious . . ." Portia heaved a heartfelt sigh and folded her hands on the table. "As you know, my family seems to think it's time I marry again. At least once a week, one of my relations invites me to dinner or a card party or something where there is inevitably a number of eligible gentlemen they deem suitable to be my next husband. As of yet, not one of them has seen fit to call on me afterward."

Julia's brow furrowed in confusion. "I thought you didn't like any of them?"

"I don't but that's not the point. It's simply, well . . ." Portia thought for a moment. "It's disheartening, that's what it is." She shook her head. "Of the three of us, Julia is the pretty one. Why, she has three men vying for her attention."

Julia shook her head. "They're only interested in the memoirs."

Veronica coughed then shrugged apologetically.

"Veronica is the clever one, and I, well, I am the proper one. I'm the one that . . . the one that's left."

Veronica patted Portia's hand. "You have money, darling."

Julia glared at her.

Veronica sighed. "And you are really quite lovely with all that dark brown hair of yours and your large brown eyes. I don't know why you think you aren't." She rolled her gaze at the ceiling. "You do have a certain wit about you as well. You can be most amusing. Beyond that . . ." A reluctant smile teased the corners of Veronica's lips. "You really don't make a very good tart."

Portia stared, then her lips twitched into a reluctant smile and the next moment all three women burst into laughter. At last Portia sniffed and smiled at her friends. "Thank you, Veronica. You do know how to put things into perspective."

Veronica shrugged in an offhand manner. "It's a gift."

Julia aimed a pointed glance at Portia. "You should have told us how you were feeling."

"Yes, I suppose. But then I also would have had to tell you"—Portia smiled in a wicked manner—"that I have enjoyed every flirtatious minute." She leaned forward and lowered her voice. "The idea came from the portion of the memoirs I read. Do you know how men react when they think they are going to be able to seduce you?" She shook her head. "I had no idea."

"Yes, but now you are going to once again be your usual, and quite charming, self," Veronica said firmly.

"I'm not going to give it up entirely."

"Nor should you." Julia nodded. "But do try not to be quite so enthusiastic in the future."

"And, darling, the right man came along once and another right man will no doubt come along again. If you have learned anything from Lady Middlebury's reminiscences you should have learned that. The last thing you want to do is make a mistake. Marrying the wrong person is one error that cannot be easily rectified." Veronica sipped her tea in a nonchalant manner. "That's what I hope my newfound brother understands."

"Oh?" Julia's manner matched Veronica's.

"I'm speaking in regards to Miss Waverly. His father tells me she is turning out to be everything he wanted." She smiled in an overly satisfied manner.

Julia's heart twisted. "I see."

"No, you don't see at all. I presented him with Miss Waverly because she meets every one of his absurd qualifications. I believe he's now finding out how totally asinine they are and that what he thought he wanted is the last thing that will make him happy." She met Julia's gaze and her satisfied smile returned. "Add to that, Miss Waverly is not the one he kissed. Is she, Julia?"

Portia gasped. "He kissed Julia? Where?"

"On the terrace," Julia muttered.

"On the *lips*." Veronica grinned. "And he was most taken aback by it."

"Was he?" Julia said as if it was of no consequence.

"He was indeed. I've never known him to be shocked by his own behavior before. Charles would have been so proud. But then Harrison hasn't been himself since he

met you." She met Julia's gaze. "Right from the beginning, he did not behave at all like his usual self. You, my
dear, are the cause of the change and I must say I like it."

Julia shook her head. "He only wants the memoirs."

"And Cadwallender just wants the memoirs as well?"

"No, he has asked to call on me," Julia admitted.

Veronica raised a brow. "And I am confident Mr.
Ellsworth wants more from you than the memoirs as
well."

"I believe Mr. Ellsworth wants more from every
woman he meets," Portia said under her breath, and the
other women turned shocked gazes on her. "You needn't
look at me like that. I may have been something of an
idiot to have flirted the way I did but I am not so stupid as
to be taken in by the likes of Mr. Ellsworth." She sipped
her tea. "Although he is most charming."

"And not to be trusted, I suspect." Veronica adopted an
overly casual tone. "I was wondering if Harrison has
apologized yet. For the kiss that is." She considered Julia
curiously. "And wondering as well if an apology is needed."

"He sent flowers and a brief note," Julia shrugged. "As
did Mr. Cadwallender and Mr. Ellsworth. But then I've
received notes from both of them nearly every day and
flowers almost as often."

Portia sighed. "A feast while some of us are in the
midst of famine."

Veronica arched a brow. "Roses?"

Julia nodded. "All of them."

Portia shook her head. "Men can be so unoriginal."

"Julia, it seems to me . . ." Veronica paused. "I don't
know how to put this tactfully."

"You've never put anything tactfully." Portia scoffed.
"Why begin now?"

Veronica grinned at her. "There's the Portia we know
and love."

Julia laughed.

"Very well then, I shall say it straight out. You can continue to deny it all you want but these gentlemen have more than literary concerns on their minds. They all want you in their beds."

"Veronica!" Julia gasped.

She ignored her. "Mr. Cadwallender has honorably made his intentions clear, and one must give him due credit for that. Indeed, I imagine involvement with him would ultimately end in marriage although I don't think he is the proper choice for you."

"I'd take him," Portia said under her breath. "I thought he was quite handsome although I suspect his funds are minimal."

Veronica ignored her. "Then there is Mr. Ellsworth who does seem indiscriminate in his desires, and I for one would not trust him with my vilest enemy let alone my dearest friend."

"One has to admit though, he is quite attractive and very famous." Portia grimaced apologetically. "I just thought that should be mentioned although I agree, Mr. Ellsworth is not the right man for you. Nor for any of us," she added quickly.

"Which leaves us with Harrison." A note of triumph sounded in Veronica's voice.

"It does not." Julia glared. "Or rather it does but to what end?"

Veronica heaved a long-suffering sigh. "Let's play a little game, shall we?"

Portia's gaze slid from Veronica to Julia and back. She smiled in an innocent manner. "I have always liked Veronica's games."

"Veronica." Julia's voice carried a note of warning and again Veronica ignored her. As Julia knew she would. Harrison was right. Her friend could be most annoying.

"Now, onto the game and the first questions." Veronica looked at Julia. "How would you react, and more importantly, how would you feel if Ellsworth were to unexpectedly grab and kiss you?"

"Why, I would be furious," Julia said without hesitation. "And somewhat revolted, I suspect. The man holds no appeal for me although I too admit he is amusing. But I would certainly slap his face."

"Excellent answer." Portia beamed. "Does she get points for that?"

"No, darling, she is the only one playing." Veronica cast Portia an affectionate smile. As gruff as she acted toward the other woman, Julia knew full well Veronica loved Portia as a sister. Without warning, gratitude for having these two women in her life washed through her. "Now, the next questions are exactly the same. Simply substitute Mr. Cadwallender for Mr. Ellsworth."

"Well, I would be most surprised if Benjamin were to kiss me."

"Benjamin?" Portia cast a knowing glance at Veronica.

"He doesn't strike me as the type of man who would take unwanted liberties. But I wouldn't slap his face." She thought for a moment. "I daresay Benjamin's kiss would be very nice."

"Good Lord, Julia." Portia stared. "Even I want more than nice."

"There is nothing wrong with nice," Julia said staunchly.

"William's kiss was nice," Veronica said in an aside to Portia.

Julia sucked in a sharp breath. "I've never told you anything of the sort!"

"Not in so many words." Veronica studied her. "Am I wrong?"

"Yes," Julia snapped.

"My apologies then." From the tone of her voice and

the look in her eye, it was obvious Veronica didn't believe her for a moment. "And there you have it. Neither Mr. Cadwallender nor Mr. Ellsworth elicits the kind of answers that would indicate further attention."

"Is the game over then?" Portia asked.

"Yes." Veronica sipped her tea. "I see no need to continue."

Portia frowned. "Aren't you going to ask about Lord Mountdale?"

Veronica shook her head. "I don't think it's necessary." Her gaze met Julia's. "Is it?"

"No, I suppose not," Julia muttered.

"It isn't? Why not? I don't . . ." Portia's eyes widened. "Oh. The kiss. Of course." She nodded. "Well, if you married Lord Mountdale all of your money troubles would be at an end."

"I would never marry any man to improve my financial circumstances," Julia said sharply. "Let alone Harrison. It wouldn't be the least bit fair to him. And he deserves far better than that."

The words hung in the air.

"Isn't that interesting," Veronica said under her breath.

Julia narrowed her eyes and glared. "Isn't what interesting?"

"How are your finances?" Veronica asked.

Julia stared at her for a moment. "Fortunately, I am not yet in dire straits. I have exchanged letters with my grandmother's landlord and he is being more than agreeable in allowing her the time she needs to vacate the cottage. I do wish she would hurry though."

"I would think it takes a fair amount of time to sort through decades of accumulation." Portia said. "Lord knows it would take me forever."

"Still, you do need to make a decision," Veronica pointed out. "About the memoirs that is, not the men. Although it seems that decision ultimately leads to a choice of men as well."

"I do need to decide the fate of the memoirs. I've never been hesitant to make a decision before. I don't know what's wrong with me now." She blew a long breath. "I admit, I am confused. This is the biggest decision I've ever made and I want it to be right."

Veronica thought for a moment. "I have an idea. It would serve you well to remove yourself from London for a few days. I have some matters that need my attention at my house in the country. I plan to go there the day after tomorrow and be back in less than a week. Why don't you come with me? Away from notes and roses and men who are nice or famous or simply annoying. It will clear your head and allow you to come to a decision." She glanced at Portia. "You should come as well."

"I would like nothing better but I can't. I have social obligations." She shuddered. "If I were to beg off, my well-meaning family would track me like hounds after a fox."

Julia shook her head. "I don't think I should either. I have any number of matters to attend to."

Veronica arched a brow. "Do you?"

"Yes, I do," Julia said, although, now that she considered it, there was really nothing pressing and no real reason why she couldn't. And the idea of peace and quiet in the country had a great deal of appeal. "But nothing that can't wait. I should love to accompany you to the country."

"Excellent." Veronica cast her a brilliant smile. "That's settled then." She turned to Portia. "And what exactly did you mean?" Her eyes narrowed. "*Julia* is the pretty one?"

\* \* \*

Julia hadn't been in the house more than five minutes when Daniels announced Benjamin's arrival. He strode into the parlor, a broad grin on his face, his eyes lighting up when he saw her. It was most flattering.

"Lady Winterset." He crossed the floor and nodded a bow. "How very nice to see you. Again, my apologies for abandoning you in the park."

"Not at all, Mr. Cadwallender. I quite understand the necessities of business. I assume it is business that brings you here today?"

"Not entirely, although I do wish to discuss my plans for your grandmother's work. If you accept my offer, of course," he added quickly. He glanced around the room. "Did you receive my flowers?"

"Yes, and I do thank you. They were most thoughtful."

"I see," he said, although it was obvious he didn't. How could he?

"Please sit down." She waved him to the sofa then took a nearby chair. "I have something of a . . . a confession to make to you."

"Oh?" His brows drew together in concern and he leaned forward. "My dear Lady Winterset—Julia—if there is some sort of problem I assure you I would do anything to assist you."

"It's really very simple. As much as I do appreciate the sentiment, please refrain from sending me even one more rose," she said gently.

His expression fell. "Yes, of course. As you wish."

"I'm afraid they make me sneeze."

He stared at her for a moment then relief washed across his face. "My apologies, I had no idea."

"How could you? It's not something that comes up in casual conversation and, as I said, the thought was lovely." She paused. "There is another thing I should mention."

He chuckled. "Another confession?"

"In a manner of speaking." She chose her words carefully. "You should know I have two other offers for the memoirs."

"Oh?" His brow rose and he was at once all business. "From other publishers?"

She shook her head. "No. One from a gentleman who feels the book will expose his family to scandal. And another from John Eddington Ellsworth."

"Ellsworth?" His eyes narrowed. "Damnation." He winced "Forgive me."

"Certainly."

"This is my fault." He shook his head. "I mentioned the memoirs to him when you first brought them to my attention. But I had no idea . . ." His brows drew together. "He wishes to publish them?"

"Not exactly." She shook her head. "What he wants is a collaboration of sorts. He's proposing—"

Daniels appeared in the open doorway and cleared his throat. "Beg pardon, my lady. A moment, if you please."

"Of course." How odd, Daniels never interrupted. She smiled at Benjamin, stood, and stepped out into the hall.

Daniels closed the door to the parlor behind her.

She studied him with a frown. "What is it, Daniels?"

"Mr. Ellsworth is here, my lady. I put him in the library."

"Good Lord." She thought for a moment. "Tell Mr. Cadwallender I shall be back in a moment. I'll see to Mr. Ellsworth."

"Very well, ma'am."

What on earth did he want? She drew a deep breath and entered the library, leaving the door open behind her.

"Lady Winterset." Mr. Ellsworth favored her with what was, no doubt, his most charming smile and started toward her.

"Mr. Ellsworth, this is a surprise." She cast him a

pleasant smile and sidestepped him, moving closer to the desk.

"A pleasant one, I hope." He chuckled.

"To what do I owe the honor of this visit?"

"I wish to discuss my plans for the memoirs in hopes that you will decide in my favor. As well as my hopes for"—he flashed her a confident grin—"us."

She stared. "You presume too much, Mr. Ellsworth. There is no us. Nor do I have any interest in there being an us."

"Come now, Julia—"

"Lady Winterset."

He shrugged. "For the moment."

She stared in disbelief. "You are overstepping your bounds, Mr. Ellsworth."

"Am I? I don't think so."

"Then you are mistaken."

"I am never mistaken about these sorts of things. I know women very well."

"So I have heard."

He took a step toward her. "You can't deny there has been something brewing between us from the very instant we met. Fate itself has pulled us together and not merely for literary purposes."

"What utter nonsense." She scoffed and stepped back. "Fate? How absurd. This is not one of your stories, Mr. Ellsworth. Nothing has been brewing between us nor have I felt anything that could possibly be termed 'brewing.' There is nothing more than a proposal of business between us."

"And I assure you I am still interested in the memoirs. Now more than ever. In truth, the more I consider the idea of a partnership with you, the more I think it will prove profitable." He moved closer. "And quite delightful."

She moved back. "I don't think so. And I have no interest in anything with you that may be remotely called delightful."

"Dear Julia." He heaved an overly dramatic sigh. "I realize you've always been the epitome of propriety, the proper wife and that sort of thing. You've always held your emotions in check as is expected of a proper lady. But those days are over. You're a widow and you're free now to indulge your wildest passions."

"My wildest passions need no indulgence, but thank you for the offer."

"The publication of the memoirs will bring a certain amount of notoriety and—"

"You said you would keep my name out of it."

"I said I would *try*." He shrugged. "These things are difficult to keep secret, you know." He smiled and again took a step toward her. "As are your feelings for me."

"Mr. Ellsworth." She huffed. "I don't mean to be rude but I have no feelings for you aside from, at this moment, complete and utter disdain." She backed up until she felt the desk behind her. The blasted man had her trapped. "And I would appreciate it if you would desist coming any closer."

"You protest too much, my dear." He cast her a wicked smile. "It does no good to try to dissuade me from what we both want." He was scarcely a handswidth away from her now. "You want me, Julia. I saw it in your eyes the other night."

Wasn't this exactly what they had warned Portia about? "What you saw in my eyes was nothing more than an appreciation for your work."

"Now that is nonsense although it is my best work." He chuckled modestly.

"Then surely you understand how I, or any woman, might be swept away by the . . . the . . . passion of your words."

"It's not the first time." His gaze traveled from her eyes to her lips and back. "I am going to kiss you now. It shall be as two stars colliding in the heavens."

"Stars colliding?" She laughed in spite of herself. "A bit overdramatic, don't you think?"

"Possibly," he murmured. "But it's a very good line. And I am still going to kiss you." He leaned closer.

She leaned back until she was practically sitting on the edge of the desk and braced one arm behind her. The last thing she needed was to lose her balance. "I warn you, I shall slap your face if you try."

"Well worth it I think."

"Very well then." She raised her hand and let it fly but Ellsworth caught it and pulled her against him. He jerked her off the desk and into his arms. "And now, Julia." He heaved a long-suffering sigh, as if he hadn't believed a word she'd said. "At last, I am going to kiss you."

"No, you're not." She struggled against him but he was far stronger than he looked. Who would have imagined a man of letters would be that solid? If she hadn't been trapped between him and the desk she might have had some room to kick him. She had no choice. He would get his kiss but the moment he released her she intended to do just that. As hard as possible and, with any luck, the vile man would limp for a week.

"Oh, but I am." He bent his head toward hers.

A hard voice sounded from the doorway. "Oh, but you're not."

# Chapter Fourteen

*By God, he was right!*

It was the first thing that popped into Harrison's head at seeing Julia in Ellsworth's arms followed immediately by a stab of jealousy so fierce it took his breath away. Even though it was obvious she was not there willingly.

Ellsworth froze and Julia pushed against him.

"Unhand her at once," Harrison said through clenched teeth.

Ellsworth released her far slower than Harrison would have liked. Julia drew a deep breath, turned, and without warning kicked the author, hard. Harrison cringed.

"Ouch." Ellsworth grabbed his leg and hopped. "Why did you do that?"

"Because you deserved it!" Julia glared at the man.

"You said you'd slap me."

"I was indulging my wildest passions! And you deserve far more than a mere kick. You should be thoroughly thrashed." She glanced at Harrison. "Thrash him, Harrison."

"Me?" Harrison stared. What was that about wildest passions?

"Yes, you. You are my friend, aren't you?"

"Well, yes."

"Then as my friend, you need to defend my honor. You keep saying that I need to be protected. This is your opportunity to protect me." She jerked her head toward Ellsworth. "Go on, thrash him."

"Whatever for? You did say you could take care of yourself," he said without thinking. Her eyes narrowed in a menacing manner and he realized his mistake. Now was apparently not the time to point out her independent nature. And he would much prefer she not direct her outrage toward him. "However, as I am your friend, if you wish me to thrash him, I shall be delighted to do so." He started to take off his coat, all the while assessing Ellsworth as an opponent. It had been years since he had engaged in fisticuffs, not since his school days. If he remembered correctly, he had received as good as he'd given. Still, while Ellsworth might be an inch or so taller than he, Harrison was confident in his own state of fitness. He could, no doubt, best the author and enjoy it as well.

"Now, now, that's not necessary." Ellsworth rubbed his leg again then straightened. "We are all civilized here. There is no need for violence." His gaze met Harrison's and there was a definite warning in his eyes. "Is there, my lord?"

"Hah!" Julia scoffed. "I feel a very great need for violence, nor do I feel the least bit civilized." She glanced at Harrison. "Well, go on."

"He may be right, Julia," Harrison said slowly, pulling his coat back on. In truth, he would like nothing better than to pummel Ellsworth into insensibility. But the look in the man's eye was unmistakable. Harrison knew as surely as if the writer had said the words aloud, Ellsworth would tell Julia of their arrangement given half a chance. "We are civilized and this should be dealt with in a civilized manner."

"Civilized?" She stared in disbelief. "His behavior was not the least bit civilized!"

Indignation colored Ellsworth's face. "I may be many things, Lady Winterset, but I am unfailingly civilized."

"What you are is nearly as arrogant as he is!"

Ellsworth grinned. "Thank you."

"It was not a compliment!"

"I say, Julia," Harrison began, "that's not at all fair."

"Very well then, if you insist on being civilized." She met Harrison's gaze and he tried not to cringe at the fury in her green eyes. "Shoot him."

"Oh, yes, that's much more civilized," Ellsworth said under his breath.

Harrison's brow furrowed. "What do you mean: 'Shoot him'?"

"Yes." A hopeful note sounded in Ellsworth's voice. "What do you mean?"

"I mean shoot him! With a pistol! Duel with him! You can't get more civilized than dueling!"

"Dueling is illegal, Julia," Harrison said gently.

"I don't care!" She glared.

"I'm afraid I don't have a dueling pistol." Ellsworth shook his head. "Do you, my lord?"

"There might be one around the house somewhere although I can't be sure."

Julia's mouth opened in disbelief.

"Would swords do?" Harrison said quickly. "I do know we have some excellent fencing swords. Perhaps I could have a servant fetch them?"

"I have to confess, I have never held a sword in my life." Ellsworth shrugged in a reluctant manner. "So I daresay this wouldn't be anywhere near a fair fight."

"Good!" Julia fairly spat the word.

"And you, my lord, would look ridiculous dueling with a man who is admittedly incompetent in sword play."

Harrison nodded. "True."

"In addition, I have legions of admirers who would not take your running me through at all well."

Harrison raised a brow. "Public outcry, you think?"

"I should hope so." Ellsworth huffed.

"I should think there would be legions of women who would applaud him and wish they'd done the deed themselves!" Julia's voice rang with outrage.

"Again, Lady Winterset"—Ellsworth grinned in an unrepentant manner—"I should hope so."

"Fine!" She crossed her arms over her chest and aimed an angry glare at Harrison. "Then do nothing whatsoever. Allow my honor to be besmirched."

"Julia—"

"My lord, I did read once of gentlemen settling a dispute by means of a duel wherein the parties involved threw billiard balls at each other," Ellsworth said helpfully.

"I have billiard balls. I shall send a servant to fetch them at once." Harrison glanced at Julia. "Is that agreeable to you?"

"No!" Julia looked from Harrison to Ellsworth and back. "It most certainly is not! Unless I am allowed to throw them myself." She glared at Harrison. "At both of you."

He gasped. "Me? What have I done?"

"All I asked for was a simple thrashing—"

"Not civilized," Ellsworth said under his breath.

"—nothing more than that." She huffed.

"Well, you did kick me," Ellsworth said. "Quite hard I might add. My leg is still throbbing. I shall no doubt have a dreadful bruise from it."

"I should have aimed higher," she snapped.

Ellsworth paled.

"I do, however, think an apology is in order," Harrison said quickly."

"Quite right, my lord." Ellsworth nodded at Julia. "Go on then."

She gasped. "You're expecting me to apologize to you?"

"You very nearly broke my leg." Ellsworth sniffed.

"Very well then." Her jaw tightened. "My apologies, Mr. Ellsworth, for not breaking your leg."

Ellsworth stared at her for a moment then grinned. "Unbridled passions. I knew it."

"Wildest passions, if you please," Julia said sharply.

Harrison drew his brows together. "I don't like the sound of either unbridled or wildest passions."

"You wouldn't," Ellsworth said under his breath.

"Unless you intend to thrash him or shoot him or skewer him, you have nothing to say about it. It's just something Mr. Ellsworth said. Something absurd." Julia waved away the comment. "I suppose it's for the best, you not thrashing or shooting or skewering him, that is. The servants would talk and it would be all over town in no time. Which would inevitably lead to scandal." She met Harrison's gaze. "And we can't have that. Can we, my lord?"

Oddly enough, scandal was no longer his greatest fear but he nodded. "I would prefer to avoid scandal." Harrison's gaze met the other man's. What was he doing here anyway other than attempting to seduce Julia? He had his money. He should be out of her life. "I suspect, Ellsworth, you have overstayed your welcome."

"So it would appear." Ellsworth drew a deep breath and bowed slightly. "My dear Lady Winterset. You have my deepest apologies. You're quite right. I misread your passions for my work for passions of another kind."

Harrison did wish the man would stop bandying the word *passions* about.

"My behavior was inexcusable. I can only offer as an excuse the fact that, as I am a man of many passions—"

There was that word again.

"—they occasionally overtake my better judgment and I may say"—his gaze slid to Harrison then back to Julia—"or do something that I may later regret. Why, I have been known to reveal matters, secrets even, best kept to myself."

If Harrison had doubts before, he had none now. The man was indeed threatening him.

"I hope, Lady Winterset," Ellsworth continued, "that you can forgive my lapse in judgment and allow me to endeavor to make amends. And furthermore, that you do not let this influence your decision regarding the memoirs. Another chance, if you please, my lady."

Julia studied him for a long moment. One might think she was weighing and measuring the benefits of a business alliance against having to associate with Ellsworth. It was extremely calculating and most admirable. Perhaps he'd been blinded by her charm or humor but he hadn't really given her enough credit for either intelligence or desperation. She apparently could indeed take care of herself.

At last she sighed. "Very well, Mr. Ellsworth. I accept your apology. And I shall continue to consider your proposal."

*What?*

"Excellent." He beamed at her. "As I am anxious to begin work, might I ask when you might decide on that? And may I persuade you to allow me to argue my case again?"

"I believe you were leaving, Mr. Ellsworth," Harrison said firmly.

She turned her annoyed gaze on Harrison. "And what are you doing here?"

"I came . . . I thought . . ." He'd come directly from his walk with Miss Waverly because he had the most absurd desire to speak to a lovely woman who wasn't an idiot. And because being with Miss Waverly made him appreciate Julia and want to be in her company. None of which he could bring himself to say. "I came to make a new offer for the memoirs."

"Then give me the envelope and be on your way."

Harrison shook his head. "I don't have an envelope."

She raised a brow. "I thought these things always came in envelopes."

"And I thought we could simply talk." He cast her a firm look. "We have a great deal to talk about."

"I would like to talk as well," Ellsworth said. "Indeed, I agree. We have a great deal to talk about. All of us."

Julia rubbed her forehead. "I would prefer not to talk to either of you at the moment. I need to consider what is best for my future. You—" She directed a hard look at Ellsworth. "You may leave." Her gaze met Harrison's. "You may follow him out and send me your new offer."

"I'm not leaving until he does," Ellsworth said staunchly. "The moment I step out the door, he will try to convince you to accept his offer and I will be"—he heaved a dramatic sigh—"devastated."

"I doubt that," Harrison said.

"These memoirs present an opportunity that will not come my way again." His gaze met Harrison's. "I would be a fool to allow them to slide through my fingers without using every means at my disposal to procure them."

"Honorable means I would hope," Harrison said.

Ellsworth's eyes narrowed slightly. "What exactly are you implying, my lord?"

"Simply what I said." Harrison shrugged. "I should

hope those means do not include actions that are less than honorable." *Blackmail. Seduction.*

Julia sucked in a hard breath. "Are you starting that again?"

"Starting what?" Ellsworth's confused glance slid between the two of them.

"Well, I was right, wasn't I?" he snapped. "Given what I walked in on."

"I was perfectly capable of handling the situation by myself."

"Yes, I could see that." Sarcasm rang in Harrison's voice.

"I kicked him, didn't I?" Her voice rose.

"And it still hurts," Ellsworth added.

Lord, she was annoying. His voice matched hers. "If I hadn't come in when I did—"

"I would have been perfectly fine!" She huffed. "I suppose now you're going to tell me what a man like him might do in a library in the middle of the afternoon."

"I see no need to tell you as you were well on your way to finding out!"

Ellsworth cleared his throat. "I say—"

They ignored him.

She stepped toward him, anger again flaring in her eyes. "And then you might want to show me exactly what he might do in a library in the middle of the day just as you showed me what he might do on a darkened terrace!"

"I might!" He moved closer. "As I don't think you have any real understanding of what a man like him is capable of!"

"You do realize I am still here." Indignation sounded in Ellsworth's voice.

"If nothing else, I daresay a man like him would not scamper off to hide like a frightened rabbit!"

"I might," Ellsworth murmured.

"I did not run off to hide like a frightened rabbit!"

"Oh? And how would you describe it?" Challenge rang in her voice.

"I came to my senses!"

"My, that is flattering!"

"I didn't mean . . ." He tried and failed to get his own anger under control. "And I . . . I sent flowers!"

"Roses make me sneeze!"

"I didn't know that! And I sent a note of apology, didn't I?"

"I would scarcely call that an apology. Brief, terse, and with no true regret!"

"Because I don't re—"

"What on earth is going on in here?" Veronica stepped into the room and shut the door behind her. "Not only could I hear you in the hall but you could probably be heard three blocks away. Now, what is going on?"

Julia drew a deep breath. "Nothing at all."

Harrison shook his head. "Not a thing."

"Lady Smithson, what a delightful surprise." Ellsworth stepped forward, a broad smile on his face. He reached his hand out to take hers but she cast him a look that said he would be risking his life were he to do so. He pulled his hand back as if singed.

Julia heaved a long-suffering sigh. "And why are you here? And is Portia right on your heels? Perhaps the entire Literary Society as well?"

"Don't be such a goose," Veronica said dismissively. "You forgot your book at the tearoom and I thought I would bring it to you, as your house was on my way." She handed her a book.

"This is not on your way and I didn't have a book." Julia's brow furrowed.

"Oh." Veronica raised a shoulder in an offhand shrug. "Then now you do." She studied the two men but inclined her head toward Julia. "Do you want to tell me what is going on here or will you leave it entirely to my imagination?"

"It scarcely matters. Mr. Ellsworth and Lord Mountdale were just leaving." Julia moved to the door. "And I have a matter to attend to."

"The matter in the parlor?" Veronica asked.

Julia stared at her friend then nodded.

Veronica cast her a smug look. "I have taken—" She smiled brightly. "Yes, indeed you do and I shall help." She opened the door, ushered a protesting Julia into the hall and joined her, closing the door behind her.

Harrison turned to Ellsworth. "What are you doing here?"

"That does seem to be the question of the day," Ellsworth said coolly. "The same as you, I imagine. I am still interested in the memoirs as well as their owner."

Harrison ignored the last of the author's statement. For now. "In spite of what I paid you, you no longer have the money for the memoirs."

"True enough, after I pay my debts, that is." He shrugged. "But surely you know how these things work, my lord. The credit of a famous author is nearly as great as that of a titled gentleman. I will have no problem acquiring the sum I promised Lady Winterset for the memoirs."

"But that was my idea." Harrison stared in disbelief.

"And an excellent idea it was too." He chuckled. "I am most grateful. It will be my most successful work yet."

"If you manage to get the memoirs," Harrison said slowly.

"I have no doubt of that." Confidence curved the author's lips. "I fully intend to acquire Lady Middlebury's book." He paused. "And her great-granddaughter in the process."

"Oh?" Harrison raised a brow. "From what I witnessed, she did not willingly fall into your arms."

"Not yet perhaps, but she will." He grinned. "I have yet to meet a woman who can resist me for long."

Harrison forced himself to remain calm. He should have thrashed Ellsworth when he had the chance. Still, there was no reason why he could not do so now. "Lady Winterset is an unusual woman. You may have met your match in her."

"Perhaps." Ellsworth studied him thoughtfully. "Would you care to wager on it?"

"I don't need to wager on it, Ellsworth."

"I know you want the book, my lord. It's obvious to me that's not all you want."

Harrison clenched his jaw. "Lady Winterset is my friend."

"Yes." Ellsworth chuckled. "That's what I thought." He crossed his arms over his chest and propped his hip on the desk. "Let me tell you something about your friend, my lord."

"I can't imagine that I am interested in anything you may have to say."

"No, you probably can't yet I am certain you will find it extremely interesting nonetheless. I have known a great many women. You would be surprised what an aphrodisiac fame is." He smirked. "I know I was."

Harrison narrowed his eyes.

"One gets to a point where one starts to recognize different types of women. Indeed, they fall into easily recognized categories."

"You're wrong, Ellsworth, I'm not interested."

"Come now, every man is interested in this. I daresay, I shall base a book on it one day. Let's see. Where to start?" He thought for a moment. "Do you recall Miss Nelson, from Lady Smithson's dinner?"

Harrison nodded, intrigued in spite of himself.

"One would place her in the category of kindred spirits, at least so perceived on her part. Miss Nelson has literary aspirations. She would fall into my bed without hesitation in the belief that we are linked by something far more romantic than mere desires of the flesh. That we are indeed kindred spirits, soul mates, another great literary couple in the manner of the Brownings."

He would never admit it aloud but he agreed with the author's assessment of Veronica's cousin.

"Then there is Lady Redwell, another of Lady Winterset's"—he cleared his throat—"friends. She is obviously impressed by fame. Given her flirtatious manner, one can imagine she would be easily seduced by the allure of celebrity. But I am experienced enough to recognize a core of restraint within her that precludes an easy seduction. When that restraint breaks . . ." He chuckled. "I should like to be the man who causes that dam to burst."

Harrison scoffed and shook his head. "You are reprehensible."

"I have been called worse." He shrugged. "As for Lady Smithson, in spite of her considerable charm and wit, she is far too intelligent to be taken in by any man. Mores the pity."

"Watch yourself, Ellsworth, she is my late brother's widow." Warning sounded in his voice. "I consider her my sister."

"My condolences." Ellsworth cast him a sympathetic smile. "As for Lady Winterset—"

Harrison gritted his teeth. "Tread carefully."

"Lady Winterset is perhaps as intelligent as Lady Smithson although I don't think she completely trusts that intelligence. She has been taken care of, you see, proper marriage and all that. I think she is still realizing she can indeed take care of herself although I'm not sure she wants to." He shook his head. "There is a look in her eye that is most compelling. I suspect she continues to learn all sorts of things about herself especially how very much like her great-grandmother she really is."

"I wouldn't wager on that either, Ellsworth." It was not too late to thrash him.

"Oh, but I am, my lord," he said coolly. "I am wagering a great deal. My future success in fact. The only thing that would increase the success of the collaboration I propose or rather, you proposed—"

Harrison narrowed his eyes.

"—would be to have Lady Winterset on my arm." He chuckled. "The public would fall all over themselves to buy the book of the true adventures of Lady Middlebury by John Eddington Ellsworth, current lover of her descendant, the lovely Lady Winterset. Scandal, my lord"—he met Harrison's gaze directly—"sells books."

At his side, Harrison's hands clenched into fists. "I will not allow you to use—"

The door snapped open and Julia stepped into the room, Veronica right behind her.

"My apologies, Lord Mountdale, Mr. Ellsworth, but I have other matters to attend to far more pressing than whatever it is we have been engaged in here so I shall bid you both good day." Julia cast them an overly pleasant smile, turned, and took her leave.

"And I have matters of my own to attend to," Ellsworth said, turning toward Veronica. "Lady Smithson." His smug gaze met Harrison's. "My lord. Good day to you both." He nodded and left.

"You can unclench your fists now," Veronica said mildly.

"My fists are not . . ." Harrison blew a long breath and relaxed his hands. "That man is a scoundrel."

"Of course he is. But he is as well a famous author." Veronica shrugged. "His literary reputation goes hand in hand with his amorous exploits to create the public role he wears so well. His less-than-sterling qualities are overlooked, given his talent with words."

"Not by me."

"Obviously." She studied him thoughtfully. "Might I ask what you are doing here?"

"I came to present Julia with a new offer." It wasn't entirely a lie. He did have an improved offer to make.

"I see. And I thought you might have come to improve on your apology."

"It crossed my mind," he said with a casual shrug.

"From what I heard, it's not the kiss itself that warrants an apology."

"Apparently not."

"But your behavior afterward."

"I realize that," he snapped. Still, what was he to say? That he'd been so stunned by his own lack of control that he could do nothing save scamper away like a frightened rabbit? That he'd been so overwhelmed by the desire that gripped him when his lips met hers that he was thoroughly confused and could scarcely form a coherent word? Oh yes, that all sounded grand. Coupled with his less-than-adequate written apology, she had every right to be angry with him, although he would dispute the frightened rabbit analogy. "I just don't know what to do now."

She raised a brow. "My, my, that is telling."

"It's nothing of the sort."

"Protest all you wish, brother dear, but I have never seen you at a loss for words or anything else."

"Then you should be ecstatic."

"And yet, oddly enough, I'm not. I can't believe it my-self. What has gotten into me?" She sighed. "I am taking Julia to the country for a few days. She needs to clear her head so that she may reach a decision on the disposition of the memoirs as well as what she wants to do about the three of you."

"The three of us?" Harrison drew his brows together.

"You, Mr. Ellsworth, and Mr. Cadwallender. He was in the parlor, you know."

"I didn't know. Damnation." He had forgotten all about Cadwallender. "What was he doing in the parlor?"

"Waiting for Julia. He had come to discuss the mem-oirs or so he said." Veronica crossed her arms over her chest and studied her brother-in-law. "When I arrived, Julia's butler informed me about the various gentlemen ensconced in various rooms. You probably didn't notice but I had him close the door. It seemed best, given the ris-ing volume of your discussion."

He nodded.

"I then made Julia's apologies and managed to send Mr. Cadwallender on his way before the chaos began in here." Her brow furrowed. "I didn't hear everything. Do you care to elaborate?"

"I'm not sure I can. Ellsworth tried to kiss her—"

"And you walked in on it?"

He nodded. "Fortunately."

"Go on."

"One thing led to another after that. Somehow she and I began arguing, I have no idea how." He huffed. "This is what happens when wild and unbridled passions are al-lowed to run amuck."

"Passions?" She stared. "Whose?"

"His, hers, mine." He shook his head. "I don't know."

She studied him for a long moment. "Admission of

passion is not something I ever imagined you saying, particularly not coupled with the words *wild* or *unbridled.* But then you've changed a great deal."

"Nonsense," he muttered, although she might well be right. He hadn't been the same since the moment he laid eyes on Julia. Past time he admitted it, at least to himself.

"Ellsworth is not your competition, you know."

"He wants the memoirs. Badly, I would say."

"That's not what I meant." She paused. "Julia is not so foolish as to be taken in by a man like Ellsworth."

"I never doubted it." Although he had.

"The one you need to be wary of is Cadwallender. He is a very nice man and I suspect very similar to her late husband."

An odd, heavy weight settled in his stomach. "Do you think so?"

"Yes, I do." She shook her head. "She hasn't said it but I would not doubt that she's noticed it as well."

"I see." Veronica was right. If the publisher was indeed like her dead husband . . . "I assume she was happy, with her husband that is."

"I would assume so," she said in a annoyingly noncommittal manner. "She's never said otherwise." Her gaze met his. "Would you like me to put in a word for you?"

"About the memoirs?"

Veronica rolled her gaze at the ceiling. "No."

"It's not necessary. I don't need . . ." He drew a deep breath. In truth, he needed every advantage he could get. Very nearly from the beginning he had accepted he needed the help of one annoying woman to best another. Now, he realized he could well use the help of one woman who was not as annoying as he had once thought her, to win the, well, the heart of another he could happily be annoyed by for the rest of his days. Good God, what had happened to him? And when? "Yes, that would be most appreciated."

She smiled slowly. "Excellent."

"You needn't look so smug."

"Oh, but I am smug. I do love being right, you know. Now"—she ushered him toward the door—"I suggest you go home and decide on a course of action. You know, have another one of your brilliant ideas."

"They don't just come to me," he muttered.

"Knowing they are a product of much thought is a great relief." They stepped into the entry and the butler immediately opened the front door. Veronica leaned closer and lowered her voice. "Devise another one of your clever plans but try not to be too proper. Julia has behaved properly most of her life and it's entirely possible she might now be interested in something more than, oh, nice. Which does not bode well for Mr. Cadwallender but does increase the threat from Mr. Ellsworth. You, brother dear, must fall somewhere in between."

Harrison stared at her. "You have a very devious mind, don't you?"

"It's a gift." She nearly pushed him out the front door. "Julia will be in the country for the next four to five days, I think. More than enough time for you to determine how you will make this end well." She nodded and the now unseen butler closed the door.

She was certainly eager to get rid of him. He started toward his carriage. Not that she wasn't right. He had a great deal of thinking to do if he was going to win Julia and, hopefully, the memoirs. There was Ellsworth who was obviously not going to give up. And then there was Cadwallender who was apparently very similar to Julia's late husband. A husband she had loved.

It was all most confusing and irritating as well. From the moment he'd heard of Lady Hermione Middlebury and her annoying great-granddaughter, Veronica had been right more often than not.

And not one of his brilliant ideas had truly turned out well.

. . . and I would place the duke firmly in that category of men.

Oh yes, Dear Reader, men do indeed fall into categories and any woman who is at all perceptive recognizes that. First, there is the Proper Gentleman and no man on earth plays that role as well as those with good, English blood. Often stiff and stodgy, they prefer everything in their lives to be efficient, well organized, and on time. They have a great deal of potential.

Then there is the Hero. His purpose is to catch you when you fall. Unfortunately, heroes grow tiresome as they come to expect you to fall and tend to be annoyed when you do not and sanctimonious when you do. No man is as arrogant as a hero.

There is the Adventurer for whom there is no mountain he can't climb, no woman he can't conquer. Do understand that I mean a spirit rather than an actual explorer. Why, I have met Adventurers who have never stepped foot outside of England.

And there are Scoundrels, either those who are merely naughty and most enjoyable or those who are truly wicked and are to be avoided. There are other categories, of course, far too many to mention now.

The men that inevitably capture one's heart are neither fully Proper Gentleman, nor Adventurer, nor Hero, nor naughty Scoundrel. Those are the men who encompass

*bits and pieces of any number of different categories. Sometimes the best, sometimes the worst.*
   *As for the duke, he was not . . .*

   from *The Perfect Mistress,*
   *the Memoirs of Lady Hermione Middlebury*

# Chapter Fifteen

What had gotten into her? She couldn't remember the last time she had raised her voice let alone lost her temper. And when had she ever spoken without thinking? It was most unsettling and not at all like her.

Julia paced the large bedroom she'd been given at Veronica's country house. The house was most impressive as were the grounds, but of course, being Veronica's, it would be. She'd been invited but she'd never been here before. She'd assumed, when Veronica had insisted she come today, that her friend would accompany her. Instead, she'd put her on the train with a note to her staff and said she'd be along the day after tomorrow as originally planned. Julia hadn't protested; it was rather nice for once to have someone else make her decisions for her. And nice as well to be away and by herself. Tomorrow, she would take a long walk and gather her thoughts, if that was possible.

Tonight, it was impossible not to think about this afternoon's confrontation with Harrison and Mr. Ellsworth. Although Mr. Ellsworth's behavior scarcely merited a second thought. It was Harrison's comments and her own responses that dwelled in her mind. She had tried to sleep to no avail and now paced the room, trying to sort out her thoughts. It was all most confusing, and while she relished the opportunity to be alone it would be nice to have someone to talk it all out with.

"Precisely why I am here," a familiar voice said behind her.

Julia turned to find Hermione lounging on a chaise near the fireplace. "Are you alone?"

Hermione smiled. "At the moment."

Julia drew a deep breath. "Thank you for coming."

"Oh, there is little I love more than staying at a grand house in the country. Although I would prefer if it was filled with convivial companions." She paused. "I could arrange that if you'd like."

"Would they all be dead?"

Hermione heaved a long-suffering sigh. "My dear Julia, for the most part my circle of acquaintances consists of the dead. Which is not the same as dull, mind you. They are quite a jolly lot and I daresay you would enjoy them as well."

"Thank you, but I would prefer not to fill Veronica's house with the dearly departed."

"I can't say I blame you. The whole idea of your coming to the country in the first place was to be alone." She studied her descendant for a moment. "Shall I leave as well?"

"Please stay," Julia said quickly and resumed pacing. "What has come over me?"

"In what sense, dear?"

"Surely you witnessed the scene in the library."

"Oh that. Indeed I did." She chuckled. "It was most impressive."

"What, pray tell, was impressive?"

"First of all, darling, you did not fall prey to Mr. Ellsworth's crude attempts at seduction. I would have thought a man with his reputation would have been a bit more subtle. In spite of the sound manner in which you kicked him, he finds it impossible to accept that any woman can resist either his charm or his fame." She smiled. "I was quite proud of you."

Julia scoffed. "Mr. Ellsworth holds no particular appeal for me."

"Yet another reason for my pride in you. And then there was the way you handled Harrison." She chuckled. "Very impressive indeed."

"I didn't handle him." Julia sighed and brushed a strand of hair away from her face. "I lost my temper. I don't lose my temper. I never lose my temper. I don't know what's wrong with me."

"I daresay you wouldn't have lost it at all if Harrison hadn't been present."

"That's absurd. I was upset by Mr. Ellsworth's behavior."

"Initially, yes. You probably would have kicked Mr. Ellsworth once you were free of his clutches whether Harrison was there or not. But I suspect you wouldn't have been anywhere near as angry had Harrison not been there. There was only one man in that room that elicited passion from you. Today, it was anger but you weren't as angry over his refusal to thrash Mr. Ellsworth as you were about his behavior following your kiss."

"Nonsense," Julia muttered, but it did seem to make a certain amount of sense.

"Yes, of course. Utter and complete nonsense." Hermione shrugged in a dismissive manner. "Let's talk about what you're going to do with my memoirs, shall we?"

"Very well." Julia resumed pacing. "I do need to make

up my mind. I have three interesting offers. Mr. Ellsworth's does seem to be the best thus far. I would receive a tidy sum, equal to that offered by Harrison."

"You do understand I do not want my work destroyed. It's all that's left of me in the world." Hermione's voice carried a deceptively offhand note, as if she didn't care.

Julia met her gaze. "I will never allow that. And that will be clear in any bargain I may strike."

"That is most appreciated. Now then we are back to Mr. Ellsworth."

Julia nodded. "His offer would include royalties from sales of your book so, with any luck at all, there would be an income in the future. It's probably the best offer thus far but . . ."

"But it would involve continued association with the man as well as the matter of his fictional versions of my adventures." Hermione's brow furrowed. "I'm not sure I trust that his adaptation wouldn't be somewhat sordid."

Julia raised a brow. "More sordid than your adventures are?"

"They're not the least bit sordid." Indignation sounded in Hermione's voice. "They might be somewhat specific as well as have a certain sensuality about them but they are not sordid."

"Probably not." Julia cast her an apologetic smile.

"And might I add, they are quite well written." Hermione sniffed. "I think I could have been an excellent writer myself." She cast Julia an unrepentant grin. "If I'd had the time."

"Very well. Then we agree." Julia nodded. "While Mr. Ellsworth's offer may be the most lucrative at the moment, everything that comes with it is not something either of us wants."

"Which brings us to Benjamin." Hermione sighed. "What a nice man he is."

Julia cast her a suspicious look. "Do you really think so?"

"Don't you?"

"Well, yes, he is very nice." She thought for a moment. "And while his offer is not as initially substantial as the others, he does think the book will be successful, which means continuing income from royalties."

"And he is a man who can certainly be trusted. You wouldn't have to worry about a man like Benjamin."

"I wouldn't think so."

"No, indeed." Hermione shook her head. "Why, Benjamin is not the sort to force himself upon you in the library."

Julia scoffed. "Absolutely not."

"Nor would he take liberties on a darkened terrace."

Julia narrowed her eyes. "Hermione."

"I would think a man like Benjamin would never let his passions overrule his innate good sense. He would never pull you into his arms and press his lips to yours until your blood fired in your veins and you clung to him because your knees were too weak to support you."

"Hermione." A definite threat sounded in Julia's voice.

Hermione ignored her. "Benjamin would never kiss you without asking permission first."

"He's a gentleman," she said staunchly.

"And very nice. As I assume his kiss would be. Julia, dear," she said gently. "You have had nice. William was nice. Do you really want nice again?"

"Yes! No." She heaved a heavy sigh.

"There's nothing wrong in pursuing what you want, you know."

"I don't know what I want."

Hermione studied her but held her tongue.

"And we're not talking about the men. We're talking about the disposition of the memoirs."

Hermione shrugged. "One goes hand in hand with the other. You can't possibly sell the memoirs to Benjamin for publication and marry Harrison."

"Who said anything about marrying Harrison?"

"I believe I did, right from the beginning," She shook her head. "You may be able to continue to lie to yourself but you cannot lie to me, dear. You have very strong feelings for him."

Julia stared at her for a moment then sighed. "Perhaps. I suppose. I don't know."

Hermione nodded in an annoyingly perceptive manner. "Marriage to him would solve all your financial troubles."

"I have no intention of marrying anyone to save myself from poverty."

"Why ever not?"

"Because it's not . . ." She searched for the word. "Right. Honorable."

"Don't be ridiculous." Hermione scoffed. "Women have always married for money. We have no other way of bettering ourselves. It's what we have always done. Why, it's what we are expected to do."

"You didn't," Julia said pointedly. "From what I've read, you certainly could have married again for money or other reasons. Why didn't you?"

"I had offers through the years," Hermione said, completely disregarding the last part of Julia's question. "Most quite attractive from gentlemen I could have easily spent the rest of my days with."

"Then why didn't you?"

"I married once," Hermione snapped. "Once was . . . enough. And, no, I did not marry your great-grandfather for his money."

Julia stared. "Did you love him very much?"

For the first time since she'd begin her visits to Julia,

Hermione's demeanor was less than her usual assured self. She drew a deep breath. "We're not talking about me."

"We are now."

Hermione rose to her feet. "You're trying to change the subject away from the fact that you've fallen in love with a man who drives you mad."

Julia gasped. "I don't know that I've fallen in love with him!"

"It's not something one *knows* like one *knows* the grass is green and one *knows* the sky is blue. Not in the beginning. It's tentative and uncertain. Why, the very uncertainty is part of the joy of falling in love. Knowing comes soon enough. Love has nothing whatsoever to do with knowledge or intelligence or rational thinking. Good Lord, if it did, no one would ever fall in love and certainly never fall in love with the wrong person. And that happens far too often." She shook her head. "I don't know why you keep trying to deny it."

"I don't either." Julia snapped then drew a deep breath. "What if he doesn't love me?"

"What if he doesn't? Knowing love at all is a miracle." Hermione fixed her with a firm look. "'Tis better to have loved and lost, than never to have loved at all."

"You're quoting Lord Tennyson now? Did you know him?"

"Not intimately but I *knew* everyone," Hermione said in a superior manner. "And those I didn't know when I was alive, I have met here. I look forward to renewing Lord Tennyson's acquaintance upon his arrival."

"That's a lovely sentiment, very poetic and all but if he doesn't love me—"

"I can't imagine that, having watched him argue with you. You can tell a great deal about a man's feelings by the way he argues. By what he says and, more, what he doesn't." She met her gaze directly. "From what I've seen, he is every bit as stubborn as you. I suspect he too rarely loses his temper or raises his voice. The fact that the two of you provoke that sort of passion in one another is nothing short of"—a wicked gleam showed in her eye—"perfect."

"Perfect?" Julia huffed. "You expect me to spend the rest of my life with a man who makes me lose my temper? Who makes me say things without thinking? What kind of life would that be?"

"Absolutely blissful." Hermione cast her a smug smile. "Which is ever so much better than nice." With that, Hermione vanished.

"I was happy with nice!" Julia said to the now-empty room.

"Content, darling, you were content." Hermione's voice drifted from somewhere unseen.

"Come back here. We're not finished!"

"Things to do, my sweet. It's rude to keep people waiting, you know."

"It's rude to vanish in the middle of a conversation as well!"

"Do try to make allowances for me, dear. I'm dead."

"Then perhaps you should act like it!" she yelled, although it was pointless. Hermione was definitely gone. For the moment. And Julia knew no more now than she had when they'd begun their conversation.

She sank down on the bed. She hadn't been herself since the day Harrison walked into her library and demanded she sell him the memoirs. She never lost control of her temper, she was never indecisive, and she was the last person anyone would call overly emotional. From the moment she'd met him her life had changed, and not for the better. Although she did have to admit she enjoyed sparring with him. Even today, there was something quite exciting in the manner in which they'd argued. Why, it was almost as enjoyable as his kiss had been. Truth be told, she wanted him to kiss her again. And again. And for the rest of her—

Good Lord! She was in love with him! With the most annoying man she'd ever met. It was nothing like the quiet, safe, *nice* sort of love she'd felt for William. This was indeed most uncertain as well as confusing and disquieting and, God help her, exciting.

As for whether he returned her feelings, it was obvious given their kiss and his behavior today that he felt something for her. It was possible it was nothing more than friendship. Still, she was fairly certain friends didn't kiss friends the way he had.

She collapsed back on the bed and stared unseeing at the ceiling. Perhaps she should take a page from Hermione's book and pursue what she wanted without hesitation or apology. Or regret.

And perhaps it was time to stop reading about her great-grandmother's adventure and begin an adventure of her own.

Damnation, this must indeed be love. Harrison stared at the pages in front of him. He had read and reread the report from his estate manager at least three times thus far and he couldn't recall a word it said. Yet he could, no doubt, recite every single word he had exchanged with Julia yesterday. He could as well recall the exact shade of her green eyes when they had snapped with anger. He could hear the sound of her laughter ringing in his soul, feel the pressure of her lips on his and the way her body had fit perfectly against him.

He pushed away from the desk, got to his feet, and paced the broad width of the library. Thank God Veronica had taken Julia to the country. He did indeed need a brilliant idea and he certainly couldn't come up with one if he had to worry about Ellsworth or Cadwallender writing her notes or popping up on her doorstep or sending her flowers. And how was he supposed to know that roses made her sneeze? It was too much to hope for that that scoundrel Ellsworth and Cadwallender, who was apparently very *nice,* didn't know about the roses. Blast it all, he had just entered this race and he was already behind.

"You're wearing out the carpet, you know." His father stood in the doorway.

"Then it shall have to be replaced," he muttered. "The carpet is the least of my worries."

"Indeed it is," his father said under his breath and moved to take a seat in one of the wing chairs flanking the fireplace. He gestured at the other chair. "Sit down, Harrison, we need to talk."

Harrison cast him a sharp glance. "Father, I have a great deal on my mind today and I really don't have time—"

"Sit down, Harrison." The order reverberated in the room. Even when his father was younger, he had scarcely ever issued orders. Harrison sat.

"Very well. What do you wish to talk about?"

"I have just come from a luncheon at Lord Ferncastle's."

"Of course." Harrison groaned to himself. Once a month, his father gathered with a group of men who'd been friends since their youth. A group that grew smaller every year and now consisted only of his father, Lord Ferncastle, and three other elderly gentlemen. From what his father had said in passing, the conversation at these gatherings consisted mostly of telling tales of their long-ago misdeeds that no doubt grew more daring and amusing and disreputable with each passing year. "How are your friends?"

"Old and getting older." He sighed. "But it's not the old that was so interesting today. Or rather I suppose it was."

Harrison nodded although his father's words made no sense. "Go on."

"Someone, I have no idea who, brought up Lady Middlebury's name." His father chuckled. "And not for the first time I might add."

"And?"

"And Lord Ferncastle had heard gossip. No, Lady Ferncastle had heard it and passed it on to her husband." His father leaned toward him and lowered his voice. "She heard about the memoirs."

Harrison blew a long breath. "I shouldn't be surprised, I suppose. It was inevitable given the number of people who know about them."

"That's not the worst part. Rumor has it they weren't written by Lady Middlebury at all."

Harrison drew his brows together. "Surely it's not being said that that blasted Ellsworth wrote them?"

"Would that it were that simple." His father shook his head. "No, the gossip is that Lady Winterset wrote them."

"What?" Shock coursed through him.

"And that they are based, not on Lady Middlebury's experiences"—he cleared his throat and cast his son a knowing look—"but on her own."

"That's absurd. Ridiculous. No one would ever believe such a thing."

"No one who knows Lady Winterset perhaps. But those who know of her great-grandmother's reputation might well believe she is simply following her ancestor's path."

"Good God!" He rubbed his forehead. "Where did this come from?"

"Who knows where it started and it scarcely matters

now. I did tell Ferncastle that I knew for a fact, given the accuracy of the pages I read, that it could have been written by no one save Lady Middlebury. Information I am confident he passed on to Lady Ferncastle within moments of our leaving the house. As she is quite an accomplished gossip, and does love knowing what no one else does, I am certain she is even now spreading my assertion as to the legitimacy of the memoirs far and wide. I can count on my other companions at our luncheon today to do the same. However . . ." His father chose his words with care. "It does seem to me, if indeed I was concerned about being named in Lady Middlebury's book, discrediting its veracity would be one way to mitigate the scandal. Which means this will spread like fire."

"Scandal sells books," Harrison said under his breath.

"Then this will fly off the shelves if it is indeed published." He studied his son for a long moment. "What are you going to do now?"

"I don't know." Harrison got to his feet and resumed pacing. "It does seem more important than ever that the book not be published. Indeed, if I were to purchase the memoirs, with nothing to fuel the gossip, the talk about them will soon fade. But if they're published . . ." He shook his head. "The scandal will be enormous."

"I'm not concerned about scandal."

"I am," he said sharply. "Julia has lived a relatively conservative life up to now. She has no idea what being at the center of a storm of scandal will mean. Everywhere she goes, she'll be stared at. People will whisper, hiding their mouths with their hands as if that will prevent her from knowing she is the topic of discussion. She won't be welcome among respectable people. Dear Lord, she'll be an outcast."

"This isn't the first time you've done this, you know."

He cast his father a narrowed look. "Done what?"

"Taken what I've said and assumed it was in reference to Lady Winterset."

"But you said—"

"I said I was not concerned about scandal and I'm not for myself. You said you were concerned about scandal but obviously that concern has nothing to do with me. There is only one person you are worried about."

Harrison stopped in midstep then pulled a deep breath and met his father's gaze. "I love her, Father."

"I know that," his father said impatiently. "But what are you going to do?"

An unfamiliar sense of helplessness washed through him. "I don't know."

"Seems to me you need a brilliant idea."

"Needing one and having one are two different matters." He ran his hand through his hair. "I don't know what to do."

The older man aimed his cane at his son. "Rescue her, my boy."

"Rescue her?" He shook his head. "How?"

"Don't ask me, I am long past the day of rescuing damsels in distress." His brow furrowed in thought. "You might start by telling her of these rumors. You wouldn't want her to be caught unawares."

"Quite right. But she's no longer in London. Veronica took her to her country house."

"Even better. There are few distractions in the country." His voice was firm. "Follow her."

"Follow her?"

"Bloody hell." His father laughed. "You're indecisive. I've never seen you indecisive before. Even as a boy you always knew precisely what you wanted and never hesitated to pursue it. If I had any doubts about your feelings, this proves it."

Harrison cast him a weak smile. "I'm glad you're so confident."

"The fact that you are not is yet another convincing factor." His gaze met his son's. "Don't let not knowing what to do prevent you from doing anything at all. Don't make the mistakes I did. Love, my boy, often requires action." He chuckled. "Go to the country, Harrison. Tell her what's happening. Tell her of your feelings for her. And tell her as well that together you can weather any storm."

He stared at his father for a long moment. "We can, can't we?"

"I have no doubt of it."

"Nor do I," he said slowly, the helplessness of a moment ago swept away by resolve. "You're right. I shall leave at once."

His father nodded. "It's scarcely two hours by train, which will give you enough time to think of what you will do upon your arrival. You will be there by evening."

"If I leave now." He started toward the door then paused. "Thank you, Father."

"I really did nothing, but you are most welcome." He grinned. "Now off with you. Like a knight of old, ride to the rescue of the woman you love."

Harrison returned his father's grin and took his leave. Within a half hour, he was on his way to King's Cross Station, marveling at the joys of an efficient staff who had a bag packed for him as well as providing the appropriate train timetable. A few hours later he approached Charles's country house. He stopped for a moment and stared at the façade.

He hadn't been here in years, since long before Charles had died. He could see his brother's grin now and could almost hear his voice urging *Harry* on. This would have pleased Charles even if Harrison still had no idea what he was going to say or do. That would have amused Charles as well.

He drew a deep breath and walked up the steps to knock. He wouldn't make the mistakes his father had even if he had no idea what those mistakes were. No, he was fairly certain, he would make his own.

But he was confident coming after Julia wasn't one of them.

*. . . and I could see it in his eyes. How he felt and what he wanted. Words are quite lovely and there is nothing more seductive than a man who knows how to use words well. Why, I have been known to fall in love over a well-written declaration of passion or a sincerely delivered assertion of affection.*

*But often, the dearest of men are not all skilled with words, written or spoken. It is not in their nature. It is very frequently what they don't say that is much more important than what they do.*

*And the look in Michael's eyes on that night when he . . .*

from *The Perfect Mistress,*
the *Memoirs of Lady Hermione Middlebury*

# Chapter Sixteen

"I beg your pardon, Lady Winterset." Veronica's butler stood in the doorway.

Julia looked up from the book of poetry she had found on the library shelves. It had been a lovely, peaceful day and while she hadn't come to a decision about anything, she was more at ease than she'd been in weeks. "Yes?"

"Another guest has arrived."

"Another guest? How odd." She put the book down and rose to her feet. "Lady Smithson didn't say anything about another guest." Although perhaps Portia had decided to come after all.

"Shall I show him in?"

Not Portia then. "Please do."

"Very well, my lady." The butler nodded, left, and a moment later Harrison strode into the library.

"Julia." He crossed the room and took her hands in his.

Her heart thudded in her chest and she stared up at him. "This is a surprise."

He smiled down at her. "To me as well. I hadn't planned . . . and yet, here I am."

She raised a brow. "I always thought you were the sort of man who planned everything."

"I was." He chuckled, his gaze meeting hers. "I don't know what has come over me."

"What has come over you?" she said without thinking. "I mean, why are you here? Not that I'm not pleased to see you," she added quickly.

"Are you pleased to see me?"

Her immediate impulse was to deny it. She summoned her newfound resolve to be more like Hermione and raised her chin slightly. "Yes, Harrison, I am."

His smile widened. "Excellent."

She knew she should pull her hands from his but couldn't seem to do so. Nor did she want to. Instead she returned his smile and said the first thing that came into her head. "Are you hungry? Would you like something to eat? You must be famished."

A gleam that did indeed look like hunger sparked in his blue eyes. "No, but thank you. A brandy perhaps."

"I shall ring for the butler."

"Not necessary." He glanced around the room. "Unless Veronica has changed things, I know where it is." He reluctantly released her hands, moved to a cabinet on the far side of the room, opened it then glanced at her. "Would you care for a brandy as well?"

"That would be lovely, thank you."

She had a dozen things she wanted to say to him and any number of things beyond that she wished to ask but now that he was here, she couldn't seem to find the words. Just blurting out a declaration of love didn't strike her at all right nor did bluntly asking him about his feelings for her.

*What would Hermione do?*

She squared her shoulders, drew a deep breath then

hesitated. There was an air of distraction about him, as if he were very far away. Perhaps this was not the right moment after all. "Harrison?"

He started, his gaze jerked to hers. "My apologies. For a moment . . ."

"Yes?"

"I thought I heard . . ." He shook his head. "I spent a lot of time through the years with my brother in this very room. There are a great many memories here. It's disquieting to be back without him."

"I am sorry. I didn't realize." She hadn't any siblings but the look on his face, of days gone past and loss and affection, clutched at her heart. "This was your brother's house then?"

"Half brother really. We had the same mother. But Charles never treated me as though I was anything less than his brother." He glanced at her. "I miss him."

"I can imagine."

"Of course. You have known loss as well." He crossed to her and handed her a glass of brandy. "Veronica hasn't changed a thing in this room. It's exactly as if Charles might walk in at any minute. I suppose I should thank her for that. There is an element of comfort in the familiarity here although I'm not sure . . ." He glanced around. "This was Charles's room more than any other. He liked the feel of being surrounded by books. By the wisdom and the humor of man he would say." He chuckled. "I don't know why really. I don't think I ever saw him with a book in his hands. He would much rather ride or conquer beautiful women or gamble until well into the morning than sit quietly with a book, no matter how interesting. Until he married Veronica, that is," he added quickly.

"From what she has said, I gather he was ripe for reform."

Harrison grinned. "Indeed he was. We were as dissimilar as two men could be and yet as close as any brothers by blood. I have no need of reform."

"Surely even you could use a little reformation."

"Charles thought I could. Even in my youth, he always considered me too stiff and stodgy and proper." He grinned. "I disagreed."

"Perhaps he thought your reformation should be in the form of, oh, I don't know, tempering your arrogance with a bit of humility?"

He stared at her then laughed. "Perhaps." He took a sip of his brandy. "I can almost feel him here, nearly hear his voice." He shrugged. "That sounds a bit fanciful, doesn't it? Especially coming from me."

"Not at all." She smiled. "Well, perhaps a bit. From you."

"I am never fanciful," he said thoughtfully.

"I didn't think you were."

He glanced at her. "Nor am I ever indecisive."

"I would imagine not."

"I decide on a plan and I follow it through." It struck her that he was talking more to himself than to her.

"That is my impression."

"I like order and efficiency and life to be as expected. I am not fond of change."

She bit back a smile. "Of course not."

"I do not shirk my responsibilities. And I am never wrong."

She raised a brow. "Never?"

"Rarely. Recently, however . . ." He stared at her as if he wanted to say something more, something important, but thought better of it. Blast it all. In spite of her feelings for him he was still the most annoying man she'd ever met.

"Yes? Recently?" She tried and failed to keep a note of

expectation from her voice. After all, why else was he here if not to make a declaration of affection?

He hesitated. "She should make changes."

"What?" She drew her brows together. "Who? What are you talking about?"

"Veronica." He swirled the brandy in his glass. "This room. This house. It's hers now. Charles is gone and she should make it her own."

"Perhaps she likes it just as it is," she said, surprised at the touch of impatience in her voice. "Perhaps she is no more interested in change than you."

"Life changes, Julia. I've always known that. What we want, even who we are. But I don't think I really accepted it until recently."

"Recently?" She held her breath. "Please, go on."

His brows drew together and again she didn't think he was talking to her. She sighed to herself. "There are ghosts here, you know. In this house, in this room."

"Ghosts?" An edge of panic raised her voice. "Don't be silly. There are no such things as ghosts. How ridiculous." Dear Lord, she was babbling. "No indeed." She had no doubt Hermione was about somewhere but surely he didn't know that. What on earth would he think if he knew the ancestor he so thoroughly disapproved of still, well, lingered? "Ghosts. Hah. Utter nonsense."

"Ghosts of the past. The specters of what's gone by." He cast her an odd look as if he were questioning her sanity. She couldn't blame him. "I'm not speaking of apparitions. That is indeed absurd."

"Completely." She uttered a strained sort of noise, somewhere between a laugh and a groan. Julia could have sworn she heard the faint sound of Hermione's laughter in the distance. With any luck she was mistaken, but her luck hadn't been all that good of late.

Harrison nodded, as if he had come to a decision. "Veronica should go on with her life."

"You think she hasn't?"

"Has she?"

"Veronica is the most confident, capable woman I have ever met. Still, I suppose no one really knows how someone else feels, deep in their heart." She thought for a moment. "It's difficult to lose someone you had planned to spend the rest of your days with."

He studied her but didn't say a word.

"However . . ." She chose her words with care. "It seems to me you can choose to grieve for the rest of your days—"

He nodded. "As the queen has done."

"Or you can accept that, well, life has indeed changed." She cast him a rueful smile. "I am not the queen."

"Have you?"

"Have I accepted that life has changed?"

"Yes. Or rather no." His gaze met hers. "Have you gone on with your life?"

She stared at him for an endless moment. "Yes." She gathered her courage. "Harrison."

"Julia," he said at the same time then smiled. "Please, go on."

"Very well then." She drew a deep breath. "Why are you here?"

He hesitated. "I thought . . . There is something you should know."

"Is there?" Surely he was going to tell her of his feelings. Why would he have followed her here otherwise? A brilliant smile came from somewhere deep inside her. "There is something you should know as well."

"I'm not sure how to say this."

"Neither am I." She shook her head. "I am not my great-grandmother. I daresay she would never be at a loss for words over something like this."

"No, you're not. It would be awkward if people believed you were." His brow furrowed. "Something like what?"

"Awkward?" She frowned. "What do you mean 'awkward'?"

"That might not be the right word." Unease crossed his face. "And what do you mean by something like that?"

"Harrison," she said slowly, "I suspect what you are trying to say is not what I am trying to say."

"What I am trying to say is difficult."

"Apparently." Good Lord. How could she have been so wrong? He was going to tell her he was marrying Miss Waverly. Her heart sank. "Go on then, say it," she snapped.

His brows pulled together. "Why are you angry?"

"I'm not angry," she said sharply. "I never get angry and I never lose my temper. Now, get on with it."

He studied her closely. "It seems to me you lose your temper frequently."

"Only with you!" She drew a calming breath and tried to ignore the sharp sense of loss and pain curling within her. "I am not angry but I am impatient. You came all the way from London to tell me something. Something *awkward*. So tell me."

"Very well." He took a sip of his brandy. "First of all, word of the existence of the memoirs has spread," he said in an overly casual manner. It was most annoying. "It's becoming quite a topic of gossip."

She stared in disbelief. "That's what you came to tell me? We knew that there would be gossip and even a certain amount of scandal connected with Hermione's memoirs. I had hoped that wouldn't happen until the book was

published but now that it has, admittedly, it is *awkward*."
She shrugged. "But there's nothing I can do about it save
decide on the disposition of the memoirs at once."

"Burning was a good idea," he said under his breath.

"Under no circumstances will I allow them to be destroyed." She crossed her arms over her chest. "This is all
that is left of my great-grandmother. It's not merely a
chronicle of her adventures but the story of her life. Her
thoughts and comments and observations of that life. Regardless of how much you offer, I will never turn them
over to you to be destroyed."

He eyed her coolly. "You've said that before."

"It cannot be said often enough."

"And I agree. At this point destroying them would be a
mistake."

"A mistake?"

"Your only salvation lies in the veracity of the memoirs."

"My salvation?" She narrowed her eyes. "What do you
mean *my salvation*? What haven't you told me?"

"The gossip isn't merely about the existence of the
memoirs but exactly who is the author."

"The author?" She stared in confusion. "My great-
grandmother is the author."

"And anyone who reads them will realize that but, as
no one has read them yet, at least not completely . . ."

Dread settled heavily in the pit of her stomach.

"The gossip is that you wrote them." His gaze met
hers. "That they are based not on Lady Middlebury's life
but on your own experiences and fertile imagination."

"Good Lord!" She collapsed onto the sofa and stared
at him. "My imagination is not that fertile. I could never . . ."
She shook her head. "How on earth . . . Who . . ."

"Who knows how something like this gets started." He
shook his head. "It's bad, Julia."

"I expected some scandal, a bit of notoriety perhaps, but this . . ."

"Drink your brandy."

"Brandy won't help." But she downed the liquor nonetheless and held out her glass for more.

He crossed the room, grabbed the decanter, and returned to fill her glass. "Are you calmer now?"

"I shall never be calm again." She looked up at him. "My reputation will be ruined. I will never be able to hold my head up in public." Her thoughts raced. "I shall have to leave the country. Go to the continent perhaps. The French don't seem to mind this sort of thing. Indeed, they relish it. Better yet, the Italians. I don't speak the language but I can learn. Yes, that's it. I shall move to Italy and never step foot in England again."

"We will not allow that to happen."

"And how are we going to prevent it?"

"I had a great deal of time to think on the way here. There are several options." He paced the room. "First of all, and my own personal choice, is for you to accept my offer—"

"And allow you to destroy Hermione's work? Never!"

"Let me finish if you please," he snapped.

"Then do so," she said, and took another deep swallow of the brandy.

"The more I have come to know you, the more I understand that regardless of the monetary compensation involved, you are far too stubborn—"

"Indeed I am." She glared at him.

"And loyal to a member of your family you have never met, which is rather admirable," he added quickly.

"I like her," she said under her breath.

"Understandable, as you've been reading her words. As I was saying," he continued. "I know you would not sell them to me because, even if I promised not to destroy them, you cannot trust that my word would be greater than my loyalty to my family." His gaze pinned hers. "Even though I have never gone back on my word."

She blew a resigned breath. "I have no doubt of that."

"However, if I simply bought the rights to publish them, you could keep the actual work locked away where no one could find it hopefully."

"That might be agreeable," she said slowly.

"And I suspect, without public dissemination to fuel the fire, the gossip would eventually die."

She heaved a heartfelt sigh. "Hermione wants them published, I think. Although I haven't asked her. I should do that." She tossed back the brandy. Her glass was again empty. She held it out to him. "If you please."

"Given you are now talking about asking your dead ancestor her opinion, I think you've had more than enough."

She scoffed. "I haven't had nearly enough."

He studied her then reluctantly filled her glass halfway.

"You said there were options."

"Yes. The next is to allow the memoirs to be published. When I first heard about the gossip I didn't think that was a good idea. Now however I have changed my mind. Once read, I can't imagine anyone thinking they were written by you."

Her eyes widened in indignation. "Why not?"

"Why not?" His brows drew together. "You just said your imagination is not that fertile."

"Well, I certainly couldn't have invented all of Hermione's adventures. She had a great many of them. But I can well imagine frolicking naked in a meadow under the moonlight. Or a tryst in a garden during a masked ball. Or finding exquisite passion I never dreamed possible in the arms of a man I scarcely knew."

He stared. "What man?"

*You!* "No man in particular." She huffed. "I'm only

saying, that while I couldn't have written all of her adventures, I could certainly have thought of some of them. I'm rather insulted that you think I couldn't."

"It wasn't a criticism of your intellect, but rather a compliment on your proper nature."

"I am much less proper than I used to be. Indeed, I am tired of being proper altogether. I'd rather have a bit more adventure and considerably less . . . less . . . *content*!"

He stared at her as if she were speaking a language he didn't understand. Or was completely mad. Not that she cared.

"I am more like Hermione than I imagined."

"Are you?"

"Yes," she snapped. "And in these circumstances I believe it would be wise for me to consider exactly what she would do." She downed the rest of her brandy and rose somewhat unsteadily to her feet. "Obviously, I can no longer put off making a decision regarding the disposition of the memoirs. I shall do so before I return to London."

"Past time I would say."

"Yes, well you have never been indecisive," she said sharply. "Until recently."

He narrowed his eyes.

"I am going to retire for the evening now. I have a great deal to think about." She straightened her shoulders, a lofty note sounding in her voice. "I do appreciate you making the effort to come all the way here to inform me of this *awkward* situation. It was a very . . ." She searched for the right words. "Responsible thing to do. For a friend."

"A friend?" He glared.

"Yes." She waved toward the door. "Now then, I am certain you are eager to be on your way."

He shook his head. "I'm not going anywhere."

"I assumed you would return to London tonight."

"I don't know why you assumed that. I have spent many nights in this house and I intend to do so tonight." He drained his glass. "I should like to speak to Veronica as well."

"Veronica isn't here."

"Where is she?"

"London, I would say." She shrugged. "She is not expected until tomorrow."

"I see." He thought for a moment. "I'm certain she would not have any difficulty with my staying the night. Unless, of course, you do."

"I don't care what you do. It's a very big house." She started toward the door. "I shall inform the servants to make up a room for you."

"I did that on my arrival," he said in clipped tones.

"Of course you did, given your efficient nature." She turned and stalked across the library and into the hall.

"Why are you angry at me?" He trailed after her.

"I'm not angry with you." She started up the stairs.

"What have I done save come all the way from London?"

"What have you done?" She whirled around. "First of all, you're following me."

"I most certainly am not. I'm going to my room."

"So you say." She sniffed and continued up the stairs.

"I am not following you."

"Why not? You followed me to the country."

"Well, I am not following you now."

"Hah!" She reached the top of the stairs and turned toward her room, acutely conscious that he was right on her heels. She reached her door, threw it open then glanced at him. "Don't tell me this is the room you always stay in."

"It's not." He stepped to the door directly across the hall. "This is my room."

"Excellent! I would hate to inconvenience you."

He snorted. "You have done nothing but inconvenience me from the moment I first heard your name."

She stared at him. "I cannot fully express how that delights me!"

He snapped open his door. "And I cannot believe I came all the way here to . . ."

"To what?"

He shook his head. "This was obviously a mistake."

"If that's the way you feel—"

"You know nothing about the way I feel," he said sharply.

"Oh? And how do you feel?"

"Confused. Annoyed. Irritated." His jaw clenched. "Confusion, annoyance, and irritation have been my constant companions since the moment I met you."

"Welcome, my lord, to my life!"

"Your life?"

"You are the most—"

"I know, I know." Impatience rang in his voice. "I am the most annoying man you have ever met. Surely a woman who prides herself on her intelligence could come up with something more original."

"I shall certainly give it my complete attention!" With that she stepped into her room and slammed the door behind her. A split second later she heard the door across the hall slam as well.

She was furious with him and wasn't exactly sure why. She quickly pulled off her gown and her undergarments and changed into her nightclothes, grateful she had told the maid last night she would need no assistance. The last thing she wanted was a servant to witness her display of temper. She threw back the covers, extinguished the lamp, and fell into bed. She lay staring into the dark and tried to marshal her thoughts.

There was no real reason to be angry with him. He had, after all, come here to warn her about the gossip when it certainly could have waited. He'd gone out of his way and, in truth, it was very thoughtful. He didn't owe this to her. He was simply being, well, nice. Very nice. More than nice. And in return she had raised her voice and lost her temper again and she hadn't been very nice at all.

She heaved a heartfelt sigh. It wasn't anger she felt. Well, it was, but it stemmed from disappointment. She had hoped, when he'd arrived, that he'd come to tell her that he shared her feelings. Not that he knew what her feelings were. She'd had every intention of telling him but the words wouldn't come. Quite simply she'd been afraid of what he might say or do. Or worse, that he didn't feel the same.

"I could use some advice now, you know," she said, and waited. There was no response but then she wasn't surprised. Obviously, this was something she needed to figure out on her own.

In spite of what she might say or hope, Julia really wasn't as much like Hermione as she wished. Hermione who had loved all her partners in adventure and had never hesitated to do precisely what she wanted. Julia had loved William who had never made her lose her temper or cause her to speak without thinking or curled her toes when he kissed her but with whom she had been content. And now she loved Harrison who elicited passions in her she'd never dreamed of and made her ache with desire she'd never imagined and might well drive her mad.

*How sad and bad and mad it was—But then, how it was sweet.*

She threw back the covers, slid out of bed, and lit the lamp. Hermione was right; there was nothing wrong with pursuing what you wanted. She pulled on her robe and summoned her courage. It was past time to take action, even if it was wrong.

Harrison paced his room, grateful for the decanter of brandy that was always on the desk in this room when he was a guest.

What had he done wrong? He racked his brains trying to think, going over every word. He'd taken her hands when he'd arrived and she did not pull away, which had seemed very good. She'd said she was pleased to see him and he'd seen it in her eyes as well. He'd talked about Charles, which certainly was forgivable. And . . . she had something she thought he should know. But what? Surely it was something quite wonderful. Why, hadn't the look in her eyes said as much?

Damnation. He had come here as much to tell her of his feelings as to inform her about the gossip; more really. Yet somehow that had slipped right by him. What an uncertain idiot he was. But then that's how she made him feel and he might as well get used to it. The woman made him ache and no woman had ever done that before. He loved her and he wanted her. In his bed and in his life forever. And it was past time he did something about it. Whether she realized it or not she'd led him on a merry chase and by God it was over. He stalked to the door, pulled it open, and stepped into the hall. Julia paused in midstep halfway across the hall, a scant two steps away.

Their gazes met and for a long moment neither said a word.

Then her chin raised slightly and she drew a deep breath. "Kiss me, my lord."

. . . in spite of all evidence to the contrary, he did like to think he was in command. But then they all do. It is part of the makeup of men. They believe they do indeed rule the world and are lord of all they survey. And we allow them to think so as we are generally fond of them and, as well, we know better.

So when Sir Harold wished to believe seduction was entirely his idea and I had to be convinced as to the merits of the endeavor, why, what was I to do? It will come as no surprise that given . . .

from *The Perfect Mistress,*
*the Memoirs of Lady Hermione Middlebury*

# Chapter Seventeen

She stared at him and for a moment wondered if she had made a dreadful mistake.

Then, without warning she was in his arms and his lips were pressed against hers. Her mouth opened to his and he angled his lips harder over hers. His tongue teased hers and desire hard and hot washed through her and she melted against him. He tasted of brandy and passion and longing and she moaned softly against him. His mouth explored her, pillaged her, claimed her. After a moment or an eternity he raised his head and stared into her eyes.

"Julia?"

"Yes," she breathed the word in answer to the question in his eyes.

He scooped her into his arms and carried her back into her room, shutting the door behind him with his foot.

She'd never wanted a man like this. Indeed, she couldn't remember ever wanting, ever needing, ever aching like this before. He set her on her feet beside the bed and again his mouth claimed hers. And the restraint born of the proper behavior of a lifetime shattered. Her hands and his were everywhere at once, frantic with desire new and unknown and too long ignored. She tugged at the sash of his dressing gown until it opened, then pushed it off his shoulders. He pulled off her robe and his lips left hers to explore the bend of her neck and the curve of her shoulders. She shuddered at the feel of his lips on flesh never before so sensitive.

He fumbled with the ties of her nightgown until she felt it fall to the floor. Cool air caressed her heated body. He pulled away to impatiently drag his nightshirt over his head and toss it aside, then gathered her close. Her arms slid around his neck. His naked body pressed against her and he took her mouth again and again, a portent of what would come. What she wanted. His mouth plundered hers and she reveled in the feel of their tongues dueling, mating, their mouths joined, the heat of his body next to hers.

Her breasts pressed against his chest, rough with coarse hair that only heightened her desire. He ran his hands over her back and skimmed along her sides to rest in the dip of her waist. Heat pooled deep in her womb and moisture dampened between her legs. His arousal lay hard against her stomach and she slipped her hand between their bodies to wrap it around his—*cock* was the word in Hermione's memoirs when nothing else would serve. Not a word that Julia would have so much as thought before reading her great-grandmother's adventures, but here and now it was—a shiver ran through her—erotic and exciting. A voice in the back of her head noted, even with her husband, she had never been so bold as to touch him in this manner but she didn't care. Bold seemed right, natural somehow with this man. As if something inside her had been waiting for him to set it free. Maybe she had changed, maybe she was indeed like Hermione but she'd never known this kind of passion, this kind of desire. Gripping and driving and unrelenting. As if she were no longer the Julia she had always been but a creature of sensation and need. He groaned against her mouth and she stroked him, relishing the feel of his arousal—his cock—in her hand.

His hands slid lower, skimming over her skin, searing a path of fire in their wake. A spark to kindling. He cupped her derriere and dragged his lips from her mouth to run kisses along the line of her jaw and down her neck. She pressed her hips against his, his cock hard between them. He pulled her tighter against him and lifted her. Her legs wrapped around him and her most intimate places pressed against the solid muscle of his stomach and throbbed. She felt his cock, hot and hard, resting beneath the crack of her buttocks. Her head fell back and he tasted the hollow of her throat and she arched toward him.

He took a step backward and they tumbled together onto the bed. Her legs fell open and he shifted to lie between them, cupping her breasts. His tongue toyed with her nipple, tightening beneath his touch. Aching need and pure pleasure sparked from his mouth to deep within her. She moaned and gripped his shoulders. He sucked at her nipple and teased it with his tongue and lightly with his teeth. Sensation flooded her. Her fingers dug into his flesh and faint whimpering sounds came from the back of her throat.

"Oh God, Harrison . . ."

He turned his attention to her other breast, cupping it in his hand.

"Julia." Her name whispered against her skin.

Again his mouth tasted her, teased her. His tongue circled her nipple then flicked over the tip. And her back arched upward and she wanted . . . more.

He shifted to lay beside her, wrapping one arm around her. His mouth trailed over her neck and throat. His free hand drifted over her breasts, exploring her, caressing her.

She'd never imagined her skin could feel so aware, so alive. She traced the hills and valleys of his chest, his stomach, with her fingertips. His hand traveled lower, his fingers tracing circles on her stomach. He hooked one leg over hers, spreading her open. His hand slipped down to rest on her mound, one finger sliding lower, barely touching her.

She tensed, her breath caught, and for an endless moment she thought she would surely perish from the intensity of her need. His fingers slid over the place where only one man had ever touched her and she shuddered with the indescribable feeling. He caressed her, his fingers slick with her own desire. The pressure of his fingers increased and she rolled her hips in rhythm with his touch. Aching need curled tighter within her.

Without warning his fingers withdrew and she whimpered with loss. He shifted to settle between her legs and she felt his erection, hard and hot, nudge her. Slowly he slid into her, filling her, completing her, and she moaned with the pleasure of being one with him. He pulled back very nearly entirely then eased into her again. His strokes were agonizingly slow, measured, and she felt every inch of him within her. She wrapped her legs around him and pulled him deeper, her body throbbing around him, his cock pulsing within her.

Gradually, he moved faster, harder. She rocked her hips against his, their movement growing faster, frantic. He thrust into her again and again and she met his passion with her own. His need with hers. Faster and harder and hotter they moved in a rhythm natural and primal and instinctive. And she wondered if the glory and intensity of the pleasure tightening within her would surely destroy her and didn't care and wanted more. Ached for more. And release claimed her, shattered her. She cried out, her back arched upward, and her body shuddered again and again with wave after wave of exquisite pleasure. He thrust hard once more and his muscles tensed against her. He groaned and his body shook with his own release for a moment or forever. Until at last he stilled and she clung to him.

For a long time, neither of them moved and she reveled in the feel of him still buried inside her. Still one with her. And nice was the farthest word from her mind.

For an eternity or a moment they lay together. Harrison struggled to catch his breath. At last he reluctantly withdrew and rolled to her side, pulling her close.

"Dear Lord," she murmured against him. "Oh, Harrison."

His arms tightened around her. He had been satisfied by intimacy with a woman before but never like this. Never as if it wasn't merely their bodies that had joined but their souls.

"I do feel, well, my apologies."

"Your apologies?" He shifted to gaze into her eyes. "Are you sorry that we did this? I realize it was unexpected. But I thought you . . . and I know I certainly, well, if you regret—"

"No, nothing like that." She shook her head. "I don't regret so much as a single instant. It's just that I, well . . ." She buried her face in his neck and murmured something too muffled to make out.

"Julia?"

She raised her head and stared at him. "I was just so . . . abandoned! I swear to you, Harrison, I have never behaved like that before."

"Never?"

"Never." She shook her head. "I don't know what came over me. I was certainly, well, I simply . . ."

"But surely, you and your husband . . ."

"Well, yes, of course, but not like that."

"Like what?"

"Wanton!"

"Wanton?"

"Yes, wanton. I've never behaved like that before. I never knew it could feel like that." She rolled over, wrapped a blanket around her, and slid off the bed. "I never! I mean I don't. Well, I wouldn't. I couldn't. And yet, I did." She paced at the foot of the bed and he sat up to watch her, shoving a pillow behind him. She was amazing. All indignant and tousled from lovemaking and confused. She'd never been lovelier. His muscles tightened.

"You're saying"—he chose his words with care—"that I make you feel wanton?"

"Yes!"

"Really?" The most absurd sense of masculine pride swelled within him. "Wanton?"

"Yes! Don't make me say it again. I've scarcely ever thought the word let alone said it." She paced. "Just as the word co—well, other words are now in my head." She stared at him. "Words like that were never in my head. And things like—" She waved at the bed. "—like this! I never even imagined!"

"Never?"

"Never! I mean, I am not inexperienced. I have well, you know, but never with anyone other than William and certainly never unmarried . . . and"—she gestured wildly—"never with the lights on. Dear Lord." She resumed pacing.

"Do you have any idea how disloyal this makes me feel as well?" She shook her head. "I loved William. And this, with him, was very"—she waved at the bed and grimaced—"nice."

"I see." It was all he could do to keep a straight face. She was so charmingly flustered. And he was so ridiculously pleased. Regardless, he was smart enough to know better than to let his amusement and pride show.

"All of which makes me think I am like Hermione and worse . . ." She stopped and stared at him. "Bloody hell, Harrison, I liked being wanton!" Her eyes widened and she groaned. He'd wager "bloody hell" hadn't been in her vocabulary until recently either.

He choked back a laugh.

She glared. "This isn't funny!"

"No, you're right, it isn't funny." He tried and failed to keep a grin from his face.

"You think it is!"

"Not at all." He threw back the covers, crawled to the foot of the bed, then swung his legs over the side to plant his feet on the floor. "I think it's marvelous."

She studied him. "Do you?"

"I do indeed." He reached out, grabbed the blanket she clutched around herself, and pulled her back to him.

"You're completely naked, you know."

"I am well aware of that." He tugged at her blanket. "And I do hate to be naked alone." She sighed and released her grip. He pulled the blanket free and dropped it. "Much better." He drew her closer and nuzzled the soft, creamy skin of her midsection.

She gasped and her breath quickened. "You're quite pleased with yourself, aren't you?"

He glanced up. Her eyes were again glazing with desire and he cast her a wicked grin. "I have never been so pleased."

She looked down between them where it was obvious just how pleased he was. She met his gaze and hesitated then smiled slowly. "Why, my lord, I believe you may be just as wanton as I am."

"I do hope so, Lady Winterset, I do hope so." He

slipped his hand between her legs, his fingers sliding over her. She shuddered and rocked tentatively against his hand, again slick with desire.

He settled his hands around her waist and drew her closer to straddle his legs.

"Harrison," she said in a weak protest that was more a moan than a word.

She rested her hands on his shoulders. He moved one hand to cup her bottom and with the other positioned his cock, sliding it against her until she made a tiny whimpering sound of need. Her body trembled and she gripped his shoulders. He lowered her onto his shaft, again hard and eager, and she moaned as he entered her.

His hands slid around her waist. He tried to restrain himself, to move at a calm, measured pace. But within moments of entering her, passion and need gripped him and he thrust into her harder and faster. She responded in kind, riding him, driving him deeper. Her muscles caressed him, gripped him, drove him on. All thoughts vanished and he existed only in the feel of being surrounded by her, engulfed by her, one with her. And the pleasure, tense and demanding, growing again. She throbbed around him and his blood pulsed in his veins. Her head dropped back, and he pressed his mouth against the base of her throat, tasting her, feeling the beat of her heart in rhythm with his own. Aching need for release spiraled tighter and tighter within him.

Dimly he noticed the bed rocking hard against the wall, the moans of pleasure that came from the back of her throat, his own labored breath. Wanton. Abandoned. Completely uncivilized.

Glorious.

He groaned and thrust upward and exploded into her, clinging hard to her as he shuddered against her again and again.

"Harrison." She gasped, her nails digging into his shoulders. "Please . . ."

He thrust again and once more and her muscles tightened around him. Her release gripped her and she cried out, shaking against him for long moments until her head fell forward onto his shoulder. He tightened his arms around her and she clung to him. Until at last his breathing resembled something vaguely normal.

She giggled against his neck.

He stroked her hair. "My God, you are wanton."

Her head jerked up and she stared at him. "Harrison!"

He grinned. "I like it."

She stared at him for a moment then laughed. "That works out nicely then."

A few minutes later, they had washed up and returned to bed. He pulled her close, her lovely bottom fitting snugly against him, his body curled around hers. Had he ever been so . . . spent? Satisfied? Content? Had anything ever felt as right as this? And he had the scandalous behavior of his father and Lady Middlebury to thank. She could be exactly like her great-grandmother if she wished but only in his bed. Only for him.

"It's the book, I think," she murmured in a sleepy voice. "I have been unduly influenced by Hermione's adventures."

"We shall have to do something about that," he said softly against her ear.

She yawned. "I won't let you destroy it."

"I have no intention of destroying it." His hands cupped the full firmness of her breasts. She snuggled back against him. "In fact, I think you should read it again." He nibbled lightly on her ear. "Over and over again."

She sighed in agreement. Within moments her breathing was even and he knew she was asleep. And, whether she yet realized it or not, she was his.

He hadn't admitted it to her but he too was stunned by the passion of their joining. He'd always enjoyed the intimacies between a man and a woman. He'd always found it most satisfying. But this, making love with Julia, was beyond his experience. It was not merely a melding of their bodies but their souls. He'd never been insatiable before but with this woman he knew he would never be able to have enough of her. Would never stop wanting her.

Then again, he'd never been with a woman he loved before. Obviously, that made all the difference. He was not merely satisfied but he was, well, happy. Gloriously, deliriously happy. He wanted to laugh out loud at the thought.

In his entire proper existence he had never once considered that wanton was to be appreciated.


Julia opened her eyes, smiled, and propped herself on one elbow. She watched Harrison sleep and her heart melted. She should be exhausted but instead she was invigorated and quite, quite happy. They'd slept together, arms and legs entwined and at some point, made love again in the dark. Slowly and lazily and infinitely sweet. The late-morning sunlight now fell across the bed and she marveled at the path that had brought them together.

If indeed she was wanton, well, there was something to be said for that. It was obviously part and parcel of loving him. Still, she had loved William. Their intimate relations had always been most satisfying. But with her husband, the heights they had climbed had been somehow smaller and not the least bit overwhelming. At least for her. The release she had experienced, on occasion, in his arms had been far less intense than the explosion of sensation and bliss Harrison had brought her. But William had always seemed quite satisfied and she had been satisfied as well. Still, she'd never imagined the difference between tumbling down a gently sloping hill and soaring wildly off a towering cliff. She tried to ignore a twinge of guilt at the thought that perhaps Harrison was more concerned for her pleasure than William had been. William had been a sensitive and caring lover but he had never ignited the fire inside her that Harrison had lit. Good Lord, maybe she was wanton. Or just in love.

That too was different. Certainly, at the moment it could well be colored by the aftermath of physical passion but it seemed whereas William had owned her heart, Harrison possessed her soul. She had no idea why or how but it was something she knew deep within her. Perhaps Hermione was right. There was nothing as passionate as a man one argued with.

Harrison's eyes remained closed but a slow smile spread across his face. "I don't even want to know what you're thinking."

She laughed.

He opened his eyes and grinned, looking not at all like the stuffy Earl of Mountdale, with whom a woman might be content, but rather a man who promised a lifetime of adventure. "I changed my mind." Without warning he wrapped his arms around her and rolled her over until she lay on top of him, arms folded on his chest, staring down into his blue eyes. "Now, my love, tell me what is on your mind."

"You, my lord, you are on my mind."

"Excellent." He leaned forward to kiss the tip of her nose. "And that is where I wish to stay."

Lord, when had she last been so happy? Still, as wonderful as last night had been, there were realities that needed to be faced with the new day. "The servants must be wondering why neither of us have made an appearance."

He chuckled. "The servants are probably already aware of why we have not made an appearance, given my bed was not slept in."

"I had forgotten about that." She sighed. "Still, we should be up and about."

"Why?"

"Well, it's late morning. I am never still in bed at this hour."

"Nor am I."

"We should dress."

"Why?"

She drew her brows together. "Harrison, what has gotten into you?"

"You have and it's quite delightful." He kissed her hard. "But you're probably right. As much as I should like nothing better than to spend the entire day right here, in bed with you, I, for one, am hungry. Ravenous really. Can't remember the last time I was this hungry." He grinned. "I wonder why?"

"Odd, isn't it?" She returned his grin. "Especially as I am as hungry as you." How had she ever thought him annoying and not completely charming and quite irresistible?

His arms tightened around her and he rolled her over on her back, kissed her once again then hopped out of bed. She caught her breath. She'd seen him last night, of course, but not standing, naked with the sunlight hitting him, highlighting the hard muscles of his chest, the way it tapered to his hips and, even in its passive state, his most impressive—she winced—cock.

He glanced around the room. "Do you have any idea where my clothes went to?"

"Under the chaise in the corner perhaps?" she said innocently then watched him stride across the room and bend over to look under the couch. Hermione was right. A man should look good walking away.

He straightened and shook his head. "Not here. Now, if I remember right . . ." He grinned at her. "I lost my dressing gown somewhere between the door and—"

A sharp knock sounded at the door and at once it opened.

. . . and he dove under the bedclothes and pretended to be fast asleep thus leaving me to face the wrath of the lady I had been told no longer held his affections. It was obvious she had not been similarly informed. You can well imagine, Dear Reader, especially given my lack of attire, that I was quite at a loss for words. Still, there was a lesson to be learned. Regardless of how discreet one may believe one's actions or the precautions taken to avoid discovery, privacy can never be completely assured.

I was, however, most grateful that she was not armed with a pistol as rumor had it that this was not the first time she had discovered a gentleman of her intimate acquaintance in the bed of another . . .

from *The Perfect Mistress,*
*the Memoirs of Lady Hermione Middlebury*

# Chapter Eighteen

"I cannot believe you are still abed at this hour." Veronica swept into the room. "Although it is probably much deser—" Her eyes widened and she sucked in a hard breath.

For a long moment no one moved in a frozen tableau of misbehavior. In some remote part of her mind not completely horrified, Julia noted that if this scene were on stage it would be most amusing and decidedly naughty, although the actors would be clothed.

Veronica's gaze fixed on Harrison, dropped from his face then quickly returned. She clapped her hand to her throat and emitted an odd strangled sort of sound, as if the words themselves were lodged there.

Harrison hesitated, apparently debating the merits of diving for cover or completely ignoring the fact that he hadn't a stitch on, was in Julia's bedroom where she was just as naked as he, and was now confronted by his sister.

"Good day, Veronica," he said in as casual a manner as he might if they had just chanced upon one another in the park. He strolled across the room, picked up the blanket that lay on the floor at the foot of the bed, and wrapped it around himself. Given his example, Julia could do no less and simply clutched the covers tighter against her chest and resisted the most absurd impulse to giggle.

Veronica gasped. "My God, Harrison."

"Yes?"

She stared. "What has come over you?"

Julia snorted back a laugh.

"Over me?" He raised a brow. "In what way?"

"The Harrison I have always known would not have been so unconcerned at being caught sans clothing!"

"Ah, yes." He glanced down as if just now noticing his state of undress. "Awkward, isn't it?"

Veronica choked. "Awkward is the least of it!"

Julia bit her lip. She would have thought being caught with a naked man would have been mortifying, not amusing, but it was perhaps the funniest thing that had ever happened to her. Hermione's influence, no doubt, as well as Harrison's complete nonchalance and total composure. It was most impressive.

Veronica, however, did not look either amused or impressed. "Julia, I demand to know what is going on."

"Well," Julia said slowly, still trying to keep from laughing, "nothing." She paused. "At the moment."

Harrison grinned.

"This is not funny!"

Julia's gaze met Harrison's and they both burst into laughter.

"I don't know why the two of you think it's so amusing." Veronica's stunned gaze slid from Julia to Harrison. "And what are you doing here?"

"Nothing." His grin widened. "At the moment."

"This is . . . well, it's . . . and I . . ." Veronica drew herself up. "Well, I'm shocked, that's what I am. Shocked, I tell you. Shocked at you both."

"Come now, Veronica," Harrison said mildly. "Of all the people I know, you are the one I would think would be least likely to be shocked by anything let alone something of this nature."

"The very fact that I am is shocking as well." She fanned her face with her hand. "But even I can be taken aback by finding a naked man, *my brother,* in my dearest friend's boudoir."

"Think what your reaction would have been had you arrived sooner," Harrison murmured.

Julia ignored him. "Now, now, Veronica. We certainly did not plan to shock you."

"Indeed," Harrison added. "You did not figure in our plans at all."

Julia cast her a chastising look. "It's not as if we expected you to arrive and burst uninvited into the room."

"That's obvious!"

"You weren't supposed to come until tomorrow."

Veronica glared at her. "This is tomorrow!"

"Oh yes, of course." Julia giggled.

Harrison shrugged. "It seems to me the cat is now out of the bag."

"Obviously, the cat's not all that's out of the bag," Veronica snapped.

"You're most amusing when you're indignant you know." He chuckled.

She narrowed her eyes.

"Well, I believe I shall go back to my room and dress."

"Excellent idea!" she snapped.

"And then I hope your staff has some sort of meal prepared." He glanced at Julia. "We are famished."

"Indeed we are." Julia nodded. "I can't remember the last time I was this hungry."

Veronica groaned.

"We have a great deal to talk about as well." His gaze met hers and her heart fluttered.

"Yes," she said softly. "A great deal."

"More than you think!" Veronica huffed.

Harrison cast Julia a last lingering look and left, closing the door behind him.

"Well?" Veronica stared at her friend.

"Well what?"

"Do you care to explain?"

"Goodness, Veronica, I daresay an explanation isn't necessary." Julia plucked an errant thread from the sheet. "I would think it's obvious."

"You and Harrison?"

Julia grinned.

Veronica sank down on the foot of the bed. "I can't say I'm surprised."

"You did seem surprised."

"Well, yes I was surprised at"—she gestured at the bed—"this. I knew the two of you were developing feelings for one another. Knowing Harrison, and you as well, I assumed there would be something of a . . . a courtship. Evenings at the theater, dinners with friends, that sort of thing."

"Oh, I imagine we can still go to the theater," Julia said in an innocent manner.

Veronica rolled her gaze toward the ceiling. "What I never imagined was his seducing you."

"He did not seduce me."

Veronica's eyes widened. "Then you—"

"I would say it was a mutual seduction."

Veronica studied her closely. "Are you all right?"

"I have never been better." She smiled at the thought of just how better she really was.

"Are you sure?"

"Veronica, I have just had the most wonderful night of my entire life."

"I see." She paused. "Not merely nice then?"

Julia grinned. "No, not merely nice. And better yet—" she drew a deep breath—"I suspect it is only the beginning."

Veronica stared at her for a long moment then nodded. "That's . . . wonderful. Truly wonderful. If you're happy about this and he's happy—"

"I am and I am fairly certain he is as well."

A slow smile spread across Veronica's face. "I knew it. Not entirely from the beginning but Harrison started to change when he first met you. And watching the two of you dance around each other, well, I couldn't be more pleased." A wry note sounded in her voice. "Although I shall surely go blind from the sight I was confronted with today."

Julia laughed.

"Now, you should dress as well and I shall meet you downstairs." She stood and her expression sobered. "There's a rather nasty business you need to know about."

"Are you talking about the rumors?"

Veronica arched a brow. "You know?"

She nodded. "That's why Harrison is here. He thought I should know as soon as possible."

"What a charming, thoughtful thing for him to do. I fear I have not given him due credit. Although he does prove my point." She started toward the door.

"And which of your many points is that?"

"What I always say about Portia holds true for Harrison as well. Those least likely to bend are most likely to snap."

Julia scoffed. "I daresay he hasn't snapped."

"Perhaps not, but he has certainly bent a great deal.

Thanks to you or thanks to love, it scarcely matters why, I suppose. The only thing that's significant is that he has changed for the better. He is not the man he was. Stuffy, staid, dull Harrison seems to have been banished. Charles would have been very pleased." She pulled open the door then looked back and cast Julia a wicked grin. "And my God, the man looks good naked."

"As soon as I heard, of course, I attempted to ferret out the source of the rumors." Veronica shook her head. "To no avail, I'm afraid. At least not yet."

Harrison and the ladies sat on Veronica's terrace enjoying the unusually warm autumn day. No doubt, one of the last they would see. In the few hours since her momentous arrival, Veronica had regained her usual composure and had even expressed her approval. Not that it mattered. His gaze strayed to Julia but then he could scarcely tear his eyes away from her. If he couldn't touch her hand or hold her in his arms or press his lips to hers, which he resisted in Veronica's presence, he could at least feast his eyes on her. Savor the way her skin glowed in the fresh air and how the sunlight painted her hair with hues of gold. And revel in the manner in which her gaze would meet and mesh with his and the secret promises that passed between them.

Veronica heaved a frustrated sigh. "Are you listening to me? Either of you?"

"We've heard every word, Veronica," Julia said smoothly. "You have not yet discovered who is behind these dreadful rumors but you are determined to do so."

"Perhaps you were listening," she said, somewhat mollified. "Indeed, I fully intend to discover the culprit responsible. I have excellent sources for this sort of thing, you know. They have yet to fail me and I will not allow failure now."

"And do not think I am not grateful for your efforts." Julia laid her hand on Veronica's. "You are a true friend and I am most appreciative."

"As am I," Harrison added. "A scandal of this magnitude will destroy Julia's reputation." Not that he really cared. As much as he had always fought to avoid scandal, given recent events, it was no longer as crucial as it once was. Besides, Julia would soon become Lady Mountdale and would then be above reproach. If she still wanted the memoirs published, Harrison would arrange for a private publication, a limited edition that could be carefully controlled. It was a solution that would solve all their problems. She had no need now to sell her great-grandmother's book. As the Countess of Mountdale, as his wife, her financial difficulties were at an end.

Veronica's considering gaze shifted from Julia to Harrison and back. "Julia?"

She nodded. "I would prefer not to be at the center of scandal."

"While I had originally planned to stay for several days, I think it would be best if we all returned to London at once," Veronica said. "This is a battle that cannot be waged from a distance."

The butler appeared at the terrace door, discreetly crossed to Veronica, and spoke low into her ear. She nodded. "Show them into the parlor."

The butler took his leave and Veronica's gaze met Julia's. "It appears you have guests."

Surprise widened Julia's eyes. "I do? Who on earth would be coming to see me?"

Veronica studied Julia. "Lord Holridge and his mother."

Julia stared. "William's brother and mother are here?"

"So it seems." Veronica rose to her feet. "I can say you are indisposed, if you'd like."

"No, don't be silly. I haven't seen them since William's death. I can't imagine why . . ." Julia's face paled. "Good Lord. Do you think they've heard?"

Veronica's voice was grim. "I can't think of another reason for them to be here."

Harrison stood and held out his hand to Julia. "Then we shall find out why they have come."

Her gaze met his. She smiled, took his hand and rose. "Yes, we shall."

"I'm not sure I shall be able to stand the two of you," Veronica said under her breath and led the way to the parlor.

They paused outside the closed parlor doors. Harrison chose his words with care. "Veronica, I know you wish to help but I think it would be best if you did not accompany her."

"Nonsense. This is my house and Julia is my guest." She sniffed. "Besides, I know how to handle people like this. I have handled you all these years."

"Precisely why I think your presence might not be wise," he said. "You do have a certain way about you that tends to exacerbate an awkward situation."

"We don't know what the situation is yet, although admittedly we can guess," Julia said in a manner far calmer than he would have expected.

"Hah! We know exactly why they're here," Veronica said. "What nerve they have. You cannot confront them alone."

"Yes, Veronica, I can." Julia drew a deep breath. "I am not the same woman I once was. The Wintersets made it abundantly clear after William's death that I no longer had a position in their family. Nor do I feel any obligation to them whatsoever. I have had to take care of myself for the last three years and I have no doubt I can do so now."

"At least let Harrison go in with you. He knows these kind of stuffy, proper people. Lord knows, he is a stuffy, proper sort himself. Besides, Holridge is a baron whereas Harrison is an earl. People like that are always conscious of rank."

"And I daresay you could use a friendly face," Harrison added, ignoring Veronica's assessment of his nature.

Julia paused then nodded. "Very well then."

Harrison glanced at Veronica. "I assume you'll be listening at the door?"

"Goodness, Harrison." She huffed. "I would be nowhere else."

He nodded and opened the door, waiting for Julia to enter first then closed the door behind them. A gentleman of about his age stood near the fireplace, a matronly woman with a grim expression sat on the settee.

"Lord Holridge, Lady Holridge." Julia nodded a greeting. "Allow me to introduce Lady Smithson's brother, Lord Mountdale."

Lady Holridge's eyes widened. "Lord Mountdale, this is an honor."

Lord Holridge nodded. "Lord Mountdale."

Harrison cast them a polite smile but held his tongue. This was, after all, Julia's affair. But he would not hesitate to step in if necessary.

"I must say, I am surprised to see you here," Julia said. "Or to see you at all for that matter."

"I have no doubt you are surprised," Lady Holridge said in a curt manner. "As you chose to flee from London. Fortunately, it was not difficult to ascertain your whereabouts."

Julia's eyes narrowed slightly. "I did not flee from London. Lady Smithson was so kind as to invite me to spend a few days of peace in the country."

"Hmph." Lady Holridge snorted.

"Lady Winterset," Lord Holridge said, then his tone softened. "Julia. We have become aware of a matter of some importance that has us greatly troubled."

"It's a scandal, that's what it is." Lady Holridge's lips pressed together. "Scandal has never touched this family and I will not allow it to do so now."

Harrison winced to himself. Hadn't he said much the same thing when he'd first heard about the memoirs? And hadn't he sounded every bit as sanctimonious and stuffy?

"Julia," Lord Holridge began before his mother could say another word. The man was obviously smarter than he looked. "We have heard that you are planning to sell for publication a book, memoirs—"

"Vile, filthy, scandalous memoirs." Lady Holridge sniffed.

"—that were either written by your ancestor—"

"A notorious tart that respectable people would not associate with." Lady Holridge huffed.

"—or by yourself based on your own"—he cleared his throat—"experience. We should like to know if it's true."

Julia considered him coolly. "Which part, Edward?"

"For goodness' sakes, Edward, we know it's true." Lady Holridge speared Julia with a look that would have made even Harrison shudder if subjected to it. "Isn't it, Julia?"

Julia clasped her hands together and considered the older woman calmly. "I am indeed contemplating the sale for publication of memoirs written by Lady Middlebury."

The elderly lady's eyes narrowed. "I knew it."

Julia cast her a cool look. This was the Julia he had first met in her library. "Then why did you ask?"

Lady Holridge sputtered.

"Julia," Lord Holridge began. "There is already a great deal of talk about these memoirs. While you say they were written by Lady Middlebury, and certainly we believe you, but given the rumors, other people will not. Have you considered the effect this will have on your reputation? Your future?"

"And the way it will reflect on William and his family?" Lady Holridge said sharply.

"I have given its impact on my life a great deal of consideration, Edward. It would be foolish not to. As William is dead, I have not given so much as a single thought as to how this would reflect upon him. Nor have I considered the effect on his family. It simply is of no significance to me."

Lady Holridge's face reddened and she looked as if she might explode at any moment into a million pieces of indignity and outrage.

"To be blunt, and I believe this situation does call for honesty, my finances are such that I have no other choice." Julia smiled politely. "And I would rather face scandal than certain poverty."

"William would be appalled." Lady Holridge glared. "My son would never permit this if he were alive."

"Unfortunately, he is not alive. And I can no longer be concerned with what he might think."

The older woman gasped. "Dear Lord!"

"Perhaps, if your son had had the foresight to provide for his widow, Lady Winterset would not be in the financial straits that have led her to this point," Harrison said smoothly. "Or if your family had not seen fit to disavow themselves of any financial responsibility toward your late son's wife this could have been avoided."

"Not my idea," Lord Holridge said under his breath.

His mother ignored him. "I absolutely forbid you to continue on this course that will lead us all into scandal."

"I believe you forfeited any right to forbid me, or indeed, to so much as ask me to do anything whatsoever, when you ceased the allowance you gave William and cut off any ties to your family." Julia's voice was as composed as her manner even though Harrison suspected she was shaking with anger.

"I will not permit you to drag my family through the muck and mire of your family's disgusting heritage!"

"You"—Julia met her gaze with an unflinching stare—"have no say in it."

"Julia," Lord Holridge said quickly. "If we were to resume William's allowance, thus eliminating your financial difficulties, would you then reconsider the publication of this work?"

She considered her late husband's brother for a long moment. Harrison held his breath. Julia smiled in a cordial manner but there was a look in her eye that he had seen before. "No."

"You are as disgraceful as your great-grandmother." Disdain rang in Lady Holridge's voice and she rose to her feet. "You shall pay for this, Julia Winterset. I shall make certain you will never again be welcome among decent people. Society will be closed to you for the rest of your days."

"Mother." Even as Lord Holridge said the word, Harrison knew it was futile.

"I knew right from the beginning William was making a dreadful mistake. I tried to warn him, indeed, I tried to stop him but he refused to listen. I told him that tarts and madness run in your family." She shook her head. "Of course he's not the first son to marry against his family's wishes. I have always thought that was precisely why he chose you. That and your pretty face."

Fire glinted in Julia's eyes. "As much as I do hate to spoil your plans—"

"Lady Holridge," Harrison said quickly to forestall Julia. "Even an impartial observer can see that it is unlikely that you and Lady Winterset will ever see eye to eye. But perhaps you would allow me to make a suggestion?"

Julia's gaze caught his and she nodded slightly.

"I beg your pardon, my lord." Lady Holridge drew her brows together. "But I am not sure I understand your interest in this matter."

"Lady Winterset has long been a friend of my family's," he said without hesitation. It wasn't a complete lie. Veronica was family. "I can assure you there has never been scandal attached to my family either."

"No, I've never heard anything about you. And I would have too." She nodded. "Your father is another matter. I understand he's named in this scandalous work."

At once he realized where Lady Holridge had learned her information. "And that is precisely my interest. You should know I have been discussing a solution with Lady Winterset that will satisfy us all. Indeed, we are very close to an agreement."

"Oh?" Suspicion sounded in the older woman's voice.

Julia's gaze fixed on him.

He did need to take a hand in this. As an intelligent woman Julia would understand that what he was about to do was in her best interests. The Lady Holridges and Ferncastles of this world could indeed make one an outcast in society. Even marriage to someone as eminently proper as he had always been would not fully redeem her for years. And no matter how much she might claim she didn't care about scandal, her response to learning about these rumors last night had been most telling. Besides, there was no longer any need for her to sell the memoirs.

"I am just as concerned about the scandal this book will cause as you are. I can assure you I have the matter well in hand." He smiled in a conspiratorial manner. And Veronica thought he couldn't be charming. "It is to no one's benefit to publish them and make them available for public consumption."

"I should say not!" The older woman glared.

"And if they are not published, the matter will fade from interest as soon as the next interesting item comes along." He favored her with his most charming smile. "Don't you agree?"

"Yes, well, you're right, I suppose." She smiled reluctantly. "I must say, I am grateful you have taken this stand, my lord."

He smiled in a modest manner.

"We are most appreciative for your assistance in this matter," Lord Holridge said in a grateful manner, and slanted Julia a quick look of apology.

"Obviously, what was needed was a firm hand," his mother said, now completely ignoring Julia's presence.

"Mother, we must be going if we are to return to London before nightfall." Obviously, Lord Holridge was eager to be on his way.

"Nonsense." His mother scoffed. "I assumed Lady Smithson would offer us accommodations for the night."

Lord Holridge groaned softly.

The door opened and Veronica stepped into the room, an overly pleasant smile on her face. "I was just passing by and thought I heard my name. May I be of assistance?"

"I was just saying that I assumed you would offer your hospitality to us for the night." Lady Holridge cast Veronica a beneficent smile, as if she were bestowing a great favor on the younger woman.

"Why on earth would I do that?" The innocent look in Veronica's eyes matched her tone. "Unless I am mistaken, you were neither invited nor expected." Harrison gave her a chastising look and she shrugged. "Unfortunately, I seem to be beset with unexpected guests today and I simply have no spare rooms."

"You don't?" Lady Holridge studied her suspiciously. "But this house is enormous."

Veronica smiled. "Odd, isn't it?" She hooked her arm through Lady Holridge's and steered her toward the door. "But do allow me to escort you out. It is, after all, the very least I can do. Any other time of course, well, you do understand. Now, you should hurry or you will miss the last train."

"Trains are disgusting, filthy contraptions." Lady Holridge sniffed in contempt. "I have never ridden on a train nor shall I ever. We came in our carriage."

"All the way from London? Imagine that." Veronica escorted her out the door, Lord Holridge trailing behind. "Then you must be on your way and I must commend you on adhering to your principles rather than surrendering to convenience and ease. . . ."

"That's that." Harrison chuckled and closed the door behind them. "I did think Veronica was going to do something that might . . ." He turned toward Julia and his smile faded. "You're angry with me, aren't you?"

Julia glanced from side to side as if looking to see if there were anyone else in the room. "Oh, are you talking to me? I didn't realize you knew I was still present."

He took a step toward her. "Julia."

"You had no right to lead her to believe the memoirs will not be published. Indeed, you had no right to interfere at all."

He stared at her. "If I hadn't stepped in, you would have said or done something to make the situation worse."

"So you were protecting me?"

"Well . . . yes."

She shook her head. "I don't need your protection."

"Perhaps not but you did need my help."

"No." Her gaze met his. "I did not."

"Julia, while you are an intelligent woman, I am an in-telligent man." He chose his words with care. "And as an intelligent woman you must admit that I know better."

"In this case or always?"

He hesitated.

"I see," she said slowly. "Then while I am intelligent I am not nearly as clever as you?"

"I am a man," he said without thinking.

"Indeed you are," she said coolly. "What did you mean when you said you had the matter well in hand?"

"I meant that, well, I do," he said staunchly.

"Perhaps I am not as intelligent as you think. Please explain. How exactly do you have the matter well in hand?"

"Surely after last night . . ."

"Yes?"

"Well, it seems to me you have no need to publish the memoirs now."

"Because I shared your bed?"

"Yes. No!" He shook his head. "That's not what I meant at all."

"What did you mean?"

"I meant that your finances will soon no longer be a problem."

"I don't see that last night changed my financial cir-cumstances in the least."

"I shall take care of your finances."

"Oh?" She raised a brow.

"Well, I assumed—"

"If you are speaking of marriage, which you have not mentioned up to this point—"

"I am mentioning it now."

She ignored him. "While I do realize you have certain

moral standards, I am a competent adult and accountable for my own actions. It is not necessary to marry me simply because you seduced me."

He gasped. "I did not seduce you."

"My apologies." Her eyes narrowed. "Of course you didn't. I was every bit as responsible for last night as you."

"Yes," he snapped, "you were."

"Because I . . . I wanted you."

He scoffed. "That was obvious!"

"I wanted to be in your bed."

"Enthusiastically, I might point out."

"Because I am just like my great-grandmother?"

"I didn't say that. In fact, you're the one who keeps saying that."

"Nonetheless, it's obvious that's what you're thinking. I see it all now. Your entire devious plan."

He stared. "What devious plan?"

"You were the one who first mentioned that other men might be interested in me because of my great-grandmother's nature. Which obviously means you were thinking the exact same thing."

"I was trying to warn you." Indignation sounded in his voice. "You're not being fair."

She ignored him. "So once you had me in your bed—"

"Again, by mutual consent."

"—and had your way with me—"

"You certainly had your way with me as well." He huffed.

"—then I would be so . . . what? Swept away by passion?"

"There was sweeping on both sides if I recall."

"That I would gladly relinquish the memoirs to you?"

"It was not a plan," he said staunchly.

"And then what?"

He drew his brows together. "What?"

"Did you expect me to follow in Hermione's footsteps? To become your mistress?"

"No!" He huffed. "That thought never crossed my mind. I thought you'd become my wife!"

"Because that's the proper thing to do after a night of passion?"

"Yes! No! That's not why at all."

"Come now, my lord, I am not the type of woman you want for a wife."

"No, you're not," he snapped.

"Then we are agreed."

"We're not agreed on anything!"

"Apparently!" She drew a deep breath. "Did you really think you could get the memoirs this way?"

He hesitated. The thought had crossed his mind.

"I do so hate to disappoint you." Her eyes narrowed. "My plans have not changed in the least. I shall sell the memoirs for publication the moment I return to London, which I intend to do as soon as possible." She started for the door. "Oh, and I do apologize that you shall have to go back on your word to Lady Holridge. You have nothing well in hand. Absolutely nothing." With that she nodded and took her leave.

For a long moment he stared at the door. What exactly had he done that was so wrong? Yes, he had made assumptions about a future together that might have been premature. And certainly it might not have been wise to indicate to Lady Holridge the memoirs would not be published. He had known that before he had said it but it had seemed like a brilliant idea at the time. And perhaps it had been presumptuous on his part to assume that she would acquiesce to his desire not to publish the book now that they had shared a bed.

But this was a woman who had taken care of herself

with no help from anyone for the last three years. One would think she would have been grateful to have a man take charge. He winced. That, no doubt, was where he had made his biggest mistake. Nor had it been wise to admit that she was not what he wanted in a wife. But what he wanted had changed. Now he wanted a wife who would drive him mad. Now he wanted Julia.

He would return to London at once. Further discussion with Julia today would serve neither of them well and she needed time to come to her senses and realize he was only trying to help. And then he would . . . court her. Yes, that's what he'd do. Send flowers—not roses—and tokens of affection and notes professing his love. He'd write poetry if necessary and he would walk in that damn park every morning if he had to.

He had come here in the first place to rescue her and he was not about to let anyone, even Julia herself, stand in the way of his doing just that. Whether she realized it or not, she needed him. And damnation, he needed her.

And he refused to spend the rest of his life without her.

*. . . therefore I was quite touched and most grateful. It was apparent, to my delight, that his lordship had been thoroughly trained.*

*It has often seemed to me there is very little difference between the training of a man and that of a dog, although a dog is usually much easier. He will learn proper behavior by little more than the repeated offering of a delectable morsel as a reward for his actions. Men are very much the same. Promise a man something delicious, something he wants quite badly, and he will do precisely what you wish him to do.*

*His lordship had obviously been taught to consider his words before they left his lips, a quality rare in most men as it goes against their nature. But dear Cedric had been well . . .*

from *The Perfect Mistress,*
*the Memoirs of Lady Hermione Middlebury*

# Chapter Nineteen

"Welcome home, Lady Winterset," Daniels said in his usual competent manner. "I trust your stay in the country was uneventful?"

"Let us say it was interesting, Daniels. Thank you," Julia said with a wry smile.

It was good to be home. Even the heavy weight that had settled in Julia's stomach when she had argued with Harrison had lessened.

He had left Veronica's last night to return to London alone. Julia and Veronica had taken the first train this morning. While Veronica was well aware something had transpired between the two of them—Harrison's abrupt departure was ample evidence of that—she was wise enough, for once, to keep her curiosity to herself. Julia was grateful for that. She had no desire to discuss her feelings or emotions or anything at all regarding Harrison with anyone, alive or dead. Hermione too had been absent.

It had been a long, lonely night and Julia had scarcely slept a wink. By this morning she had realized that in spite of his smug, superior attitude he was indeed only trying to help and doing so in the only way he knew how. The fact that ultimately he had treated her like an incompetent was annoying but somewhat understandable. The blasted man did indeed think he knew best. She suspected now the anger she had directed at him had more to do with her fury at her former in-laws than his well-intentioned actions. She had already decided to forgive him as his heart was in the right place and even offer him an apology of her own. Not that she had done anything really wrong, but she shouldn't have taken out the anger triggered by William's family on him. Besides, he had pointed out her financial circumstances were a direct result of their own actions. It was thoughtful and most appreciated.

She pulled off her gloves and removed her hat, handing them to the butler.

"There have been several callers in your absence," Daniels said. "Mr. Cadwallender, Mr. Ellsworth, Baron Holridge and Lady Holridge." He paused. "I told them you were away."

"But you didn't tell them exactly where I was?" she asked, even though she knew the answer.

"Absolutely not, my lady." A firm note sounded in the butler's voice. He was too well trained and protective to have told any of her callers exactly where she was although Lady Holridge was right. Determining her whereabouts would have taken little effort. "And your grandmother has—"

"Julia!" Grandmother appeared at the top of the stairs, a beaming smile on her face, and gracefully descended. "What a charming little house this is."

Her grandmother's smile was contagious and Julia's heart lightened. "Eleanor! How wonderful that you've come at last. I was nearly ready to fetch you myself."

"For good or ill, I am here now." She reached the foot of the steps and enfolded her granddaughter in a heartfelt embrace. Then she stepped back and studied her. "Oh, dear, as bad as all that?"

Julia widened her eyes in an innocent matter. "What?"

"Come, come, darling, I know all about it." She tucked Julia's hand into the crook of her elbow and led her into the parlor.

"What, exactly, do you think you know?" Julia said cautiously.

"Well, I know you've fallen in love with Lord Mountdale." She chuckled. "I do so love the irony of that."

"Because his father was once involved with Hermione? Yes, I suppose." Julia frowned. "But it's not at all amusing. I am quite distraught."

"Perhaps if you hadn't been so stubborn and proud you wouldn't be so distraught. Although both questionable qualities do run in our blood. Mores the pity." She seated herself on the sofa then patted the spot next to her. Julia obediently sat. "Now then, have you forgiven him for doing what he thought was best even if he was perhaps wrong? Although I must say, I too would have been hard-pressed to stay quiet under the circumstances."

"Eleanor." Julia chose her words with care. She wasn't entirely certain she wanted to hear the answer. "How do you know about any of this?"

Eleanor raised a brow. "How do you think?"

Julia braced herself. "Hermione?"

"Who else?" Eleanor shook her head. "My mother has spoken to me nearly every day since the day she died. We did not part on good terms." She sighed. "I was angry with her for a very long time. Of course, she was living in France and it's quite easy to remain angry with someone when you don't see them and can ignore their letters." She met Julia's gaze directly. "But it's very hard to ignore someone who is dead and is present whether you wish them to be or not."

"I have noticed," Julia said faintly. It was one thing to suspect whose voice Eleanor heard, it was quite another to confirm it.

"She can be most persistent."

"I have noticed that as well."

"I can't say I ever forgave her as much as I came to re- alize her actions had nothing really to do with me." Eleanor grimaced. "And then I asked her to forgive me." She shook her head. "But I wasted so much time. Time, my dear, is something you never get back."

"I suppose not."

"So, do you intend to be stubborn and justifiably out- raged or forgive him and get on with your lives together?"

Julia smiled. "I may well have already forgiven him."

"But you have not yet told him?"

"Not yet, but I will."

"Excellent. And you will waste no time in doing so?"

"I intend to tell him when next I see him."

"See that you do. Forgiveness is a difficult thing, both to seek and bestow, and only grows more difficult with every passing day." Eleanor shook her head. "But time is precious. One day you think you have all the time in the world to forgive or do whatever it is you wish to do and the next you find there is no time left at all."

Julia studied the older woman curiously. "What are you trying to say?"

"Nothing you don't already know." She smiled and patted Julia's hand. "You have decided to forgive him. You will do so as soon as possible and that will be the end of it. Or rather the beginning, I think."

"Eleanor." Julia paused. She wasn't entirely sure how to ask this. "Why is Hermione still here? Shouldn't she be, well, somewhere else?"

"Heaven, you mean?"

"Yes, I suppose. I have been reading her memoirs—do you know about the book of memoirs she wrote before her death?"

She shook her head. "I knew nothing about them until my brother died. She and I agreed that you should have them. That you needed them."

Julia nodded. "Because I needed the money they would fetch."

"There was that, of course, but more . . . It's difficult to know who you are without knowing those who came before you. It's also very easy to repeat mistakes of the past if you have no idea what they were." Eleanor thought for a moment. "The memoirs are only the beginning, of course. You should know this, the history of your family. It's past time, I think."

Julia nodded. "Then please, do go on."

Eleanor drew a deep breath and began "My father died when I was barely a year old and my mother then chose to live her life by her own rules. At first glance it would appear that, in doing so, she wasn't very good as a mother. But she did love her children." She paused. "When I lost the man who was arguably the love of my life—"

"My grandfather?"

"No," she said simply. "He had died several years earlier, and make no mistake, I did indeed love him. However, the love I am speaking of was lost because I was unwilling to forgive something that had nothing to do with me although I did not realize it at the time. And when I did forgive, it was too late. He had married someone else." She shrugged. "Around that same time your mother met and married your father and I retired to the country. They were indeed made for each other and I did not think my presence in their life was necessary. In that I now see I was wrong. She still needed me and I was too lost in my own misfortune to understand that. It caused a rift between us that never truly healed." She blew a long breath. "My mother—Hermione—died a few years later and began her visits to me. It seemed better for your mother to believe I was mad than to think I had abandoned her." Eleanor met her gaze directly. "Which in truth I had."

"Surely she didn't think—"

"I don't know what she thought. I didn't try to find out." She shrugged. "I always thought there would be time, you see. Time to be closer and time to know you. She never brought you on those rare visits of hers, protecting you from your mad grandmother, no doubt. But I always had the feeling she and your father were so close there was little room left for a child."

"They were wonderful. I couldn't have asked for more caring parents," Julia said indignantly, even if she had long ago acknowledged, if only to herself, that her role in her parents' lives was peripheral at best.

"Of course they were." Eleanor smiled. "And you should pay no attention to anything I say." She heaved a heartfelt sigh. "I am very old, you know, and my mind is not what it used to be."

"I doubt that."

"You were asking why my mother's spirit still lingers."

"And you have changed the subject."

"Indeed I have. A privilege of age, my dear." She nodded. "Unfortunately, there is no answer. My mother and I have discussed it at length through the years. Initially, we assumed she was here to set things right between us. Once that was accomplished and she remained, we had no idea why. Nor does it really seem to matter although I do think she would like to move on to wherever it is she is going." She shook her head. "I hate to think she is doomed to wander the earth forever."

"She does seem to be having a good time of it," Julia said wryly.

"On the surface, perhaps." Eleanor shrugged. "It's most interesting that she has revealed herself to you."

"She once said something about my needing her."

"That makes sense, I suppose. I have needed her for all these years and needed as well to make amends for my anger with her. Odd to think I scarcely knew my mother at all until her death."

Eleanor thought for a moment. "In the thirty-some years that she has been gone, that she has been with me, I have come to realize while the manner in which she lived her life might have been scandalous and unacceptable in a moral sense to most people, she was a good person."

"I think so." Julia nodded. "Her memoirs are very candid and, as far as I can tell, she was always very kind and generous and never deliberately hurt anyone."

"And deserves to rest in peace."

"Yes, she does." Julia paused. "Do you think there is something we can do to help?"

"I wish I knew. If she is here because in some way we need her, I suppose all we can do is allow her to help us. Lord knows, she has saved me from being lonely all these years. Harriet was an excellent companion but even the dearest friendship pales in comparison to the love of family." Eleanor met her gaze. "But now I have you. Thank you, my dear."

A lump lodged in Julia's throat. "I should have insisted you join me years ago."

"And I shouldn't have been so stubborn about doing so."

"Stubbornness"—Julia grinned—"runs in the blood." She sobered. "You will always have a place with me."

"Thank you, my dear. That is lovely to hear." Her green

eyes twinkled. "As I am confident I have a few good years left."

"Many good years." Julia hesitated. "I am curious about one thing you alluded to. You needn't answer, of course, and it's probably presumptuous of me to inquire."

Eleanor raised a brow. "My, this sounds interesting. I am so glad we no longer discuss the weather. Thanks to my mother, there are scarcely any secrets you have that I am not aware of so it is only fair that you inquire as to mine. Besides, it's no doubt part of the story and should be told."

"If you're sure."

"I am." She studied her curiously. "Do ask me anything you wish."

Julia chose her words carefully. "You said you lost the love of your life because your forgiveness was too long in coming." She paused. "I was wondering . . ."

"What he did?"

Julia nodded.

"Ah, well that." She sighed in resignation. "It was a very long time ago and scarcely matters now. And there is probably a lesson to be learned about the timeliness of forgiveness." Eleanor drew a deep breath and gazed unseeing across the room or the years. "He had never married, was really something of a rake, a most adventurous and scandalous sort. Not at all the type of man I had ever been attracted by. I was a widow, good Lord. I was in my fortieth year and never imagined I would fall in love again. And fall quite hard I might add. I had never felt that way about any man, never imagined the passion and intensity of it. To this day it still lingers in my mind, in my heart perhaps."

"What happened?"

"Well . . ." Her voice was matter of fact, as if she'd come to terms with this so long ago it was no longer of any significance. "I discovered, long before he knew me, when he was much younger, he had had a liaison with an older woman of some notoriety." She met Julia's gaze and smiled wryly. "The man was Harrison's father and the woman was my mother."

The irony did not escape her.

The very thing that had torn her grandmother and Lord Kingsbury apart—his affair with Hermione—was the very thing that had brought Julia and Harrison together. Julia had fallen in love with the son of the man who had broken her grandmother's heart because he had had an affair with her great-grandmother, whose memoirs had brought she and Harrison together. It was both convoluted and confusing, but one thing was clear, at least to Julia. Regardless of what Hermione's ultimate purpose might be, or how old Eleanor and Lord Kingsbury now were, it might not be too late for them although Eleanor had expressed no desire in that regard. Indeed, immediately after her shocking revelation she had begged off further discussion, citing her age dictated a need to rest. Julia was beginning to suspect her grandmother used her age to her advantage when she deemed it necessary.

Julia had spent the remainder of the morning writing necessary notes and reassessing her finances. The outlook was somewhat brighter now that she no longer had Eleanor's expenses to consider. But the need for money had certainly not vanished, simply diminished for the moment. In spite of her declaration to Harrison, she held off writing to Benjamin to tell him of her decision to sell him the memoirs. Even if she were to marry Harrison, which at the moment was not at all a certainty, she had grown independent enough to want her own finances. Still, if they were to have a future together, it would not begin well if she completely ignored his wishes. At the very least, she should discuss it with him before taking any action whatsoever.

But would they have a future together? She'd waited all morning to hear from him and it was already past noon. In spite of her best efforts, she was only paying half-hearted attention to the figures and papers on the desk before her. She had expected, at the very least, a note of some sort by now. Or flowers—even roses. Or an unexpected visit. The fact that he hadn't contacted her was most disquieting. After all, how could she forgive him if he gave her no opportunity to do so? She couldn't ignore the thought that perhaps he had no wish to see her. That he had come to his senses and decided their night together was nothing but reckless, ill-considered passion. Or that he had realized the type of woman he had initially planned to wed was still what he wanted. And hadn't he admitted Julia was not what he wanted in a wife?

Regardless, resolve tightened her jaw; she was not going to allow him to walk out of her life without so much as a by your leave. If he had indeed decided what had passed between them was a mistake, he would have to tell her to her face. She would give him the remainder of today to do so. Tomorrow, she would take matters into her own hands. Odd that she'd had difficulties deciding on the fate of the memoirs but this decision she had no hesitation about whatsoever.

"Lady Winterset." Daniels appeared at the library door. "You have—"

"Do be so kind as to step out of the way, Daniels." Veronica's voice sounded behind the butler. Daniels hesitated but his training won out. He would never stand in the path of a lady, and no man in his right mind would stand in the way of a determined Veronica. He moved aside. Veronica stepped into the room, Portia close at her heels. "Julia, we have the most interesting bit of news."

"*I* have the most interesting bit of news, you mean," Portia said with a triumphant grin then looked around. "Why, I have never been in your library before. It's not very big, is it?"

"No, it's not." Julia rose. "Perhaps we should go into the parlor before I hear this interesting bit of news."

"There's no place for both of us to sit in here." Portia glanced around, leading the way. "You really should get another chair, Julia. Or a larger library."

"I have no room for another chair and no money for a larger house."

"Good Lord, darling, that is an ugly lamp," Veronica murmured on their way out of the room.

A few minutes later they were seated in the parlor. Veronica insisted that Julia ring for tea even though Portia was fairly bursting with excitement to tell her news. Or, more likely because of it.

"Very well," Julia said at last. "What is it?"

Portia paused in the manner of an actress about to deliver the most important line of the play. "Well, I was at a dinner last night. You know, one of those ones my cousins are continually having in hopes of introducing me—"

"Do get on with it, Portia," Veronica said impatiently. "If you don't tell her right this very instant, I will."

"You do take all the fun out of things." Portia heaved a long-suffering sigh. "Very well then." She paused dramatically. "As I—"

"She knows who started the rumors about the memoirs," Veronica blurted.

Portia's eyes widened with fury. "Veronica! How could you?"

"I don't know." Veronica sank back in her chair and

waved her hand helplessly in front of her face. "Something just came over me. You were being so blasted slow." She glared at the other woman. "You, Portia, could try the patience of a saint."

"And you are no saint," she snapped.

Veronica shrugged. "Obviously."

"Nor am I." Julia drew a deep breath. "So, *Portia,* if you would be so kind as to tell me the name of the culprit who began all this, I shall be eternally grateful."

"Well." Portia appeared somewhat mollified.

"Now!"

"John Eddington Ellsworth," Portia said with a smug smile and a flourish of triumph in her voice.

"And isn't that interesting?" Veronica nodded in a knowing manner.

"Surely you must be mistaken." Julia stared. "Do you know this for certain?"

"I am as certain as anyone can be about something like this." Portia shrugged.

"Go on, tell her the rest," Veronica said.

"Very well. As I started to say before I was interrupted . . ." She cast Veronica a look of annoyance. "I was at dinner last night, seated next to a very nice gentleman, another candidate, although I will admit this one had a certain amount of potential. The conversation turned to mutual acquaintances and your name came up."

"And?" Julia held her breath.

"He said he had heard you had written a scandalous book. Of course I denied it and demanded to know where he had heard such a thing." Portia sighed. "I don't know why men are always criticizing women for gossiping as they seem to do so very much themselves."

Julia clenched her teeth. "Get on with it."

"I am." Portia huffed. "Anyway, he said he knew it to be the truth because he had heard it directly from Mr.

Ellsworth himself. They belong to the same club, you see, and were discussing Mr. Ellsworth's work. And Mr. Ellsworth told him personally that he was close to an agreement on collaborating on a book that you had written based on the life of your ancestor as well as your own experiences."

"I see." The oddest sense of calm settled over her. Which was probably good since Julia had never before truly wanted to strangle the life out of anyone. And had never before imagined that not only could she do such a thing but she would enjoy it. She was grateful as well that the author wasn't here this very moment.

Portia and Veronica traded glances.

"We knew you would want to know," Portia said.

"We also knew you would want to do something about it at once," Veronica added.

"Oh, I do indeed wish to do something about it."

"Excellent." Veronica grinned. "As I took the liberty of sending a note, in your name, to Mr. Ellsworth requesting him to call on you this afternoon. It said you had come to a decision about the memoirs and wished to discuss it with him. He should be here any minute."

Julia narrowed her eyes. "That is indeed a liberty."

"Don't look at me like that, Julia Winterset," Veronica said. "You need to nip this in the bud before it goes any further and the only sure way to do that is to confront this man immediately. I should think threatening those parts of him that he is no doubt most proud of would be the place to begin." She leaned forward and met Julia's gaze. "I knew full well, and Portia agreed—"

"I did indeed." Portia nodded.

"—that you need to take action immediately and if left to your own devices you would probably ponder the situation and consider what to do next in a sane and rational manner."

"We don't think sane and rational is the way to handle this." Portia shook her head. "We think overt anger and the threat of severe physical violence is called for." She straightened her shoulders. "And we are prepared to help."

Julia stared at her friends. "As much as I appreciate your offer, I have no doubt I can handle Mr. Ellsworth without assistance." She stood. "Now, as he will apparently be here shortly, you should take your leave."

"Oh, I don't think so." Veronica settled back in her chair. "We have no intention of leaving."

"We intend to remain right here in the event you might need us," Portia said. "If nothing else, to provide you with moral support. While we don't think you will truly resort to physical violence, we are prepared to assist with that as well." Her determined gaze met Julia's. "I was raised in a family with seven other children, four of whom were boys. And while there was no lack of affection, indeed my cousins one and all treated me precisely as they treated each other. One did what was necessary to survive. As a child I was considered somewhat scrappy. While I have had no need to engage my—"

"Scrappiness?" Veronica's eyes widened in an innocent manner.

Portia ignored her. "—*skills* in recent years I have no doubt they would be recalled should I have need of them."

"If you are required to bash Mr. Ellsworth over the head, you mean?" Veronica said with barely concealed amusement.

"Yes. I wouldn't hesitate to do so. Nor . . ." She pinned Veronica with a firm look. "Would you."

"Of course I wouldn't. I would quite enjoy bashing Mr. Ellsworth over the head. But then we expect that of me." She smiled in an overly sweet manner that would certainly strike terror into the heart of Mr. Ellsworth or any man so foolish as to cross her.

"There will be no need the bash him over the head," Julia said sternly. "As much as that does have a certain amount of appeal. But I would prefer to meet with him alone."

Julia's maid discreetly came into the parlor with the tea cart and the women fell silent. She quickly placed the cart and took her leave. Daniels might be in charge of only a small staff but he ran it with efficiency.

"We expected that." Veronica began as soon as the maid was out of hearing, her voice as determined as the look in her eye. "Which is why we intend to listen at the door where we will be close at hand should you need us."

Julia suspected even if she were to bodily throw her friends out of the house, they might well listen at the window.

"Very well." She sighed. "I shall meet with him in the library. But there will be no interference from the two of you."

"We wouldn't think of interfering," Veronica huffed.

"Absolutely not." Indignation sounded in Portia's voice.

"Hah. I don't believe either of you for a moment."

"Nor should you." Veronica grinned and glanced at Portia. "And you said I was the clever one."

Portia ignored her. "We will, however, agree not to make our presence known unless you need us."

"Or we think you need us," Veronica added.

"I will not need you."

Veronica shrugged. "One never knows."

"And while we wait for Mr. Ellsworth . . ." Portia poured a cup of tea in an offhand manner. "You can tell me everything that transpired while you were away."

Julia raised a surprised brow. "I assumed Veronica would have told you."

"She alluded, she implied, and she hinted but she really didn't say much of anything."

Julia stared at Veronica. "How very unusual of you to hold your tongue like that."

"I didn't think it was my place." Veronica sniffed. "Besides, there has been no time. The moment I met Portia she told me what she had heard and we came to tell you without delay."

"Were it not for the importance of the information we had to bring you I would have been beside myself with curiosity." Portia sipped her tea and studied her over the rim of her cup. "Now that we have accomplished that . . ."

"You are beside yourself with curiosity?"

"From the minor details Veronica has revealed, I gather Lord Mountdale followed you to the country?"

Veronica shuddered, no doubt at the thought of how she had discovered Harrison's presence.

Julia nodded "He came to tell me about the rumors."

"Did he?" Portia's gaze slid from Julia to Veronica.

"She might prefer not to discuss it, dear." Veronica considered Julia carefully. "From my observation, it did not end well. Unless . . . have you have heard from Harrison today?"

"Not yet." Julia sipped her tea. "And if I don't then he shall hear from me. As for not ending well . . ." She cast her friends a pleasant smile. "That remains to be seen."

# Chapter Twenty

"Bloody hell."

Harrison stared at the note in his hand then glanced at the clock on the mantel. Thank God, Veronica had had the foresight to have a footman deliver this message to him at once. He shouldn't be the least bit surprised that Ellsworth was behind the rumors, although one did wonder what he hoped to gain. Nor should he be surprised that Veronica and her cohort, Lady Redwell, had taken matters into their own hands and were even now luring the author to Julia's. He had no doubt that when cornered, Ellsworth would reveal Harrison's part in the author's proposal regarding the memoirs. The man was not to be trusted. And while Harrison could, and fully intended, to stand by his actions with Lady Holridge, as he could certainly argue he had simply acted in what he believed were Julia's best interests, he could never explain his involvement with Ellsworth.

Upon his arrival home last night he had discussed the disagreement with Julia with his father and what he should do now. The older man had agreed that actively pursuing Julia coupled with thoughtful tokens of affection and his unrelenting presence was, if not brilliant, at least a fairly good idea. But Harrison had been beset by other matters demanding his attention today and had not yet had time to set his plan into motion. Now, it seemed there was no time at all. He had to reach Julia and tell her about what admittedly was a dreadful error in judgment before Ellsworth did.

He threw open the library doors, but before he could take a step was nearly knocked over by a large, furry creature bounding into him. He staggered backward, under attack by the beast who planted huge paws on his chest and took a swipe at his chin with an inordinately long, wet tongue.

"What in the name of all that's holy is this!" He pushed the creature down and backed away.

"It's a dog, of course." His father grinned and stepped into the library. "Sit, Browning. That's a good boy."

The dog—Browning—obediently sat at Harrison's feet but his tail continued to wag frantically, the rest of his body wiggling with his tail, a furry mass of barely restrained enthusiasm.

"I can see it's a dog." Harrison stared at the creature. His head came to just above Harrison's knee. He was solidly built, Harrison could attest to that, with long gray fur and white markings, and was perhaps the most absurd animal Harrison had ever seen. "But what kind of dog? And why is it here?"

"It's a Scotch bearded collie," his father said proudly. "I have a friend who breeds them."

"Why? It looks like a doormat." Browning wiggled even more if possible and stared up at him. "And it's grinning at me."

"He's a very friendly dog. And quite smart I've been told."

"He can count to ten and play the violin for all I care. Why is he here, no doubt shedding on my carpet?"

"You said you wanted one. For Lady Winterset."

Harrison stared. "What are you talking about?"

His father heaved a long-suffering sigh. "Last night, when we were discussing how you could get back into Lady Winterset's good graces, you mentioned that she liked dogs. I distinctly remember you saying that presenting her with a dog might be a thoughtful gesture. So"— Father gestured at the beast with a flourish—"I acquired Browning for you to give to her."

"But he's . . . he's . . ."

"Irresistible?"

Harrison studied the grinning creature. There was something, well, happy about him. He reached out and petted his head and he could have sworn he heard the animal moan in delight. "Why Browning?"

"You also mentioned she liked poetry. Robert Browning is my favorite poet and I feared, left to your own devices, you might name him something less dignified."

"I doubt that I have ever seen an animal less dignified than this one." Harrison chuckled in spite of himself. "He is somewhat irresistible, isn't he?"

"Trust me, Harrison," his father said in a sage manner. "She will adore him and adore you for bringing him to her."

He met his father's gaze. "She can scarcely stay angry for long with a man who is this thoughtful." He grimaced. "Even if he has done something she might consider reprehensible."

"I hardly think that business with Lady . . ." Realization dawned on the older man's face. "She knows about you and Ellsworth?"

"Not yet. I was just about to go tell her myself before she finds out from him."

"Then what are you waiting for? Off with you, my boy. Ride to the rescue once again. Try to do a better job this time." He handed his son a leash. "And take Browning. He might turn the tide in your favor."

"Although I doubt even the most irresistible creature will make a difference, I will bring him along." He blew a long breath. "I shall need all the help I can get."

"Lady Winterset." Mr. Ellsworth beamed and started across the library toward her.

"Stay right where you are, Mr. Ellsworth," she said coolly and closed the library door behind her. As annoying as she had initially thought it would be to have Veronica and Portia on the other side of the door, right now, she was grateful they were there. After all, if she did indeed strangle him, she could never dispose of his body by herself.

He stopped in midstep; his confident expression faltered. "As you wish." He paused. "I was quite pleased to receive your note. You have made your decision then? About the memoirs."

She smiled pleasantly. "Ah, yes, the memoirs. Precisely what I wished to discuss with you."

"Excellent." He breathed a sigh of relief. "I should like to begin work at once. I have been giving the memoirs a great deal of thought. First, of course, I shall need to read them fully as I have only Mr. Cadwallender's assessment as to their—"

"Mr. Ellsworth, it has come to my attention that the memoirs have become the topic of a considerable amount of gossip."

"We should have expected they would not remain secret. But it scarcely matters, they shall be public knowledge soon enough."

"Oh, but this gossip isn't just about the memoirs but, rather, about the author."

He chuckled. "Well, your great-grandmother was well known in certain circles."

"Indeed she was, but the rumors I am hearing do not give her the credit due her." Her voice hardened. "The talk is that I am the author and that they are based as much on my own experience as on Lady Middlebury's life."

Concern showed on his face. For a moment she could almost believe he was innocent. "Nasty business, gossip."

"Isn't it though?" She sighed in a dramatic manner. "I can't imagine how such a thing could happen."

"And yet these things do happen." He shook his head. "Still, I suppose, the situation can be salvaged."

"Oh?" *Salvaged?* If ever a man deserved to be strangled it was this man. "Please, do go on."

"I believe we can use this to our advantage," he began, the most infuriating note of eagerness in his voice. On further consideration, strangling was too good for him.

She widened her eyes in an innocent manner. "I'm afraid I don't understand."

"My dear Lady Winterset—may I call you Julia now? As we are going to be partners?"

She smiled her assent but didn't trust herself to speak. Not yet.

"Well, my dear, as you know, scandal sells books. The scandalous affairs of a woman long in her grave, while certainly interesting and profitable, are not nearly as lucrative as the amorous adventures of a living, breathing lady. An exceptionally beautiful lady, I might add."

"So." She chose her words with care. "This rumor is your doing then?"

"Well." He smiled in a modest manner. "I must admit

it was a stroke of genius. As clever as any story I have written."

"Did you give no thought as to what this might do to my reputation?" In spite of her best efforts her voice rose. "My life?"

"Yes, of course. It will change your life completely. You will no longer be the nearly impoverished widowed Lady Winterset but Julia Winterset. Authoress, adventuress, and—"

"And nothing! How dare you presume to take such liberties with my life!"

"Nonsense." He scoffed. "Why, my dear Julia, you shall be famous. We shall be famous together."

"I don't want to be famous. And I certainly don't want to be anything with you. I want to be . . ." What did she want? A life with Harrison? Love? Children? All of it? "Happy!"

"There's no reason why you can't be both. I am famous and happy as well."

"You are a nasty, contemptuous creature." She narrowed her eyes and took a step toward him. He wisely backed away. "As for your stroke of genius, it will do you no good whatsoever. I have no intention of letting you anywhere near the memoirs or anywhere near me!"

"You needn't be so indignant." He shrugged in a nonchalant manner. "It's not as if I am the only one whose actions were, perhaps, questionable."

"Perhaps?" She glared. "Perhaps?"

"Others are just as responsible as I am."

"Don't try to lay this at someone else's feet." She crossed her arms over her chest. "It's your doing entirely."

"Not entirely." Mr. Ellsworth paused for a moment, no doubt to find the right words and not out of any sense of regret or loyalty. "This was not my idea in the first place."

She gasped. "Surely you're not trying to blame this mess on Mr. Cadwallender?"

"Don't be absurd. While I have no doubt Cadwallender's new enterprise will be a success, he simply doesn't have the imagination for a scheme like this. Besides, he is entirely too nice."

She cast him a narrowed look. "What scheme?"

"To acquire the memoirs."

"I am losing what little patience I have left, Mr. Ellsworth. Explain yourself."

"It was Lord Mountdale's idea. At least in the beginning."

"What do you mean?" The most awful feeling of dread settled over her.

"Lord Mountdale offered me a tidy sum to propose to you that I purchase the memoirs and incorporate them into a book of my own. I thought it was a brilliant idea." He shrugged. "Once I had Lady Middlebury's book, I was to turn it over to him."

"I don't believe you," she said, even though she had thought it odd that the sum the author had offered was precisely the same as Harrison's initial offer. And wasn't there more than the figure that had seemed familiar?

She circled around Mr. Ellsworth, pulled open a drawer, and found the envelopes containing his offer and Harrison's. She pulled both offers out and laid them on the desk. Studying them side by side, it was apparent the figures were written by the same hand on the same paper. Her heart lodged in her throat. There was no denying it. Harrison had thought to trick her into giving him the memoirs.

"I gather you believe me now," Mr. Ellsworth said.

She nodded, ignoring the queasy sensation in her stomach.

"Although I suppose it scarcely matters." He rolled his gaze toward the ceiling. "He reneged on our arrangement. Oh, he did pay me what he had promised but he no longer wished to continue." He chuckled. "I, however, still thought the idea of combining my skill with Lady Middlebury's adventures was excellent and had every intention of pursuing it."

She stared in disbelief. "But what purpose did starting the rumors serve?"

"To get rid of Mountdale, of course." He scoffed. "I saw him kiss you at Lady Tennwright's and, worse, I saw the way you looked at him. I knew you would never agree to my proposal if you were involved with him. I thought if you were embroiled in a scandal, he would scamper off into the woods like a good little earl."

"And then?"

"And then he would be so preoccupied with the current scandal he would no longer care about the scandals of decades ago. And I could have the memoirs."

She considered him for a moment. "But how could you afford them if you no longer had his lordship's funding?"

"I had thought to convince you to form a true partnership."

She scoffed. "Surely you are not speaking of marriage?"

"Marriage?" His shook his head. "It did strike me that marriage would be one way to get my hands on the memoirs but no." His expression brightened. "Would you have considered it?"

"Absolutely not!"

"That's for best then." He grimanced. "It's possible I have a wife somewhere. I did however think though, that the right man—"

"You?"

"I am considered quite dashing and more than ordinarily charming. And I do have a certain amount of fame."

She ignored him. "The right man, what?"

"That you might, with the right man, be lured into following Lady Middlebury's path."

"I am sorry to disappoint you." She drew a deep breath. "So you initially took money from Lord Mountdale, then decided you liked the plot he came up with for yourself. Then thought a scandal would eliminate him so you could get the memoirs by seduction?"

He grinned. "Brilliant, isn't it?"

"It's the vilest, most despicable thing I have ever heard."

He chuckled. "It will make an excellent book."

She gasped. "You wouldn't!"

"Of course I would, and indeed I will." He sniffed in a haughty manner. "I should get something for my troubles."

"Your troubles? What troubles? You deceived me, you spread unpleasant lies about me, and you tried to seduce me."

"None of which was particularly easy." He paused. "Well, the seduction part wasn't. I still have a bruise, you know."

"Good! I only regret that I—"

The door burst open and a large, furry beast bounded into the room, paused as if deciding his next move, then trotted up to Julia, sat at her feet, and gazed up at her in an adoring manner.

"Browning!" Harrison hurried after the creature, Veronica and Portia right behind.

Julia stared at the animal, apparently some sort of dog, large and furry and quite adorable. She leaned over and rubbed his head. He grinned up at her. Julia glanced up at Harrison. "A dog? You brought a dog?"

"For you. To accompany you in the park," he said staunchly. "Roses make you sneeze." He cast a hard look at Mr. Ellsworth. "Mr. Ellsworth."

"Lord Mountdale." The author beamed. "What a surprise to see you here."

Harrison's eyes narrowed. "Is it?"

"We were just talking about you," Ellsworth said.

"Oh?" Harrison's voice was cautious.

"Mr. Ellsworth was just leaving," Julia said, and sent a silent message to Veronica.

Veronica hesitated for a moment then nodded. "As were we. Do join us, Mr. Ellsworth."

"There is nothing I would like better. Good day, Lady Winterset, Lord Mountdale." He nodded and strode out of the room.

"We're leaving now?" Portia said under her breath to Veronica. "But it's about to get even better."

"Precisely why we're leaving." Veronica herded the other woman through the door then glanced back at the dog. "You there."

The dog, Browning, looked at her with obvious amusement.

"You too." She snapped her fingers. "Come along. I shall give you a glove to chew on. I understand Portia's new gloves are quite tasty."

Browning considered it for a moment, then trotted out of the room. Veronica closed the doors behind him.

For a long moment Julia considered Harrison, her expression calm and unreadable. His stomach twisted. This was not a good sign.

"Julia," he began at last. "There is something we need to discuss."

"Is there?" she said coolly. "I can't imagine what that might be."

"You can't?" The oddest mix of hope and caution

washed through him. Perhaps Ellsworth had kept his mouth shut after all.

"Unless, of course, you're referring to your less-than-honorable plot with Mr. Ellsworth to trick me out of the memoirs?"

So much for hope. He chose his words carefully. "Yes, well, that was what I wished to talk about."

"And what, pray tell, did you plan to say?"

"I didn't have a plan."

"Ah, well, you probably have already exceeded your number of plans for today."

"I . . ." Surely she couldn't be too angry with a man who had presented her with an irresistible dog. "I brought you a dog."

"Part of a plan?"

"Well, yes, I suppose. As well as an apology regarding yesterday." It was never easy to apologize for doing what one would probably do again given the same circumstances. "Even though I was doing what I thought was best for you, I did indeed, perhaps, overstep. I should have remained silent."

"Very well."

He studied her cautiously. "Very well?"

"I accept your apology."

"You do?"

"Yes, you were right."

"I almost always am," he said without thinking then winced. This was not the time for arrogance.

"I meant, as you were only trying to improve the situation, I should not have been angry. You did mean well. You also defended me when you mentioned why my finances were a problem, and I am most appreciative." She narrowed her eyes. "I do not mean to imply that your actions were correct."

"I did what I thought was necessary," he said staunchly.

Her brows pulled together. "Do you ever admit when you are wrong?"

"Yes, on those rare occasions when I am wrong." He drew a deep breath. "And admittedly I was wrong in my association with Ellsworth."

"I see." Her voice was cool and collected. "You were wrong then to lie to me and deceive me?"

He shook his head. "I never lied to you."

"You're right, my lord. How could I have been so foolish as to charge you with lying? My apologies." Anger flared in her eyes but her tone was calm. Deceptively so. It was most unnerving. "You paid someone else to lie to me."

He couldn't deny her charge, so ignoring it seemed best. "I did not deceive you."

She stared in disbelief. "So, even though you paid that vile man to wrest the memoirs from me by trickery, because you did not do the deed directly, you do not bear the responsibility? You did not deceive me?"

"I admit I set certain actions in motion but I realized my error almost at once and withdrew my support of the plan."

"The fact that you changed your mind—"

"I came to my senses," he said staunchly.

"Oh, bravo, my lord!"

"You needn't be sarcastic."

"Sarcastic is the very least of what I need to be."

"This is not entirely my fault, you know."

"Oh?"

"I came to you initially with an excellent offer that you refused to so much as consider."

"You're right. This is my fault entirely." She clasped her hands together in an obvious effort to remain calm. "It would have been so much better for all concerned if I had simply been swept away by your charm and had acquiesced to the wishes of the wealthy and proper Lord Mountdale without pause, without question."

"It certainly would have been easier," he said under his breath.

"I do apologize that it's been difficult for you. Tell me, Harrison." Her words were measured. "Just when did you make this arrangement with Ellsworth?"

"When?" Oh, she would not take this well.

"Yes, when?"

There was nothing to be done about it now so he had better just say it. "The day after Veronica's party."

"I see." She paused. "Then the very day, scarcely twenty-four hours, after the evening in which you had professed your desire to be my friend, you hatched a scheme to trick me into giving you, albeit indirectly, my great-grandmother's work."

"Admittedly, it does not sound good when put that way."

"And what way would you put it to make it sound better?"

"You must give me some credit for calling a halt to it."

Her eyes narrowed. "Why did you?"

"First of all, one could argue that it was wrong, in a moral sense."

"Which didn't stop you from initiating it."

"I might well have been caught up by the brilliance of the idea—"

"Brilliance?" She snorted with disdain. "Perhaps if one was a master criminal."

"It seemed brilliant at the time," he said sharply. "But I didn't realize that when I told Ellsworth to acquire the memoirs by whatever means necessary—"

"Whatever means necessary?"

"Barring illegal or illicit methods, I said that specifically. However, I did later realize that he might well assume . . . seduction was allowable."

"You encouraged him to seduce me?" Her voice rose.

"I most certainly did not." He huffed. "It did not even occur to me that he might attempt to do so in his efforts to get the book until much later."

"Ellsworth's reputation with women is not a secret."

"And I agree, I did not take that into account. It was perhaps a miscalculation on my part."

Realization dawned on her face. "Then when you warned me that gentlemen who knew of the memoirs might assume I was as free with my favors as Hermione you were thinking of Mr. Ellsworth?"

"Yes." He nodded. "I was trying to protect you."

"You were trying to protect me from the man you had paid to get the book by whatever means possible?"

He huffed. "That too doesn't sound good when you say it that way."

"None of this sounds good in any way it's said whatsoever."

"I was trying as well to protect my family's name. I was trying to save my father from scandal. You can scarcely fault me for that."

"And yet I do." She shook her head. "Is it your responsibility to protect everyone?"

"Apparently!"

"Using whatever means you deem necessary?"

"Yes." He drew a deep breath. "If you had been sane and rational and accepted my offer when I first came to you, none of this would have happened."

"None of this?" she said slowly.

"Yes! There would be no Ellsworth, no scandalous rumors, no need to fly to the country to warn you."

"To protect me, you mean."

"Yes!"

"If I had accepted your offer at the beginning, none of this would have happened."

"That's what I just said."

"And you would prefer that none of this had ever happened?"

"Yes! I would prefer that none of this had ever happened!"

"You would rather that nothing had ever changed. That your life had stayed precisely as it always was?"

"Exactly. My life was respectable and properly managed. My mind was clear and without questions. I had no doubts about my behavior or my decisions. And my temper was rarely displayed."

"Then I suggest you take your leave right now and go back to your proper, respectable, well-managed life. And do not return." She met his gaze and fury blazed in her green eyes. Her voice was hard. "As far as I am concerned, none of this has ever happened."

"Excellent." He stepped to the door and yanked it open.

"And Lord Mountdale?"

"Yes?" He glanced back at her.

"I am keeping the dog."

"Good! I suspect he sheds."

He was already seated in his carriage when he realized exactly what he had said.

*"I would prefer that none of this had ever happened!"*

He groaned and buried his face in his hands. How could he have said such a thing? He didn't mean it of course, not the way it had sounded. It was only because the woman drove him mad. This wasn't the first time he had said something that didn't sound at all like what he had intended to say. Yes, Ellsworth and the rumors were nothing short of disastrous, but all that had transpired had not been bad. Indeed one could argue that while his life had changed, it had done so for the better.

He had come to like Veronica and accepted her as the sister he'd never had. He had grown closer to his father and had talked with him in a manner he could never remember having done before. His life had become, well, interesting.

If none of this had ever happened he wouldn't have come to know Julia. He wouldn't have discovered that what he thought he wanted in his life, wasn't what he wanted at all. He never would have found what he did want. And he wouldn't have fallen in love.

He was going to have to fix this. Pity he had no thoughts as to how to go about it. Not a single brilliant idea raised its questionable head. No matter. He would find the answer, he had no choice. He was not about to spend the rest of his life without her.

Veronica kept saying he had changed and even he could see it. But obviously he had not changed enough. Or perhaps he couldn't really change at all. Could he ever stop doing what he thought was necessary to protect the people he loved? Of course not. Although he could temper his actions he supposed, take into account the concerns of others, consider that he might not always be the only one who knew the right course of action.

Still, would he have to spend the rest of his life apologizing to her for doing what he thought was best?

Bloody hell, he hoped so.

*. . . as it would have been a grave mistake on my part not to have forgiven him.*

*One could argue his offense was too egregious to forgive but I did not see it so. Few men's actions are not the result of how they have lived their lives up to that point, the decisions they have made, the responsibilities they have lived up to and those they have failed. Balance must always be considered between intent and action. His intentions were not to cause harm even if the result of his actions was most upsetting. And he deeply, sincerely regretted his behavior.*

*Forgiveness, Dear Reader, is as infinite as love in that once bestowed does not mean it cannot be given again. A wise woman knows when a man deserves another chance and when she would be a fool to allow him back into her heart or her . . .*

from *The Perfect Mistress,*
*the Memoirs of Lady Hermione Middlebury*

# Chapter Twenty-one

Browning sat on the floor at Julia's feet, his chin resting in her lap, gazing up at her with adoring black eyes. With one hand she scratched behind his ears, the other toyed with her grandmother's pendant hanging around her neck. Eleanor had insisted she wear it today, saying a pretty bauble always lifted a woman's spirits. Not that it had done so. Still, it was a nice thought.

Nicer still was the animal who had already laid claim to her heart. Browning was an excellent gift and very thoughtful even if he was part of some sort of plan to get back into her good graces. Although why he was named Browning escaped her as he was not brown but gray and white. And he would be in her life long after the memory of Harrison's dark blue eyes or the feel of his arms around her or of his lips on hers had faded. Not that she suspected they ever would.

Her anger had not vanished since yesterday but it too had faded, to be replaced by an ache in her heart so deep it caught at her breath. She had scarcely slept at all last night thinking about what Harrison had said and done and why. Her grandmother had said she would feel much better in the morning, but here it was morning and she didn't feel at all better—just tired, and listless, and very sad.

Harrison was, well, who he was. The kind of man who considered it his duty to protect those people he decided needed protection. Who would do what he thought was necessary even if it was wrong. It was what was expected of him, indeed, what he expected of himself. That, in itself, was not a bad quality. The question was could she accept it? Not that it mattered now. He regretted everything that had happened. Everything including her.

"Lady Winterset?" Daniels said from the doorway. "There is a gentleman requesting to see you." Her heart leapt but Daniels shook his head. "It is Lord Kingsbury."

Harrison's father? "Very well. Show him in."

A moment later the elderly man, with the assistance of a cane, hobbled into the room. The man was nearly as tall as his son. One could see, in his day, he was every bit as handsome and now remained most distinguished. In spite of his age, he still had an air of roguish charm about him and a definite wicked twinkle in his eye. Browning immediately bounded over to greet him, tail wagging in enthusiasm. His lordship chuckled and patted the dog's head.

Julia rose to her feet. "Good day, my lord. I must say this is an unexpected pleasure."

"I do hope you're not disappointed."

"Why would I be disappointed?"

"I thought perhaps you might be expecting a different member of the family." He studied her closely. "Was I wrong?"

She ignored his question and indicated the chair nearest him. "Do sit down, my lord."

He settled into the chair. She sat on the sofa; Browning returned to sit at her feet. "Why are you here, my lord?"

"I have come to plead my son's case."

She raised a brow. "Your son's case?"

He shook his head in a mournful manner. "He's in a sorry state, I'm afraid."

Her heart tripped. "Is he?"

He considered her for a moment then smiled. "As are you, I see."

"Nonsense," she said. "I have never been better."

He laughed. "My dear young woman, I don't believe you for a moment. If I did I would take my leave at once. No, I would say at the very least, you haven't slept."

"I have a great deal on my mind." She shrugged. "There is nothing more to it than that."

"Of course not." He smiled. "Surely your inability to sleep isn't because you're miserable."

"Not in the least."

"Nor could it be due to confusion."

"I have never been less confused."

"Or attributable to being caught in a maelstrom of emotion and loss and even, dare I say it, heartache."

"I'm not caught in anything and my heart has never been better."

"My, that is a shame," he said under his breath.

She huffed. "Lord Kingsbury, I have no idea what you are trying to say."

"Then I shall endeavor to do better." He thought for a moment. "I have made a great many mistakes in my life. Among them, the premature turning over of family responsibilities to my son. Not that he was not more than capable, even then. But he has become somewhat narrow-minded, even arrogant, in his belief that he alone knows what is best for all concerned."

She scoffed. "I have noticed that."

"His heart, however, is usually in the right place, but perhaps you've noticed that as well?"

"Perhaps."

"I do not want my son to make the mistakes I did." He paused. "Are you aware that I knew your grandmother?"

"Did you?"

He nodded. "She was quite wonderful. I have often thought . . . well, it scarcely matters now, I suppose. She's gone and I am very nearly at the end of my days."

Obviously he thought Eleanor was dead. Julia started to correct him then caught herself. She would have to talk to her grandmother before she told him otherwise.

He blew a long breath. "When I met Eleanor, I had no idea she was Hermione's daughter. My liaison with her had occurred some fifteen years before I met your grandmother. Eleanor was a widow and I never imagined, I never connected the names although the eyes . . ." He nodded slowly. "I should have known by the eyes. You have her eyes, green as fine emeralds and as endless as the night."

She bit back a smile. "How very poetic of you."

"I have my poetic moments." He smiled absently and continued his story. "Eleanor was devastated when she found out about her mother and me. To be expected, of course. I was rather shocked myself. She said she never wanted to see me again. I had hurt her deeply. She couldn't forgive me and I couldn't blame her. I didn't know what to do. I was as miserable and confused and lost as Harrison is now. So I did nothing, which was very stupid of me." He shrugged. "The next thing I knew I was married to Harrison's mother and Eleanor had vanished from my life."

"You never tried to find her? When your wife died, that is?"

"I had no right. Besides, it was too late, she was gone." He smiled wryly. "It seemed somehow as though events were coming full circle when you came into Harrison's life and he fell in love with you." He met her gaze. "There has not been a day since the moment I lost her that I have not regretted allowing your grandmother to walk out of my life, and I will not watch history repeat itself."

"You do know what he did?"

"I do. Quite simply, it was wrong. However, while his methods were questionable, he was only trying to save me from scandal." He leaned forward. "That kind of loyalty is commendable."

"I suppose one could say—"

"Furthermore, at that point, he scarcely knew you at all and, in truth, owed you no allegiance whatsoever."

"Well, yes, if you wish to—"

"And you must give him some credit for calling the entire thing off."

"And I do but—"

"But what, my dear?"

"But . . ." She met his gaze directly and ignored the lump that lodged in her throat. "He wishes none of it had ever happened." She drew a deep breath. "None of it would include me."

"My dear Julia." His voice softened. "You drive him quite mad. This is not the first thing he has said to you that was not entirely as he intended it, nor, I suspect, will it be the last. He is indeed miserable and confused. He has no idea what to do, which in itself is not the Harrison I know, and says a great deal about not only his state of mind but his feelings for you. He is beside himself trying to come up with some sort of brilliant idea to win you back." He grinned. "God help us all."

She chose her words with care. "It seems to me what someone says in the heat of the moment is often what one truly feels."

"Does it?" He considered her curiously. "And it's always been my experience that nothing said in the heat of the moment can be completely trusted. Words are both awkward and dangerous. And what comes out of one's mouth might not be at all what one meant to say."

She met his gaze. "Do you really think so?"

"My dear, no man who truly wished none of this had ever happened would be as unhappy as my son is today."

She shook her head. "I don't know . . ."

"You can certainly choose not to forgive him and never see him again." He paused. "If that would make you happy."

She heaved a heavy sigh. "Or I could forgive him, I suppose."

"And allow him to spend the rest of his life trying to make amends." Lord Kingsbury nodded. "It would certainly serve him right. Fit penance for his crimes I would say."

"It does seem appropriate." She thought for a moment. "Is he truly miserable?"

"I have never seen anything like it." He nodded. "All he wants now is to make up for it all."

"He did get me a dog."

"Entirely his idea, I might point out."

She smiled in spite of herself. "You're lying, my lord."

"But I do it so well. And it's not a complete lie. A dog is not something I would have thought of. I tend to lean more toward jewelry as a gift of apology."

"You should reconsider that. It's not nearly as charming." She cast an affectionate glance at the dog. "Why is he called Browning?"

"Robert Browning is Harrison's favorite poet," Lord Kingsbury said staunchly.

She laughed. "I doubt that."

"He is trying to embrace poetry. For you."

"Is he?" How very sweet of Harrison. In spite of his arrogance and annoying nature, there was something endearing about the man. But then she already knew that.

"He is indeed." Lord Kingsbury nodded. "Admittedly, I am lending him a guiding hand. Browning is my favorite poet as well." He thought for a moment. "'How sad and bad and mad it was—' "

Her grandmother's voice sounded from the doorway. "'But then, how it was sweet.' "

Lord Kingsbury's eye widened. He struggled to his feet and turned toward the door, his voice barely more than a shocked whisper. "Eleanor?"

She smiled. "Albert."

He stared in disbelief. "I thought you were dead."

"Not quite yet."

"Very nearly everyone we once knew is."

"Apparently, we are made of sterner stuff."

"I assumed that you too . . . You seemed to have vanished from the face of the earth."

"Admittedly a mistake on my part. One of many." She shrugged. "And water under the bridge now as they say."

He studied her for a moment. "Do you still wish me dead?"

"Goodness, you are an absurd man. I never wished you dead." Her smile widened and her eyes twinkled in a wicked manner. "Simply dismembered."

He stared at her for a long moment. "Is it too late?"

"For dismemberment?" She glanced pointedly at his cane. "It scarcely seems necessary now."

He smiled slowly. "You have not changed at all."

"Nonsense." She scoffed. "I have changed a great deal. Why, I am as old as time itself."

"And yet just as lovely as I remember." He gazed at Eleanor with a look that said he did indeed see the woman she once was.

How sad to think of all the years lost because she was slow to forgive and he didn't know how to make amends. Julia's heart caught.

"You didn't answer me. Is it too late?"

"As we have both agreed we are still alive, I would say it's not at all too late."

"I have much to make up for," he warned.

"We both have much to make up for." While her words were directed at the older man, her gaze strayed to Julia. "I was a fool to have delayed forgiving you when it was only truly my pride that was injured. I have regretted it for thirty years."

"Will you allow me to make amends now?"

"My dear Albert, we have wasted a great many years. I should hate to waste any more." She moved toward him and held out her hand. "I would propose we go on from here."

He took her hand and raised it to his lips. "My darling girl, there is not a day that I have not missed you."

Eleanor fairly glowed with newfound happiness. "What a wonderful coincidence, my dear man."

The two long-ago lovers stared into one another's eyes and Julia realized her presence was not needed. She edged toward the door.

"If you will excuse me . . ."

"Before you go," Lord Kingsbury began, "there is something I have wondered since we first met at Veronica's."

"Yes?"

"Although I am most grateful that you decided to sell Hermione's memoirs, as none of this would have happened otherwise, I am curious as to why you simply didn't sell your great-grandmother's jewels." He nodded at the pendant around her neck. "That necklace is most distinctive and I remember it well. It was given to her by a prince if I recall and is no doubt quite valuable."

Eleanor sighed. "I told you to take it to a jeweler."

"I haven't had the chance." Julia stared. "All of your treasures then? Are they all—"

"True treasures." Eleanor lifted a shoulder in a casual manner. "Of course."

"Mrs. Philpot said they were paste."

"Goodness, darling, if one is going to allow the world to think one is mad, it's best not to let anyone know the madwoman in the cottage has a king's ransom in jewels." She met her granddaughter's gaze. "Although, as they are not my jewels, perhaps I am not the one you should be quizzing about this."

"Perhaps not." Julia nodded, exchanged a few more words then took her leave, closing the parlor doors behind her. It wasn't as if Eleanor and Albert needed a chaperone after all. A girlish giggle sounded behind the doors and Julia grinned. Although perhaps they did.

A few minutes later, she stood in the middle of her bedroom and drew a deep breath.

"I know you don't do parlor tricks," she said, "and Lord knows, you have never appeared on command, but I do need to speak to you. Now."

"Very well," Hermione said a fraction of an instant before she appeared, sitting in her usual spot at the end of the bed. "You called and I came." She shrugged. "I do hope you're happy but do not expect it to happen again."

Julia ignored her. "I need to ask about, well, your legacy."

"The memoirs you mean."

"No. Money, jewels, that sort of thing."

Hermione wrinkled her nose. "It's really most impolite to discuss money."

"You have my apologies."

Hermione sighed. "Go on then."

"What happened to your money? Why did you leave nothing of value when you died?"

She bristled. "I rather thought my memoirs were of value."

"That's not what I meant."

"I know what you meant and I did." She shrugged. "The small fortune I inherited from my husband went to my son, as was expected. Unfortunately, while he did not squander it, he did not nurture it either and, as you know, there was nothing left when he died. My jewels, quite an extensive collection I might add, went to my daughter."

"Real jewels?"

"Goodness, darling." She sniffed. "How could you ask such a thing?"

"Then all this time that I have been juggling accounts and trying to determine what to do about my financial woes," Julia said slowly, "the solution to all my problems has been in my grandmother's hands the entire time?"

"So it would seem."

"Why didn't you tell me?"

"You didn't ask."

"I don't need to sell the memoirs then?"

"Not if you don't wish to."

"And there is no need to marry anyone because I need money?"

"Not at all." She paused. "And the fact that Harrison has a tidy fortune has never played a part in how you feel about him, has it?"

She shook her head. "No."

"His wealth has simply been a pleasant attribute, like dimples or curly hair. And much more attractive now that you don't need it." She studied her for a moment. "What are you waiting for, Julia?"

"What do you mean?"

Hermione heaved a long-suffering sigh. "To begin with"—she ticked the points off on her fingers—"you no longer need Harrison's money now that you know the value of the treasures that are as much yours as they are Eleanor's. So that aversion you have about marrying a man for his money is no longer relevant. You, my dear have independent wealth."

A weight lifted off her shoulders. "And I have you to thank."

"Think nothing of it." Hermione waved away the comment. "Secondly, you have learned a lesson from your grandmother's mistakes."

"About forgiveness?"

"And balance as well." She shrugged. "Forgiving an act that had nothing to do with you or something that was well intended even if ill conceived against a lifetime of regret."

"I should forgive him."

Hermione raised a brow. "I thought you already had."

"What if it's too late?"

"It's not but to make certain you should waste no time."

Julia stepped toward the door then paused. "But what about Miss Waverly? She is the type of woman he's always wanted for a wife."

"You needn't worry about the proper Miss Waverly." Hermione smirked. "I have it on very good authority that this morning, when her maid went in to awaken her, she discovered the young woman had run off with a footman." She leaned forward in a confidential manner. "A very handsome footman I might add."

Julia stared. "Veronica was right. Those least likely to bend . . ."

# Chapter Twenty-two

"Julia," he began. "My methods may have been questionable but I believed, at the time, the end result was worth the, well, more deceitful aspects . . . damnation."

Harrison glared at the suit of armor positioned to one side of the fireplace. He'd had it moved here from its usual place at the foot of the stairs because it was nearly Julia's height and provided an excellent substitute Julia. He was not about to speak to her again until he knew exactly what he wished to say.

He resumed pacing the parlor. While he realized it might seem too efficient to practice a speech of apology and affection it also seemed wise, given the last two times he had tried to speak with her. It might also be wise to face up to one's own limitations. As much as he prided himself on his intelligence he apparently had no idea when to restrain from expressing every opinion he had ever had. He was not a stupid man, yet she made him feel somewhat stupid, a feeling only enforced by his actions. He had no intention of going to Julia until he knew exactly what he was going to say. Obviously, he could no longer trust his intelligence, or lack thereof, in her presence.

Harrison paced the length of the parlor, drew a deep breath then stopped before the armor.

" 'To err is human, to forgive is divine'. Alexander Pope." He paused and cast the substitute Julia a knowing look. "One of Britain's greatest poets, you know." He groaned. That was bloody awful. He sounded like a schoolboy giving a recitation. He had no idea how to do this. How would Charles have handled this? Or his father?

*"Listen to your heart and not your head."*

Very well. He drew a deep breath then addressed the suit.

"Julia, from the very beginning, I have behaved not at all like my usual self in some ways while in others I have been entirely true to my nature. I apologize for the absurd scheme I initiated with Mr. Ellsworth and I assure you nothing like that will ever happen again. I apologize as well for my interference with Lady Holridge however, while I cannot guarantee I will never again do what I think is appropriate under the circumstances, I do promise to try not to interfere and to attempt to take your concerns into account."

That was good, that was very good. He thought for a moment then continued.

"As for the memoirs, if you wish to sell them for publication, I have no objection. I have learned there are far more important things in this life than preventing scandal." He paused for a moment. Out of the corner of his eye, he caught a movement in the mirror over the mantel that partially reflected the door. His heart skipped a beat. How long had she been there? His head said to stop at once and acknowledge her presence. His heart disagreed.

He smiled to himself and continued. "I know you value your financial independence, and if the sale of the memoirs will make you content in that regard so be it. For good or ill, they are your legacy."

He didn't dare look toward her reflection for fear of meeting her gaze. This was going entirely too well and there was one more thing he needed to say.

"You should know as well, that I did not love you the moment we first met. I found you obstinate and annoying and far too intelligent for a woman. But some time after I asked for your friendship . . . By the time I kissed you on the terrace, my fate was sealed." He cleared his throat. "I cannot imagine living my life without you by my side. And should you agree to be my wife"—his gaze flicked to hers in the mirror—"I shall spend every day of my life trying to make you happy. And in doing so I shall be happy as well."

"You will make a lovely couple," Julia said, "you and the suit of armor, that is."

"She's everything I ever wanted in a wife. I simply didn't realize it until I met her."

"She seems rather less than the proper, correct, well-bred lady you wanted. Goodness, Harrison, her knees are showing."

"But you must admit they are lovely knees although they could do with a bit of polishing."

"Ah, but she does seem an independent type that might not wish her knees polished."

He shrugged. "Her independence is what makes her who she is. I would not now change her if I could."

"Even if she isn't what you wanted?"

"She isn't what I wanted only because I could never have imagined her. Now, I can't imagine anyone else."

"No?"

"I love her."

"I see." She considered him for a moment. "How long have you known I was here?"

"How long have you been here?"

Her brow rose. "Answering a question with a question? Very well then. I did hear you expound on the divine nature of forgiveness."

"It's poetry, you know."

She bit back a smile. "I am aware of that."

He grimaced. "I can't say I shall ever love poetry."

"Nor do I expect you to."

"I have recently discovered I have a great many flaws and failings."

"You are human after all."

"Will you marry me then and correct all my flaws and failings?"

"No."

His heart sank and he swiveled to face her. "No?"

"No." She shook her head. "I have no desire to correct your flaws and failings. They make you who you are." She smiled. "I would not change you even if I could."

"But do you forgive me? My flaws and failings that is."

"Well, you did give me a dog."

He smiled slowly. "I did."

"He's a grand spirit. I already love him."

"How could you not?" His smiled widened. "He is irresistible and named after a poet."

"And I love you as well." Her gaze locked with his. "How could I not?"

"In spite of it all?"

"No, my dear man." She walked toward him. "Because of it all."

He moved toward her and pulled her into his arms. "And I love you as I never imagined, never dreamed, I could."

"Then Veronica was right. She said I would suit you." She slid her arms around his neck. "But she was wrong as well. She said you would never suit me."

"I do love it when she's wrong. I shall have to remind her of that." He brushed his lips across hers. "And remind you as well how nicely we suit. Every day for the rest of your life I think. I intend to make you absurdly happy and completely content."

"Don't be silly. I shall never be merely content with you." Her green eyes gazed into his and his breath caught and his heart leapt. "You, my love, for now and forever, are my adventure."

# The End

*Three weeks later . . .*

"Lovely ceremony, I thought. Quite touching really."

At once Julia was wide awake and struggled to sit up. "Where have you been? And why are you here now? You do realize this is my wedding night?"

"Happy, darling?"

"Blissful but . . ." She glanced at Harrison sleeping beside her and lowered her voice. "Do be quiet. You'll awaken him and I have no idea how to explain you."

"I rather think he's too exhausted to awaken." Hermione flashed her a wicked grin. "Indeed, he's sleeping like the dead."

"That's not the least bit amusing."

"Really? I thought it was most amusing, given that I really am expired whereas he is simply"—she chuckled—"expended."

"Now is not the time." Julia tried to pull her thoughts together. "There is something I must tell you and I'm not sure how to say it."

"My, this doesn't sound good."

"It's not." She drew a deep breath. "Your memoirs seem to have disappeared. I can't find them anywhere."

"Imagine that."

"Odder still, neither Benjamin nor Portia nor Harrison can find the selections they had."

"That is odd." She shrugged. "Well, I'm certain they will turn up eventually."

Julia studied her. There was something decidedly different about Hermione tonight. "Will they?"

"I have no idea." She nodded toward Harrison. "You do realize he will always be somewhat stuffy and proper?"

"I do."

"And that proper English gentlemen and their wives usually have separate rooms?"

Julia grinned. "In that respect, I doubt he will ever be entirely proper. Nor do I intend to allow him to be."

"Excellent." Hermione paused. "Are you going to tell him about the circumstances of his birth?"

She shook her head. "No. It would serve no purpose save to take him down a peg. And I suspect I shall have other methods of doing that when necessary."

"You love him and that's how it should be. Julia . . ." Hermione hesitated.

"Hermione," Julia said slowly. "What is it?"

"Oh dear, am I that transparent?" She glanced down. "No, delightfully solid I would say."

"Why are you here?"

"I have something to tell you as well and now that the time has come I too have difficulties finding the right words." She drew a deep breath. "As lovely as my afterlife has been, and I have had a grand time, I have learned, and learned really isn't accurate." She thought for a moment. "I'm not sure how to describe it. One minute I didn't know and the next moment I did."

"Know what?"

"Why I have lingered here and why my time is now at an end."

"Of course, that's it. That's what's different." Julia stared. "You look ten years younger."

"Fourteen actually. I was four and twenty when my husband died. I had thought I would join him when it was my turn but having fun with my old friends, meeting new ones, going to parties and routs and balls was apparently my penance." She shook her head in amazement. "I find it hard to believe. I had everything here that I had enjoyed in life except the one thing I wanted most. But I couldn't leave, you see, until I had fixed what was, however indirectly, my fault."

At once Julia understood. "Grandmother and Lord Kingsbury?"

"That's why I talked to her all these years." She smiled an odd sort of half-hearted smile. "I tried to be a better mother in death than I was in life."

Julia nodded.

"Then when you inherited the memoirs and you needed me, well, I had to be here. But my work is done and all at last ends well." She rose to her feet. "Have a wonderful life, my dear child."

"Aren't you coming back?"

"You no longer need me. My daughter has been reunited with the love of her life and you have been joined with the love of yours." She smiled. "And I have earned the right to be reunited with mine." Hermione paused for a long moment. "I lived forty-three years after he died. I had a lovely life full of adventures and affection." She sighed. "But I would have traded all of it for one more day with him."

Julia swallowed hard. "I know."

"Yes, darling, at last you do." She cast a smile at her great-granddaughter's new husband's sleeping form. "You know exactly how I feel."

"Will I ever see you again?"

"Certainly someday. But it will be a very long time from now. When your adventure"—she nodded at Harrison—"and his is at an end."

Julia swallowed hard. "I will miss you."

"My dear child, I will always be with you in your heart, just as I will always be with my daughter."

An ache burned the back of Julia's throat. "Do you really have to go?"

"Darling, I want to go." She fell silent for a moment. "Did you ever finish reading my book? Did you ever get to the end?"

She shook her head.

"Ah well," she said in a lofty manner, "it was an excellent ending in which I imparted the lessons of a lifetime."

Julia smiled. "Anything I should know?"

"My dear child." Hermione faded from sight. "You already do."

*At the beginning of this volume I said I had no regrets and when I wrote those words I believed them to be true. Now, as I have set to paper the adventures of my life I find there are indeed regrets.*

*I regret I did not know in my youth what I know now. I regret that I made assumptions about the unrelenting nature of time. I regret that I was not as clever as I thought I was. And I wonder if these regrets are unique to me or if they are universal as they seem so very human.*

*Still, I have learned much. I know that the person in the midst of the crowd may be the most alone. I know that true love makes no sense and cannot be denied and lingers even after death. I know that it is indeed the adventure that makes life worth living. And I know the grandest adventures of life pale in comparison to the greater adventure of love.*

*That, Dear Reader, is the most important thing I have learned. And the true lesson of the life of a perfect mistress.*

from *The Perfect Mistress,*
*the Lost Memoirs of Lady Hermione Middlebury*